P9-DBT-560

JULIAN APPROACHED HER,
REACHED OUT FOR HER

DISCARD

She immediately struck his hands away hard. He reached again, dodging her defenses this time with awful ease and blinding speed and grabbing her around her lower jaw with the palms of both hands. Once he had her face cradled and firmly trapped within his hands, he jerked her forward into his body, even as he swooped to catch her mouth with his.

Asia planned just how hard she would bite through his lip. She was even trying to decide between upper and lower when the unexpected scorch of his kiss slammed into her from all sides at once. In all of an instant, her entire body recalled what he had made her feel. Her mind recalled it best of all. The memory was vague about "how" it had happened, but the "what" was clear enough. Pleasure beyond anything she could have imagined. *He* had made her feel that. He had powered through her rigid, cold body, just as he was doing in that very moment, until she had melted and collapsed. Asia felt her entire body sagging against his as her knees literally went weak. Just from such a simple kiss.

CHICAGO PUBLIC LIBRARY
RODEN BRANCH
6083 N NORTHWEST HWY
CHICAGO, IL 60631
DEC 2009

Also Available from Jacquelyn Frank

The Nightwalkers
Jacob
Gideon
Elijah
Damien
Noah

The Shadowdwellers
Ecstasy
Rapture
Pleasure

The Gatherers
Hunting Julian

Published by Kensington Publishing Corporation

Hunting Julian

THE GATHERERS

Jacquelyn Frank

ZEBRA BOOKS
KENSINGTON PUBLISHING CORP.
http://www.kensingtonbooks.com

ZEBRA BOOKS are published by

Kensington Publishing Corp.
119 West 40th Street
New York, NY 10018

Copyright © 2010 by Jacquelyn Frank

All rights reserved. No part of this book may be reproduced in any form or by any means without the prior written consent of the Publisher, excepting brief quotes used in reviews.

If you purchased this book without a cover you should be aware that this book is stolen property. It was reported as "unsold and destroyed" to the Publisher and neither the Author nor the Publisher has received any payment for this "stripped book."

All Kensington titles, imprints, and distributed lines are available at special quantity discounts for bulk purchases for sales promotion, premiums, fund-raising, educational, or institutional use.

Special book excerpts or customized printings can also be created to fit specific needs. For details, write or phone the office of the Kensington Special Sales Manager: Attn. Special Sales Department. Kensington Publishing Corp., 119 West 40th Street, New York, NY 10018. Phone: 1-800-221-2647.

Zebra and the Z logo Reg. U.S. Pat. & TM Off.

ISBN-13: 978-1-4201-0425-7
ISBN-10: 1-4201-0425-X

First Printing: January 2010
10 9 8 7 6 5 4 3 2 1

Printed in the United States of America

R0422961836

Chicago Public Library
Roden Branch
6083 N. Northwest Hwy.
Chicago, IL 60631
(312) 744-1478

Chapter 1

Julian.

Even watching him from a good distance, Asia Callahan could feel the off-the-charts testosterone roiling off the man. It actually had nothing to do with the fact that he was everything "tall, dark and handsome," like something a lame romance writer might stuff into some dopey story about rakes and swooning or whatever. In truth, it had everything to do with his inherent chemistry, which absolutely reeked of sex, lustfulness, and all things outright carnal. It was as off the charts as a man could get, bordering on inhuman, in Asia's opinion. The fact that he had good looks to go with it was merely adding insult to injury, and purely coincidental.

Or just lethal.

Asia adjusted her focus slowly, ignoring the ache in her neck as she watched Julian in action through her high-tech night-vision binoculars. He walked with a sinful ease of grace, she noted, for someone so tall and relatively heavy with muscle. Not Mr. Universe heavy, but quite definitively buffed out. Military built, she'd guessed. By now she'd seen him with his shirt off enough times to be pretty familiar with the contours of his upper body. He wasn't slender or lean or even merely athletic; he was built like a brute . . . except that in absolute contradiction to his size and body mass, he moved like a god. Smooth, easy, and effortless, and even the slightest casual cock of one hip just oozed a sophisticated style and refinement that a mere brute could never pull off.

Too bad he was a cold-blooded murderer.

Or that was the going theory. One she was highly inclined to believe after spending so much time studying his every move. It had nothing to do with the fact that he kept vampire's hours, sleeping all day and trolling the night. It wasn't even because he used women like toilet paper, discarding them just about as fast as he got them to drop their panties for him. After all, Asia was a firm believer in women who owned their sexuality. If these crazy chicks wanted a man like Julian to stick it to them, well, that was their right. If he were any other man, she'd say more power to them . . . or perhaps even "get out of my way."

The ones who came crying after a man like that later on—the pathetic ones who thought he was capable of more than a night or two of mind-blowing orgasms—in her opinion, they deserved what they got. Tears and girly emotions had no place in Julian's scope of interest. And honestly, any time one of them got to walk away with the breath still pushing through their bodies, they ought to consider themselves damn lucky.

Still, she could almost understand their mistakenness. Julian's smile alone was not only sexy and compelling, it was enough to make anyone on the receiving end of it feel as if she were the only woman in his world. Hell, she was how many yards away? Even *she* felt like she was the only woman in his world, and he didn't even know she was there.

Not that Asia was known for being the swooning, sentimental type. No, no, no. No one would ever accuse her of having touchy-feely emotionalism or equally girly crap like that. She'd seen way too much in her life, done too much and been too many places to have even the littlest smidge of a star in either of her eyes. So instead of getting weak in the knees or panting and drooling when she saw Julian pull his smooth routine on the women who seemed to flock to him like vultures to a fresh kill, all she saw was a hell of a lot of masculine sex appeal and a man who knew how to use it to further his own untrustworthy agenda.

Surprise, surprise.

Unfortunately, for about a baker's dozen of women to date, his "agenda" had ended in highly suspicious and nefarious disappearances. There had even been a pair of bodies along the way, both men who had been closely associated with a couple of the missing women. Just because there had been no female bodies in his wake didn't mean he wasn't guilty as the walking sin he was, it just meant he had a really good hiding place for the—

Asia pushed away the finality of that train of thought. She reverted to her analysis of her target. Julian was, among these many other things, a nomad. He'd moved through seven states in as many months, finding large cities and enjoying them with a perverse and obvious relish, rather like the way he enjoyed his women . . . with the arrogance only a genius criminal mind could attain. He thought he was so clever. He thought he was miles above detection.

Asia, however, had detected him.

Much to the embarrassment of a few police departments across the United States, she alone had made the connection between Julian and the missing women, painstakingly tracking back over an all but trackless trail, making sure she found proof that he was in every single city on every single date of every single disappearance. Once she had established that, she had taken her proof to the FBI, who hadn't even known the cases from city to city were linked. After all, he didn't fit any profile any of them had ever heard of. Rarely did a serial killer cross state lines as he had done, and when one did, and subsequently escalated at the rate of Julian's pace, he usually began to get sloppy. At that point they would be indulging in their own twisted, worked-up emotions, prey to stressors and triggers that would send them spiraling out of control.

Also against the usual profile of a serial killer was Julian's remarkable sexuality and control. Often sexual dysfunction was key to this sort of mentality; rape was the only way they could find their sadistic pleasure. But Julian lured woman after woman to his lairs again and again, made thorough love to them, and then . . . he let them go. He didn't have a type he stuck to; he didn't have a tried and true lure. He didn't do anything where anyone could see or hear. He never left as much as a drop of DNA, his or theirs, to guide his hunters back to him.

How was that even possible? How did women simply enter his apartment, never be heard from again, without leaving a trace that their paths had even crossed? How had Kenya simply faded from existence, as if she didn't have a sister dying in increments every day because she was nowhere to be found?

Asia's sister had very likely been Julian's tenth victim.

And if Asia hadn't personally seen Kenya with the bastard the night she'd disappeared, she would never have gotten this close to him. Every time she looked at him, she could see the last image she'd had of her sister as Kenya had stood draped against that gorgeous body, winking at Asia from around his side, so proud of her conquest as she'd brazenly fondled his ass.

It was pure fortune she'd even been there at all. Asia wasn't the nightclub type. Oh, she had been in more of them than she wanted to count; clubs, bars, and seedy piss-water places trying to pass themselves off as one or the other. People seemed to have a jones for sticky floors, meat-market socialism, and tawdry lighting backed by music that whined, droned, or throbbed. She had never enjoyed it, never wanted to tolerate it, and never had a choice, it seemed, as she ended up in them time after time. But the night of her disappearance, Kenya had begged and pleaded with her to come out and "relax" and "loosen up" and try to have a good time. What her sister had really wanted was a tough-assed bodyguard in the form of a lethal sister to keep the losers off her while she scoped for something rare and fine to take to bed for the night.

She had found Julian.

A rare find indeed. In a club packed with male meat, Asia's beautiful, rambunctious sister had managed to pick the one and only psychopathic killer in the lot.

But he had a pattern, just like they all had patterns. It had taken some time, but she had figured it out. He picked a city, spent a few weeks getting comfortable and fucking everything in a skirt. Then he picked exactly two women in each city to do . . . whatever it was he did with them . . . before moving on to a new location. Asia wanted to be clinical and methodical about what this man had likely done to those girls, but she still cringed and shied away from definitively saying he murdered them. Not because she didn't believe he was fully capable of such an act, because she did, but because one of those women was her sister, and while she knew in her gut he was responsible for every one of the disappearances, she had no solid proof he had actually killed them. For all she knew and the evidence showed, he could be some kind of collector, keeping them captive and alive somewhere . . . anywhere.

This was her only hope.

Asia set aside her night-vision goggles and checked her face in her rearview mirror to make certain she hadn't disturbed the dramatic sweep of color and sparkles decorating her lids and lashes. The cool blue of her eyes was dramatically enhanced by the effect of midnight blue liner and lash coloring, as well as the blue-violet shades of her shadow. Her hair had been twisted back into a simple coif, but shimmering ribbons of silver hung from it in long coils. She got out of her car, the damp Florida air striking her legs as her heels hit the pavement. She then turned toward Pussy Willows, the nightclub where Julian was working as a bouncer, per his usual MO, as well as general eye candy in order to attract the young, beautifully single women the club needed to lure in eager and recently paid males to spend time and drink their money.

Asia had spent the past half hour watching these girls flirt with danger and come on to almost-certain death, all the while knowing that Julian had only taken one victim since arriving in Fort Lauderdale and that, if he stuck to his meticulous schedule, he had only four days remaining before he moved on. He was probably growing a little itchy for his second victim by now.

Asia was determined to be that second and very last victim.

Julian smiled at the buxom blonde with his usual flirtatiousness, one shoulder back against the door-jamb as his gaze drifted down the line of potentials who wanted so badly to gain admittance to the exclusive hot spot. The blonde was cute, but a bit too tawdry for Pussy Willows, which was aiming for just a touch more class than her overtly tits-and-ass approach to her wardrobe. She continued to flirt outrageously with him in hopes he would give her and her girlfriend the nod and let her in, but Julian could tell her patience was wearing thin after twenty minutes of being unsuccessful. The midnight hour was bearing down; he could smell the coke and X lifestyle on her, pressuring her to have fun and get wasted already. She clearly wasn't used to not getting a response to her "charms," and it was ticking her off as her ego took a beating from his indifference.

He would have taken pity on her, but the club manager had already been out twice that night to dress Julian down for his choices of admittance. If Vernon arrived a third time with his nasty, derogatory attitude in tow, Julian might end up sacrificing his prime position at the club door in order to belt the shallow, prejudiced bastard so hard his head would snap clean off his neck. Since this would be in antithesis to his goals, it was best if Julian didn't provoke such an encounter by letting the under-par girl through the door.

Still smiling, he leaned forward toward the girl in question. "Beat it, sweetie," he drawled. "My boss is a dick and he won't let me pass anyone who isn't wearing designer and diamonds."

Not that Julian was completely certain what that was supposed to mean. From his perspective, clothing and jewelry weren't the clues that led to an outstanding woman, but it seemed to ring true to the other bouncers and since it was crucial that he fit in, he had to follow their lead. He wasn't there to make waves and stand out.

He was also aware of the fact that it was only his charm, his looks, and his accent that made the phrase come off as helpful instead of as the insult it really was. The blonde nodded and sighed in resignation, muttered a curse, then grabbed her friend by the arm and walked back down the line away from the club. Vincent, the other bouncer, liked to call the reaction "sour grapes." It was just another reference that went over his head and, like many others, gave the impression that he was a bit simpler-minded than he actually was. Some put it down to a language barrier due to his heavy accent, just as many liked to think he was as vacuous as he was beautiful, the combination more comforting to them somehow. He let the impression stand, just like he let all the others stand. People could think what they would. He had nothing to prove to anyone and would just as soon be left to himself so he could keep to his own business.

Julian heard her before anyone else would have, the determined click of her heels against the cement walkway drawing his attention almost immediately. There was confidence to the stride, not the mincing steps of a woman wearing heels too high for her to manage. These were high heels, but she managed them very well indeed. When she came around the hedges, he realized it was probably because she was already used to walking on legs that were insanely long and another few inches couldn't possibly matter. The extent of her legs was imminently obvious because her skirt covered barely more than a scant portion of her upper thighs, the silver fabric shimmering along her amazing body with every single step. She wore no bra, the firmness of her breasts not needing one in the least. Her nipples were slightly erect, obvious under the fabric that ran over her skin with the intimacy of the flow of water against it.

She forwent the line, the action of a woman who knew who and what she was, and ignored the rude complaints and remarks hissed at her as she bypassed those who were waiting like the good little lemmings they were. This woman, Julian realized, waited for no one. Her diamond tennis bracelet and matching anklet satisfied one of Vernon's requirements, and he was willing to bet that scrap of silver she was pretending to wear as a dress more than fulfilled the other. Either way, he didn't give a damn what Vernon thought or said.

She was perfect, and she was what *he* had been looking for.

By the time she made it halfway up the line, he began to catch her fragrance. He caught it all, everything from her shampoo and cosmetics to the clean perfection of light lemon and verbena. Even better than all of that was the sweetness of pure female, everything sexual and exotic to her gender in specific, kept in pristine balance and calling to him in every way. To Julian's surprise, his body began to react quickly and eagerly, an out-of-control response that was very unlike him and, thereby, all the more exciting for its uniqueness. Maybe it was the beautiful smell of her that enthralled his senses and translated so strongly into his quickly hardening sex, but when those riveting blue eyes roamed over him and just as obviously dismissed him without any impression on her coolly stunning features, that was when he knew it went much deeper than that.

The color around her eyes was striking, but it was also annoying to him. He wondered what she looked like when her face was scrubbed as clean as the rest of her body smelled. She was dusted with sparkles over every inch of her bare skin, of which there was quite a lot. Her ebony hair was also lightly glittering, but in his opinion did not need the artifice. The jet locks picked up the lights outside of the club, turning them holographic with color. He itched with a sharp, insane desire to know how long it was. Long, he guessed, and it would be quite straight. There was a touch of something about her features that hinted at a possible Asian heritage, but it was far too vague for him to be certain.

The woman struck an impatient, autocratic pose when she reached the velvet rope, her eyes sweeping over Vincent just as dismissively as they had Julian. Julian was already there, disengaging the link to let her through, yet standing in her way to prevent her passing.

"ID?" he asked.

She carried no purse that he could see and if she had pockets in her dress he'd be damned. She was obviously of age and he was just as obviously baiting her, his teasing smile meant to charm her into breaking her hardcore attitude.

"Back off, Lurch," she said dryly, pushing a finger into the center of his chest until her long fingernail dug deep into his flesh. "We both know I'm old enough to be here. I'm not giving some fluffy piece of candy an eyeball at my address. You'll have to be satisfied with what you see."

She dropped her hand to indicate her stunning figure with a careless sweep of her fingers.

"Julian," Vincent warned in a sharp whisper, "let her in."

Julian frowned at the command and ignored the other bouncer so he could maybe provoke her into touching him again. The contact had been positively electric, charging up every nerve ending in his body and making him rather regretful that he hadn't tucked in his shirt that night. He would have loved to see how she reacted to knowing he had a hell of an erection just from her approach. She probably wouldn't appreciate it the way he did for its uniqueness, but it might have gotten a pause from her, or at least a fiery reaction of indignation he would have loved to feel and witness.

"What will you do for me if I let you pass?" he asked archly, definitely risking his job and not caring any more than he had a few minutes earlier. This was what he was there for. *She* was what he was there for. Now that he had his target, there was no longer any reason to wait around for another.

She placed a hand on a curved hip, the opposite one jutting out as she rested her weight back on her heel and slowly looked him over.

"Look, I realize you are used to that smarmy charm working on the little girls who come in here, but I am neither a girl nor charmed, so back off before I call Vernon out here and get your ass fired."

"Go ahead. I would rather quit than pass up an opportunity to stand in your path."

She smiled at that, a slow curving of her lips that very obviously did not reach her beautifully cold blue eyes. "That sounded almost regal and sincere. You practice that one in the mirror?"

"No, actually, it *was* sincere. Doesn't majesty deserve regality?"

She tilted her head and studied him, looking briefly perplexed, an expression that finally did make it to her eyes. He realized these American women were not used to men who spoke in such ways without coming off as insincere or obviously . . . what was the term she had used? *Smarmy.*

Julian turned aside at last and offered his arm to her.

"At least let me buy you your first drink before the undeserving throng tries to sweep you away?"

"Thanks, but I don't drink," she said as she ignored his arm and breezed past him. "I'm just here to get laid."

The remark set up a cheer from those in the front of the line who had overheard her, and Vincent chuckled into his fist. Julian was barely paying attention to him as he kept his focus on the sway of her behind under that slinky silver fabric while she walked away in bold, sexy strides. "I believe," he said softly aloud to no one, "I could consider that an invitation."

Julian dismissed the other bouncer and the line of people outside and instantly followed his target. The club had what Vernon liked to call a "comfortable" crowd. It was just enough to look popular and wildly fun, but not so much that it felt like an icebox jammed full of meat. Julian never took his eyes off her, and it wasn't difficult at all to track her. The silver of her dress had much less to do with that than the fact that she was wickedly tall for a woman and that every inch of her became a magnet to everything in the room with a penis.

"Shit," he muttered when he saw the room shift to accommodate and then crowd her arrival. She blew off the first few predators with a cold warning look and a sharp, silent palm to ward them off, but Julian realized she had dressed to attract what she had claimed she wanted, and before long she would have her pick of the room.

He frowned as he thought of all those other men moving aggressively into her sphere. Not that competition worried him, because he hardly considered them as such, but he realized he didn't think he was going to like watching her play the game of social flirtation and invitation as she searched for someone to invite to her bed.

Julian found himself suppressing a severe vocal reaction at the thought of her offering herself to anyone but him. Even muted, the possessive and feral sound startled a few nearby patrons, and he curled his fingers into fists in an attempt to get control of himself. It was to be expected, he told himself sternly. He had stayed longer than he should and his patience was wearing thin as his next target had eluded him.

But now, he was certain, she was here; a vision in silver looking for a man to mate with. The odd thing was that despite her declaration of such a goal, he sensed no sexual readiness from her. He could smell not a hint of active pheromones spiking in search of a target of their own. Oh, he could scent the rush of her adrenaline well enough, and he heard the excited pounding of her heart, but there was something more akin to fear and anger in that mix than there was of sexual predation. But perhaps that was just a matter of allowing herself time to sit back, relax, and slowly open herself up to the possibilities.

However, Julian was going to be her one and only possibility. He would see to that. He hadn't come this far and waited this long for his prize only to be turned away by mere attitude or be pushed aside for a simple human male.

Julian walked by her as soon as she sat down on the raised stool at a lone little round table. Surrounded by others, yet alone in the sea of humanity, for a moment she seemed ill-fitted to her surroundings. She was perfectly turned out and confident as hell, but he somehow got the impression she was just there to do what she had to do to get what she wanted, not because she enjoyed very much about it. It baffled him that someone so striking would have to resort to such raw tactics to find physical satisfaction. Men should be spilling out of every crevice to get close to her, just as they were doing now. Julian found it fascinating that she wasn't already marked by another.

Not that this would have stopped him. It hadn't before and it wouldn't now. Especially not now. He just found it curious. He had to assume it wasn't for lack of trying by others, and taking into consideration her brusque, bold nature he could only conclude that this was the way she wanted it to be. Brief, easy, and detached.

Intriguing.

Such a complex ego and personality would certainly make for some interesting challenges, he made no mistake about that, but he was definitely spoiling for a challenge.

From *her*. Not from a thousand other male idiots who wouldn't know what to do with a woman like this if given a map, a guide, and a way to cheat. Besides, she smelled good enough to eat, and he was realizing just how damn hungry he really was.

In all of this time . . . encountering so many women and experiencing them at their most primal and most vulnerable, and he had never reacted like this. Julian began to realize there was a significant reason for all of it—the possessive urges, the jealousy, and most of all the uncontrolled response of his entire psyche just to her distant presence. The way he had been so juiced up by the simplest touch of her fingertip should have tipped him off instantly, but he'd been caught between his needs for his second target of the month and the press of time. He hadn't seen it at first. Now he began to understand what he was standing in the shadow of.

If Kine could see him now, he'd make Julian suffer for every moment he had touted how he didn't need a *kindra*. But at that time he hadn't fully appreciated how powerful certain instinctual urges could really be, and he was quite sorry now for not showing them their due respect. He was becoming more regretful by the second as his skin literally began to tighten with the need to get closer to her. She called to him on a visceral level and he knew that although resistance was inconceivable for him at this point, the pull was completely one-sided until he did what he had to do. However, it would require gaining her trust in order to betray it.

Not an easy task for many reasons, her obviously jaded and acerbic personality being the key sticking point.

Julian moved over to the bar across from her and watched very carefully as she took pleasure in blowing off a few more men before deigning to be a little charming to one or two. She was holding a very select court within a half an hour and Julian studied each of her choices carefully. Each one was handsome, carried a fit build, and was obviously full of confidence. A lot like him, if he thought about it, but she had dismissed him for some reason. It occurred to him that her dismissal had been rather purposeful in its way.

She had gone out of her way to cut him much more sharply than she did others.

Yet her parting shot had been very leading.

Julian pushed away from the bar and crossed to her. He stepped through her court and held out a hand in invitation although he had yet to see her dance. He didn't verbalize his request and didn't back away when she ignored him for a while to finish her current conversation. Then she turned her head and looked up at him. For a moment there was something very hostile flashing in the cold depths of her ice blue eyes, and then she cocked a brow in question.

"Back again?" she asked almost wearily. She leaned back in her chair, liquid silver fabric drawing tight over her fine breasts. He felt every man in range zero in on the detail and it grated harshly on his senses as they reacted with sexual arousal in varying degrees. Each and every one of them was determined to be the one she took home with her. Half of them were already hard in anticipation of it.

He needed to withdraw her from this throng before his temper began to chafe. As well trained as he was in controlling his more volatile emotions, he was in deep and alien waters now. He'd never experienced the brutality of impulsive feelings that he was currently being thrashed with.

"Again?" he echoed softly, meeting the chill beauty of her gaze. "I never left. However, it is time I asked you to dance."

"Time?" she asked archly.

"Well, yes. You challenged me earlier. I took up the gauntlet. The next step would be to convince you that I am the one you want to take to your bed tonight. I imagine dancing with you, and therefore obtaining time for private discussion, is one of the best ways to secure that in this environment."

"Hey!" someone protested his forthright supposition.

She held up a hand to stay the protester's chivalrous intent.

"Dancing will convince me to fuck you?" she queried just as bluntly. "You must be a hell of a dancer."

"Only one way to find out," he said.

She contemplated the proposal with amusement on her lips, then got up and walked past him, once again refusing to let him touch her even to guide her to the dance floor. That was okay, though. He would be touching her soon enough.

They reached the floor and he took the choice away from her abruptly, grasping her wrist and tugging her in close and tight along his body. She was tall and incredibly fit beneath her curves, her strength showing itself in a flare of resistance for a moment before she seemed to make herself relax against him. He understood instantly that it wasn't a real relaxation, the low tension in her spine and legs radiating clearly into his psyche. He had expected her to be uptight, so he didn't understand why she would try to affect otherwise. Why, he wondered, did she make herself curl against his body when she wasn't yet ready to do so?

He tested her, dropping a hand into the low, sweeping curve of her spine as it spread out over her sweetly turned bottom. He moved her in tight to the tempo of the music, swaying her sharply and deeply into the bend of his hard body. His very hard body. He made the state of his arousal known, letting her feel the thickness and weight of it through both their clothing, figuring she should share in the state since she'd caused it a good forty minutes ago and it hadn't eased since. But that was okay, too. He was enjoying the sensation.

The deprivation. He wasn't looking for easy relief; he wanted to drag it to him kicking and screaming, and he knew she would be the perfect resource for the battle he craved.

Julian turned her quickly around in his arms, giving himself the cushion of her rear for his hips as he curved an arm around her ribs under her breasts. He moved them both to the low, pulsing throb of the music almost as reflex. His full attention was elsewhere. His nose drifted down the line of her neck as he drew in that delicious verbena cleanliness. Feminine musk rose from her skin beneath her dress, the heat of the press of so many bodies making her warm considerably and creating the rich aroma in abundance. It was agonizing and gorgeous all at once. He longed to draw her away somewhere alone so he could indulge without all the harsh outside influences of smoke, alcohol, and overused synthetic perfumes worn by others.

"This is quite an argument," she said with a flirtatious rubbing of her backside against his zipper. Julian's hands swept down to her hips, holding her there against him as he let her warmth burn into him until he ached. She did not argue in the least, instead taunting him in seductive slides and wriggles.

Julian grabbed her around her slender throat, tipping her head back against his shoulder and engaging her ear with a rough-voiced warning. "Don't think you will play me like this and then just walk away with a toss of these sweet shoulders and that tart attitude of yours."

"I can do whatever I want. It's a free country and I owe you nothing." She turned in his hold, reaching down to flick a saucy finger up the length of his erection. "I think I've given you enough already."

Then she tossed her shoulders and whirled out of

his hold, making as if to walk away. Julian didn't let her get that far before returning her with an almost elegant catch and spin back against him. He settled her firmly in place, his hand back over her bottom although quite a bit more blatantly this time.

"Tease," he said gruffly against her ear. "Why are you being so purposely cruel to me? What have I done that so offends you?"

"Why would you think I am offended? Can't stand some simple hard-to-get? Grow a thicker skin," she advised. "Toughen up."

"I am plenty tough enough. Hard as steel, in fact," he hissed against her cheek. "More so than I have been for a very long time."

"Mmm. Sure," she scoffed. "Guy like you? You probably take home some airheaded tart every single night. Maybe I'm just not interested in being one of the crowd. Ever consider that?"

"You wouldn't be. I can promise you that. You would be the very last woman I would ever bring to my home. There would be you and no other after you."

Asia couldn't decide if that was a threat or a deadly promise. Still, she had to force herself past her knowledge of the game he was playing with her. She was pushing him too hard. She needed to be his choice, just as he was promising. She needed him to take her with him, and she prayed he would try to do to her what he had done to Kenya. She didn't have an exact plan per se because she didn't know exactly what it was he had done, but she was not going to leave him until he told her where her sister was. He would pay, one way or another, but above all else she had to know what had happened to Kenya.

Large hands slid over her hips and waist, and she shuddered at the sensation. It was horrifying, how a caress could be so logically repulsive and yet physically compelling all at once. In truth, she felt the crawling of her skin because she knew what he had done, but it was almost as if . . . as if the rest of her body was disavowing that knowledge just so it could respond on a purely molecular level. Without her permission, she felt the draw of him that so many other women must have felt. But that was okay, she told herself. She wanted to feel everything exactly as they had. She wanted to do everything exactly as his other victims had.

She had already made mistakes, like avoidance and cringing when his touch had so sharply reviled her. When he had reached in offer to get her to dance, she had been flooded with the irrepressible rage of wanting to hurt him in an act of vengeance. Asia needed to control that fury. She wouldn't allow herself to destroy her opportunity with wild emotion.

So now she took slow, even breaths and let him press his prodding erection against her pubic mound as they swayed in a rhythm contrary to the music around them. He seemed oddly out of control, like his patience was worn very thin. Was it because he was off schedule and he was eager for his latest kill? His words promised her he wasn't just looking to get laid. He wanted to get it all off. Whatever it was, he wanted to use her completely to satisfy his needs—both carnal and homicidal, if that was his goal. She could feel it in the desperation of his touch and the way he wouldn't let her move away from him again.

"That's quite an unbelievable promise," she whispered with a sly grin as she snaked two fingertips down the back of his neck in a meandering path of stimulation. "I could be the worst lay in town."

His laugh of disbelief was flattering and resounding. He was convinced otherwise and he made no bones about it.

"If this was only about sex, I might be worried," he conceded, "but it isn't."

A stupider girl would have taken that charmingly accented phrase as a promise of depth and romance. Many of them probably had. Thirteen of them at the very least. It disturbed her to think her sister had fallen so foolishly into such candied promises. Kenya was not so naïve to be swept away in such ways.

"Then what is it about?" she dared to ask.

"Oh, much more than the physical. Even beyond the spiritual. Once you learn the truth of that, perhaps you will not be as harsh and jaded as you are."

"You call it jaded; I call it having my eyes wide open."

"I call it a shame. The pain you American women suffer at the hands of your foolish men only proves to me how lacking they are as a sex and species."

"You are of their sex and species," she reminded him with a laugh.

"I am something very different than you have ever known before. This is another promise I can make. In my culture, you would be quite treasured. *I* would treasure you."

Yes, of course you would. You would kill me, stuff me, and mount me, getting off on the memory of my screams and death throes again and again as you treasured some trophy from my body.

Asia smiled in contradiction to her poisoned thoughts. "You haven't even asked me my name," she noted.

"Nor have you asked mine. I imagined you would ask when you were interested, and you would give when you were ready. I am in no hurry. I don't plan on losing track of you anytime soon."

Asia suppressed a shiver and simply smiled up into his pine green eyes again, rather creeped out by her own morbid thoughts. She wasn't afraid that she couldn't handle him, it was just how wretchedly sincere he sounded just then. It made her want to scream inside and out. But Asia Callahan, renowned as one of the very best bounty hunters and martial artists in the biz, always got her man, and this one was the most important catch of her life.

Maybe even her sister's life.

"Let's go," she said quite suddenly, her fingertips trailing slowly down the back of his neck in a sensual invitation. "If we're going to party, I want to get started. Now."

Julian raised a brow at her sudden and swift change of gears. There was no denying how genuine the invitation was—she did indeed want to get going—but he also sensed she had a not-so-hidden agenda, and it made him hesitate. Oh, had he been anyone else he would have believed the bold beauty he held against his body and her invitation to play, but he wasn't just anyone else and she wasn't just any woman.

The question was—who exactly was she?

It didn't matter. It *wouldn't* matter, he thought fiercely. He had to have her and he would do everything to see that he made her his.

"My place or yours?" he asked roughly as her touch powered through him in racing spears of energy. It could all sound almost normal. Almost real. Julian craved what she offered so artfully, his heart racing to know her and how she would feel in the throes of lusty, energetic screams. "Never mind. You'll come with me," he told her in the very next breath.

She gave him another of those enigmatically simple, shallow smiles that never quite thawed the icy calculation in her eyes. Julian did not pay that any mind. She was voluntarily allowing him to take her somewhere private, and that was all that mattered.

He swept her outside of the club, keeping her tight and close to his body. He ignored Vincent's leer and thumbs-up and hastened his prize to the rental car he had chosen a month earlier. He knew the racy design earned him status in the eyes of some women, and he also knew it would make no impression on this woman in particular. He rather enjoyed that idea. It was indicative of a woman who, for all her fine embellishments, was not dependent on material things. He thought of how useful that would be as he ushered her into the vehicle and hurried to get behind the wheel.

"I need to stop at my car for my purse," she informed him quickly, leaning her warmth against the length of his arm and trailing fingertips against his chest. He nodded curtly and threw the metallic beast into gear.

Asia snagged her bag from her car, not bothering to check what she already knew was ready and waiting for her within it. Even if he hadn't stopped as she had requested, she was prepared for that, too. This was just added insurance.

Julian Sawyer was going to regret the day he'd ever laid a hand on her sister.

Chapter 2

Asia was quite familiar with where Sawyer lived and lurked. She knew the entire layout of his rather classy apartment, from the broad living room to the wood-paneled kitchen, and especially the roomy back bedroom where he had taken so many of his nightly conquests. Of course, they hadn't always made it that far into the apartment. Julian did have the annoying habit of keeping all his shades tightly drawn, so it was only with parabolic microphones that she had learned as little as she had. Tonight that privacy was a deeply felt blessing. If there were newly aware Feds out there watching, she was going to keep them forever guessing over what was really going to happen. She might have preferred the anonymity of her own hotel room, but any agents worth their salt would have followed them there just as easily. At least she knew exactly how well versed he was in sealing his privacy.

The door closed and she tossed her purse down on a nearby chair as she turned and fully confronted the enemy. She wriggled a little slink into her carriage, reminding herself that she was supposed to be there for a good fuck and she needed to keep up that image until she was able to finally make her move. If that meant getting down and dirty, then so be it. Asia would do anything if it gave her even the smallest chance of restoring her sister to her.

Anything. Even if it meant completely seducing the repulsive beauty of this sociopathic Casanova.

Julian shut the door and dropped his keys on a side table, his eyes riveting onto her as she stood in a pose of proud display for him. Her Amazon's body tantalized and teased, she knew, the provocative cling of her clothing an amazing lure to his innately male sexual need for visual stimuli. She had watched him and knew his every last preference. He didn't care for any particular hair color, it seemed, but he tended toward women with long hair. He loved the long-legged ones most of all. He seemed to react very strongly to willfulness, enjoying fire and a bit of fight. Above all, he liked aggressive women. It wasn't hard to figure out that Julian Sawyer was looking for either a rough ride or a good fight to get himself off.

Asia tipped one spaghetti strap to the very edge of her shoulder, silver sliding low against her breast and threatening to run free from the nipple it clung to.

Julian's eyes ran dark, like evergreen as they fell to the tempting, teasing display, and she could swear he made a deep, dangerous sound of need and blatant desire. She recalled that she had noted him to be an eerily silent and methodical lover. She had heard woman after woman cry out in satisfaction, attesting that he actually knew what he was doing, but outside of his breathing she'd never heard so much as a groan from him. In fact, he'd been unnaturally quiet and still. She wondered if she should be flattered or afraid of anything different from the norm. Perhaps the more he was provoked, the more likely he was to lose control. Perhaps it was his sexual response getting out of his control that set off his psychosis. The thought only encouraged her to goad him. She wanted him to snap. She wanted him to give her a reason to open up hell on him.

She reached to push aside the opposite strap, but in a quick flash of movement she barely saw, he crossed to her and caught the thin strips of silver fabric, closing his large hands around her arms and shoulders as he kept her dress from sliding free of her body.

"No," he said deeply at her surprised and questioning look. "When I see you naked for the first time, it will be as a lover, not as a stranger. You will tell me your name first."

She hesitated at the dictate, knowing it was a very visible pause by the way he frowned so seriously. If he had been anyone else, she would have thought she'd hurt his feelings. But in all the time she had been stalking him, the one thing she had noted above all else was that Julian Sawyer was a man of very few emotions. He was always calm and always steady. Perfectly controlled at all times. Except for tonight. Tonight he was different. Different for *her.*

"Asia," she offered at last, the firmness of her tone warning him that was as far as she was willing to go. "My name is Asia."

He digested that for a moment, and she wondered how long it would take before he considered his condition satisfied and subjected her to the slightly chilly air-conditioned atmosphere of the apartment.

"Asia," he echoed, his large hands sliding smooth and warm up over her shoulders until, she realized, he had resettled the straps of her dress into a less precarious position. The unpredictability of his actions disturbed her a little. This wasn't how he had been with the others before her; he had shown no interest in speaking to them. Asia tried to remind herself yet again that a difference was a good thing. Something had set each pair of women of the past seven months apart from all the others. She needed to be set apart if she was going to be among that select class of victims.

In keeping with her character of the night, however, she dropped her hands onto her hips and cocked her head as she bent a knee forward enough to rub her leg between his thighs where it settled against them.

"I thought you were out for a fuck," she noted bluntly. "You can skip the Mr. Romance routine. I don't need it."

He studied her carefully a moment, reaching to trail his fingertips up along her throat. "I think you do need it," he observed. "I think you have a great many needs you'd rather not share with me. You want this to be uncomplicated and straightforward, where it cannot be."

"Sure it can," she forced herself to say even as his uncanny words made her heart race beneath her breast. "You are a man. I am a woman. As long as we have all the interlocking parts required—and I admit, a fair amount of skill would be nice as well—we can get straight to where we both want to be. You haven't had a hard-on for me for this long because you want to talk to me," she pointed out.

That earned her a wry smile, Julian's expression a bit sheepish and fearfully endearing as he ran a hand back through one side of his dark hair. She had thought it was black, but up close she could see it was the darkest possible brown. It bothered her suddenly that there was so much about him that was appealing. It was like roses. Something so fragrant and beautiful that you couldn't help burrowing your nose into it shouldn't have things like thorns and bees to hurt you. She appreciated how naïve and unlike her such a thought truly was, but just because she rarely indulged them didn't mean she didn't have them.

"My needs go well beyond those of my physical body," he said to her, those green eyes flicking up from their low position in his bent head. She felt snared by that look, her throat tightening with a strange sense of having gotten in way over her head. She wanted to laugh aloud at the ludicrous idea as soon as she had it.

"Well, mine don't," she countered, realizing she didn't sound as convincing as she should have. She reached out to cover that up with her touch, having already realized how easily it distracted him. She snaked her arms around his neck, drawing herself in tight and snug to his body. "Your physical body will suit me fine," she whispered softly as her lips brushed against his ear.

Julian groaned softly as she wriggled against him, his hands tightening reflexively against her shoulders. Before she knew it, he had turned his face against her neck and was . . .

Sniffing her?

Asia's brows lowered in a perplexed expression of disbelief as she felt him breathe deeply and sigh an extraordinary exhalation against her pulse. Even more unusual was the fine tremor she felt run through him.

"Such a sweet invitation," he breathed against her softly, his nose nuzzling against her pulse. "Too bad it is a lie."

He had her by her throat in an instant, his hand locking hard and fast around her as he kicked her feet out from under her and sent her slamming down to the floor on her back. He controlled the entire action, however, keeping the impact minimal, if not shockingly violent, as he ended up with his grip shy of throttling her and his face mere millimeters from hers. He had thrown a leg over hers, firmly pinning her to the hardwood floor as she instinctively reached to grasp the wrist of the hand at her throat.

"For a woman who wants to fuck so badly, you smell decidedly clean of sexual arousal," he growled harshly. "What game is it you are playing? Why are you here?"

"I don't . . . Are you out of your mind?" she rasped, the pressure of his hand just enough to warn her of his strength and the possible consequences if she ticked him off enough. "What the hell are you talking about?" Indignation seemed the way to go. Maybe a little fear. The more she was threatened, in actuality, the calmer and more in control Asia got. His kindness had rattled her much more than this would. *This* she understood.

This was what she had wanted.

She thumbed the catch on her ring, then grabbed his wrist again so the micro-fine needle injected into his skin. He would mistake the sensation for the cut of her diamond. In a sense it was exactly that. The heavy narcotic serum flooding into him would make him hers in an instant.

"I am talking about this . . ."

To her shock she felt his hand sweep up under her dress. His fingertips dipped into her panties below the waistband and it was all she could do to keep from freaking out as thick male fingers skimmed over her denuded mound and dove with intimacy between her nether lips.

"Warm. Damp, to be certain," he observed, "but in no way bearing the heat or wetness of a woman longing for sex."

"You're blaming me because you haven't done anything to turn me on?" she demanded incredulously.

"Your scent is fear-scent, and yet not. You smell of a hunter. The predator. The *ziniprano*. Tell me, *zini*," he said in a heated, fierce whisper of threat as he wedged himself in between her legs, "if it is a fucking you so desire, will it matter to you how it comes about?"

The intent behind his devious invitation and the hard actions of his heavy body over hers triggered a hell of a lot more than fear in Asia. She knew she needed to wait, if only to see the narcotic hit him like a ton of bricks, making all of this infinitely easier, but she couldn't. His intimate touch grew deeper as he spread her legs wide around his hips and Asia learned that there were just some things even she couldn't do.

"I don't know," she countered in a rasp of pent-up fury and hurt. "Why don't you tell me how you did it to my sister, first?"

He went still in surprise, just as she had hoped for, leaving himself wide open for her free hands to make their mark.

Asia was a jujitsu master. She had achieved black belt status at a very young age, and had only increased in degrees until the time she had become the sensei of her own dojo. The art of self-defense, the art of power in small movements. This was what she used to drive rigid fingers into his throat and eyes simultaneously. She took satisfaction in his roar of agony as she used the ripple of her fit body to buck him off her at the first available opportunity. She spilled his significant weight onto the wooden floor and pounced on him in fisted, violent strikes.

She hadn't expected him to be an easy target, and he did not disappoint her. She didn't even know how he had grabbed her and thrown her, but the next thing she knew she was getting floor burns on her bare legs as she skidded and tumbled away. She rolled up to her feet in smooth continuity, her hair whipping back as it spilled free of its twist. She ignored it, even though it was now a liability, and focused on her giant adversary as he growled with ferocious anger and crouched as if preparing to charge her. His following hesitation was a godsend. The more time he took, the more time for the drug in his system to take effect.

"What is this?" he confronted her with a roar of fury. "Why do you play this brutal game with me?"

"Because you are nothing but violent, evil filth, and this is what you deserve! You stole the single most precious thing from my life, as well as those most precious to the lives of countless others, and it's time you paid the price for that!"

"And you are going to make me pay, *zini?*" His laughter irked her as it rolled in irritating waves of derision over her. "Little warrior. So cold-hearted, no? To play such a game as the bait just to lure me in close. For what? What is this imagined slight I have done to you?"

"My sister, you prick!" she screamed, months of pain and fear suddenly overriding all of her cold control. Hot fury and unwanted agony burned in her throat and clenching fists. "You stole her! I want her back! You will give her back to me, or so help me, I will kill you!"

Why isn't the drug working? Damn it, Justin had guaranteed it would! She'd watched him test it on a gorilla, the injection taking under sixty seconds to drop the beast completely.

"I doubt that is how this will end," he said flatly. He seemed confident of that as he straightened and strolled directly across the room.

She fought. With everything she had and everything she knew, she beat him off her again and again. But every time she made a strike that should have taken him down, he simply shook it off and kept coming at her. It was as if he didn't feel any pain at all, except she knew that he did when he grunted or bellowed out from her critical hits. Fighting in heels lent disadvantages and advantages, not the least of which was the stiletto she drove deep into the back of his thigh, shedding first blood as she yanked free.

That was when everything changed.

She had pulled free with a spin so by the time she came full around, her fists raised in a pose of defensive aggression, blood poured down the back of his leg as he stumbled briefly to a knee.

At least she thought it was blood.

It was *pink*.

Not a thin or light red, not red of any variety or shade, but a brilliant carnation pink bordering on fluorescence.

The sight made her do a double take, the shock of it taking a moment to sink in as she stood frozen at the ready. Julian stood up slowly and turned around, his malachite green eyes glittering with a dangerous resignation. Asia had never known true and utter fear before, she realized. She knew that because she was feeling it right then when she finally understood just why the drug had not and would never work on Julian Sawyer.

He wasn't human.

Julian didn't know why he felt so betrayed by the acts of the gorgeously violent woman he was suddenly facing, but he did. He felt it bone deep and beyond. It was finally clear to him the reasons why she was there.

Apparently, her sister had been Chosen. One of the thirteen he had taken over most recently. Asia had sought him out on purpose, set out to lure him in any way she could, and had primed and pimped herself for vengeance. His unexpected reaction to her and the way it had muddled his senses and reflexes had almost provided the key opportunity she would have needed. But that was over now. Reality was settling cold and sober onto his shoulders, resigning him to acts of inevitability.

She would be his fourteenth and his last. If there had been any doubt, which there had not, it would have been out of his control the moment she drew blood and so obviously realized he wasn't what she had expected him to be. His cover was completely blown. Useless. If *she* knew he was responsible for the disappearances of those women, then it was a sure bet that others did, too. That irked him, simply because he took such pride in how flawlessly he conducted his work.

Now he needed to evacuate, and the law demanded she be dealt with without delay.

Julian took advantage of her momentary shock to charge her. He snatched her up and then drove her down to the floor. He didn't have time for grace or caution, though he tried to buffer her impact by cupping a protective hand around the back of her head. She hit hard, her breath jolting out of her like the explosion of a burst balloon. Then the drive of his weight on top of her hit her, preventing her from drawing in new oxygen. The advantage was all he needed to dive into the numbed aura radiating all around her lithe body. He could see the energy field surrounding her in vicious violets and furious reds, swelling in proportion to her anger and rage as she gave off the passionate power of her emotions. He could use them as the pathway into her, but he needed something quite different in order to open a pathway out of there.

Closing his eyes, a dangerous risk around his ferocious *zini*, he focused his mindheart on catching up the lighter tendrils of color around her. Few and far between though they were at the moment, he snared them nonetheless. Winding it around his mindheart like spun cotton sugar around a cone of paper, he gathered them more and more. When her breath came again, it was with a wide-eyed gasp. She was staring into the nothingness of her own personal energy as her anger was converted against her will to a completely different type of passion.

It was better when it was voluntary. It was so much more beautiful when the Chosen was open and willing, relaxed and ready to feel the pleasure transition could bring. She blindly reached for him, her hands fisting in his shirt as she fought his manipulation.

"Relax," he whispered to her softly as her body arched and contorted in a combination of resistance and starting pleasure. "You cannot fight this, Asia. Humans do not have the power at first. Your psyche is strong, your will is a thing of sheer beauty. You could sate the appetites of a thousand needy souls. I sensed it from you the moment I saw you. But it will be so much more than that. So very much more."

Once she was completely caught in his psychic webbing, he knew she would be helpless to resist or to physically fight him any more, despite her significant warrior skills. That had been a surprise, of course, but certainly made sense. The more aggressive and driven the personality, the more powerful the aura and all the energy it could exude. Julian pushed up away from her body a little, though he found himself loath to do so as his mental strokes along her essential energy translated in sensual writhing of her delectable form. His eyes drifted irresistibly down, over her chest where her nipples were poking out rigidly beneath the soft silvery fabric of her dress. The scent of her changed in strong degrees, and the arousal that had been missing from her "act" now permeated her skin and tissues with rich, musky intensity. It was positively delicious. So was the feel of her within his mindheart. His mindheart was the magnet, and her lust, need, and passion were the metals. His growing control over them began to manipulate them into amplifying the one thing he needed from her right then.

Pleasure.

Pure, anything but simple, and so very exquisite as it radiated stronger and stronger from her, it fed him until he was glutted with the delicacy of it. He became more than a little drunk with the incredible power of it. He was physically aching and blood flooded hard and hot into long-starved tissues. Julian sensed a certain measure of starvation from Asia as well. She fought her headlong tumble far better than any before her that he had ever seen. She was clearly used to powering through denial, to depriving herself of the pleasures of the body despite how she was so well made for it. The tragedy of that was in the fact that she was resonant with the raw talent for loving. Everything about her screamed a level of sensitivity and passion unlike anything he'd known before, and he craved intimate knowledge with that part of her. Not like this. Not with the forcible connection of minds, auras, and emotions where she had been given no choice, but with all the power of voluntary physical release and need that he sensed she was capable of.

"Oh God!"

She cried out and followed it up with a gasp as her

knees blindly rose up on either side of Julian's hips, cradling him in the amazing heat of her core when her sudden surrendering movement settled him deeply against her. She couldn't know how very long it had been since he had known such carnal pleasure. Even so, this was like nothing he could remember. The sheer heat of her overwhelmed him and he was pulsing almost violently with need as her legs snaked around his and pinned him tightly to her while she began to cant her hips up against him. The searing heat of her sex burned through the fabric of his trousers. She rubbed against his turgid cock like a cat in heat, which, he supposed, she was. A heat of his making.

Not hers.

That was what made the bodily pleasure he felt so very wrong. There was an act in this society where one person forcibly used another for physical sex. A deviant act they called rape. This did not exist in his world. In truth, there were much worse things than such an extreme violation to be found within his world. Still, he was keenly aware that what he was doing could be construed as a mental form of rape, because she had not been willing when it had begun, but he'd had no choice, and the penalty for breaking certain laws would have been far harsher on her than this choice of the moment. At least this path would give her bliss unlike anything she would have ever felt in her human existence.

Julian moved to draw away from her grasp, but was surprised to realize just how strong she was. She clung tightly to him, dragging him back down until his nose was firmly burrowed between her breasts, his sense of smell overwhelmed by that heated aroma of pure, aroused woman. Her fingertips raked through his hair as she writhed harder and moaned in low, rich need.

God, he needed her to let go of him, Julian thought as his own arousal began to feed back into the draw of hers through his stimulated mindheart. He could not be this close to her when she broke. Even now she was reaching a fervor as she rubbed in frantic strokes all around his captured body. She would climax soon, opening the Gate. He wouldn't allow her to be thrown into Justice Hall with her legs spread around him like some kind of nightfly. She deserved much more respect than that. From him. From those who forced him to steal her away like this.

Besides, if he felt her come against him, he was quite certain he wouldn't be able to hold back the urges surging through him to join her. He would waste himself like a lowlife residue rider, and that was simply unacceptable.

Julian's powerful mind grabbed hold of her fatly woven pleasure, stalling it until frustration made her squirm and loosen her grip on him. Inevitably, she sought to touch herself, desperate to jolt forward what he held in abeyance. He surged back away from her, well aware of how his body ached so badly he could hardly see straight. But that was okay. There would be time for more after. After she learned to accept what would become of her. He watched, completely mesmerized, as her hands parted in opposite directions over her skin, one diving beneath her top to fondle a breast and the fat, thrusting nipple so easily seen under the silver. The other headed between her legs, scrabbling to get under her skirt and to touch herself all at the same time. Julian carefully resituated himself, ignoring his own discomfort so he could sit her up between his legs, his chest bracing against her back as her hair rained straight and black between their bodies. Grasping her wrists, he released his hold on her psychic pleasure. She began to build up again instantly, the sharp climb making her cry out as her hands left her body in order to crawl up his arms. She clung to his biceps as he smoothed her little dress back into place. The unbelievable beauty of her body would be his and his alone, he thought with determination. He needed her to be this way at this moment in order to make passage, but he would give them no other part of her unless she volunteered it. Even so, she would be his.

His.

Julian felt her reaching for the jolting crest of her orgasm, his mindheart overwhelmed with the rush of it. He gathered it all, channeled it into a hard, boring tunnel of energy, and then let her explode. Asia screamed as climax rippled in hard, senseless waves through her mind and body. But instead of the sharp high and dramatic drop she might be used to, this continued on and on, until she couldn't even breathe anymore. Her nails gouged into Julian's upper arms, but he bore it quietly as he guided them home.

Chapter 3

Julian reached to gently turn her raised knees to one side, protecting her from the eyes of the Ampliphi as they abruptly appeared before them, seated on the floor in the center of Justice Hall. The Gate was still brilliant around them, more so than usual as all the excess power of Asia's energy spilled out in the form of an azure and lavender light. Smoke scudded out over the intricately tiled floor of the Ampliphi chamber. Then, with a last gasp for breath, Asia collapsed weakly against Julian, the energy that Gate travel had taken from her leaving her drained in spite of her plentiful resources. This was as much his fault as anything. She had so disrupted and disturbed his focus that he had not finessed the portal of travel so it wouldn't burn her out so much. As it was, listening and feeling her reach that crest as she had undulated in beautiful, bursting pleasure had just about undone him. He had never seen anything like it in his entire career.

Not in his entire lifetime.

Considering he had conducted the sexual energy of a great many human women in that time, that was truly saying something.

The Gate resonated with one last glow around them and then disappeared with a hard, vibrating snap of cut-off energy. Julian turned up his eyes to the Ampliphi as he cradled his unwilling prize between his hands and thighs, holding her tightly against his chest.

"Julian, why have you returned?"

The six beings around him were always magnificent to see. Over time they had evolved so they could spend much of their time as pure psychic energy, even in spite of the energy crisis. It was such an amazing accomplishment that it deserved all of one's respect and awe. Only the Ampliphi were this powerful, and only their advanced age, experience, and wisdom could have allowed for them to achieve such a grand state. They were proof of what miraculous things could be done with a minimum of energy.

However, the strain of starvation showed on them just as it did all of Julian's people. At the moment, though, they were all glowing quite a bit more vigorously than usual because of the explosive flood of energy Asia had brought into the room. Their silvery auras were brilliant to look upon. Julian couldn't help the flash of possessive jealousy that raced through him when he realized that they had been exposed to the fallout of Asia's climax. No one had intended to steal from her, but her crest had been so powerful and effervescent that it must have been forced onto the unsuspecting Ampliphi. Julian struggled to keep from resenting their fully flushed appearances and silvery glow that nearly blinded him in that moment.

Energy was not to be hoarded selfishly, he knew. Still, he found himself strongly despising the idea of having to share any part of Asia with anyone else.

Julian tried to dismiss the possessive impulse. He focused on the Ampliphi who had spoken while pushing aside the telltale emotions spinning through him that he knew they could easily identify in his aura.

"Ampliphi Kloe." He greeted his sponsor first, as respect and tradition demanded. Then he turned his attention to the leader of the Ampliphi. "Ampliphi Christophe," he greeted with equal respect and a grave nod of his head. "I have conducted this woman across against her will."

His announcement was greeted with one or two bright flashes of irritation. He had expected they wouldn't be happy, but there was nothing he could do about that now.

"You have been compromised," Ampliphi Rennin noted, disapproval sharp in his tone.

"To what extent, I do not yet know," he acknowledged. "But I suspect it to be only a minimal exposure of attention. She did not know I was not human. Cleaners will need to be sent behind me. Blood was shed."

"We can see that," Ampliphi Christophe noted, drawing Julian's attention to the blood dripping heavily onto the floor beneath his leg. "This is very disappointing, Gatherer. Only seven months? You have never been discovered so quickly before. This is a setback we as a species cannot afford."

"I am aware of that, Ampliphi. I beg your forgiveness. However, my circuit as Gatherer would have ended anyway. This woman is *kindra* to me."

He felt the surprise that rippled through the august body of beings. He hardly faulted them for it. He was in just as much shock as they were over the development.

"Impossible!" Ampliphi Kloe swirled in angry violet. *"Kindra,"* she scoffed. "More likely you make excuses to drop your responsibilities."

Julian bristled at the accusation. He was used to

Kloe's bitter ways, but she was calling him a liar and it would not be tolerated. He didn't care who she was.

"How can you be certain?" Ampliphi Sydelle spoke up. There was movement to her right and Julian became aware of Gatherer Kine's presence over her shoulder. He wondered why the Gatherer was home instead of in the field.

"This cannot be explained. It cannot be quantified," Julian said carefully. "I know many believe the *kind* to be a myth, but anything written about so much cannot be make-believe."

"She is human," Sydelle countered dismissively, ever the arguer. But she did not argue to undermine so much as to test his faith in his position.

"Are humans not our salvation in every other way?" Julian demanded. "We are doomed to die without them. They were chosen because of how close they are to us in makeup, minds, and emotion. Why not a human? We rely on their spirits for everything else, why can there not be *kind* among them?"

Julian's heart raced with fear as the Ampliphi exchanged lightning-sharp bolts of energy between them, debating back and forth in silence with each other. Then, with a bright emanation, Christophe ended the speculation.

"This you speak may be all true, but if she came over unwillingly I am going to guess she has not acknowledged this connection between you. We will let you acclimate her and guide her. We will let you woo her as you will. However, if she rejects you, then we know she is not *kindra* to you and she will go the way of the others who have come before her. Do you accept?"

"Yes," Julian answered with quick and sure eagerness. Whatever doubts they might have, he knew the truth.

"Well, this is disappointing," Ampliphi Kloe said with

a frustrated emanation. "You are our best Gatherer, Julian. Also, this woman has enough energy to feed thousands of us."

Julian was on his feet in an instant, his hands curling into fists as he stood over Asia, his feet braced on either side of her as she lay in an exhausted slump on the floor between them. His sudden aggression lashed out at the council of Ampliphi in streams of indigo, whipping energy he could not manage. He was so thoroughly juiced with Asia's psychic plentitude that he was having trouble controlling the abundance of emotion it created.

"You'll not deprive me of her," he said soft and low, the furious threat behind the calm words quite evident on the basis of his energy alone. "Not even you can do that if she is truly *kindra!*"

"Easy, Gatherer." Christophe tried to soothe him, tendrils of gentle pink power extending to touch Julian with a sense of fairness and compassionate understanding. "We have already given you our terms and we will hold up our end. If you are *kind* to one another, the residual of what will come between you as you live your daily lives will be enough to energize your entire colony. Believe us when we say we hope you are not wrong in your supposition. I think Kloe is merely disappointed that our best Gatherer is seemingly now defunct. She is rather proud of her most accomplished student, you know."

Julian did know, and he felt quite foolish for reacting in such an openly hostile manner, but Kloe had a way of bringing that out in others. He understood it was also Asia's influence that made it so, but that didn't make him feel any better for treating a mentor in such a distrusting manner.

"I did not want this," he said, meaning to speak to

himself but finding the thought out in the open. He realized it was fear of the unknown and overwhelming future that prompted his impulse to reject. But even as he spoke, he knelt down beside the woman who had rent his life into shreds within the space of a human hour. She had sought him out for all the wrong reasons, believed all the worst of him, and would wake to a very different world than she had known. Julian supposed it was only fair that both their lives had to be destroyed in order to place them on an equal plane where they could rebuild something together. "She will not be easy. She did not volunteer in any fashion."

"Just the act of bringing her around will feed thousands," Kine mused wryly.

"You had best get on with it, then. It wouldn't do for this to begin among us," Ampliphi Greison said sagely. "In one cycle she will return to this chamber where I will make final judgment as to whether she is fit to stay among us or not. This lies on your shoulders, Gatherer. She must freely give what we need or she will be wiped and returned to her home."

"You would destroy her entire mind," Julian protested.

"Just her memories of who and what she is. Her memories of this place and of you. She will be a danger to us all if I did not. So I suggest you not fail in your endeavors to win her over."

"No. Of course not." Julian wasn't certain if he felt sincerity or sarcasm behind Greison's suggestion. He rarely found himself in agreement with Greison, but the Ampliphi was right: Asia had to come around or they would rob her of everything she was.

But he would be damned before he would tell her as much. If she came around it would be because she wanted to, not because she was being blackmailed into it.

Julian moved in an attempt to gather her up, but suddenly the displacement of energies he'd ridden overwhelmed him and sent him tottering off balance. It was all he could do to brace himself with both hands against the floor. The weakness and disorientation annoyed him, but it would pass. The true irritant lay in showing the flaw to the noble gathering behind him. Of course, he highly doubted any of them had experienced the differences between life on Earth and life here Beneath. The flux of power alone was as nauseating a ride as a gravity-defying, record-breaking roller coaster. The analogy amused him for a moment when he realized it was Shade's fascination with the human inventions that had brought the example to mind. His coworker was obsessed with the damn things, and it had clearly rubbed off.

"Gatherer, you are weakened," Greison noted with rankling dispassion. "I shall contact your Companion to come and assist you with your burden."

"No!" Julian was up and whirling on the Ampliphi in a heartbeat, the action only worsening his fluctuating equilibrium. Still, he held himself strong and steady. "Do not."

"Nonsense. You require assistance. There is no shame in that. This is what a Companion is for," Rennin said dismissively, reaching for the bell that would summon Julian's Companion.

"Please, I beg of you, do not do this in this manner. I . . ." He hesitated when the desperation in his voice caused their energy to beat at him with curiosity. "I would not wish to reveal the future to my Companion in such a coldhearted manner."

Julian could tell they did not understand. It was

very likely that they wouldn't, even with an explanation. The Ampliphi, like so many of his people, were quite disengaged from their emotions much of the time. Compassion chief among them.

"Julian, you are being oversensitive," Ampliphi Sydelle scolded him.

"Too much time exposed to humans, no doubt," Greison considered.

"No," Julian retorted sharply. "I merely suggest that it would be cruel to force my Companion to so abruptly face the one who will replace her."

"Ridiculous. Ariel knows she is not your *kindra*, and as such expects this day may be in her future. We assigned her to you. You never made a commitment, and even if you had, it would have been foolish of her to accept it at face value," Kloe scoffed.

"Julian would never make a false promise," Gisella defended him, making him recall why he had always been partial to her, even though she had not been the one to mentor him. Then she turned to him and reminded him of why the Ampliphi so irritated him at times. "Ariel is your servant. You are her master. She is to obey you in all things and accepts this as her place. You do her discredit to attribute nonsense to her sensibilities."

"I beg your humble pardon, Ampliphi, but you don't know a damn thing about Ariel. You haven't been Companioned with her for sixteen years as I have. I doubt any of you have had more than cursory contact with her in all of this time. Ariel is . . . insecure. Possessive, you could say. She will not take this well."

That was understating matters. Over the years, his long, continued absences when his Gatherer duties took him to Earth time and again had germinated small seeds of jealousy and loneliness into full-blown and often debilitating characteristics in Ariel. Characteristics he could have had her dismissed for a long time ago. Perhaps he should have done. Unlike his methodical compatriots, however, he had not had the heart to tip her over the edge by confirming her every doubt that she would never quite be enough for him. Since he was so rarely present in this realm anymore, it had not been much of an issue to leave her to do her work as always.

It would be now.

His days as a Gatherer were on hold for quite some time, if not permanently. Asia had seen to that in more ways than one.

"If this is the case, why did you not approach us with this? You ought to have shed the defective girl immediately. These types of distractions are the last thing our Gatherers need. We have rules and bounds for a reason, Julian." Sydelle shifted in a rare show of irritation. "Companions are assigned to ease your cares and needs, not compound them. We will have her ejected from your living spaces immediately."

"You will not."

Few dared to countermand the Ampliphi, least of all in such a resounding and dire tone of voice. The chamber fell quite quiet, energy ebbing away from Julian now as his own surplus flared hard with his temper.

"You will allow me time to gently and thoughtfully prepare a longtime Companion for her transition to retirement. She will not serve me so long only to be dismissed in shame at the very end. She deserves better, for, despite her weaknesses, she has done her service well and thoroughly. It is not Ariel's fault that her trainers did not see the flaws in her confidence that made her unsuitable for a role as Companion. She hid them well, even from her own awareness, I assure you. It was years before the cracks became large enough for me to see them. This transition will be done with respect and in private. I will not force her to keep composure in front of you all even as she helps to carry the end of life as she has known it into her own home. She will be rejected, evicted, retired, and obsolete in all of an instant. That instant should be between her and me alone."

Julian did not wait to see if they agreed or disagreed with what amounted to a command. Despite his position and power, he risked much taking authority with the Ampliphi in such a manner. He doubted anyone else would have been allowed to get away with it.

He knelt again, this time in all steadiness, because so much balanced so precariously on his strength in that moment. He lifted Asia tight and close to his chest and rose smoothly to his feet. He exited the chambers in a few sharp strides.

"He was ever willful," Sydelle mused.

"His unflagging confidence is what made him so ideal for the role of Gatherer," Kloe said with no little amount of smug pride. She was the one who had insisted on his training, grooming him from the first day. She would not let them revise all her hard work at this late date.

"He should be checked for this," Rennin grumbled. "It does not do for him to think he can get away with—"

"He will be more powerful than us all one day," Christophe interrupted sharply and definitively, quelling the debate before it began. "If any of you doubted that, those doubts must end with the taking of his *kindra*. Without her, he would be formidable.

With her, he will be nigh unstoppable. There are no limits to what he will accomplish."

"He needs to win her first. Stealing her from her life will not make an easy way of it," Rennin mused. "To be his match, her will must be equal to his own. They could just as easily destroy one another."

"Do not look so eager for the prospect, Rennin," Christophe warned. "You may fear your future if you must, but you ought to fear all our futures if something significant does not happen soon to interrupt the disaster we are rushing toward. Losing Julian will only make it happen all the quicker."

"God forbid it," Sydelle whispered with the dreadful respect their situation called for.

"God may yet grant your wish," Christophe sighed. "But until then . . ."

He reached for the bell. He fed energy into the ring, sending out a distinctive frequency. Every being among them had their own toned signal. They knew it instinctively, felt the pull to answer the call of the Ampliphi whenever it was sounded. They were born with it, their auras resonating it. Only the six bells in the chamber could create the match. It could not be duplicated any other way.

Within a moment, the Ampliphi's call was answered, a rush of energy displacement at the center of the chamber rolling off the newcomer in dark, overwhelming waves. It was so different from Julian's righteous and bright abundance of energy. But then, Julian spent much time feeding from human energy.

This one was from the very bottom of the energy food chain.

Greison narrowed all of his energy on his Gatherer, studying him silently for a long space of time. The others waited patiently as he ordered his thoughts.

"We have a task for you," he said, the gravelly resonance of his voice echoing throughout the Hall.

Julian entered his home quickly, closing the door against curious stares that rankled so easily. He didn't even bother to locate Ariel, knowing she would be on him in just moments once she sensed his arrival. He swiftly made his way to the second level of the structure and carried Asia into the unoccupied room he maintained for visitors. He had no sooner set her down than the excited greeting burst along the walls.

"Julian! Julian!"

Ariel ran into the room as he turned to face her. She rocketed her soft, rounded little body up against him and hugged him until he was throttled by her strength and her excitement. Her hair hung damp against her back and wrists, telling him she had been bathing. Her robe, in fact, was damp, as if she'd leapt straight from the bath and donned it.

"You're home! I wasn't expecting you at all! No one warned me. I will ready your things as soon as I—"

"Come now and be easy." He chuckled softly against her temple. "There is time for everything. Mostly there is time for you to take a breath."

"Then you aren't leaving again right away?" she asked eagerly as she clung to him and looked up into his eyes.

Julian hesitated. He didn't mean to be evasive, but he didn't want to lie to her, and the bald truth would be like slitting her gut wide open. In the time it took him to struggle for the right words, Ariel's head tipped to the side and she caught sight of the woman in the bed behind him.

"Julian, who is this?" she asked, her enthusiasm

bleeding out of her swiftly and suspicion creeping into her voice—along with an instant emanation of jealousy. She gripped at him a bit more strongly as her eyes narrowed on Asia. "You've brought home a guest? A Chosen? Shouldn't she be with the Ampliphi receiving residence?"

"Ariel, let's go inside and talk for a moment," he invited her gently.

"No." She bit her lip and stubbornly drew back to cross her arms over her body. "Tell me here and now, why is she here?"

"Because this is my home, Ariel," he reminded her a bit sharply as her petulance boded ill for the coming conversation. "She is my guest because I choose her to be. But also . . . she is a special woman." He turned slightly to look at Asia, unable to help reaching out to touch her foot.

"I'll just bet she is," Ariel hissed with her entire being, the lash of her fury laced with pain. "The only reason for bringing a Chosen home is so you can bed her, Julian! I can sense the lust on you already! You reek of her!"

"Enough!" he said harshly, turning back to her with a hard motion.

"No! How could you do this?" Ariel's warm, tragic eyes filled with tears. The energy of her emotions sank into him. Julian found himself already overfilled with Asia's vitality, so it didn't affect him as much as it had at other times when Ariel had pulled out cards of guilt and betrayal. It helped him steady himself for her inevitable hurt. "This is my home, too," she whispered painfully.

"Not any longer," he told her softly.

Ariel gasped, his information so unexpected that she froze in wide-eyed shock. She stared at him as if she hadn't heard him right, but she quickly realized that she had.

"No," she breathed. "No! I-I didn't mean . . . t-to make you angry!" She vibrated with clumsy panic, her heart racing wildly in fear.

"Ariel, I am not angry," he said as gently as he could. "I am not punishing you."

"Yes! Yes, you are!" she cried, her hands gripping the front of her robe, her body hunching into itself as if seeking protection.

"No, Ari. Ariel, she is *kindra* to me." Julian paused only long enough to watch the awful impact that bit of news had on her. He was truly sorry to hurt her, the pain flooding out of her tasting bitter on his tongue and flitting against the walls of mental protection he had to erect against her. However, she had to face the fact that her life was about to change and her plans and fantasies concerning him would never see fruition. "I'm sorry, but this is the way things have been dealt. You have been an excellent Companion for all these years, and I should like you and me to always be close, but the arrival of my *kindra* means it is time for you to retire. It's beyond time for you to find companionship for yourself. There are so many out there who would—"

"I don't want them! I want you!" She flung herself into him, wrapping him in the clutch of her arms like a vise. Her hands gripped his shirt so hard that the fabric popped at its seams. "Please. Oh, please, Julian don't do this! She's nothing! An *alien!* What does she know of you? What can she appreciate of the gift you are? I know! I know *everything*. What you need. What you like. I even know what you desire!"

"Ariel, stop this," he commanded her, overpowering her and putting her away from him. "You have always known we are not meant to be committed. You have served your role as Companion with loyalty and devotion. Let's not end this in a way that will cause us pain and hardship." He paused, judging the stubbornness and anger radiating off her. "And no, Ari, you do not know what I truly desire. If you did, and if it mattered to you, you wouldn't be thinking and acting so selfishly. Maybe she doesn't know anything of me, but she will. Once she does, everything here will change. Don't you want to see our people healthy and happy?"

"I don't care about anyone else but you," she whispered.

"Then I am more convinced than ever that you don't truly love me, Ariel. If you did, you would never say such a thing. You would never feel such a thing. Now, please . . . the Ampliphi will give you a beautiful new life where you will be treasured by many just as you deserve." He reached out and gently brushed back her hair for a moment, trying to ease the rigid betrayal etched into her features. "In three days they will come for you, and you must be ready. Go and begin. I don't expect you to care for my *kindra*. I would not be so cruel to you. If it is too hard for you to remain these three days, tell me now and I will see you escorted to Justice Hall as soon as you wish."

Ariel stood for a moment, her arms wrapped tight and tense around her body, her bitter gaze shifting from him to the woman in the bed behind him.

"I will serve out my time," she said with wintry emotions oozing off her. "If I am to be banished, I would at least appreciate some time for our good-byes. Will you give me that much?"

"Of course. It is a hard adjustment for us both, Ariel. Don't mistake my firmness as being uncaring. I simply have no other choice. Not anymore."

"Yes. So you say."

With that vague agreement, Ariel turned and walked out of the room, the slump in her defeated posture making Julian's mouth sour again. He looked back at Asia, more aware than ever of how far he would have to come with her.

Julian turned to sit in the lone chair in the room, the only other piece of furniture there was. He exhaled long and slow, his head bowing so he could rub at the tension in his neck while he waited for Asia to awaken.

Chapter 4

Asia opened her eyes with a slow, sticky flutter, as if she didn't have the energy to complete the task. It only took an instant for memory to rush in on her, and fury and outrage bolted into her rapidly afterward. She surged upright into a sitting position . . .

. . . and promptly flopped over onto her chest and face, her whole body wobbling in on itself like a tragically overcooked noodle. She found her nose buried in a gossamer fabric of white that clung softly to her face even as she tried to get strength under herself to at least roll back and breathe some fresh air.

It was the touch of smooth fingers around her throat and shoulder that finally made the action possible. The stroke of that touch against her skin made it scream with sudden sensitivity, but Asia gritted her teeth against the unwanted sensation as she was turned over. She didn't need to look up into those jade eyes to know that the hands belonged to her heartless enemy. Julian Sawyer. He pressed a palm to the bedding beside her ear and brushed aside her wild hair as he leaned over her. Darkest brown curls slid into a loose arrangement against his forehead. She wished she had the energy to reach up and snatch the charmingly obnoxious lock right out of his forehead. Even more, she wished she could knee the bastard right in the crotch. He was leaning over her in a vulnerable enough position, but she simply had no strength.

"What did you do to me?" she demanded, surprised to hear the breathy weakness in her own voice. Then, in the very next instant, she began to recall very vivid snatches of exactly what he had done to her.

Well, not *exactly*.

But enough to know without a doubt that it had been his manipulation that had caused her loss of all control. He had ripped away all of her defenses in a heartbeat, prying her open and gutting her for his own fascination and inspection. She remembered the waves of unbelievable pleasure, the crippling need as he had tormented her. Asia especially remembered the embarrassing way she had writhed beneath him, all but begging him to do what she would never have wanted him to do.

She fought the urge to cry like some kind of weak, whimpering heroine in a movie who waited around for someone else to save her. Asia had always saved herself. No one would take that from her, especially not the man who had already stolen her dignity from her. Dignity and oh so very much more.

"I'm sorry," he said, sliding a hand under her head and slowly rearranging her on the comfortable bedding. The bed felt rather like being cradled in a hammock, only somehow firmer. Certainly a much larger and more stable environment as he knelt halfway onto the surface beside her. "I had no choice. Had it been up to me, I would have done this properly. However, when you drew blood, proper became impossible."

The memory of bloodying him made her smile . . . until she recalled the color of that blood.

"You're an alien?" It sounded utterly ridiculous even to her, so she didn't resent his laughter. But it was the only explanation she could come up with.

"No, *zini*, I am not. Alien to your world, perhaps, but here *you* are the alien."

Panic infused her as her very worst fears were confirmed.

Dorothy wasn't in Kansas anymore.

"Holy hell and damnation," she uttered. "I've been kidnapped by aliens?" She scoffed and reached up to hit him, push him or, damn it, even flick him. Anything to reflect her fury with him for putting her in this preposterous position. All she managed was a weak flop of her hand against his chest. He made it worse by chuckling again.

"I never would have taken you to have such an imagination," he mused.

"Get away from me," she said. "When this drug wears off, you prick, I'm going to kick the shit out of you."

"I thank you for the forewarning. It is most considerate of you. However, you are not drugged. Merely exhausted. To be honest, I am rather surprised to see you awake. It is nothing plenty of sleep cannot cure, of course. Then you will be free to kick my ass if it is what will make you feel better. Experience tells me, however, that it is not likely to help you."

"Yeah, well, I'll have fun with it just the same," she grumbled. She paused in her temper, finding even strong emotions to be exhausting. She took the moment to look around at her surroundings. Above her was a sharp, conical ceiling, the shape and material quite surreal. It was as if it had been hand-woven. Some kind of fibrous material turned in progressive, tight patterns all the way up until it reached a perfect point about twelve feet above her. The shape reminded her of the cap to the tower where Rapunzel had been kept prisoner in her storybook as a child. She had always hated those "princess in a tower" stories. She supposed she had been an empowered female even as a child, circumstances making her old and wise before her time. Kenya had been a little more fanciful, but that was because Asia had raised her to provide her with a little more opportunity to be free to follow her dreams and desires.

"Where am I?" she asked at last, though she dreaded hearing she was on some kind of funky, pointy spaceship.

"You are Beneath," he said, as if that explained everything.

He looked like that was all he was going to say for a moment, but then seemed to reassess that plan. Asia realized he had judged her capable of handling the truth, no matter how shocking it might be to her, and she couldn't help but feel surprised that he had intuited what so many men around her could never seem to figure out. Even the ones that had known her for years couldn't help the constantly annoying urge they seemed to be born with to protect her from things that were, in the end, really quite trivial, or to condescend to her because of her gender. It gave her a chill that a stranger seemed to get what they had never been able to comprehend, and she'd barely had a real conversation with him.

"I know this will be hard for you to believe, and you will only be convinced when you see it all for yourself. After all, to you I am not worthy of trust and I am a lowlife beneath the capability of truth. I realize this is your perspective. Just the same, I will explain.

Earth . . ." He hesitated when he saw her eyes widen slightly at the reference to Earth as a place separate and apart from his pending explanation. "Earth is both much nearer and much farther than you may comprehend. We are Beneath. Beneath Earth." He sat on the edge of the bed and held out a flat hand, palm down. "Think of it as levels of existence. Earth is a plane, or some would call it a dimension. Located here. In this sense, you have to imagine that Earth is actually flat. It's a flat space running in an infinite line on its particular plane, one dimension within the universe, so to speak. There are planes both above and below the plane you know. Humans have a sense of them, actually, and mistakenly refer to them as Heaven and Hell. Heaven and Hell are actually very different dimensions beyond what I am about to describe, but let's not confuse the issue. There are three planes above Earth, and three below. Each runs parallel to the one above or below it. You are here." He indicated a plane far and low from the hand representing Earth. "Beneath. The lowest plane below."

"Great. I'm literally in the lowest level of hell," she ground out. "I suppose you are going to tell me it all 'looks just like Earth'?"

"Hardly that," he said with a frown. "In fact, I must warn you not to go outside of this house without me at first. It can be very dangerous for one who is unfamiliar with the nature of this place."

"How convenient," she said with snide sarcasm. "If I believe you, I might stay here cowering in fear of the unknown and not attempt escape. Nice try."

"I'm quite serious," Julian said sharply. "This is no ploy. I have no reason to keep you within these walls except to keep you safe from outside harm. It is not as though you can run back home or escape to some-where else."

Asia couldn't help but feel a little bit rattled by how off-the-cuff confident he seemed of that.

"And you just happen to speak English here?" she asked shrewdly.

"No. I know English from my time in America and other countries of Earth. Those who are native Beneath speak a language of the mind and of energy. Again, your species has a sense of it in things like body language. It may take a little time, but you will come to comprehend us quite well eventually."

"Like hell I will. There isn't going to be any 'eventually.' I want to go back home."

"You cannot."

She'd known he was going to say that. Thirteen missing girls backed the truth of his words.

Shit!

"Kenya! She's here? Beneath?" she demanded, struggling to sit up and being frustrated by the lack of her body's response.

"Yes, *zini.* Not in this village at the moment, but she is Beneath. She is safe, alive and really quite happy, I assure you."

"You'll forgive me if your assurances don't mean squat to me," she hissed at him. "My sister loved her life just the way it was. She loves me. There is no way she would willingly go anywhere without me."

"Well, she isn't without you any longer, now is she?" he pointed out. "However," he added baldly, "she was not unwilling when she came here. Unlike your cir-cumstances, she readily volunteered to come."

"You are a liar! This is all a bunch of bullshit! Let me up! Let me go!"

She shoved against him, her fingers batting against him like ineffective little moths.

"I do not lie. I may conceal certain truths, but I do not lie." He had the nerve to sound highly offended. "In time you will speak to Kenya for yourself. For now, I can prove nothing to you until you rest and regain your strength. Take your time. If I am lying, you can prove me a liar just as well later as now. I will not harm you. I will not . . ." He hesitated and seemed to edit himself. "There will not be a repeat of what happened before without your permission. Had I any choice I would not have taken you like that. But there are laws here. Chief among them is that no one who learns of us can remain on Earth. The damage and danger it could cause to every plane would be horrendous. It is the one universal rule among the planes. Earth is to remain unaware of us . . . at least empirically. As I said, you have a sense of our existence. The trouble is that, as a species, humans are too volatile to enter the planes en masse. Very delicate creatures live in these places in a very delicate balance. These balances have been disrupted before, and even now we suffer for it. But I will explain that another time. Please rest."

He reached out to caress a thumb over her cheek, and Asia was glad to have the satisfaction of jerking away from his unwelcome touch. His tenderness was just as disturbing now as ever. She watched him rise away from her and there was a creak of ropes as his weight left the bed. As soon as he was gone, she inspected her surroundings. There was no solid door to the room. He had passed through a curtain of dense, heavy beadwork that shined and glittered like strung gems. The bed, she realized, really was like a hammock. Ropes secured it to the woven walls at several points on three sides, the only open side the one he had left from. The room was round, like the single leaf of a clover, except where it connected to what must be the rest of the house. It was unusual, to be sure, but hardly beyond the scope of a creative architect. Why anyone would want to build a round house was beyond her, but it had certainly been done before.

Otherwise, the room was quite bare. It was clearly meant to only be slept in. She did notice that there were no windows, making it very much a prison to her. That made her very suspicious of his claims that this was a "home," rather than someplace he took his kidnapping victims to. She had to admit, his explanation was creative. It was a bit unnerving, however, to realize that the alien psychopath might also be delusional. Odds were they hadn't gone anywhere that a car couldn't get to. He might be . . . different, but that was not proof that he was being truthful.

The only question she had, as her exhaustion caught up with her and began to drag her back under, was whether Kenya was really nearby and if she was truly okay.

When Asia awoke later on, she had no concept of how much time had passed. All she knew was that she was awake, able to move like normal, and starving.

As if he had read her mind even before she had awakened, Julian came in bearing a tray of very unusual foods. She recognized only half of the things there. French fries and corn on the cob. Strange combination for an alien menu, she thought, looking up at him questioningly.

"I got attached to certain Earth foods," he explained almost bashfully. "It's frowned on to bring them here, but it's not illegal, so I stock up on my favorites. They are very unique to your realm. I thought you might find a little comfort in their familiarity. The other two dishes are called *htinni* and *yogu*. Both are local fruit and vegetable dishes. They are among the most flavorful of this culture."

He set the tray down on the bed beside her, and the look she shot him was positively scathing. "If you think I'm going to eat anything you give me, you are out of your freakin' mind."

"It isn't drugged," he assured her, taking up a liberal clump of fries and eating them with obvious enjoyment. "Salt. I think it is the salt that makes both of these things so delicious. It is a shame it is so bad for human health. And yet, salt is a key part of your makeup. Is that not curious?"

"Yeah. Fascinating," she said, not sounding the least bit intrigued.

He ignored her sarcasm, spooning up one of the two stranger dishes for himself. It was orange in color, steaming and fragrant like spice and curry was fragrant, but looked a bit like baby food. It was probably exactly that. Baby food spiced up to seem strange and alien.

Julian did not avail himself of any more of her food to prove it wasn't poisoned. She wouldn't eat either of those untouched dishes, if she considered eating at all. He looked for a moment like he wanted to say something more to her, but then he simply turned to leave. It wasn't until he reached the beaded curtain that he finally spoke up.

"You have the run of the house. I must leave for a short time, but you need to remember not to go outside as yet. I will take you out when I return. Please heed me at this if nothing else. I only ask a little patience, and then I will show you my world. I would stay, but I have to . . . I have things to attend to. If you need anything, Ariel will be here."

He hesitated again, his pause quite pregnant with things he wanted to say but did not. It only served to irritate her. He left her wondering who the hell Ariel was. Figuring there was only one way to find out a lot of the answers she needed, she pushed the tray aside and slid cautiously to her feet. She tested herself out for aftereffects of drugs, but she felt quite normal. She wasn't unusually thirsty, weak, tired, or even hungover, which supported his claims that he had not drugged her in the first place. But it was clear he had done something to her. She had gone on a hell of a trip, as though loaded up on Ecstasy, and it had been disturbingly out of character. She brushed a hard hand at her cheeks as they flushed red in anger and embarrassment. He would pay for stripping away her dignity like that. She would see to it.

She waited a few minutes before she cautiously inched up to the curtained doorway. She hadn't heard a door close, so she couldn't be certain he had left as he'd claimed he was going to. He could be testing her to see if she would attempt escape. He had to know she would. He seemed able to intuit a great deal about her, so she had to assume he would anticipate her desires to go against his command and try and break free of him somehow. She slid quietly through the curtains, for the first time noticing she no longer had shoes on and that the floors were woven tight and hard beneath her feet. There was no splintering to the webbing beneath her, despite the fact that it looked almost like a layer of braided vines. The surface was treated, making it silky smooth while providing traction with its meshed texture.

As she crept through the house, she realized that

the woven material made up all the solid surfaces: walls, flooring, ceilings, and anything of substance to the architecture of the home. It was just weird enough to make her stomach clench with doubt and questions, but it wasn't enough to convince her. As she searched slowly and quietly around her would-be prison, she encountered two bedrooms besides the one she had left. One had a decided feminine touch, the other was more dark and masculine. Not so much the color differences to the bedding, but also the nature of the décor. Julian had a history of taking rather posh, showy apartments in his travels, so it was hard for her to picture him in this more rustic environment. She did not step into the room, something inherent in her telling her to keep far from his bed and his belongings. She already knew him intimately enough, thanks. But she did take a moment to notice there were no photographs or artwork of any kind, not that she could figure how to mount such things on round walls. It was not absent of personal touches, however. There was a kind of personalization just in the way the bed and a slung-up chair in one spot were obviously designed for the specific comfort of one man. It was strange, however, that she saw no tables and no lights in any of these rooms. If there was recessed lighting, she couldn't find it.

She was wasting time, Asia lectured herself sternly. It was time to find out just how far Julian would let her go before bringing down the hammer. Would he let her make it all the way outside? It would be easy enough to explain away a suburb or remote cabin to fit his delusions, but it would be easier for him to leave her questioning. As yet, there was no sight of any windows. She found it curious that the place wasn't pitch-black. In fact, it seemed warmly and diffusely lit from just about everywhere, although for the life of her, as she moved on through the house, she could find no switches, lamps, or bulbs to account for any of it. She quickly denied the idea that it was anything but some designer's clever trick of technology and architecture.

Things got really peculiar, however, when she reached the end of her search at a central circular opening in the floor. But where anyone else would have a spiral staircase leading down to the next floor, this was a wide, spiral, and gently graded . . . slide. Or ramp. It depended on how you looked at it. Perhaps it was designed for someone in a wheelchair? But wouldn't an elevator be easier? She carefully stepped onto the slide and realized the mesh material provided much better traction than she had given it credit for. It made for a smooth, quick descent. When she reached the bottom, though, she looked back up and had sympathy for anyone who wasn't in decent shape and sporting a good sense of balance when it came to the climb back up.

Turning her attention to the newest floor, she became instantly aware of the presence of another person nearby. It was hard to miss, actually. The sound of feminine sniffles and softly hitching sobs was rather hard to overlook. Unable to help herself, fearing someone else might be in trouble in this surreal situation, she followed the sounds to the nearest room. Stepping through another beaded doorway, she found herself in what had to be a kitchen, although it wasn't like anything she'd ever seen before. It seemed a strange cross between modern and primitive. There was an open fire pit, the shape and size of which reminded her of a normal-sized sandbox in a child's backyard. It was roomy, about waist-high to the woman who was removing a pot from the grill set over the flames. She turned and threw the pot angrily into a basin full of fresh, sudsy water. It distracted Asia from trying to figure out exactly how the smoke from the freestanding fire was being vented out of the room.

"Are you Ariel?" she asked.

The other woman didn't seem surprised to realize Asia was there. In fact, she didn't even look up to acknowledge her. However, Asia knew she had heard her because she'd gone very still. She was a very pretty young woman, a redhead with a braid of hair that hung in a thick rope down to just below her bottom. She was slim in some places, but busty and lushly curved over her hips. She certainly wasn't shaped like so many of the perfect-sized women Julian had taken back to his apartment night after night. She hadn't thought him capable of being anything other than too shallow to appreciate a woman shaped in some other fashion.

Then again, she was standing in his kitchen looking very domesticated. She was probably his wife. She certainly looked miserable and beaten down enough to find herself married to a beautiful man who did nothing but run around on her night after night, even going so far as to bring one home with him. Probably more than one. Maybe even fourteen. The little fool probably loved him to death and would likely tolerate anything he said or did just to stay close to him. The very idea made Asia ill.

The bang of a serving ladle joining the pot in the basin drew her attention back up sharply to the woman in question, who rounded on her with obvious anger in her eyes.

"You know nothing!" she spat, her accent far heavier than Julian's. "You appreciate nothing! You make to judge me? After you rob me of my life?"

There was a certain sharp, ringing sound that

always seemed to occur when a knife was drawn in a kitchen. Ariel grabbed what was obviously a blade from the countertop nearest her and Asia was instantly on guard, holding out a hand.

"Whoa! I didn't do anything!" Asia instantly measured the space of the flooring, the distance to dangerous points like the knife and the fire pit. "You can keep your life just how you like it, whatever it is. Just show me the door and I am out of here."

Ariel curled a lip in derision so obvious and so harsh that, for the first time, Asia took note that her ears were . . . weird. The lobes were actually pointed, or rather came to a point. They seemed just as soft as anyone's, as the gems she wore through them made them wobble a little when fury shook her entire frame.

Then she seemed to stop, her emotional display calming considerably as a smile ripped through half her mouth. Asia couldn't call it a friendly expression.

"The door is just behind you," she invited in an almost silky tone.

Asia wasn't an idiot. Had the girl denied her access or barred her aggressively, she would have wanted out more than anything, but this nicety in the aftermath of such a bold flare of hostility made her hesitate as she looked over her shoulder. The door was like the door to a vault, the hard, gunmetal gray steel locked with a central wheel. Like a pressure door on a submarine, when the wheel turned it sent bolts sliding into the steel frame around it that had been securely riveted, woven, and wholly integrated into the materials of the walls.

The wheel lock was on the inside.

A strange thing if someone was trying to keep prisoners in. Ominous if they were trying to keep others or help out. The feel of being in a carefully, if oddly, constructed fort began to settle over her. But here was the question. Would the door open?

It meant turning her back on Ariel, but the other woman had tossed the knife in the basin with the rest of the dishes and gone back to her angry, sniffly process of ignoring Asia's presence.

"What the hell," she muttered with a shrug. She wasn't going to fall for the old "don't step over this line!" command some kidnapping monster laid out for her. She owed it not only to herself to get the heck out of there, but she owed it to Kenya. He might have been lying about her being alive and nearby just to get her to comply, but she needed to believe that he hadn't.

Asia crossed to the door in just a few strides, grabbed the wheel, and turned hard. The bolts retracted sharply, the vibration pounding up her arms through the metal she touched. She was actually surprised it hadn't been locked. Not one to look at a gift horse like a dentist, she yanked the door open and immediately rushed outside.

She half expected Julian to be there waiting to stop her, but she had hoped to get a few useful screams out to draw attention or something.

Well, Julian wasn't there . . .

But she sure did scream.

Chapter 5

Understandable, considering she had expected to run out onto a porch or a lawn, not into dead, cold open space. The ledge outside of the door was no more than a stride wide and there were no railings. She plummeted over the edge and screamed. Things flashed by her, but she was locked in panic that kept her from thinking. The fall seemed to last forever, but she knew it would end any instant.

It did.

She hit something flexible and soft that creaked and stretched like elastic as it flexed to decelerate her, rather than stopping her all at once.

"Hold on to the net!"

The instruction rang clear enough through her rattled mind and she grabbed hard for the fibrous webbing around her. Good thing, too, because it began to retract with alarming speed and if she hadn't been holding on she would have been flung free of it. It took a minute or two, but the nauseating bounce of the elastic net finally came to a stop and she lay on it, her heart racing madly with more emotions than she wanted to be feeling just then. Just ever, she amended. She would happily live the rest of her life never feeling this way again. Scared. Glad to be alive. Terrified over what she was mixed up in. And for the first time, she began to feel like she was in a situation where she was out of her depth enough that she might not be strong enough to protect herself, never mind her kid sister. That, above all else, was the worst feeling Asia had ever known in her life.

"Asia! *Zini*, are you all right?" The rushing, breathless fear in Julian's voice so matched what she was feeling that she couldn't help but look in his direction. She opened her eyes for the first time since her impact and saw she was, indeed, in some kind of huge net that was made of the same stuff his house was made of, except where that was hard, this sprang and flexed. It was just strange enough for her to begin to feel her convictions about what was happening to her crack a little. She saw Julian kneeling on a nearby ledge, reaching a supplicating hand toward her in a combination of wanting to reach something too far away and to keep her calm all at once.

"It's okay, Asia. The net will hold," he assured her rapidly. "Just move to me and don't—"

Look down.

She realized that was where he was going when she looked down through the wide squares of the netted web and saw nothing but clouds. Granted, they were strangely beautiful clouds, but it came down to the fact that they looked quite insignificant should she keep falling. They would not catch her, as the net had. At first she didn't question that they were magenta and burgundy in color. It was just like at sunset or sunrise. Only, after a moment, Asia realized she could feel the sun on her back somewhere above her.

Adding perspective to just how far away the clouds

were from her was a pair of snow white, sheer cliffs that were way off to the sides on her right and left. She knew it couldn't be snow, however, because the wind that sang and howled through the enormous gorge was too warm. But more important than all of that was the sinking understanding that it was a free fall into total oblivion for at least a mile. She couldn't tell exactly. There was no ground under her. If the net had not been there . . .

Asia swallowed and was suddenly grateful she hadn't eaten. She closed her eyes as the urge to vomit rode over her for a long, hard moment. She began to shake, simply giving in to the fact that she had every right to be scared halfway to hell. After all, she had almost fallen straight to hell and beyond.

"Asia, look at me."

She'd never thought she'd be so grateful to hear the calm, rich smoothness of Julian Sawyer's tone of voice. Like so much about him, it was innately sexy and compelling, but right then it was strong and familiar in a situation that, she was beginning to realize, was as unfamiliar and as alien as it got.

She looked at him and tried not to think that he was rather far away. She focused instead on the position he was in as he knelt on a ledge where parts of the net had been secured.

"Listen, *zini*. These nets are strong and secure and are designed to hold the weight of a person or an animal." Since Asia had begun to realize that the way he hesitated, thinking before he spoke, was a rich clue to when he was omitting important information, she couldn't help the chuckle that erupted nervously from her chest.

"*A* person. *An* animal," she noted the distinction, her hands clutching the net all the harder. She knew by the grim set of his mouth that she'd hit it on the head. His nod was superfluous.

"Yeah. For a woman of your weight and size, it isn't a problem, okay? But I can't come get you. You can crawl or, better yet, roll slowly over this way. It is important that you don't test the elasticity of the net too much. It is designed to break away if something struggles within it long enough."

"What the fuck kind of a safety net is this?" she demanded with a gasping of instantly fearful breaths as she was unable to help looking back down into burgundy-clouded oblivion.

"It has its purposes," he assured her, the amusement lacing his voice pissing her off enough to push through her paralytic fear of the moment.

Asia reached out to her side, secured a hand around the net, and rolled just as she might do across the dojo mats until her opposite hand could come around and grab new net.

Asia couldn't possibly have known how thickly Julian's heart was lodged in his throat as he watched her bravely begin to come toward him. When he had heard her scream and looked up to see her streaking through the sky toward a fifty-fifty chance at death, he'd thought there wouldn't ever be a plane of existence capable of containing the energy of sheer terror that had gripped him. He had used that lash of violent fear to guide her fall as best he could away from ramps, buildings, and bridges that would have broken her to bits had she begun to hit and bounce off them. He risked much by doing so, and by taking her to the nets. Intended to catch children or domesticated animals, they were strong enough and resilient enough to catch a lighter adult. However, as he had mentioned, anything beyond that made the nets break away.

She did not yet realize that there were men and beasts in this plane that made the design necessary. Everything about the way they lived was designed to protect them from those dangers around them. Julian realized he had made a terrible mistake by not being straight and blunt with her about that. He should have stayed and shown her. He had thought she would be safe with Ariel there, but clearly he had been wrong. He hoped Ariel was not hurt. Asia had proven herself a resourceful fighter. Enough that she might outmatch his more domesticated Companion. He had not considered that she might harm an innocent woman in her need to be free. He had rather hoped that speaking with Ariel might have actually calmed her and made his story more believable until he could show her the truth for himself.

"Excellent," he praised her softly as she moved surely and securely, never releasing the netting from both hands at once. Julian tried not to think of how far she still was from him, his heart racing to think any harsh movement might make the net snap away. The men on the planking beside him had all reached out to hold the netting near its moorings, just in case it loosened. The net would need to be replaced with a fresh one after this, but that was all right so long as it served its purpose now.

"She's a brave one," Shade commented from his right side where he gripped the netting. "Most freeze the first time this happens."

"She did freeze," Kine drawled from his left. "She just recovered quickly. He's right. She's gutsy. A little reckless by the looks of it, but she's got balls."

"You're in some serious trouble," Shade said.

"I was aware of that the moment I saw her," Julian informed them levelly. "Then there is a whole part where she thinks I am a psychopathic murderer. She tried to kick my ass because she thinks her sister was one of my victims."

Kine barked out a laugh at that. "I've always loved that phrase. Humans use the best phraseology sometimes. Clearly your ass remains unkicked, but has her opinion of you improved?"

"I doubt it. I think she was trying to escape my evil clutches just now."

"Good God. If you're evil and a psychopath, then she's going to positively hate Kine," Shade mused.

"Or better yet, Daedalus." Kine chuckled.

"Will you both keep your voices down," Julian said. "I have enough work ahead of me without her overhearing my degenerate friends."

Shade glanced over Julian's head to look at Kine. "He must be talking about you," he remarked.

"Clearly," Kine said.

Julian ignored the byplay and focused on the appearance of icy blue eyes only a few yards away now. She paused a moment to catch her breath. Not because there was any real exertion involved, but because she appreciated how much danger she was in. At least she believed him that much. Then again, he thought as he looked down at the bottomless gorge, she hadn't had much choice when presented with such empirical proof. She was lying on her back, her little silver dress wound snug and tight to her body from her rolling progress. He was all too aware of how her skirt had ridden up over her rather delectable backside, revealing the bare shape of her ass in the form-hugging thong every time she rolled to her belly. Considering the multitude of men around him that were appreciating the view, he was having a difficult time keeping a cap on his anger and jealousy and focusing instead on getting her safely in his grasp.

For the moment he watched as her expression changed from tension to one of total, unabashed awe. He looked up and realized she had probably just appreciated the view of all that was above her for the very first time. He tried to imagine what it must be like, from her perspective, to see an entire colony strung between the two sides of the cliffs. Since she had hit nets at the very bottom level, all nineteen other levels were stretched across above her. The colony itself was several miles long along the gorge, but when it grew, it grew downward. Each level had many ramps, bridges, and grades leading up to the next in strategic places. The clover-shaped houses with their conical roofs and basements on each leaf had to seem very strange to her. He could tell exactly when she began to appreciate how deadly and dangerous the fall from his top-level home had been. She looked at him when the crisscrossing bridges and roads above her made her realize just how impossible it had been that she hadn't hit any of them; that she hadn't been skewered by any one of the numerous pointed roofs, most of which were tipped with iron spikes.

"I know," he said in a low, calm voice. "I will explain everything to you when you are safe." He curved his fingers to beckon her closer. "It's just a little way now."

By now she was also noticing the crowds of men who stood along the edges of the walkways watching this drama slowly unfold. She was sharp and clever, and he knew it wouldn't take long for her to realize . . .

"Where are the women?"

She gripped the net until her knuckles turned white and Julian could see her pulse pounding in her throat as she swallowed back her panic in order to demand an answer from him. Had she been one of them, she would have felt the ripple of uneasy and bitter emotional energy that echoed through every male in earshot of the query.

Then again, had she been one of them, she wouldn't have needed to ask the question.

"They are usually safe indoors at this time of day," Julian said meaningfully, giving her a look that said she should have been safe inside as well.

"Oh, like that domesticated little bitch who tried to kill me just now?" she asked sharply, the accusation lashing through Julian like a whip of poisonous fire.

"She did what?" he thundered, suddenly surging up to his full height. Almost simultaneously, Kine and Shade reached out to take hold of his wrists. It was a reminder for him to keep his emotions under control. If he let his energy lash out, it could endanger her in her still precarious position. What he wanted more than anything was to grab her out of that deathtrap and hold her so tightly to himself she wouldn't be able to breathe for a week. Then he wanted to find Ariel and kill her.

"Easy," Kine warned softly as rage tremored through him. Julian felt both men quickly absorbing the energy he was giving off, but it wouldn't be long before they would be glutted, especially with such powerful surges as these.

"Asia, come to me," he commanded her in a hard, barely civil voice. "I will have you safe right now." *Right now. Not a moment to waste or spare.* There was no brooking disagreement with him, and as obstinate and independent as she was, she must have sensed there was an even greater danger to defying this command than there was below her and the net. She rolled a few more times until he could grab on to Kine with one hand and reach to pluck her free of danger with the other. He swung her onto her feet on the planking, and all of the men released their hold on the netting and stood up.

Julian could feel them all around him. Their envy, lust, and jealousy almost overpowered him. He knew they did not want or mean to feel this way, but he also realized just how stunning his prize was and how lucky he was to have found something so rare; something most of them would never have the pleasure of knowing or even coming close to in their lifetime.

Julian ignored her stiff resistance to his touch and held her very tightly against his body. He very carefully kept himself in check from feeling the heat and awareness that wanted to rush over him just because she was close to him again. This would only cruelly provoke those surrounding them.

"Asia," he said carefully, "this is my village and these are my *kiṇ*. Like in your world it means family, although here it is more about spiritual kinship than blood or physical relationships. My *kin* will always be easy to identify by the black mark of the spearhead just here." He touched his wrist where it had been burned black by a hot spear point as a child. The accidental scar had somehow, long ago, become a symbol of kinship and loyalty as man after man of their colony had taken spears to their skin in a show of solidarity. It had started with his best friend Lucien, who had done it to solidify his friendship with him after Julian had suffered through a great betrayal, and it had caught with the entire village after that. Now it was a ceremonial rite of acceptance into the community. You did not belong unless you carried the mark of the *kin*. "My *kin* will always aid you and guide you from danger. Once you believe you can trust me, you may believe you can trust them as well."

Asia looked around warily at the throng of men, and Julian didn't blame her. She was rather like a favorite dessert on a cart that everyone hungered for, but was disappointed to find out it was already reserved for someone else. On the plus side, the wall of male energy around her made her actually burrow more willingly against him. Anchoring her to his side, he forwent any introductions beyond that, hoping his friends would understand as he moved forward and pushed through the crowd. They left the worst of it when they left the lowest tier and climbed the curved ramp to the next. Julian couldn't help the impulse he had to lock a hand possessively around her far hip, pressing his forearm against her backside in an attempt to keep the lower levels from staring at her ass as she rose higher above them in that tiny little dress.

Asia shot him a look, but didn't say anything. She was actually very grim and quiet as she slowly took each step with him through the wending, curving levels of the village that literally hung in midair.

"God, this place should have rails at least," she said hollowly.

"There are reasons for that. We have a very good sense of balance. I can tell you do as well. Most of the paths are wide enough for two to walk safely side by side as we are doing."

"Wait."

She stopped and pulled away to face him, her steps cautious and careful as she wrapped tight arms across her middle.

"Everything you said . . . about the planes and stuff. It's the truth, isn't it?"

"I told you, I do not lie."

"Well, excuse me for not believing my kidnapper," she snapped at him. The accusation made him wince, but he was quick to nod in agreement.

"You are right. What I did was an abduction. I would have preferred otherwise, as I said, but it doesn't change that you were brought against your will." Julian moved a step closer to her, catching her around the back of her neck as he drew her to within a breath of touching against him. He let his heat and pent-up emotions flow softly and silkily over her, let them permeate her stubborn mind. "Had it been my choice, I would have shown you the ways of this world in slow, gentle days; I would have brought you the future in long, drugging connections you would have quickly become addicted to. I would have brought you to me again and again until you were bare and open and begging for me to take you . . . here."

Julian had almost lost track of what he was talking about as the sultry smell of her had quickly risen into his senses. He had spoken of the education and Conduction of a Chosen one's passage, but for her, as his *kindra,* it would have been much, much different. He knew that, at the moment, she was so tightly walled away from him that she was not allowing herself access to the place within herself that craved and starved for him, her *kindri.* It rode him in hard ripples of frustration and irritation that he could be so close to her, and yet so unwelcome. But here was where he belonged. Here he must very soon make a claim if he was going to prove his announcement that she was *kindra.* Not that many would doubt him, but it had been tried before, someone making a false claim to *kindra* in an attempt to cheat the lonely Fates.

"I hope you can forgive me the method but come

to appreciate the opportunity and its unique pleasures," he said softly.

"You mean pleasures like falling out of the sky?" she
retorted.

"You wouldn't have fallen if you'd listened and
stayed inside where it was safe!"

"Again, forgive me for not obeying my kidnapper,"
she shot back snidely. "And when that twit in your
kitchen pulled a knife on me, I figured I'd best take
her up on her invitation to show myself the door!"

Ariel.

Julian saw a thousand shades of red rush into his
vision all at once, and he locked tight hands around
Asia's arms when the entire village trembled on its
deep moorings. The village rode the energy wave as it
was designed to do, diffusing and distributing it evenly
so no one was jolted too hard or thrown off balance.
Asia grabbed on to him for stability. Julian heard the
sounds of masculine grunts and groans as the power
of the emotional outburst filtered through them.

"Oh my God, this place is a deathtrap," Asia gasped,
clinging to him hard now as she began to tremble in
nervous terror. Julian closed his eyes briefly as he
tried to control his temper yet again. The last thing he
needed was to feed every man around them hostile,
aggressive emotional energy. The entire village could
erupt into chaos.

"Listen to me," he rasped out against her forehead
as he turned and pressed his lips against her in a brief
kiss that made her stiffen in resistance to the affection,
as small as it was. "This village has hung here for hundreds of years. The material we use to build it is almost
indestructible. There are men here who do nothing
else but see to the integrity of each level so everyone
who lives here remains utterly safe. I would never allow

you or anyone else I call *kin* to stay here for a single second if I thought it was unsafe."

"There are no rails. No ropes. What do your children do?"

"I will explain all of that."

"When?" she demanded harshly, trying to pull away now that her initial anxiety had passed. "When will you explain Kenya?"

"Now. All of it. But inside where you will be safe. Please," he added, flooding her with the energy of his good intent until he felt her relax just a little, though she still stood warily in his grasp.

"I thought you said it was safe," she said, turning her head to look down over the edge of the walkway to see the levels below them. Asia swallowed hard and turned her cool blue eyes back to him.

"It is . . . for those who were raised here. I took my first steps on these walkways. I was born to walk them and am native to the world that drops above and below it. You are not. It will take time for you to feel that same security and natural ease. Before long, you will not even notice any longer that there are no ropes or rails to hold on to."

She frowned even as she gave a reluctant nod. "I still don't see why you don't have them."

"You will," he assured her.

Chapter 6

Asia was not so sure.

Just the same, she didn't see that she had very much choice in the matter until she learned the lay of the land a little better. The lay of the air, she corrected herself. She had never been afraid of heights before, but this was honestly asking a lot of even the bravest soul. Those clouds in the distant beyond below them would break now and again and she still saw nothing solid with which she could judge the distance to the ground. She had to wonder just how high they were that they were *above* a cloud line.

Julian took her arm and carefully turned her to his side. He walked her to one of the weird conical clover houses nearby and entered. She instantly realized it was some kind of eatery by the smell of the place when she followed him in, the aroma of food surrounding her. But otherwise, despite the thick crowd of men at the tables all around the circular rooms, it was eerily silent.

Or so she thought. Their entrance somehow made everything all the more silent as dozens of pairs of eyes became riveted to them.

"Remind me to get you a decent dress to wear," Julian muttered as he guided her toward an empty table.

"How about I remind you why I have no wardrobe to change into?" she countered sharply.

"Done," he relented with a chuckle as he sat her down, the comeback actually making him smile.

She had to admit, the building seemed very sturdy and it was easy to forget they weren't on the ground. Again, there were no windows or visible light sources, but the room had a sunny feel to it all the same. She'd have to ask him about that. After she got more important answers first.

"Okay, I'm listening," she challenged him immediately.

"You're also hungry. I can tell you ate nothing I brought you."

She watched him turn to look for a server. A waiter at the counter saw him, but only stood where he was for a moment as he made eye contact with Julian. Then he promptly turned his back on him and walked away, ignoring his obvious need.

"Well, that was rude," she noted with a scoff. "So much for your *kin*."

Julian just gave her an enigmatic smile. Slowly, she became aware of everyone dropping their attention back to their meals and . . . well, there was still no conversation. There was no music or anything else but the sound of movement, eating, and dishes being touched or moved. There was, however, a strange little buzz all around her, sort of like a ringing in her ears. Asia wouldn't be surprised if she'd given her head a good jogging when she'd hit that net and now her bounced brain was complaining about it.

As quickly as she thought of the whole incident, she

just as quickly pushed it away. It made her heart hurt to remember the harrowing free fall.

"Okay, so talk. I guess I believe the whole plane thing. I mean, the colored clouds and bottomless pit kind of convinced me. Just tell me why I am here and why everything is so . . . weird."

"You think this is weird?" he countered. "You should try growing up this way and stepping into an Earth culture sometime. They are so vastly different from one another, too. From the primitive to the technologically savvy. The violence, prejudice, and hatred so many engage in so often is quite overwhelming. Debilitating, even." He frowned at that. "Even something as simple as walking on solid ground. I was raised to fear rock and soil under my feet."

Asia laughed at that incredulously. The sound of it seemed terribly loud to her in the muted room, but not many seemed to take notice of it. "But you find air to be safe?"

"So will you, one day. Trust me. If you wish to survive in this world, you will keep off the grass. Keep off the ground."

"Why?" she demanded.

"Think of it like this," he said carefully. "This village is like a safety zone. Stepping outside of it would be like . . . like wading your way down your Amazon River; it is deadly, dangerous, and pretty much an act of suicide. It's fairly impossible to achieve success, from what I understand. Think of why that is and apply it to the ground here."

"It's dangerous because of the things that live in and around it. The animals and snakes and stuff."

"Also, the river itself. Poisonous flora. Sucking mud. Insects. The real danger, however, is that everything deadly that is there knows exactly how to hide itself.

To the uneducated, the blend and blur of the jungle is just pretty to look at. In truth, predators lurk along nearly every inch. Even the bite of the tiniest mosquito can be deadly if it carries a disease like malaria. You can take nothing for granted."

"Okay, okay," she breathed. "I get it. Don't walk on the grass."

Just then, the waiter who had rebuffed Julian appeared carrying a serving tray full of hot, delicious-smelling dishes. He set them down as if he knew exactly who wanted what, then left without a word. Oddly enough, the setting reminded her of going to a Chinese restaurant. Strange but wondrous dishes steamed attractively. She didn't recognize any of it, but it was colorful, hot, and fragrant enough to her starving belly for her to not really care so much about being unacquainted with the food.

Julian reached to take a plate and she watched him fill it before he set it in front of her. Even the plate was unusually shaped, the curves of it in the shape of an eye instead of the conventional round or square she was accustomed to. Asia wanted to take umbrage at the way he served her without even asking her what she wanted or thought she might like, except everything he chose was exactly what she did want.

"Let's start with your sister," he said as he picked up his own plate. He dished up something that was a brilliant blue color. She was glad she didn't have any of that on her plate. Blue food just seemed wrong somehow. However, his proposal quickly made her forget about the color of the food.

"Where is she?"

"Visiting another colony at the moment. She will be back soon. I have sent for her and I expect she will arrive by midday tomorrow." He regarded her as he picked up the dual-pronged fork by his plate. "It was the soonest I could manage. I hope you can believe that. Checking on the arrangements for her early return was why I left you just before. Otherwise I would not have abandoned you to your own devices." He paused and a dark, dangerous expression passed over him. The activity in the room seemed to hiccup again, attention turning their way in uneasy glances of brooding eyes.

"Okay, this lack of females thing is creeping me out," Asia said in a sharp whisper. "And why isn't anyone saying anything?"

Julian raised one dark brow in surprise. He looked around the room and then seemed to recall she wasn't from around there.

"Actually, the room is rather noisy," he told her. "Just not on the vocal level you are expecting to hear. There is much conversation, laughter, and other things like it. More than is usual," he noted. "Everyone is feeling quite energized and excited by your presence here."

Asia gaped at him as if he had lost his mind. She looked around the room and tried to see and hear whatever it was he was hearing, but all she heard was the sounds of eating and that persistent buzz.

"It will take time for you to hear it all," he reminded her. "We speak in different ways here, although you will find a few who can use English and other Earthly languages. Most of my friends, in fact. We all work . . ." He hesitated and made a face that etched his handsome features with a hardness that seemed wry and almost bitter. "I should begin with telling you the nature of my people. You see, we look very similar to humans. Some slight differences are not immediately or always obvious."

"Ariel had pointed lobes," she said as she stabbed at something that looked like meat on her plate. She shrugged off her leery sensations and ate it. It was actually quite sweet, although it was tart underneath after a moment. "But I have watched you for a while and you don't seem different in any way."

"Don't I?" he returned, looking amused. "And how long is a while?"

"Nonstop? These past few weeks. Took me a while to catch up to you after I backtracked your trail all the way to Oregon. I didn't get to see you nab your first girl in Lauderdale, but I knew when I saw the missing persons report that it was you."

"Holy shit." Julian uttered the earthly profanity, looking completely shocked. "You were able to track me back seven months? How the hell did you do that?"

"It's actually easy . . . if you're a bounty hunter and you know how to do it. Once I had tracked you back to just before you took my sister, to New Orleans, I had a feel for your routine. After that it was cake."

"A bounty hunter? You're a bounty hunter?" He actually had the nerve to lean to the side and scope a look down her body, as if that had anything to do with anything.

"Great. Even aliens are chauvinists," she muttered, making an irritated dive at more food.

Julian sat back and grinned at that. "This is a ninety percent male society, *zini*. It's hard for us to be otherwise when we outnumber our women two hundred to one."

The ratio made her choke. She coughed into her hand as her wide eyes darted to the heavy male patronage around her. "I thought you said the women were indoors."

"They are. All fifteen of them, if I include you and

discount the children beneath the age of sexual maturity."

"Fifteen?" Including Ariel in that count, that meant she knew almost a fifth of the female population already. "And this city has three thousand men in it?"

"Give or take. I didn't get a recent count yet. And it is the same in all of the colonies along the gorge. Some larger . . . some smaller. You see, this is one reason why I go to Earth plane, Asia. If I do not find very special women who are willing to trade away everything they know in order to come and help us, my people will be extinct in a matter of a few generations."

Asia paused mid-chew as that information sank in and choked her. She was on her feet in an instant and running for the heavy steel door that led to the outside. She didn't even care about the nonexistent railings or the height or any of it. When the first man stepped in her path to impede her, her reaction was unthinking and automatic. She hit him and he contacted the floor hard, his breath leaving him in a satisfying whoosh even as she ducked under the grab of another male. She struck him in the throat and about a half dozen other soft spots before he fell away. After that, others quickly backed away from her.

"Asia, stop!"

Julian's commanding bellow hit her just as her hands closed around the circular door handle. She did stop, panic burning in her chest but logic telling her there was nowhere she could run just yet. She didn't know anything about where she was. She was a prisoner of her ignorance.

A prisoner in a village full of men who needed women to breed with.

"No!" he said sharply as he came up behind her. "It's not what you are thinking. Not . . . not entirely."

"Not *entirely?*" she demanded as she turned to face him, still clutching at the door as her pulse pounded in her chest and temples. It was a nightmare! She'd been kidnapped by aliens so she could pop out babies for them. It sounded like a horrible sci-fi movie!

"I won't deny that there is an essential need for fertile women here. The evidence of that is right in front of your face." He indicated the ring of men behind him who were all staring at her in that creepy dark and silent manner. The ringing buzz in her head was getting worse and she was getting a headache. It was all too much for her to process and conceive of, even as she struggled to figure out how to survive the insane situation she found herself in. It only grew worse with every word he uttered. "But there is much more to it than that," he said. "Certainly there is much more to you and to me."

"You and me?" she echoed, stunned and aghast. Mocking her captor while facing down a crowd of his friends was truly unwise, but she couldn't help the snorting laugh of derision that escaped her. "There is no 'you and me,' you sick freak! You're a psychopathic monster who stole me and my sister for . . . for . . . *breeding stock!* You and me? Sweetheart, I promise you now, the only 'you and me' will be the one where *you* are laid out dead on the fucking floor because of *me!*"

Julian stood with his male *kin* at his back, looking like a king in command of a personal army as a shadowed fury whipped over his features and tightened into his clenching fists. Asia couldn't help an anxious swallow when he began to stalk across the distance between them. The movement was precipitating action on her part. Survival instinct raged and screamed in the echoes of her racing heartbeats. He approached her, reached out for her, and she immediately struck his hands away hard. He reached again, dodging her defenses this time with awful ease and blinding speed and grabbing her lower jaw with the palms of both hands. Once he had her face cradled and firmly trapped within his hands, he jerked her forward into his body, even as he swooped to catch her mouth with his.

Asia planned just how hard she would bite through his lip. She was even trying to decide between upper and lower when the unexpected scorch of his kiss slammed into her from all sides at once. In all of an instant, her entire body recalled what he had made her feel. Her mind recalled it best of all. The memory was vague about "how" it had happened, but the "what" was clear enough. Pleasure beyond anything she could have imagined. *He* had made her feel that. He had powered through her rigid, cold body, just as he was doing in that very moment, until she had melted and collapsed. Asia felt her entire body sagging against his as her knees literally went weak. Just from such a simple kiss.

When his tongue stroked her lips to request entrance, everything changed.

Fire ignited over her face, only to drop in molten, liquid need down through her throat and chest. The desire to taste of him overwhelmed her and she forgot everything about everything. Nothing could possibly matter. Not in the face of this amazing sensation. She opened her mouth and with a quick winding of her arms behind his neck she surged up into him. She sank her tongue between his lips and tasted him long and deep and aggressively until she could feel his hands sweeping around to her back and gripping her so tightly she could barely draw breath.

Asia was no stranger to sex or any of its components. She used it in short, sharp bursts to take off edginess or when batteries and a vibrator just couldn't cut it. It was, to her, a perfunctory and often dissatisfying act that she had learned to go longer and longer without. Whether it was her coldness or poor choices of partners that made it that way, she had never bothered to examine.

But this was a completely different level of physical intimacy, and she knew it right away. The scorch marks across her soul were telling enough on their own, but there was the sheer physical heat that really burned her to awareness. Everything, from the touch of his hands to the tangle of his tongue, was like wrestling with pure fire. Her back abruptly hit a wall as his hands slid over silver silky fabric and the eager, begging skin and nerves beneath. She cried out in relief and pleasure when he finally cupped her breasts in his large, hot hands. He ground his hips forward against her, introducing her to the huge and solid bulge behind his zipper, and she was wildly overcome with the urge to scramble up his body, spread her legs around him, and beg him to do her.

But before she could follow the madcap impulse, he jerked away from her, ripping his mouth from the kiss and dropping his hands from her breasts. He took two steps back, each one jolting over her like rejecting slaps. She fought the rushing surge of desolate tears that welled into her eyes, and confusion beat through her. Half of her wanted to know why he had left and longed for him to return; the other half wanted to know what in hell had just happened to her.

"There will always be a you and me," he rasped, his voice gravelly with his caged need as his hands fisted again. Numbly, Asia realized he was gripping himself to keep from grabbing her again. "Understand that, if nothing else." He paused to take a steadying breath, giving her the time to blink dazedly at the way every man in the room seemed to be withdrawn into himself and most had turned away to afford what little privacy there could be. "Listen carefully," Julian warned her. "We are not human. Though we are corporeal and as you see us now, the central core of our existence is in the pure energy we gather and harvest to nourish our life-forces. Our young, especially, are in need of this energy and feed from the elders of us like babes nursing at a mother's breast. But we are weak. Starving. Colony after colony of us."

As if he couldn't help himself, he stepped close to her again and reached to stroke warm knuckles over her cheek, then turned his hand to run slow fingertips down her throat. His gaze seemed riveted to his own actions.

"Several decades ago a terrible plague ripped through this world. All were touched by it, but because it fed on the hormone estrogen, our men were best able to fight it off and recover. Our women were decimated by it. Then it came again a few decades later. And then again, until we are as you see us now." He lifted a hand to indicate the room filled with grim male visages who listened to him explain all of this to her. "But it is worse than what you suppose, Asia. Far worse than just a matter of being unable to breed more children. You see, our women were, like the women of your own world, the more vibrant and positively emotional sex. They stimulated us in ways that produce things like passion, love, enjoyment, frustration, determination . . . the list goes on and on. These emotional energies are what recycle the energy of this plane so it can be fed into us full of nutrition and vitality once more."

Julian drifted his warm touch across her bare shoulder and she was shocked to find how quickly her pulse shifted in excitement. The reaction confused her as well. She was starting to believe he wasn't an axe murderer, but she shouldn't be standing there literally panting for him when he was no better than some kind of kidnapping sex slaver.

"Yes, I suppose that is as good a description as any for what I do," he agreed stiffly, making her gasp aloud.

Can he read my mind? Is he reading my every thought?

"No, *zini*. You are speaking out to us. Your energy is so profound that we can hear you well, even though you don't yet know how to hear us. The louder the emotion in your thoughts, the better we can hear you. It radiates all down your body"—he paused to drop slow, hot eyes down the front of her figure until she imagined she could feel them burning into her skin—"and emanates out to us like an animated conversation. Soon you will learn how to hear us in this way." He took hold of her wrist where she held it guardedly across her chest, a way of shielding her sudden sense of exposure. "But let's return to my duties to these colonies and on Earth. You wanted to know what happened to those women? Why I chose them and not any of the others?"

Asia nodded, unable to make herself engage in the conversation in any other way. She was already feeling cornered and overloaded with information and input. She was the center of so much attention, and while she was used to that as an instructor, it was a very different feeling when she thought that what they wanted from her was quite a bit more intimate than jujitsu lessons. Worse, she was trapped by her lack of knowledge of where she was and a healthy dose of respectful fear for navigating a world that was alien to her.

She watched Julian turn his head to look back at the others in the tavern. After a moment, they all broke apart and returned to their tables and meals, but Asia was still very aware of their focus on her and Julian. Still, it was better now that they weren't a wall of intensity crowded around her.

"I am a Gatherer," he began abruptly as he turned back to catch her gaze with his own. "Gatherers were created a long time ago to hunt for energy resources needed to feed us regularly. It was a temporary solution, and one that had to be handled very carefully. You see, the most powerful resources of convertible energy are things like . . . like birth or death, joy and faith, war and . . . sex. Especially the sexual climax of a woman. Orgasm is harder and more complex for your sex to achieve, but it has a dynamic outburst of power that can energize hundreds of us at a time.

"Think of Gatherers as conductors. We . . . channel all of this from your world to ours. Unfortunately, the process of creating, and then what it takes in order to conduct it, is draining and sometimes even debilitating to the host. Just like rage or passion or any powerful emotion is draining. But because we then conduct it away from the human host it becomes even more exhaustive. Because of this, each human woman can only be a host once. To use her more than that will burn her out. It will make her ill and weak, perhaps even put her in a coma. If I choose improperly, it could even kill her."

"That's what you were doing? When you brought home those girls every night? You were . . . conducting their energy to here?"

He nodded. "They were volunteering, although they didn't know exactly what for. Each came to me seeking an experience of pleasure, and I gave that to them in trade for the energy outburst that, if I didn't guide it to here, would simply have been wasted. As long as I choose the right women, no harm comes to anyone and it is a mutually satisfactory arrangement."

"Okay," she said slowly. "I can buy that. But what about those fourteen? The ones like me you brought here."

That earned her a vague little smile. "Those thirteen women," he said distinctively, clearly omitting her from the pack, "are the Chosen. You see, every so often there is a human female who has such a powerfully energetic psyche and such an overabundance of psychic energy and an insatiable sensuality that she could withstand conduction repetitively and hardly feel the difference in herself. Your sister, for example. She has such a vibrant life-force that it is quite blinding. She was the most brilliant example of psychic plentitude that I had ever seen . . . until I saw you. I am not surprised you are related to Kenya. It shows in the strength of your auras.

"When I discover a woman capable of being Chosen, I take her for several nights. I carefully test her strength and ability to make repetitive donations of power. Then, once she falls asleep, I make her dream of this world. I include everything. The beauty, the dangers, the needs, and the hard, harsh realities we live with. This is what I wanted to do with you, as well. It is an informative introduction. Then I make a proposal. I make sure they realize that once they come here they can never come back. If they come here, they will be needed for their energy and, if they so choose, their fertility. But that last is a personal choice, Asia. None here are forced to breed any more than they would be in American society."

"And you are trying to tell me my sister agreed to this? A life of . . . of fornicating for a society of energy parasites?"

The look that billowed across his features was dark and quite dangerous. Asia had to admit it probably hadn't been wise to describe his people in such an unflattering manner, but she couldn't believe her sister would willingly whore for a bunch of aliens!

"Your sister," he hissed softly into her face, "is a generous and beautiful soul. In this trait, clearly you differ." It was meant harshly, and Asia didn't want it to sting as badly as it did, but it smarted fiercely just the same. Why would she care what his opinion of her was?

"Go to hell," she spat back at him.

"Already there," he rebounded, reaching to grasp her by an arm. He jerked her roughly away from the door, and then opened it with his free hand. Asia couldn't help but envy the easy strength he did it with. She was no weakling, but it took the entire weight and momentum of her body to open or close one of those heavy doors.

When her feet were once again rushing over the unguarded walkways, she stopped struggling against his grip and quickly grew grateful for it. It still shattered her nerves to be so close to the edges of the paths. One almost deadly fall was enough to last her the rest of her life. Repeats weren't necessary.

"I'm trying very hard to remember that you have had no exposure to this culture like you should have," Julian growled, obviously angered by her remarks still.

"Don't do me any favors," she snapped.

His response was to speed up his steps and jerk her along. He was incredibly surefooted, she had to admit, as he walked the paths as if he were striding down the center of a six-lane highway. They abruptly stopped at another hut and he disengaged the heavy door and locks. He shoved her in ahead of himself and she stumbled over the saddle of the door. Catching herself quickly, she went to blast him for his rough handling. She was sick of it and refused to allow it for another second.

But before she could do that, she realized almost instantly that this place was somehow very different from a home or a pub. It took only a moment of her attention for the smell of the place and the racks of the beds to sink into her awareness. She covered her mouth in horror as she took in the sight of dozens of sick and obviously dying people. Mostly men, as expected, but there were women and a frightening number of children as well. The smell of decay and infection surrounded her, chased by the aroma of antiseptics trying to keep up with what was demanded of them.

"Oh my God. . . . Is this . . . that plague?"

"No!" he said roughly, his green eyes turning dim with pain. "I would never expose you to something like that."

The queer thing was that his intensity and fear for her safety in his response were so believable. Why did he care so much about what happened to her?

Because he needed a woman, she recalled. They all did. She was like some kind of precious commodity, like a rare diamond, that needed to be guarded and protected at all costs. Only to them, she was far more fragile than a diamond.

"This," he said with a sigh, "is starvation. Energy starvation. Energy is everything, Asia. It powers every single function of every living thing, and when the resource wanes or disappears, there is no longer any force there to propel things like . . . immune systems. Nervous systems. Respiratory, circulatory, ambulatory. It goes on, starting with one and cascading to all of the rest. Those hardest hit are the children who don't know yet or have not the strength to steal their power from others." He walked over to a bunk about chest high, and that buzzing sound filled her head again as he stroked back the hair of the pale-skinned little boy lying there. That was when she realized that buzz was the energy field they were using to communicate. Asia comprehended she could even determine that she was very aware of the power of Julian's field, and the whimpering weakness of the boy who tried to respond. She suddenly wished she could understand what he was saying to the child. Did he know the boy personally? Watching small fingers curl around Julian's branded wrist made him seem so damn tiny compared to the large, vital male standing over him.

"I don't understand," she whispered softly. "You are in perfect health, Julian. I saw many others who looked robust and fit enough. If you can conduct energy between worlds, why can't you perform the simple act of feeding these children?"

"I am in perfect health because I need to be to do my work. I also get the first taste and blush of every ounce of energy I conduct. If I allowed myself to give away my strength and energy, I would fall as weak as these, and then who would give them what little they get now? Energy is shared out in a very specific order. Our leaders, the Ampliphi, and Gatherers are at the top of the chain. Then come the soldiers and the laborers who keep the colony secure, sound, and safe. By now, what remains is not very much, but it must go first to any natural-born females if the village has them. They are our future. Without them we may as well starve." The point was hard and cold and left weighted on Asia as he turned to look at the boy. "By now all that is left is residue. Energy comes in grades, Asia. The beautiful flush of a woman in pleasure or in joy feeds pleasure and joy into those who drink of it.

When that is used up, what is left behind is all those little taints that so many of your Earth females cling to even in the best of moments. Insecurity. Anger or vengeance against someone. Dark emotions and darker motivations. It hurts to feast on these things all of the time, but we do it or we starve. But it affects them, Asia. The elderly, the young boys, the infirm or handicapped, and of course, those who are criminal among us. These are fed this last residue in hopes it will be enough, but as you see, it never is."

"But . . . you just need . . ." Asia swallowed down her abject horror. "You need more Gatherers. Or . . . or you should move your people to Earth!"

He laughed at that, but it wasn't a kind or humorous sound. "Yes, because humans would be so welcoming of anyone or anything that was different than they were," he retorted derisively. "All it would take is one child getting cut on a playground and it would be over. And do you not understand how selective Gatherers must be? If all we needed was any human or emotional energy, we could walk around all day funneling it at the rate your race pisses it away! But you are so volatile and violent, shifting from one emotion to the next in such rapid order it can hardly be followed. If I were a cruel man I would show you what the smallest residue of that filth can accomplish, never mind explosions of it. But still we take what we can of it because we have no choice. It must be pure and it must be powerful and it must have the right motives. We have been through every experimentation and option, and this was the only one that was safe and sound enough to leave no host harmed and feed the greatest number of our people the best level of energy available. Every colony has a Gatherer. Every Gatherer hunts for energy for their village in their own way with their own expertise. That energy is fed to the Ampliphi and they distribute it to everyone else in even and fair shares. And now, because of you, this village has lost its Gatherer."

"What?" she exclaimed. "But you're right here!"

"Yes, I am, aren't I?" He turned to face her, his features cut like stone. "Right here. And do you think this is where I ought to be? Do you think me standing here arguing with you is how to best serve my *kin*?"

"I'm not the one forcing you to be here!" she cried.

"Don't you think we know we cross the line when we steal away women like you? Look at him, Asia, and tell me you blame me for the affront! Better still, tell me you would prefer that I had been the serial murderer you suspected me to be and would rather your sister had died in torture and violence instead of living in a place where she is lushly craved and worshipped. The human women who agree to come here are like angels to us. Saviors. They don't just have free will and the rights they've always known, but they have the adoration of a starving people and the desire of hundreds of men who need them. They have their pick among them, or none of them at all if it suits them. As for breeding, we would prefer that be put off a while, actually. Pregnant women have a much distorted sex drive, and the sharing of energy from them must cease at the end of the first trimester to protect the growing child and the mother it will make demands on. As much as it is a gain to bring new life to us, it is also a hard deprivation to lose that resource.

"As for more Gatherers . . . each colony can only have one at maximum. It is a hard duty and requires a certain level of strength, power, training, and—"

"Hotness?" she filled in for him, raising a brow as she slid her eyes over him in pointed appraisal.

"Yes. Sometimes it takes a measure of personable ability," he argued, although with a small smile. He gave the boy a friendly nudge against his nose and turned away from the bunk. "Not everyone here can pass for human. Not every man here can train to fight to the point where they can completely protect themselves against discovery. We must always be anonymous and avoid detection at all costs. That's why I move constantly through a country I have chosen. And we can't stay more than an Earth year. It starts to affect us. Some Gatherers have become . . . sociopaths. Some become like you. Hard, harsh, and jaded to a point of dysfunction."

"Dysfunction! I function just fine, thank you very much," she burst out in a fast, low voice that hissed through her teeth. "I own two successful businesses and train dozens of people in the martial arts every day."

"You hunt down evil men and women by sinking into their worlds and their habits until you can think like them and anticipate what they will do next so you can catch them. Asia, that would jade and embitter anyone, but for a woman like you, with such a stunning emotional aura and the outstanding potential for passionate expression, it's like pumping poison into a mountain spring. It's polluting and a waste of a pristine resource. But don't worry, *zini*. Given time and a different environment, I have faith that you can recover from all the taint your society poured into you."

He was reaching out for her again, and to Asia's surprise, she had no urge to pull away this time. His hand closed around the back of her neck and he drew her flush to his body.

"Now," he whispered softly as he touched dry, gentle lips against hers, "let me show you how you are so special compared to all of the other women."

Asia anticipated him. She could feel the sexual aggression pouring off of him in waves that were tumultuous and raw despite his tenderness of the moment. She stiffened and shot a glance to the nearest tiers of bunks and the children within them.

"Julian," she murmured in protest, an unexpected flush infusing her cheeks.

"Trust me, Asia, they need you just as much as I do."

Julian covered her lips warmly, kissing away her awkward hesitation in a single, burning moment. Her hands came up to grip his thick, powerful arms as his hands locked hard against her back and dragged her deep into the bend of his body. It was just as much of a shock to her as the first kiss had been. The approach, the need, and the response were so alien to her.

Here, you are the alien.

His words echoed into her head and she realized just how true it was. Not because she was such a different species, a different culture, but because she thought so coldly and so darkly in comparison to him. And why? Was her entire species on the edge of death and obliteration? Not imminently, no. She griped about things like disrespect, dysfunction, and social malfunction. He faced death and disease and knowing he was getting first taste of all the best energy while a boy he knew and others like him lay dying of starvation.

"Julian," she whispered against his mouth, her heart hurting with a powerful compassion for him and all of those with him. As he kissed her with deeper and deeper passion, burning new and powerful paths of need along the surface of her skin, she finally believed her sister had volunteered to become a part of these people. Kenya had always been free and wild, and had always hurt when others had hurt. The environment of Beneath was the perfect lure for a girl like Kenya. She had a cause, the power to help, and more men to choose from than she could have ever imagined. Kenya actually used to joke about wanting to go to Alaska where men outnumbered women almost ten to one. Hearty, sexy, rugged men, she hoped. But she'd always followed it up by jokingly realizing she wouldn't be very attractive if her tits froze off the minute she got there.

Julian choked out a laugh against her mouth and Asia gasped when she realized he must have heard her thoughts again. Or felt them. Or whatever it was he did.

"It's both. It is hearing and feeling at the same time," he explained softly as his lips trailed over her cheek. "Think of it like whale song. It's sound, emotional thought, and vibration all together. Now," his mouth slid back over hers to brush against her lips as he spoke, "the more you feel, the louder you get." He lowered his voice to the barest whisper. "Rather like the way you screamed when you came for me."

This time Asia felt her entire body burn in a fierce blush. But it was the sudden wash of her memory to his reference more than it was outrage or displeasure. She felt silly for feeling that way. But at the same time she liked the scorching need rushing down through her every organ and the sudden curve of hunger that bent her body into his. Now that she was far less inclined to think of Julian as the ultimate villain, she was quickly made aware of all those irresistible male temptations he was gifted with that no longer seemed so sinister or deceptive. Perhaps she was not as quick to toss away her life as Kenya was, but that didn't mean—

Asia jolted back away from him in sudden, sharp realization. Again, the memory of her sister brazenly stroking her hand over Julian's backside invaded her like a horrid pestilence.

"Oh God. You slept with my *sister!*"

"The hell I did!" Julian shot back in equally offended explosion. "What gave you that idea?"

She got instantly snide, her hands fisted in violence against her hips. "Oh, I don't know. Maybe because I listened to you screw everything in a skirt every night for three weeks! God, you and your slick charm! I can't believe I fell for that!"

"You listened? But did you see? Better yet," he ground out, pushing his face into hers as he seized her by the shoulders, "do you remember? If you had been outside the night I took you, what would you have heard, Asia? A woman moaning softly with pleasure? The increasingly wild cries?" His voice lowered so only she would hear him. "The begging for a deep, hard fuck?" A tremor racked him and Asia knew without a doubt that there was nothing wrong with his memory. She knew he recalled every moment she had done every single one of those things. "I haven't been with a woman in a very long time, Asia," he confessed to her hotly, scorching her with the wash of his breath against her face. "There are none here, remember? And the energy it takes to become sexually aroused is a luxury I cannot afford. It would be selfish and would be like stealing food out of the mouths of these babes."

He turned her sharply so she saw the entire room of sickly patients, his big body looming up behind her as his hard, gripping hands never once let her go, no matter how often they kept shifting over her arms, shoulders, collarbone, and throat.

"Do you think I would do that?" he demanded in a growl next to her ear.

"But . . ." She struggled to turn back, but he held her tight. It forced her to whisper harshly over her shoulder to him. "You were aroused with me. You are even now," she pointed out. She thrust her bottom back against him to prove her point, giving his very obvious erection a rather saucy rub between her cheeks.

"God," he gasped on a suddenly hitching voice as his hands locked down on her hips and forced her to repeat the wicked motion. She didn't want to feel the steaming of her skin that happened in response to feeling him like that, but it seemed she had no choice over how her body wanted to behave. Then he cupped her chin in a big palm and drew her attention to the boys in their beds. "Look," he rasped. "Look at them. See why you are different to me. See why you are the only one I can indulge in this with."

She looked.

And she saw.

Right before her eyes she saw pale skin flush with color and limp bodies began to squirm. Dull eyes instantly began to brighten. Groans and stirring started from other beds and areas as well, the whole infirmary seeming to suddenly rouse and come alive from under its pall. The male attendants caring for them began to hurry about to tend to them and answer their calls.

"If I did you up against this wall behind us," he whispered wickedly, "they'd be eating and trying to walk and wanting to play for the first time in months. Do you see? You are special. To me. You are *kindra*, Asia. It means you are my one true mate. My ultimate match. My soul and my body recognized you instantly, and that is why I reacted with you like I have not felt in so very long a time. It burned no energy to feel arousal for you, but instead created it. Every rush of heat and breath you feel, every throb of pleasure and beating of your pulse generates a power that feeds them. But it won't just be sex, *zini*. It will be laughter, happiness, joy of all kinds. It will be resentment, suspicion, and anger. You have a right to feel it all, but be certain you never throw it around carelessly. You remember the tremor from before? That was because I became angry with you and let my control of it slip. At the moment, your influence on me has me drunk with emotion, need, and power, and it is all I can do to manage it and give you what you are demanding from me all at the same time."

"So you never had sex with any of those women?" she asked, her disbelief loud and clear. Still, she remembered how she had trapped him to her body, begged him to take her, and yet he had withheld. Even though he believed this thing about her being his *kindra* and made it sound as if that somehow gave him special rights to her, he had still denied himself when he could so easily have taken.

"None. I wanted nothing of any of them except one night of rich, abundant energy. They believe other things happened, but they did not. You will have to take my word for that, for I have no way to prove it to you."

Well, not that it mattered, she told herself sternly. It would if he'd been with Kenya, and she'd tell her the truth of that soon enough, perhaps. But it wasn't as though he didn't have the right to screw anyone or anything he wanted.

"Does Kenya think you and she . . ." She trailed off. Even if it was a fantasy implanted in her sister's mind, it would still be just like the same thing. One thing she refused to do was to poach or share a man her sister had claimed first.

"No. She was Chosen, remember? She got the entire truth in the end. The pleasure she shared with me was a mental gathering of energy I conducted back to this plane. I never touched her physically."

"I'm not so sure the mental touch is not still too intimate," she said quietly.

"You tell me, Asia. We've shared it between us already."

He had a point. At this stage, she and Kenya were on equal footing.

"But it is not Kenya that I desire," he whispered against her ear, his tongue touching a sensitive spot oh-so-briefly. "Keep that always in mind."

Julian stepped away from her and reached for the door.

Chapter 7

Julian drew a deep breath of fresh air as he stepped onto the planking outside. His entire body ached for the woman he'd left behind and it was well beyond the level of pain at this point. He leaned back against the infirmary's exterior wall and forced himself to breathe and to calm his painfully raging body. God, she had no idea what it felt like just to touch her, never mind the shocking pleasure of her kiss and the sinful bliss of feeling her rub tauntingly against him. She couldn't possibly know what it was like to live always on the edge of starvation and in nearly total emotional denial, only to suddenly be swamped with the glut of power and feeling she provided. Julian couldn't believe the scope of this need he felt. He could count on three fingers how many times he had had actual physical sex. The conduction of orgasmic energy—well, that rolled into far higher numbers, and he had learned much more from those encounters than he had from the physical ones. He had learned the depths of a woman and how it could sometimes be so mystical and endless.

For the first time he felt as though he was facing a physical possibility that would not only match the mental but far, far surpass it. To say it was intimidating would be understating matters. To say he craved it with every fiber of his being was an equally weak description.

It was also clear she had no trust in him whatsoever. It was quite alien, actually, to be treated with distrust and suspicion. He wasn't used to being disbelieved and having his every action questioned and dissected. At least, not outside of Ampliphi chambers. Justice Hall was the place for such things to happen. This . . . this he would be bringing into his own home.

Julian glanced up several more levels until he saw the bottom of his house. Therein dwelled yet another problem he had to attend to. Ariel. Her deception and betrayal of loyalty to him broiled him with temper and a rage he had to work very hard to control. He'd already shaken the village with it once. He couldn't afford to infect so many men with his hostility. So long as Asia was beside him, feeding him energy, he would be too rich a resource as well. The problem was she triggered his temper so easily, converting energy into anger that, frankly, the colony did not need.

After a moment, Asia stepped out after him, her movement cautious as she kept away from the edge of the planking. She turned and saw him there and he confronted her cold, hard gaze. They were two such different creatures, and yet so much the same. Different parts of similar beasts, he thought. He was becoming well acquainted with his more savage tendencies ever since she'd stepped into his sphere, and she was a ruthless sort of predator herself, dogging him and hunting him for flaws and answers until he would likely drop from exhaustion.

"Julian," she said quietly, her eyes softening briefly, "I feel for the plight of those boys . . . for all of your people. But this place . . . I don't belong here. This isn't where I want to be."

"You do belong here. And how can you know if you want it or me when you have given neither the respect of your time and attention? Will you not even try before you so cavalierly dismiss us all?"

He didn't mean to be so harsh, but it wasn't as if he was in much control over himself at the moment. He was trying to manage far too many volatile emotions. To top it off, she was swamping him with her desires to abandon them all. To escape. To flee as fast as she could.

It was much colder than he had expected of her, even from one so jaded as she was. Was his *kindra* really so selfish a creature that she would shrug off the sick and the dying so simply? The thought made his rage take over and he lashed out at her, rather than ejecting it to poison the others around them.

"It matters not," he hissed. "The law says you cannot go back. You know too much. You have seen too much. To send you back would be a liability to us and millions of others. No individual's desires are worth the risk to an entire species. Suck it up, sweetheart. You're here to stay."

Julian pushed away from the wall and began to walk toward home. He heard her make a sound of outrage before she rushed after him. Quite bravely, he mused, for a woman who had overshot a walkway once already that day.

"You arrogant bastard!" she shouted to his back. "You can't keep me here! I have a life!"

"You still have a life. Be grateful for that."

That gave her a moment's pause that made her fluctuate between regret for those whose lives were at risk, and the understanding that there was a potential threat in his remark. If she could only understand just how voluble her emotional energy was, how easily she spoke what she didn't want others to hear.

"Are you threatening me?" she demanded. "Are you saying that you'd have me killed or something if I don't play your whore?"

Julian stopped short, causing her to ram into him. He whirled to catch her arm, keeping her from stepping back into open air. She gasped in fear as she realized she'd almost fallen again, but when he pulled her into himself with a harsh tug, she realized quickly where the real danger was.

"You insult me and yourself to refer to a mating between us in such a way. And no, I would not have you killed. I would be incapable of ordering any harm to my *kindra*. It would destroy me to see you hurt. But," he added, the word falling with hard dread, "the Ampliphi would sacrifice us both in an instant to keep this world safe. Never doubt that. And so you understand just what that means, I will tell you that each village has a ruling family. As well as Gatherer, I am the leader of the ruling family of this village. I suppose you would call me a king in your world. The Ampliphi is my council, just as they are council to every king of every colony of our species. We who rule aspire to become Ampliphi one day. But while we as rulers are autonomous to a certain point, there are bounds even we may not cross lest we come under Ampliphi justice. I assure you, Asia, as valuable as I am to them, they will see me destroyed before they will see you destroy them. Think of what that means, I beg of you, before you toss your selfish desires around so carelessly."

"It's not selfish to want what I worked so hard for! My school . . ."

"Will be run by others or will disappear, but little boys and jaded, stained men will live and be redeemed."

"Stop trivializing my life like that!" she wrenched out, tears gathering sharply in her eyes as she clenched her fists. "You don't know the hell I went through to make my life! You don't know what it took to make Kenya the woman you so admire! Goddamn you!"

"You're right," he countered softly, "I don't know any of that." Julian reached out to catch the lone tear that escaped her fierce control. "But I want to know it all. I want to know everything about you, Asia."

If only she would let it be that simple, but Julian knew she wouldn't. Still, that was okay. He had never been the sort to seek an easy way out, although in this case, the easier it went for him, the better for his people.

"Let's start with I don't belong to you," she said angrily. "Not you or any other man on any other world. You do not and will never own me! You might force me to stay here, but you won't force me to be your . . . your . . ."

Julian knew just how terrible his warning expression must have been to make her check her tirade when it had so much momentum. But, damn it, he couldn't stomach her cheapening their connection again. Maybe he should have let her, because what she did instead all but gutted him.

"I can do whatever I want. I'll be like Kenya. A sex goddess for thousands of men to admire! I'll fuck whoever I want whenever I want and have a jolly time of it. Your people will get plenty of my energy and I won't have to look at you ever again!"

No.

No, no, no, oh no, she did not just say that.

But she had, and like lighting a very, very short fuse, there was no way to stop the explosion to follow and no way to get anyone to safety.

Julian tried. With all of his might he tried to use

logic to tell himself that she did not mean what she was saying; that she was simply lashing out to hurt him as she felt he had hurt her, but it was no use. Logic couldn't prevail and he had been holding back too many thick, seething emotions for too damn long. Everything rushed out of him in a reactive energy wave that nothing could stop and none could brace against. All of his fury, jealousy, and even his passion for her blew out of him like a geyser. He threw back his head, clenched his body tight, and released a primal, roaring scream up into the air.

The entire village bucked and rolled with the impact of it, the lurching walkway sending her toppling into him and grabbing hold of him. He could feel her wrestling with her fear of falling from the wobbling walkway and being face-to-face with so much obvious rage that she had purposely caused. There were two very solid thumps on the planking behind and in front of Julian, and he knew immediately that it was Kine and Shade.

"My God, you're all insane," Asia gasped, obviously realizing the two men had jumped down from a higher level to get to them.

"Julian," Kine said carefully. "You have to calm down." He frowned at Asia. "What the hell did you say to him?" he demanded.

"Oh, screw you," she snapped back. "I'm sick of being made to feel like I'm the designated asshole around here. You can all go to hell."

Julian felt her shove away from him. In his state of emotional nausea it felt like simply more rejection, another threat of abandonment. He fought the irrationality of it, but this was powerful stuff he wasn't used to reining in.

"God, she's gonna get us all killed," Shade hissed from behind him.

"Stay where you are," Kine commanded her.

Too late.

The buck and roll was the most violent yet, but worse was the echoing cries of angry men from level after level of the village.

"Asia," Kine said cautiously, trying to use a kind voice when he clearly wanted to force her to do his will. "I know you can't appreciate the delicate balance emotional energy plays in this society as a whole, but at the very least understand that the connection between you and Julian unleashes uncontrollable emotions. Julian is handling them well because he spent so much time managing the influence of human emotion, but he is obviously not able to maintain it if you persist in taunting him!"

"Everyone will feel and act on his rage and fury; *that* is how powerful it is, Asia. It's infecting the whole colony and he can't control it! Please do something," Shade begged her. "Apologize or take back whatever it was you said. . . . Just do something to help!"

Julian was half crouched in a tight knot of animalistic rage. In his mind, all he saw was Asia giving herself joyfully to one man after another after another. Possessive need choked him and he emitted a low, dangerous growl.

Asia went very still. If there was one thing a woman like her had a true sense of, it was when danger was close at hand. Still, she faced the thing she had created with straight shoulders and a fearless aplomb. Even through the haze of his emotional breakdown, Julian could smell the way she quickly shed all of her fear and saw the anger in her aura dissipate. It was a beginning. Her body language and intent were no longer screaming hurtful images at him of how she would take other men by the dozens rather than ever come to him. His imagination hardly needed the help, however, as her threat rang sickly through his wild mind. Julian struggled to regain control, groaning as the rush of negativity battered out of him in awful waves.

The sudden touch of her hand against his chest was like an anchor in a squalling tempest. It drew all of his focus, that simple sensation of touch. Then a second hand followed, sliding gently against his throat before grasping the back of his neck. She leaned close to him and he could feel the intense wash of her glorious body heat, and the divine scent that was purely Asia. He groaned again, this time with the utter pleasure the simplistic stimulation of his senses gave him. His mind was slowly clearing and calming. He could see her reaching for him, pulling him down to her beautiful mouth.

Julian suddenly stopped her, one hand locking around the wrist that drew him to her and the other grasping her by the chin.

"Not," he rasped roughly, "unless you mean it. I'll not be charity to you or take affection as mere damage control."

She paused a moment, obviously to think about it. Cool blue eyes regarded him for a long moment. "Will you take it as an apology for being purposely cruel to you? Because I was, and it was beneath me."

"Aye," he breathed as he lowered his head, "I'll take an apology."

And an opportunity. The chance to burn onto her memory the way it could be between them if only she would welcome it instead of fighting it so hard. Ignoring the presence of his friends, he grabbed hold of her like a drowning creature would cling to driftwood, molding her to his body in hard, fierce need. She bent to match him, her flexible body easy and soft in his grasp as he devoured her in a passionate kiss. Her mouth opened under his and he rumbled out a sound of appreciation for the opportunity to dive deep within and drink of her erotic and splendid taste. He did not set a goal to kiss her until he was sated, because he knew he would never reach that point of satisfaction by the path of mere kisses. He couldn't pause to explain to her how he, like so many of these males, had waited all of his life for her. He had never believed it would happen, and had never stopped cradling a tiny flame of hope that it would. Now he knew God was testing him for every time he had doubted and scoffed against this gift. He was going to make Julian earn what he had dared to treat so dismissively.

"Release it," he heard Kine mutter under his breath. It was a reminder that damage had been done to them all, and now he must pay the price of repair. They both must. Julian uncapped the place inside himself where his passion raged and eagerly devoured every tiny tidbit of pleasure she deigned to give to him. Had he a better choice, he would have kept the baldness and starkness of his need and relief in reserve. It was a deep exposure of his most private feelings. But Kine was right. After releasing so much violence into the village's supply of energy, he needed to counterbalance it with strong, stunning joy. Since he knew Asia was not likely to allow him to rip it from her abundant surplus, he had to take it from himself.

He turned his full attention to the taste and feel of the beautiful creature in his arms. What he wouldn't give just then to be alone with her in a room with secure footing and, mercifully, a bed. It wasn't that he wanted to take anything from her, but that he wanted to give. She wasn't just a convenient body to slake his drought of thirst. She wasn't just a pool of resource others needed to drink from in order to survive. She was *kindra*. A queen. A soul mate. A true Companion. To him she would be where he would rest his body and soul from now . . . until the very last of his breaths.

Now all he had to do was convince her he was worthy of being the same to her.

She drew back for breath, but he quickly caught her and kissed her with firm, meaningful intent. When he lifted his head she was flushed and soft all across her face, her cool eyes suddenly looking very hot.

"What was that for?" she asked in a rush of air.

"An apology," he said. "For what you've lost. I'm sorry you are so angry about what you left behind, but I swear to you I will show you something so much better. There are dangers and terrible things just like on any world, but it can be joyous and beautiful, too. Rewarding. You will see."

"Maybe," she said carefully.

"Will you at least allow me the chance to convince you?"

"Maybe," she said again, but this time there was a mischievous smile twitching at her lips.

Julian released her carefully, making sure she had her feet settled right. He turned to his friends. "Patrol every level for the next hour to make certain there are no lingering effects." He looked up at his home again. "And send two guards to my home."

Julian reached down to take Asia's hand in his and led the way up to his house.

Chapter 8

Asia had so much information and sensation running through her mind and body that she was barely paying attention as she followed him through the threshold of the steel door to his house. A foolish mistake, given that a known enemy lurked within. However, Julian's dramatic outcry and curse snapped her to full alert. He released her hand and rushed into the kitchen area, the beaded divider clacking and swinging violently as he burst through it.

There, lying in a crumpled heap in a pool of her own blood, was the young Ariel. She had a knife embedded in her back, near her right shoulder and collarbone. She had been rather pale to start with, but now she was ghostly white and barely drawing breath as Julian reached down and turned her over gently into his arms.

"Ari? Ariel?" he called to her softly as he stroked a bloodstained finger over her neck and throat in an attempt to rouse her.

Asia felt an unbelievable rush of irritation as she watched Julian touch the other woman so very tenderly and with an obvious affection. Who the hell was this woman to him, anyway? Why was he being so kind to the same treacherous bitch who had tried to kill her with her devious invitation to walk out the door? What happened to all of his gushing words about how he couldn't tolerate any harm done to her?

Well, he was looking pretty damn tolerant just then. "Honey? Wake up."

The endearment compounded everything Asia was feeling and she felt choked with hostile emotion. It confused her as it rushed over her. She had seen wounded criminals before and had always afforded them human compassion and aid whether she wanted to or not. Why was she so against doing the same for this girl who had clearly been a victim of a brutal assault? She was lying there all but dead and all Asia could think of was that the way Julian was touching her made her want to crush the twit with a string of offensive linebackers. Asia gripped the edge of a countertop at her back until her fingers ached and her knuckles were white as she struggled to fight back the hectic, irrational emotions. *What in hell is happening to me? What has Julian done to me?*

Besides kiss the bejeezus out of her? Asia simply had no way of answering the question. She was still trying to grasp the concept that she was trapped in this world with this man whether she liked it or not.

She certainly wasn't prepared to like it, never mind start to crave it.

Ariel opened her eyes. Soft and brown, they seemed suddenly vulnerable and innocent, and Asia instantly felt bad for being so harsh in her thoughts just before. After all, it had probably not even occurred to someone who'd been raised in a single environment all of her life that someone would be unable to navigate something as simple as the walkways and ledges beyond the door.

"Hey, sweetheart," Julian said gently as he cradled the weak girl close. "Can't turn my back on you for a second," he teased as he waited for her to fully focus on him. "What happened? Who did this, honey?"

Asia frowned. There certainly was a lot of "honey" and "sweetheart" flying around the room. Clearly Julian had a few more details he needed to explain to her, and Ariel's significance in his household had damn well better be one of them.

Then Ariel blinked and weakly raised a hand.

"She did," she croaked, pointing to Asia.

Asia saw Julian's entire body stiffen and his head whipped around so he could narrow an accusatory green glare on her. She was so shocked by the accusation that all she could manage was a sharp, disbelieving laugh for a minute. Then she realized Julian was actually willing to give the ridiculous story credence.

"That is a hell of a nasty fucking lie! Don't tell me you believe I would stab some girl in the back for no good reason!"

"To escape," Ariel rasped. "I tried to stop her."

"Okay, now you have to know she's lying her ass off," Asia shot out sharply, her hands dropping hard on her hips. "I wouldn't need a damn knife to lay her out and you know it."

Julian hesitated, turning his head indecisively between the two women.

"Asia, she can't exactly stab herself in the back. Why would she even want to?" he asked.

Well, heck. He had a point. It was pretty damning to look at. Except she knew she hadn't done it.

"Let's just get her some help. You can accuse me all you want, but let's keep it to assault and not murder. She doesn't look good at all," she grumbled in grudging awareness for the duplicitous twit's life. *Go ahead, save her, heal her, get her on her feet so I can slap the shit out of her on even ground.* "Ground" being a relative term, of course.

Julian's expression was grim as he nodded with agreement. He set Ariel down on her side, wincing when the girl groaned with pain and weakness. Then he hurried back to the door so he could step out and call loudly for help. Left alone with her accuser, Asia frowned down at the girl.

"What's your game?" she demanded.

Ariel didn't respond, but Asia most certainly did not miss the woman's smug little smile. That was when she knew Ariel had somehow set this up so she could get rid of Asia's presence in Julian's life. She remembered the outburst the girl had sputtered earlier, and she realized that she was a direct threat to Ariel's relationship with Julian. Was Ariel his wife? Was she being cast off because of this *kindra* business?

As soon as she thought it, she realized it couldn't be. She couldn't say she knew Julian well at all, but instinct told her that a man who fought so hard to honor the needs of his people would never make a false promise or break a sworn vow. Whatever she was, whatever her relationship to Julian, this deceptive girl was willing to do whatever it took to eliminate Asia as a threat—even risking her own life in the process. It was the act of a completely unhinged mind and it made her heart stutter to think Julian kept such a creature close by. If he was as critically important to his people as she had begun to comprehend, someone this unstable put thousands of lives in jeopardy. That knife could just as easily have ended up in Asia's back . . . or worse, Julian's.

Asia slowly crouched down over the twisted young woman and very carefully engaged her ear.

"I come from a world of violence and deception the likes of which you will never understand any more than I comprehend this world in its entirety, and you should be grateful for that, you fool. But you will grasp one thing very clearly, Ariel. I am a woman who hunts men who murder and rape and decimate people's lives just for the joy of how it makes them feel. I have hunted women who have slaughtered their own young, driven knives into the hearts and testicles of the men they swore they loved. I have hunted children who sell drugs to babies and who burn down houses because it gets them off to see the destruction and the aftermath of people's ruined lives. If you think for one tiny little second that you and your sneaky little tricks and lies are going to get the best of me, you are in for a world of shock, *honey*."

She stood up over her and looked down on Ariel's wide stare of surprise and saw the small inkling of fear that was finally reflected within it.

"Stay away from me and stay away from Julian, Ariel. As I understand it, there are hundreds of men out there who are desperate for a woman. Take my advice. Get well and choose one. Choose all of them. Choose anyone but Julian. Got it?"

"I think she's got it," Julian said, his voice dark and heavy behind her.

Asia turned slightly on her heel and shrugged a shoulder at his brooding expression of disapproval. "I hope so. Anyone who is willing to rig up a way to stab themselves in the back just to turn you against me is only one step shy of taking the knife to my throat next, and only two steps from yours. It's called: 'If I can't have him, then no one can.' It's really quite a pre-dictable psychology."

Julian's frown deepened as he looked down at

Ariel. He said nothing in reply because others began to spill into his house to retrieve the dying girl. Julian left Asia alone for a while as he set out to see Ariel was comfortable and well cared for in the infirmary.

Left to her own devices, Asia took the time to slowly explore his home. Her inspection earlier had been distracted and cursory. This time she took the time to appreciate the details. Overall it was a casual and rustic environment, not what her culture would expect of a king's main residence. But then again, he was also a Gatherer, and clearly he spent a great deal of time on the Earth plane. An absent ruler. How did such an arrangement work? From what she had divined, he was gone for months, perhaps even years at a time. How did a man run a colony if he wasn't there?

Then again, Richard the Lionheart ruled all of England while gallivanting into Crusade after Crusade. But he had left someone in charge in his stead. Who had Julian chosen for such an important task?

It was so surreal. The man she had been stalking was nothing she had thought him to be. He was a king, for heaven's sake! She had thought him a low-life piece of murdering scum. How could she have been so wrong? Surely there had been signs that he wasn't a killer?

Asia nodded, acquiescing the point. There had been plenty of signs; she just had not wanted to see them. She had made an assumption and a mold and had forced Julian into it. Granted, the fact that he had made so many women disappear had helped . . . but she had seen the clean class of his lifestyle and the authoritative confidence of his demeanor and seen an organized predator and an arrogant psychopath instead of the thoughtful man he truly seemed to be. It was almost creepy, how many of the qualities that made a king could also be attributed to the psychopathic mind. To be fair to herself, it wasn't often you found royalty bouncing at a long chain of clubs.

Asia returned to the scene of the "crime" and stepped carefully over the blood on the floor to enter the kitchen. She slowly inspected the place for a clue as to how Ariel had managed to stab herself in such an awkward and difficult spot.

"Anything?"

Asia couldn't believe she startled. Even more, she couldn't believe he'd come into the house and room so quietly. She turned to look at him with surprise. "I didn't even hear the door."

"That is because you left it open. I think I need to explain to you the importance of securing every door behind you."

"Because every man in town is going to be driven mad with lust for me and will be banging the door down?" she asked snarkily.

Asia could tell by the harsh bunching of his shoulder and chest muscles that it had been a very poor joke. She winced when he exhaled a bullish huff through his nose as he worked to control his spiking temper. It was such a keen reaction that she could have sworn she felt the presence of it prickling over her skin.

"I'm sorry. It was a bad joke," she said quickly. "Tell me why I need to shut the doors. I will do it, but I would like to know the reasons why instead of being expected to simply obey your commands."

He nodded at that, submitting to her point. "Because twice a day, at sunrise and at sunset, the *okriti* are on the move. They are vicious and powerful predators sized just a bit bigger than I am. They are clever and resourceful, for all they are animals, and those who are caught outside or with unsecured doors end up slaughtered and dragged off for the local *okriti* herd's dinner. When you came out and fell into the net before, it was barely past sunrise and the safety time was not begun. That was why you saw no women out. They are no match for the *okriti* and so are restricted indoors at these times. Our males are no match for them either, individually. This is why I was with my friends." He narrowed serious eyes on her. "The *okriti* are only one of those dangers I mentioned. It is because they roam the lands in heavily populated herds that it became necessary to build our castles literally in the sky. They dislike heights. They also have a poor sense of balance."

"No rails," she said softly. "That's why you have no ropes or rails. You want them to fall if they come. And," she lit up with understanding, "that's why the nets break away! The beasts would struggle mindlessly and make them snap, keeping them from climbing back into the village."

"Very good," he remarked as he leaned against the wall. He looked down at the tacky pool of blood between them. "Just the same," he said softly, "every now and then one of the *okriti* will get lucky and someone suffers for it. Blood is shed and the screams . . ."

There was much more to his dark tone than just the information he was imparting to her. She could see the thoughts churning in his head as he mapped his gaze over the crime scene. Asia crossed her arms beneath her breasts and gave herself a tight little hug. There was nothing else she could say or do to help convince him she didn't do what she had been accused of, so she didn't bother to repeat herself.

"I have someone coming to help clean all of this up," he said after a minute. "I wanted to show you something before—"

"Who is she?" Asia heard herself interrupt him sharply and suddenly. The urge to know was terrible and insistent. "Who is Ariel to you? Why was she here? Does she live here? With you? Is she your lover or . . . or your wife?" She hadn't really believed that last possibility until it rushed past her lips. Despite her earlier logic about his honor, doubt began to infect her like a plague. Was Ariel the one who rightfully belonged here? Was she being cast aside because of some arcane belief or practice? Her mind raced with questions as she tried not to think the worst of him. It was the least she could do when she was hoping that he wouldn't think the worst of her.

"She is not my wife," he said carefully, the hard look he flicked over at her telling her very clearly what he thought of such a dishonorable supposition being attributed to him. "Nor was she ever my lover. She did live here. She has been my Companion for sixteen years. A Companion is assigned to a Gatherer to care for his home and belongings while he is away from this plane so he doesn't have to worry about such trivialities and can focus on what he is supposed to do. It is a job, a chosen profession just like any other. One with a great deal of ceremony and regulation to it." He paused a long moment. "She has believed herself to be in love with me for quite some time, despite my attempts to discourage her. I think she might like the tragedy of it. The unrequited love of a working girl who serves the king. Perhaps, though, in her mind, the fairy tale ends differently than it did when I came home carrying the beautiful woman who is my *kindra,* signaling the end of her life with me. She was to be retired after today. It is a respectable way to live for a girl like her."

"A girl like her?" she echoed. "But she is a native

female. I thought you said you treasured your native women more than anything."

"We do. Ariel is no exception. She could have chosen any number of mates, or even to have a child which she would have been free to raise here, but she denied herself to those who called for her, as she had the right to do, and kept herself to herself."

"You mean she pined for you. She played the role of your wife and convinced herself you would come around if only she remained patient enough and loyal enough."

"I suppose she did," he said grimly. "I have been away time and again, and my time at home was spent in conference with the other ruling houses or the Ampliphi. I knew she was a bit dependent, but I never suspected it had gone this far. Had I truly comprehended that, I never would have left you alone with her. I never would have exposed you to such danger."

Asia moved carefully toward him, her carriage still a little stiff and wary as she skirted the evidence of Ariel's madness.

"Are you saying you believe me? You believe I had nothing to do with her injuries?"

"You were merely a catalyst, Asia. No, I do not believe you stabbed an innocent girl in the back and then proceeded to pitch yourself off the walkway."

"What makes you believe that?" she persisted.

"Because you said so and I believe you," he said with a simple shrug. "I think I would know if you were trying to deceive me. Also, listening to you threaten her reminded me of how dangerous and clever you really are. You would never do something so ham-handedly and without cause. Everything I have seen of you has been centered around not just your survival instincts, but your unflagging sense of justice.

Your pursuit of your sister, your vengeance against me when you thought I had harmed her, and your profession as a bounty hunter. You even teach others how to protect and defend themselves. The world you come from may have jaded and embittered you, *zini*, but you never stopped fighting it."

Asia didn't respond or argue with him about that. She did have to remind herself, however, that his uncanny perceptions of her character were aided by his extraordinary and unusual talents. When normal people saw her, all they saw was the hard-ass. The bitch. The stern sensei who guided and did not coddle. They rarely saw beyond that to see what Julian could see. It felt exposing and she felt vulnerable for it, but in a way it was a strange comfort to have someone other than Kenya starting to see beneath her surfaces. At the same time, she wasn't all that certain she wanted it to be him. He made her feel so strangely. Everything seemed so volatile when she got close to him, as she was doing now. The only real comfort was that it was just as disruptive to him as it was to her. Still, as far as comfort went, it was a poor one.

She had almost instantly regretted going for his throat on the walkway earlier. Somehow she had instinctively known the words flying past her lips were the best ones to wound him deeply and leave him debilitated. Seeking vulnerabilities was, after all, one of her greatest natural skills. However, she had not stopped to consider how it would affect everyone in the colony, in spite of the fact that he had already warned her what his temper could do. She had even felt a smug satisfaction when she had felt that first rumble of resulting vibration. It had only lasted a second before she'd realized just how insane it was to provoke him, but she had felt it just the same. Then his accusation of selfishness on her part had rung back at her, even before his friends had dropped in to snap her back into line.

A kiss had seemed the least she could do to make it right, but he had surprised her when, even through such loss of control, he had refused to settle for an illusion. Again, that unflagging sense of honor within him had reared up, making him refuse any half-hearted attempts to placate him.

But it hadn't been an illusion. Something very wild happened to her when he touched her or kissed her and, it seemed, the more she learned about him, the more she reacted to him. If he was feeling similar impulses, Asia was beginning to appreciate the difficulty he must be having keeping himself focused and in control. She was also beginning to appreciate his mental fortitude and the importance his people played in how he controlled his actions.

"Do you at least empathize with how all of this feels for me?" she asked abruptly. "You keep asking me to have compassion for your situation, the feelings of those around you, and the unfortunates being affected by this blight your world is suffering, but is it really that selfish of me to want you to show just a little understanding that, sometimes, some people just don't take to change very well? I'm . . ." She hesitated, but she realized by the way he was studying her that he would read her need and desires off her in other ways even if she didn't speak her mind. "I'm used to being in meticulous control of my life, Julian. I am used to having the strength and knowledge it takes to navigate my world. You plunge me into chaos and then frown on me when I don't adjust fast enough to suit you? It's unfair. It's cruel, actually, when on top of it you tell me, 'Tough luck, you can't go back.' It doesn't exactly promote warm and fuzzy feelings, you know?"

Julian actually smiled wryly at that, his jewel green eyes steady on hers. "It is strange to hear myself accused of that kind of unfairness and impatience." He shook his head slightly and lowered his gaze a moment. Asia had the keen sensation of understanding that it was a gesture of self-effacement, rather than negation of her claim. "Perhaps because I, much like yourself, have become something of an automaton in my life. Feelings and emotional outbursts require too much energy, so we get used to an affected calm and careful placidity that does nothing to excite us or vitalize our personalities."

"But I thought giving emotion away was giving energy to others," she interrupted him.

"Not all of it, Asia. It's true, we recycle what we can, but it degrades so rapidly . . . and to expend it frivolously means we will starve ourselves. So we stay a steady course. This gives me the appearance of measured consideration, politeness, and endless patience. This is how I am seen. However, since your arrival . . ." He shrugged and, as she neared his reach, he immediately extended a hand to touch against her shoulder. It was a light caress, but the manner of its tracing and the intensity of his heated eyes made it resonate far deeper. "Perhaps it will help you to know that my life, too, is being changed dramatically because you are here. I will be dismissed from my duties as a Gatherer. I will never again be allowed to make passage between planes without express Ampliphi permission. It will be expected that my focus is to be solely on the colony and, more importantly, on you."

"Because I am such an important and rich source of energy? They expect you to keep me content like some kind of bird in a gilded cage so I don't think about running away? After all, the only choice they have given me is to remain trapped in this world or to die if I try to escape it," she said, unable to delete all of the sarcastic bitterness from her tone.

"By my soul," he whispered softly, "I curse the very idea of you seeing this in that way. But I don't deny the truth for what it is . . . just as you should know it is not death that awaits you. You can return to your plane any time you please." Asia knew there was a dreadful *but* coming even before he opened his mouth. "But the process to get there is almost a fate worse than death. You must believe me when I say you would never wish to take that path."

"Wonderful. Stay trapped here or meet this fate worse than death. Some choice. As if I ever *had* a choice."

"I cannot change how this all came about, Asia. You'll never understand how much I regret that," he said, running frustrated hands through his hair.

"Or maybe I already do," she noted with a gentle arching of her left brow. "If there is one thing I understand at the moment, it is regret." She stepped even closer to him when his frown darkened fiercely. She reached out and touched his chest, for the first time taking a moment to appreciate the feel of the man beneath her fingers. She felt him startle at the voluntary intimacy of her touch, his eyes quickly darting to hers and rapidly shadowing with the need he was constantly struggling to keep in abeyance. Asia had noted the voluble emotions before but had simply balked at any understanding of what he wanted. Especially the realization that it was *her* he wanted.

She was not known for her ability to be affectionate, passionate, or anything of that sort, but her strangely powerful responses to him made her act out of character as she caressed the expanse of muscles curving over his chest with attractive masculine strength. The slightly spicy and very delicious scent of him fell against her until she was tempted into drawing a deep breath full of it.

"If you have a point to make, Asia, make it quickly," he breathed into the sudden intimacy forming between their close bodies, "because my attention becomes fickle when you are standing this close to me. I lose control of where it focuses itself."

"Hmm. You mean you begin to prefer my body over my brain? You ignore the intelligence and fixate on the T and A?"

He snorted out a laugh of wry denial. "I wish it were that simple. I wish physicality was all this was about, Asia. Then it would be a matter of physically sating myself on you and moving on, wouldn't it? But that isn't the case, and I assure you, I am no more prepared to lose control of myself to this than you are."

That made her go rigid and wary.

"Lose control of myself?"

He drew in a breath that was long and unsteady, but somehow he had never seemed stronger or more determined. His eyes were so green and so intensely fixated on her that a wicked shiver trotted down her spine. She was abruptly reminded of the way he had wiped the floor with her in just a few distinct moves in his apartment; the sleek confidence of his movements and the hard, measured strength he had used. Then she recalled how he had touched her with sharp intimacy, no hesitation and all male dominance as he had confronted the lies in her act. It made her understand it was indicative of how ruthless he could also be as a lover, yet she simply couldn't grasp why she would suddenly realize that.

"There is nothing to compare the matching of *kindri* and *kindra,* Asia. And I must warn you that the stronger the personalities of the mates, the stronger the volatility of the mating. When this happens between us, it will be an explosive event. It will always be that way. And, if you permit it, it will feed joy and pleasure into the entire colony. With you and I here, together, none in this village will ever starve again." As soon as he finished the pronouncement, he inhaled her scent, his nostrils flaring with the intense action. Asia's entire body seemed to clench all at once and her heart began to thrum a hard, harshly racing beat. He wasn't even touching her. All he had done was breathe in! But it had been all about the way he had done it, those green eyes going so dark in response to his intake of her scent they were like some kind of mysterious underground pool.

That was all it took. Just the look he was giving her and the base way he took her in with his senses had made her entire body seize up in response. She couldn't deny it as it stunned her, shocking her because she had never felt anything like it before. Hell, not even remotely like it. She was almost surprised she even knew how to recognize it for what it was, recognize it as something she had once craved so very much back when she'd still had hope for herself and for others.

Julian leaned in closer to her, lowering his head until his nose brushed her cheek and temple. "I consider myself a man of deep control and even deeper rationality, and when I tell you that I anticipate this with trepidation, I mean to say that I fear how far it will push both of our limits. As I said, I cannot cause you any real harm, *zini,* but there is so much that can be done that can be made to hurt in wonderful ways . . . and I am beginning to realize you don't have a single clue as to what I mean."

The remark was far too intimate for her and she

jerked back away from him, crossing her arms over her breasts and grabbing hold of her shoulders.

"I don't—" she sputtered in an attempt at denial.

Julian moved so fast she was pinned between his hard body and the near wall before she had even said the second word of her protest.

"Oh, no," he told her in a whisper against her ear that was quick and hot, just like the body pressing against her. "You're no wilting virgin or shy miss, this I know. I've seen you strut your sexuality and know you are intimate with it. But here is the puzzle; I don't think anyone else has been. Not truly. Maybe they've tried, maybe you had some experiences resembling pleasure, and no doubt you are always in command of your sexuality, indulging it here and there as needed, but you've never quite known the real truth of passion, have you? One human male after another fell very short of the mark, did they not? Tell me, Asia, how many men did you try before you finally gave up? And how long ago was that?"

"I'm not answering that!" she gasped, trying to turn and wriggle free. "You don't know anything!" He couldn't possibly know all of that! She hadn't even been thinking about any of it.

"You don't need to think of it or even project it. I am your mate, Asia, and I can smell the ways you have been used and disused. I can tell that the fools who tried to satisfy this richly honed and beautifully crafted body were inept and lacking the one thing you have needed more than anything."

"What's that?" she heard herself asking, her whole body feeling like it was perched on tenterhooks. Did he really know the answer she'd never discovered?

"They weren't me," he said with a low growl of claim before he bent to catch her mouth.

Chapter 9

Yes!

All of her body and soul cried out the agreement, the acknowledgment that he was so very right whether she wanted him to be or not. His kiss was everything that he was: a little rough, a lot of dominance, and exotic with an alien power over her that she didn't understand. When he kissed her like this, plundering her mouth with deep, slow strokes of his tongue around hers, she was overrun with sensation and a hum of vitality that was like getting an electrical shock. Asia didn't know what it was that made him so very different than other men—at least not in specific—but whatever it was hummed into her on a fast, fierce frequency straight to the very center of her being. Once it reached the deepest core of her body, it flash-flooded her in an all too liquid rush of arousal that made her blatantly wet with need. Suddenly self-conscious, she squirmed in his caging grasp, but he was unrelenting as he lifted away from her lips.

"No more fighting, Asia," he said softly, his breath hot against her wet lips, "me or yourself. Relent to what you feel. Relax and release, and what you will experience will blow us both away."

"I don't want to be blown away," she rasped out, clenching her teeth when she heard the fear in her own voice. She was rapidly losing control of everything around her, and no matter how good this part of it felt, it was still writhing too violently out of her grasp. "I won't be ruled by the equivalent of adolescent hormones and impulsiveness!"

He laughed, the sound rough and bordering on manic. He pressed his weight fully against her, rippling in a long, lithe line of hard muscle and a heat that penetrated her in waves. With the aroma of him so abundant around her, she couldn't seem to help the need to breathe him into herself deeply, just as he had done. Then she became very aware of the aroused state of his body, of just how hard and hot he was beneath the denim of the jeans he was wearing. Human clothing, she thought inanely, on an alien male.

The thought made her gasp and she looked up into his eyes in anxiety.

"Are you different f-from human males?" she blurted out before she could curb the impulse. The smile that curved sinfully over his lips made her entire body flush hot with an almost naughty sense of anticipation and a craving for something different and wild.

"Now, see," he murmured low and smooth near the rise of her cheek as he bent to rub his lips against her in teasing grazes, "a question like that proves to me that you aren't at all as disinterested as you wish you were. What would it matter to you otherwise? You want to know this because you want to make love with me."

Asia opened her mouth to retort with one of about a dozen different lies, but just then his mouth slid against her ear where it brushed and toyed in breathy kisses until her skin erupted in goose bumps and her nipples turned into aching hard points. Of course, the suggestion that she wanted him in her bed had a lot to do with it as well when she realized just how right he was. He made her feel in ways no one else ever had. He made her feel in ways she had once craved very much. How could she deny herself a pleasure she had thought didn't exist for her?

But what if it still didn't? What if all of this glorious play that so stimulated her ended in the usual disappointments? How could she bear that? How could he or the thousands of people he claimed were awaiting her energy survive such a crushing disillusionment?

"I am almost insulted," he whispered softly to her. "Do you forget so soon the way you called the Gate to us? Do you forget what I made you feel then?"

Asia gasped and realized she had. She had been so humiliated by her behavior and the way he had manipulated her that she had shut off the implications of what she had been made to feel.

"But you didn't touch me," she recalled in a soft voice. "You never laid a hand on me. How did you . . . ?"

"A woman of such energy as yours? Her power and pleasure are centered within her mind, in as much as it lives in her body." He drew back and she saw his momentary frown flitting through his eyes. "I am sorry it was such an impersonal event. It should have happened differently. I would much rather have . . ." His eyes slid almost closed, neglecting to hide all the things he was thinking he should have done to her to draw out those kinds of responses from her. "I have the power to touch and weave the energy of your mind's pleasure centers with just the command of my thoughts and aura." He smiled a bit devilishly. "I can always make you come, Asia, with just a thought."

Well, how could she blame herself for going completely breathless after a claim like that? Especially after having seen and felt the proof of it?

"But . . . I've had orgasms before. I know my own body, you know. I'm not a child or a prude," she said in a rush. "Still, I've never . . . not like that. It was so powerful. If you didn't have those abilities, I promise you you couldn't . . . It wouldn't happen like that." She exhaled at the end of the statement as if she had just made a terrible confession. "I'm not the passionate woman you or your people seem to need. You've made a mistake."

"Asia?"

She let her eyes drift up to his.

"If that's a truth, it's about to change. And this time you will know how good change can be."

The hot promise was followed by an even hotter kiss. He broiled against her with increasing heat from his body, the shift of his strong legs and wicked hips burrowing him tight against her. His hand slid over her hip and drew her snugly forward into him as he shaped one cheek of her backside through the slick silver of her dress. She felt herself rush in wet response between her legs, dampness saturating her underwear and making her shiver with the realization of how blatant a sign of arousal it was. Julian chuckled softly, continuing to rub himself restlessly against her.

"No more blatant than this, eh?" he queried as he fed the feel of his cock in all of its hardened glory against the feminine mound concealing his mate. "Should I take you like this, *zini?* Up against the nearest wall, only steps away from the spilt blood of your defeated enemy?"

"Julian!" she cried, trying to sound aghast and horrified but sounding more like she was inviting him to do just that.

"Don't be so shocked. You're a warrior from head to toe and your victories will always be a source of empowerment for you."

"But she was your friend. . . ."

"If she were my friend and a true Companion, she would never have betrayed me by trying to cause harm to my *kindra*. There isn't a man in this colony who would dare to do such a thing to me. I don't think you fully appreciate what she was trying to do to you by staging this."

"I don't appreciate any of this," she said without force or anger, just a lot of confusion. "I don't understand why she would do this. I don't understand why you want me. I don't understand what it is you expect me to do when I know I just can't do it!"

"Now that doesn't sound like the woman who thought she could take on a serial killer all by herself," he noted with a wicked smile.

"Well, I—" *Well, hell.* He was right about that. He had her so far off her mark that she was completely on the defensive. What she needed, what she wanted, was to get back in the game.

She escaped his grasp and bolted into the next room. She couldn't truly run away from him, she knew, but she could at least give herself distance from him and the mocking aroma of Ariel's neon pink blood pool. Unlike human blood that was tinged with the rusty smell of iron, this was sweeter, like being in a room full of sugar, and she couldn't bear the idea of what the pathetic creature had done all in the name of rescuing a life turned upside down.

What was *she* going to do to rescue a life turned upside down? Shed blood like Ariel? Go insane? Rip out her hair? Where would any of that get her?

"Oh God," she rasped, pacing the room quickly as

he came through the beaded curtains to confront her wild emotions.

But before he could speak there was a resounding clanging sound at the front door. She gasped, wondering what fresh hell was being thrown at her now.

"Will you please relax." Julian sighed. "It's just someone at the door."

"Well, excuse the fuck out of me for being a little on edge! Didn't you just tell me there are huge creatures out there that—"

Asia broke off when he opened the door to reveal the huge creature standing outside. A good seven feet tall and entirely transparent, the thing flickered like a weak movie on a moving movie screen. Asia was so stunned by the thing she almost missed Julian's reaction. He quickly knelt and dropped his head, his complexion going dramatically pale. All of a sudden, like a wave of water dashed in her face, she could sense the fear and worry coming off him. He reached out and snagged her wrist, yanking on it until she fell to her knees as well. She was too numb to really do anything else.

"Ampliphi Kloe." He greeted the faded figure with soft respect in his tone. "How may your Gatherer serve you?"

Kloe ignored his protocol and manners and went straight for Asia. She flicked a faded finger against Asia's cheek rudely, the sensation more like a sparkle than a touch.

"Here less than one of your Earth days and already there is violence and murder in your wake."

"Murder!" Julian was on his feet instantly and trying to wedge himself between Kloe and Asia. "Ariel is not dead!"

"She is not," the Ampliphi agreed, "but not for lack of

trying." There was accusation in her eyes as she stared at Asia. "You will take this one to the holding colony."

"No! She didn't do this thing!"

"There was a victim stabbed in the back and she was the only one here, is that not so?"

"Yes, but—"

"Then the matter is clear. She is no better than nightfly, so she will live as one."

"Wait a minute." Asia spoke up, getting quickly to her feet when she heard the derision in the creature's voice. "Are you sending me to jail? That sicko bitch stabs herself and I'm getting sentenced without a trial or anything?"

"Asia," Julian hissed, trying to hush her.

"No. Fuck that. I never asked to be here. I've done nothing wrong. I'll be damned if this—whatever this thing is—is going to pass judgment on me like she's deciding on paper or plastic at the checkout!"

"Insolent," Kloe stated with obvious distaste. "Ignorant. He hushes you because I am Ampliphi. I am the first and the last power of all the colonies. My will is done and not questioned!" Ampliphi Kloe turned to Julian. "Very well. Take her to the colony, as instructed, and you may take the matter up with the Ampliphi come dawn."

"Yes, Ampliphi," Julian said quickly, bowing his head to her as she moved out of the doorway like a ghost and glided down the pathway. Julian wasted no time in slamming the door and spinning the wheel to lock the posts into the steel.

"'Yes, Ampliphi'?" Asia demanded. "Is this your idea of protection, because it kinda really sucks!"

"You will be quiet!" he roared suddenly, whirling to get in her face. "Have you no appreciation for the amount of trouble you are in?"

"What I appreciate," she said through her tightly clenched teeth, "is that I went from being summarily sentenced to a trial by jury. That's what I appreciate!"

That seemed to draw up his temper, to the point where he looked utterly perplexed. "Yes," he said carefully. "That much is true." But then he frowned darkly again. "But it is not the improvement you think. The Ampliphi are notorious for backing one another almost without exception."

"Oh. Well, I suppose the key word there then is 'almost.' That implies that sometimes they do make exceptions. We'll just have to see to it this is one of those times."

"Good God, you are the most bullheaded creature I have ever met!" he exclaimed. "Regardless of what the dawn brings, you must now spend the night in holding. You do not comprehend what this place is like and what can happen to you there!"

"Then enlighten me," she demanded, her hands on her hips.

"It's a colony full of criminals! Use your imagination! These are women with nothing to lose except . . ." He looked her up and down sharply. "God! You're going to get yourself killed!"

"Nice. Way to have faith." She squared off with him. "I am a master in jujitsu and I hunt criminals for a living, Julian. I can handle myself."

He laughed at that, pacing a short distance and running a hand through his hair. It wasn't the body language of someone who was comforted.

"*Zini,* you don't understand. This isn't like human prison. These women, these nightfly, have committed such horrible crimes that we've had to lock them away! We, who are dying for lack of females, have locked them away."

"I think you need to explain the term 'nightfly' to me," she said carefully, not at all liking the panic she was reading off him.

"We cannot afford to dismiss even a woman of pure evil from among us. You understand? Even the most evil womb is precious to us. Women do not have the death penalty. Instead, they become . . . breeding stock. Nightfly. You would call them whores or prostitutes. They barter their fertility for the right to live and the means to live well, albeit in confinement. Gilded cages, of a sort. We cannot use their poisoned energy, so they are isolated from all of the colonies, but if raised right, their get can be useful members of this society. It is a distasteful way to mate and get heirs, and only those of us who are driven to utter desperation will submit to paying for the use of a nightfly."

"What makes the difference, Julian?" she asked softly, knowing she was about to infuriate him with the query. "What makes the difference between a nightfly and what you have made of my sister?"

"The difference is freedom, respect, and honor! Nightfly do not have a choice in who buys their fertility. They are not free to come and go from the nightfly colony. There is shame attached to having nightfly parentage, although it is understood there is often no other choice. If Ariel has done what you are accusing her of, she will become nightfly. She will be sentenced to bear children for the men who choose her. Those men, in return, will pay for the gilding in her cage. One of my two friends whom you have met is the son of a nightfly. He struggles with that side of his genetics constantly. His mother was the most notorious woman in the history of all the kings and colonies. A foul murderess and insurrectionist. Her name was Diolite. Only one man ever dared to pay the price for Diolite's uterus and her whelps." Julian shook his head. "It must have been like thrusting into a poisoned pool. I cannot imagine it."

It took a moment for Julian to realize how still she had gone so suddenly. He frowned as he sought for the reason for the repellant body language from her, his eyes and mind both searching her.

"This disturbs you?" he asked.

"Disturbs me? What you speak of is a heinous act called rape and forced reproduction! 'Disturb' doesn't even begin to touch on what I'm feeling!" Asia swallowed back against a rushing tide of bile lurching from her stomach.

"Every woman in our society knows what the consequences of foul behavior are, just as the men know capital punishment awaits them for any number of crimes. They are the ones who choose to commit those acts regardless. It cannot be called rape or forced when the person who is committing the treachery is aware of the penalty they are flirting with. It is a conscious and aware selection of fate. They understand they are tempting it when they try to get away with a crime, so how do you find it forced on them? And before you judge this society, Asia, remind yourself just how close we are to the eradication of our species. You have no comprehension how distasteful it is to the men of this world to treat a woman with anything less than the most gracious and honorable respect! To us the female body is a temple where we are blessed with the opportunity to worship, and the woman herself a goddess bestowing wondrous favors of passion, brilliance, and energy. Your sex is our salvation and our satiation, the ultimate prize we can earn if we are dutifully respectful and honorable enough to earn her attention and favor.

"For the Ampliphi and rulers of the colonies to be

forced to realize a woman has committed crimes and heinous acts is the most dreadful betrayal you can possibly imagine. Rare and precious as they are to us, as reverently as we treat them, they would throw it all back in our faces? They are somehow unsatisfied to the point that they commit treachery for some reason? What is it we don't give them that they could possibly want, what is it that measures as enough reason to betray that status among their people?"

"You tell me," she countered hoarsely. "Tell me what your women crave that makes them risk being sent to a penal colony that will make them into breeding machines."

Julian snorted at the terminology.

"Machines? What do you think of us? That we force a child on a woman every instant of her fertile years? A man purchases a nightfly for five years, in which time he is due a single child . . . unless the nightfly desires to have another with him during that period. You see? Even our punishments give respect to the woman. In those five years he must feed her, clothe her, and keep her in complete comfort. Her health needs become his responsibility. A single complaint of substance from the woman nullifies his chances to get a child on her. And if he fails to impregnate her in his allotted time, for any reason, he must release her regardless. Those five years will be the only ones he is ever allowed, no matter how powerful or wealthy he is. Five years, one opportunity. Once it passes, it can never again be renewed, and then his only hope of a child lays on the voluntary choice of a woman being courted by, at the very least, two hundred other men.

"The nightfly gets her five years with a single man living in whatever luxury he can afford for her before she is chosen for another man a year later. As far as punishments go, it is as gentle and spoiling as can be without giving her the freedom to commit more acts of crime or evil."

"Easy for you to say when you aren't the one being forced to have sex with a man not of your choice."

"There's that word 'choice' again," he said bitterly. "The choice was made to commit the act to thrust her into the situation in the first place."

"What about me? My choice? They are going to heedlessly make me a nightfly!"

"We could never destroy a healthy woman. It's like cutting off a crucial limb to do something so reckless," he agreed quietly.

"So tell me, Julian, where in all of this would it have been my choice? I was never aware of your laws or punishments. I never asked for any of this! You and your precious Ampliphi would make me a whore, rape victim, and baby incubator for no reason other than the fact that someone shed blood while I was in your house, and you don't see anything wrong with that?"

"Of course I do!" He lurched forward to grasp her by her shoulders. "Why do you think I am so terrified for your safety? As long as you remain in holding you are not nightfly, but if I should fail you tomorrow in front of the Ampliphi . . ."

"Wait a minute. I don't even get to defend myself?"

"No, Asia. You will remain in holding until the Ampliphi say otherwise. It will take us most of the day to get to the holding colony as it is."

"Most of," she said almost numbly before moving toward the kitchen. "Then we don't have much time. We need to find out how she did this so you have solid proof tomorrow. But I . . . but then we'll be consigning *her* to become nightfly," she realized softly.

"It will be either you or her," he reminded her

gently. "The criminal must serve her punishment. It's the only way the Ampliphi will be satisfied. But if it makes it any better, she is not likely to spend all her years in the nightfly colony. Just a designated amount of time parallel to her crime."

Asia nodded, realizing that this wasn't home and there was a very different justice system to be reckoned with. If she didn't find the proof she needed, then Ariel would get her way. Asia would be sent out of Julian's life for good, forced into a prison where any man who could pay the price would have the right to get her with child.

"Asia, I have warned you that there are dangers here. What you are seeing now is what is ugly in my world. Let's quickly figure out how she did this so I can start to show you the beauty of it as well."

Chapter 10

Lucien knew his friend was in a great deal of trouble, and that was all it took to send him hurrying through the colony. The way he leapt from one walkway to the next with determination attracted the attention of Kine, who dropped into the space behind him, following closely.

"Gatherer," Lucien greeted him briefly.

"Lucien. Heading for Julian's?"

"Why, are you come to witness the carnage?" Lucien stopped short to turn on Kine, almost forcing the other man to run over him. Catching balance on an unrailed walkway was no small trick, but Lucien knew Kine was capable and in no danger.

"I've come to help," Kine said defensively. "Why would you assume otherwise?"

"It's not enough for the Ampliphi and their Gatherers that Julian's going to be forced to step down because of his *kindra,* they have to come and obliterate him besides? Are you here to spy for Sydelle and her cohorts so they are prepared for the morrow?"

"No! If any of the Ampliphi is friend to Julian, it

would be Sydelle," Kine said defensively of his mentor. "She is softer than the rest. Wiser, too."

Lucien took the distinction with a small, grudging nod. "But Kloe is not his friend any longer. The jealous bitch couldn't wait for this girl to slip up in some way. She's a vengeful, bitter creature, everything opposite to the man she mentored."

"That is very likely true. Kloe was very displeased when she claimed Asia as *kindra*. But it is more like she is doing this to get him back rather than destroy him, Lucien. If he fails to prove the claim of *kindra* in time, then Asia will transition to Chosen and Julian—"

"Julian will be sentenced to death for lying about her being his *kindra*. That is the law. Those who covet and try to steal a woman all to themselves by falsely claiming *kind* will die for their trespass. Now she is to spend an entire day traveling to the colony, and the second day will be spent traveling back if she is so lucky as to be exonerated. That will leave him with no time to prove his claims." Lucien squared his shoulders. "But what is more likely is that you are right. Kloe wants him back. She doesn't want to train another and she doesn't want to lose that which she has all but owned for all these years. If his *kindra* goes to jail, it nullifies his claims, sparing his life and destroying hers."

"Lucien, you haven't seen him with her . . . you haven't felt it. She is *kindra*. Neither Shade nor I have doubt of it. If he loses her . . ." Kine didn't have to continue the thought. They both knew it would destroy a king to lose his destined queen. Kloe would win . . . only to lose. She would have an empty hull of a man for her trophy, and a potentially innocent woman would be cursed to the bitter life of a nightfly.

"Well then, we'll have to see to it this doesn't happen." Lucien turned and started back into determined strides.

Kine kept close all the way to Julian's door. Lucien gave a cursory bang on the door to announce himself before throwing the wheel and pushing his way into Julian's home. When they stepped inside it was to Julian standing in the doorway of his kitchen, holding aside the beaded curtains for a woman who crouched over a pool of spilt blood.

Julian straightened when he saw them, frowning at them. "*Kin,*" he said in greeting. "I think next time I would appreciate you waiting for me to bid you enter."

Lucien waved the directive off, the black spear-point mark on his wrist flashing as he did so. "We are here to help you. To find evidence if needed— to escort you to the holding colony if also needed."

The dark-haired girl hovering over the floor finally looked up at that, a pair of icy blue eyes narrowing on him with a distinct lack of appreciation for his offer. He didn't blame her. She was in an untenable position, victim to things she didn't even begin to understand. After a moment, she turned back to the blood before her.

"She bled herself nearly to death, but it shouldn't have been nearly so bad if the knife was left to plug the wound and she lay still. But look." She pointed to the wide scrubbing swirls and finger streaks, like some kind of grotesque child's finger painting, with no sense or apparent definition to it. Julian's *kindra* smiled a little when he frowned at the mess. "She moved. A lot. Scrubbed her hands all around in her own blood."

"She's covering something up," Lucien realized.

"Blood trail, so we can't figure out where she did it and how." Asia rose in a single lithe movement, the hands resting on her hips pulling the scrap of silver she wore tight across her shapely backside. It accented the amazingly long length of her legs, as well as their obvious strength. Lucien suddenly found himself very envious of his friend. She was extremely beautiful and exotically tempting.

Lucien quickly checked his reaction. He cursed himself and cut his gaze to Julian. Sure enough, his friend and *kin* was glaring at him with no small amount of anger. Lucien held out his hands like a surrendering man. His friend had a right to be possessive, but it was irrational for him to expect a colony of deprived men to not notice how striking his mate was.

Unaware of the havoc she was causing between lifelong friends, Asia stepped deeper into the kitchen. "Lord. It's like she was making a snow angel in her own blood. Sick. Guys, help me look through this mess. Take it inch by inch. All we need is a gravitational drop. A drip," she clarified when they all looked at her blankly. "Blood drips as you travel, pools as you lie still. The directionality of the drip will tell us where this fiasco started. That will lead us to the evidence we need to catch her."

All the men quickly entered the room, heeding her warning to watch their step. The fire roaring in the pit was already drying the blood fast to the floor. That was a good thing, Asia thought. It was solidifying evidence. And despite how much Ariel had tried to cover it up, she knew they would find something eventually.

Asia took a moment to glance at the new male in the room with them. Julian hadn't seen fit to introduce him to her as anything other than *kin*. He was almost as tall as Julian, but there was a huge difference between beefcake like Julian and rock-solid beef like his *kin*. This was a man who did nothing with his time except to perfect his body as a weapon. She could see it in the way he moved, for one thing. And for another, he was the first one she'd seen with a weapon. Hooked onto his belt was an engraved steel crescent, big enough to sit in a large palm and gleaming sharp on the outside curve. Attached to one of its corners was a brilliant metal wire that looped round his entire waist and was attached to a ball on the other end. The ball was hooked behind the crescent, forming a deadly belt. She had no idea how he used the thing, but she had no doubt it was a killer . . . and so was he.

"What are you doing?"

The sharp demand startled her, just about as much as the tight hand around her arm that jerked at her did. Surprised, she looked up into Julian's dark and angry eyes.

"I'm looking—"

"At Lucien," he cut in sharply.

"Oh, is that his name?" she snapped back. "Thanks for the intro. And yeah, I was looking at *Lucien*." She stressed the name. "Or more specifically, below his belt." She only let a beat pass, knowing from experience that she could only bait him so far. But he deserved it if he thought he was going to pull this caveman bullshit on her. "At his weapon," she finished, giving him a smug little smile. "And I do mean the one made out of steel, not flesh."

Lucien was glad she was getting a laugh out of this, because every other man in the room was waiting with a sick feeling in his gut to see how Julian was going to react to this torment.

"Listen, I barely want anything to do with you," she said. "What in hell makes you think I'd want anything to do with him?" She jerked her thumb to indicate Lucien. Then she seemed to second-guess herself with a look. "Well, there's always a sparring partner. But otherwise, I don't have any use for the whole lot of you!"

Kine spoke up almost timidly. "Except to look for blood drips."

"Yeah, that, too."

She went back to doing exactly that, working her arm free of Julian's lax grip as she did so. In utter silence, everyone else went back to the hunt. Lucien exhaled fully and silently. He'd be damned if he knew how she'd pulled that off. He or Kine would have been missing an eye by now had either of them been caught staring at her. Lucien was already in trouble for just a momentary glance. Well, actually, it was the reaction after the glance he was in trouble for. But he didn't waste time worrying about it. He'd set Julian straight later, after this was settled and the man had had the chance to lose himself in his *kindra* for a while.

"Wait." The single word brought all heads up except for Kine's. The Gatherer slowly crouched down and touched a finger to the floor. "I think this is it."

Asia stepped over to him carefully and crouched down with him. A neat trick in that skirt, Lucien found himself thinking. But somehow she pulled it off.

"Yes!" she cried when she saw the minuscule drop of blood. "This means she came from this side of the room." She quickly stood up and began to examine the tall storing cabinets that stood there side by side. "Oho," she said a moment later. "Clever bitch! I know how she did it!"

Julian was by her side in a flash, peering at the spot where she had touched her fingers. It was a space, very tight, between the two cabinets. And very obviously, something had been forced between them.

"She jammed the knife in here by the handle. Then I guess she threw herself back against it. The wood is all torn up here and I'll bet the knife has matching distress on it as well."

"I'll head down to the infirmary and get the knife before it disappears," Kine said, quickly navigating the morbid room and leaving the residence.

"Yes!" Asia cried victoriously, jumping up to impulsively hug her *kindri*. The act was so obviously pleasing to Julian that Lucien had to smile. But unlike Asia, he knew that celebration was premature. The Ampliphi, while wise and fair about most things, were also just as stubborn and flawed. The nature of the sometimes volatile energy they must feed from had its way of making them unpredictable. It all went through the Ampliphi first, then was filtered and meted out. It was made stronger and cleaner. It was amplified, just as their reverent name suggested. The amount of power and fortitude needed for them to do what they did was immeasurable, and so was the list of effects, both adverse and positive, they suffered from as a result.

But they were usually wise and fair. He knew Julian was hoping this evidence was enough. Flouting Ampliphi Kloe's sentence was going to be a heavy insult to the bitter female. Even if they won the day, it might not bode well for the future of the village to have an Ampliphi angry with their king.

Julian became aware of Lucien's thoughts and concerns even as he gratefully absorbed Asia's voluntary hug. He wished he could just lose himself in the sensations of her eager affection, but Lucien's worries were too strong, and too well founded. No one knew Kloe as well as her Gatherer did. He was well aware of her shortcomings. Kloe's attitude toward the humans they were forced to rely on could be chilling at times. She saw them as little more than cattle, disdaining to credit them for their spirits and their souls. Oh, she knew they had them, but she was fixedly convinced they were savages, not worthy of the roles they were being given in their society. Luckily, she also knew they had no choice but to depend on them to help replenish their world. She grudgingly gave respect for that much.

But Kloe was part of the reason they were so strict about which humans came into their world. He had been told time and again to learn their nature and weed out the violent ones. But Asia was only violent when she felt she had to be, when she felt she was in danger or backed up against a wall. It was highly unfair of Ampliphi Kloe to pass so summary a judgment without looking into the details first.

"We can't clean any of this away. It must remain as proof for us to use tomorrow morning," Julian said soberly. He put Asia away from him. "We should leave the room so nothing is damaged or affected by us."

He took hold of Asia's hand and led her out of the room, but when he went for the door, she pulled back against his grip.

"No way. I am not leaving here. I'm staying right here to make sure no one messes with the only evidence I have that can save my ass."

Julian frowned at her. "You can't stay, Asia. You've been ordered to go to the holding colony. We can't afford to disobey a direct command from the Ampliphi if we hope to win them over to our way of thinking tomorrow. We need to act as respectfully as possible."

"If it makes you feel better," Lucien added, "I will find Shade and have him and Kine sleep here tonight and guard your evidence."

"It does make me feel better," she said warily, "but are you sure they can be trusted?"

"I am positive," Julian said. "They are Gatherers, two of the best men I know, and very trustworthy friends. They will protect your innocence with their lives."

"Oh." Asia was beginning to see just how seriously

things were taken in Julian's world. "Well, then, I guess we better get going to this holding colony."

"We will, after we find you some appropriate clothing," Julian countered. "It is a trying journey," he explained lamely, making it all too clear why he really wanted her to change. Asia had half a mind to taunt him a little, but the truth was she was sick of showing her ass every time she took a wrong turn.

"I think Corla is about her size," Lucien said with a smothered grin. Julian was being unwittingly entertaining at the moment. Lucien had never seen him so off his mark before. Jealousy, possessiveness, outright hostility—all caused by a single woman. "Corla is my sister," he explained to Asia as a way to keep himself from tormenting his friend.

"Oh, well thanks. That'd be great."

"I'll be back shortly, then we can begin the journey to the holding colony."

Lucien made his exit, and Julian led her into the living area. His mouth was set in a grim line and he turned her toward him.

"This is a dangerous journey," he told her. "All travel between colonies is."

"You said Kenya was traveling from another colony," she said, suddenly breathless with fear. "Just how dangerous? In what way? Is it the *okriti*?"

"That's one of the dangers, yes. But don't worry. She is well protected. She will be here waiting for you when this is all over and done with." Julian moved stiffly away from her.

"Wait . . ."

"I can't wait, *zini*. I must arm myself and prepare for this journey."

"Well, I hope you plan on arming me as well."

That got his undivided attention. He turned back to her.

"You still don't get it, do you? You don't know how to use any of our weapons, *zini*. They aren't like what you would find on Earth. There are no nine-millimeter handguns here. We won't contaminate our people with such easy weapons of opportunity."

"And *you* still don't get it," she retorted, her long fingers curling into fists. "All I need is a damn stick about a yard long and I'll be able to take care of my own damn self! Stop underestimating me and stop treating me like some delicate butterfly you have to protect in a jar. You'll just end up killing me!"

Her temper was justified, he realized, because that was exactly what he was doing to her. "I'm sorry. I cannot help myself. Please appreciate how I am used to treating women and why. I don't mean to be insulting."

"I know you don't, and you aren't really. It's actually refreshing to be around a bunch of men who don't think slapping their wives around is an Olympic sport. But you have to let me take care of myself. Hell, I may even be able to protect *you*."

"I worry," he said, the words sudden and soft as he closed in on her, his amazing body heat washing up over her like a Caribbean tide. "In fact, I feel as though that is all I have done since you arrived."

"Well, tone it down, will you? I'll stay on my guard. I'll be very, very careful. Okay?" She shifted. "To be honest, I'm in more danger from your precious Ampliphi than I am from anything out there." She gestured to the door.

"Don't you think I know that?" he demanded sharply. "There are things going on here that you have no concept of. What you see happening around you and to you has almost nothing to do with you."

"Nothing to do with me?" She gaped at him, utterly aghast. "Your friends want to force me into a lifetime of sexual and reproductive servitude! That has a lot to do with me!"

"I meant the motivations behind this!" He lurched forward and grabbed hold of her, jerking her up against him. "Every moment that ticks away, every resistance you thrust up between us wastes drops of precious time for me. I have made a claim of *kindra,* and it is accepted . . . for now. But if I do not prove that claim by the time the sun sets two days from now, they will take you from me and send you to live in the general populace and I will be labeled a liar and deceiver for trying to take a woman for myself under false pretenses. King or no king, that is a crime that carries the penalty of death, Asia."

Asia swallowed visibly, her blue eyes wide with an answer she already knew as she asked, "What do you mean 'prove that claim'? How d-do you prove I am your *kindra?*"

"You already know," he noted as he bent to brush his nose against her temple, breathing her in all over again. "I will make love with you until this entire colony is flush and full with the fallout of our energy. I will make you feel orgasmic pleasure you could never find with anyone else. When we connect, you will change me into a being whose energy and power will be immeasurable and," he lowered his voice so it drove into her with hot, thrilling impact, her entire being flushing with liquid heat, "will be yours to thrive in and play with for all the years of our lives. But if I fail to do this, if I fail to please you as I have been created to do, Asia, then I will lose you to a wealth of others and that, by far, will make death seem like a mercy to me."

His fierce intensity and conviction finally made Asia

realize just what she had done to him when she had threatened him with that very thing earlier on the walkway. Somehow she had managed to throw into his face the worst fate imaginable to him.

And she had barely known him half a day.

All the information she had gathered about him on Earth had been false and was completely unreliable, and yet within only hours of being exposed to the true Julian, she had learned so much. She had learned how best to hurt him even before she had learned how old he was or what his favorite color was. What did that say about her? Had she really become so cutthroat and vicious? She had been so careful to raise Kenya in a way that had protected her spirit from the harsher realities of the world, yet she had seen to it she wasn't ignorant of them either. But Kenya had looked at the world as full of possibilities, while Asia looked at it as an ongoing act of damage control. She had no faith in her fellow man. She always anticipated the worst in people.

Lord, she'd become a bitter bitch, she realized. And Kenya's disappearance had only hardened her all the more.

"Asia . . . I agree that you are a victim of our laws and that our legal system is failing you horribly by threatening to make you nightfly. God, the very thought of it makes me shudder to my everlasting soul. Your freedoms mean everything to you and we would be wrong to take them away when you have really done nothing wrong, but . . . you have to understand we are protecting both of our worlds the best way we know how—even when committing such an atrocity." Julian closed his eyes briefly, his grip on her tightening in reflex to his wildly plunging thoughts. "You see, Asia, this entire situation we find ourselves in—the eradication of our women, our failing energy, and our dying peoples—this was all caused by one woman, a long, long time ago, who accidentally jumped across dimensions from another world to ours. When she begged to go home we couldn't deny her pleas. After all, nothing like this had ever happened to us before and we didn't know the ramifications. . . .

"But despite swearing up and down that she would never speak of this world she had found, after we found the way to send her back and returned her, she talked to someone she shouldn't have. A man. A brilliant man placed high in the esteem of scientists of his dimension. He recreated the conditions that had called the Gate to the woman and together they came back here. You could say they were the parents of the method we use even now to travel from Beneath to other dimensions. But . . . he was also patient zero of the plague that has more than likely destroyed us. In the physiologies of the men and women of his world, it's nothing more than the equivalent of a cough with sniffles. Here, for our women, it was utter devastation. We knew then we could never trust another alien to keep silent once they had the slightest hint of our existence, and so we decided that no means were too severe to keep them from spreading that knowledge. This is why we cannot return you or anyone else to your plane with the knowledge of this place intact in your mind."

"But don't you risk other contaminations every time you or the other Gatherers stay among us?"

"Earth is the one dimension we know of where your contaminants are harmless to us and ours are harmless to you. This was extensively tested before we made the choice to recruit your women. However, it is your violence and paranoia that threaten us most. Our repopulation techniques are not risk free by far, but they are the least dangerous to us as a whole. This is also why we follow the letter of our laws and rules with what appears to you to be single-minded devotion. How can we not when we are all touched by the results of what it cost us to be lenient in the past?"

He reached up to brush at Asia's dark hair where it was feathering over her ear. He watched her carefully as she processed everything he had told her. Julian had taken a great risk by laying all of his cards out on the table about how dangerously low they were on time to prove her to be truly *kindra*, but he couldn't afford having her shut down against him because she didn't understand their extreme laws and reasoning. She was right. There were many flaws and disagreeable solutions in their justice system, but hers was little better. However, both of their societies were doing the very best they could with the benefit of their peoples in mind. One day, perhaps, it could be different.

And now it felt like everyone was a threat to him, even his best friend Lucien, the man he entrusted the entire colony to whenever he went to Earth plane . . . until he made his claim on his *kindra*. He couldn't even find sympathy in himself for Ariel and her coming fate. Her plotting had been an unforgivable act, one that might have deprived the entire colony of the richest energy source known to their breed. Starving children's faces swam through his head, hazed in the red of his fury and the burning orange of his desperation as his deadline seemed to loom and mock him.

Trying to control the chemical and emotional storm his proximity to Asia was causing inside him, Julian forced himself to take several steps back from her. It was almost suffocating to be that close to her and yet never close enough. Equally maddening was knowing that she did not yet feel the same intensity. Oh, a few minutes ago she had been feeling it, but then her mind had latched on to their conversation, desperate for some way to throw up defenses against him yet again. It was a war between them, exhausting and fruitless . . . challenging and critical. The fates of thousands hung in the balance with every battle they fought against each other. He'd been engaged in the struggle for only half a day and already he was frustrated and feeling worn out.

Julian would rather lose himself in the pulse and power of Asia and spend his time and energy making sweet, unbearable love with her. He wanted to stamp his claim onto her and spend hour upon hour embedding his essence into her until no one could mistake her for anything other than his *kindra*.

Then, after he'd selfishly indulged in her for a few years, after he had seen his village fed and glutted from his passion with her, he wanted to put his child inside her and watch her grow even more lovely and delectable with every single moment of her pregnancy.

"Stop it," she breathed in a rasp of fear. "You want a kind of woman I just can't be! I'm never going to be someone who takes contentment in being the lover and treasure of a man. And I don't want to be a mother! I won't have babies! Why can't you understand that?"

Julian didn't smile, although he wanted to when he realized she had just heard his unspoken thoughts and desires. She was already coming in tune with him, whether she wanted to consciously or not. Soon she would be unable to resist him any longer. Soon she would cling to him and beg him for the pleasure of his body.

"I understand perfectly," he said with a renewed calm that had him exhaling a long breath. "But what I am craving at the moment is merely a part of the primitive instincts the males of my kind are born with, and I can't help the urges I have to claim my mate and reproduce. Still, these things are not all I want from you. You are more than a body to my mind and my heart, but until I claim you and secure you to the satisfaction of my impulses, they will continue to overwhelm me from time to time." Julian dared to step forward again, closing the distance between them until her scent, still flush with her arousal of minutes ago, rolled over him and through him.

"I am torn between my desires," he informed her. "I want to show you the beauty of my world and prepare you for my society, to prove to you that it is worthy of a woman as powerful and strong as you are. I want to share my needs, yes, but even more I want to share the needs of my people with you. And not just for energy, *zini*. They need a dominant and authoritative queen to rule and guide them. When I think of Kenya and the kind of person you created her to be, I see so much potential in what you can do to shape and mold a frightened and struggling class of people. Don't you see how well suited you are for being the mate of the king? You teach. You know how to fight for what is yours. You are lush with energy and passion, righteousness and determination." Julian felt his heart pounding even as he described her for them both, his excitement and anticipation overpowering him. "You would defend what you love with every ounce of power in your soul. Look how far you have come for the sake of your sister alone. I wonder what you would do for the multitude of people in this colony who will earn your love and devotion if only you give them enough time."

It was unspoken, but Asia heard loud and clear the question that followed as it raced through his mind.

What can you come to feel for me if only you would give me enough time?

Asia had no idea how to react to the query—nor could she react to any of his other questions and suppositions. He was demanding far too much from her far too soon.

And yet . . .

And yet she couldn't deny the powerful draw of him. She felt more just standing in his sphere than she had while fucking with other men. His kisses alone stirred her to a point that felt like the very brink of orgasm. Even now her whole body craved the feel of large, purposeful hands curving intimately over her body. And she knew when she looked up at him through her lashes that he was fully aware of everything she was thinking and desiring. She was assured of that an instant later when he growled low in his throat and leaned forward to nip at the side of her neck with the lightest brush of his teeth and lips, driving her full of goose bumps until her breasts hurt with the stimulation.

"Stop that," she whispered in a rush of breath she could hardly control. "You keep toying with me until I can't even see straight, and I know it's on purpose!"

"You're damn right it's on purpose," he said roughly. "Everything I do has a purpose now that holds you at its center. I've never made a secret of the desire I feel for you. I've never concealed my motives. I never will. And I won't back off, Asia, until you're mine and mine alone."

"I'm mine and mine alone!" she retorted hotly, stiff and repellant against him all of a sudden.

"I'm yours and yours alone," he said softly against the skin beneath her ear, nuzzling and tasting her until all the rigidity melted out of her body. "I am yours to do with as you please . . . whatever you please . . . whatever pleases you, *zini.*"

His hands drove up between their pressed bodies, sliding slick and quick over the glide of silver until he surrounded both her breasts with the pressure of his intense hold. He slipped his fingers around the points of her nipples and then closed them into firm little vises between them. Asia strangled on the gasp lurching through her throat, her back arching to give him more of herself even as her hands fisted in the fabric of his shirt and pushed him away.

"Will it please you to have my mouth on you here?" he asked in a breathy wash of words against her ear. "My tongue dancing on every nerve before drawing you in deep so I can suck you hard? You seem the tough sort, Asia. Will it be nibbles or bites that arouse you most? Is it the anticipation of the sensation that makes you shudder like this, or do I already please you so easily?"

Asia wanted to rail at him and deny him in every way she could possibly come up with, but she was paralyzed with the sensations of bliss and buoyancy that lifted her up into his touch, her whole body writhing to feel more and more. He was right; she was shuddering in hard shivers, a cross of delight and shock as her body responded to him with an easy fire. Somehow his thigh had slid between hers and she was brazenly rubbing herself against the hard muscle she now rode. She felt abruptly empty and aching, desperate to be filled by him, urgent with her need for him.

The surrender of her body was so complete and so overwhelming that she was struck dizzy with the effect of it. She writhed up against Julian with wanton need, her heart racing until her pulse was pounding in her ears.

"Why do I feel this way?" she asked as she burned for his every caress and now the need to touch him in answer as well. Her hands weren't at all hesitant as they began to chase paths over the well-shaped muscles of his chest. "Oh my God, it's like . . . it's like I have no control!"

She saw a frown flash over him, but it was a fleeting expression. All that remained of it were light furrows in his forehead as he bent to stroke his lips over her breastbone.

"You do have control, Asia. Merely ask me to step away and I will end this. But what you are feeling is the call of the *kind*. Similar to an animal in heat, our bodies respond to the proximity of each other with pure sexual drive . . . an increasing condition with every touch and every kiss we share."

Julian shared his kiss with her once more, devouring her lips and mouth until they were both gasping hard for breath. Heat was burning Asia everywhere at once, the need to be the central focus of his every attention driving her to an act of haste. She reached up for his hands, grasping hold with desperate fingers, then slid them all the way down the length of her shimmering dress, straight to the hem. She dipped both of their hands beneath the hem and then retraced her path in reverse. Her skin came alive with a scream when she felt his hot, huge hands melding to her. He broke free of her guidance, his palms curving over her ribs and back.

She couldn't possibly know what the feel of her skin was doing to him. It was something he had wanted so badly for what seemed like ages. She was so smooth, so deceptively soft. He could feel her strength flexing close beneath it, though, and it sent him into a spiral of need for her. Need for everything about her. Yes, it was the call of *kind*, but it was so much more than that. Couldn't she see that? Couldn't she feel it?

"God, I want to rip this little silver nothingness to shreds," he growled with impatience as it caught

against his fingers and impeded his path back around
to her breasts.

Caught up in the moment and the burning need to
feel his touch on her, she abruptly reached to grab
the back of the dress and with a too simplistic pull
sent it flying off over her head. A flutter of silver fabric
in the corner of her eye was all that was left of it.

"God help me," Julian said in soft desperation as he
looked at her nearly naked body in its entirety for the
first time and found it difficult to simply breathe, never
mind have a single complex thought or reaction. As he
had promised her, everything he was feeling was primitive and raw, instincts as base as they came. She must
have felt it, sensed it, or somehow heard it as it wailed
savagely through his mind, but whatever the reason,
she made a sound of complete agreement. It was as
if she were contemplating the perfect meal on a completely empty stomach and he could feel the appetite
rolling off her in great, heavy waves. His entire body
clenched in anticipation. This was what he had been
waiting for. This was what he had been craving since
the moment he had first understood she was his *kindra*.
It had taken so long, and yet under half a day for it
to finally strike her with equal intensity as it struck him.
Now she wanted him as she was supposed to want
him. Now she had the same hunger that he did.

At last.

Julian skimmed hot, famished eyes down her body,
reminding himself that he had the right to all of what
she was showing him, all of what she was offering him.
He could see the pale pink of her nipples in contrast
to the warm tones of her skin and was amazed at how
wrong he had been about their color. But now that he
could see their light, pearl pink color and their
beaded thrust, he realized how perfect she was just

like that. Unable to resist a moment longer, Julian bent his head to catch her between his teeth and against the flutter of his tongue.

Asia couldn't have known how keen his sense of taste was. It was so sharply honed that he caught the full flavor of her skin, her perfume, and her perspiration in a single tasting. The mélange might have been confusing to some, but not to him. Oh, he would prefer her without cosmetics and artifice, but there would be time to express those desires later. For the time being, he liked the mixture of their cultures and their worlds on his tongue. He could imagine what she would taste like all over the rest of her skin, just as he had done every time he had kissed her neck, ear, or even her lips. The smell of her rising off her flesh was pure divinity. Pure excited female.

"Can you imagine how it will be?" he demanded of her even as he gnawed gently at the point of her breast and reveled in her clutching fingers in his hair and her gasping response. "We'll complete the act of the *kind*, making love so intensely it will take days for us to recover. Can you imagine that?"

"Yes. Oh, yes, Julian," she panted quickly against his hair as her fingers gripped the strands harshly. "I pray you are right about this. I hope so much that there's no disappointment."

The remark gave Julian sharp pause, cutting through the haze of need and craving that so ruled him. He raised his head, lifting his lips from her flesh, and tried to meet her eyes. The blue depths were closed off from him, squeezed tightly shut as if she were desperately trying to hold on to a fantasy. A dream.

Not a reality.

Julian reached up for her chin, his grip a bit brutal as

frustration warred with his need to stake his claim. She resisted him, as always, her eyes staying screwed shut.

She had no faith in him, he realized a bit numbly. There was no trust in her whatsoever. She didn't believe for an instant that what she was feeling would last or carry her through to fulfill the promises he was making her. And despite the urgency of those raging instincts within him, Julian proved how truthful he had been when he had claimed this was not all about the physical. He stepped away from the exquisite offering that she was, rejecting her half-baked efforts at learning what it meant to be *kindra* to him. Despite all he had said to her, she simply didn't understand . . . and she didn't believe. Without that belief in him—*in them*—a mating between them would ring false and empty. Oh, it would satisfy the Ampliphi and the claim of *kind* between them, but he refused to take portions of her now, only to be snapping up scraps of her later as they went. He could not be satisfied like this, and neither would she. So long as she fought the real depths of the role she was meant to play, she would circumvent the overwhelming possession of the *kind* mating. Until he had her trust, he realized, he would never have *her.*

Frustrated and aching from head to toe, he extricated himself from Asia completely and walked away to a safe distance. Well, relatively so. There would never be a distance between them that would act as enough of a buffer to shut down their physical desire for one another, especially not now that the connection was moving along at a raging clip and calling them to one another in screams of need.

"Dress yourself."

Chapter 11

"Dress yourself."

The command was harsh and hot, coming from him on a voice full of unrelieved need and finally making her fully aware of the fact that he intended to put an end to their interlude. To say she was shocked was a poor representation. Flabbergasted was more like it. An impact that was quickly chased by a hundred other emotional reactions just as wildly skewed and confused.

"But . . ." She couldn't even fathom how to argue with him just then. All she knew was how viciously deprived she felt without his heat and passion burning into her. One of her nipples was abraded by his teeth and tongue, making it far more sensitive to the air of the room and making her so very aware of how it had felt to have him there. The long length of her body curved restlessly with unspent passion; she longed to draw him back to her and sought in her mind how she could do that—even as she struggled with the sense of relief rushing through her. Discombobulated by the conflicting desires, she sought Julian's help and guidance.

"I don't understand you!" The snap in her voice came off harsher than she meant it, but frustration was getting the better of her. She reached to scoop up her dress, jerking it on over her head so roughly she was lucky she didn't tear the delicate fabric. "You've been harping on me since daybreak about how much you want to make love to me, and when you finally get the chance, you walk off and treat me like I have the fucking plague! What kind of sick game is this?"

"Why don't you tell me!" He rounded on her, getting up in her face. "You bitch at me about how you aren't just a body for mating with and making babies, but you throw yourself at me offering nothing but your sex to me! Tell me why I shouldn't be confused and pissed off!"

"I . . ." Asia suddenly saw his point and she felt a little sick in her stomach. "I couldn't help it," she argued lamely. "It just comes over me when you touch me. And it isn't against the law for me to get turned on when that's what you are trying to do to me! You want to talk about confused? You start pawing me, get me all wound up, but somehow it's still not enough for you! If you want to fuck, then let's do it! Let's feed the masses, Julian. Put all your troubles and worries to rest. C'mon, I'm game."

He laughed. It was a bitter, hard sound, but it was a laugh just the same. "You just don't get it. I'm beginning to think you never will."

He turned his back on her and started up the spiral ramp leading to the upper level of the house.

"Hey!"

She hurried after him, reaching the landing just as she grabbed hold of him around one bicep and yanked really hard to turn him toward her. He emitted a frustrated growl, all but roaring in her face as he came around to face her.

"I thought you said you didn't want to be nightfly,"

he hissed at her, all but knocking her back with the level of rage he was emanating at her. "If that's true, then why would you whore with me?"

"*Whore?* Did you just call me—"

She didn't even finish. She hauled back and punched him in the head before she could even think about checking the impulse. What she didn't realize was that his anger, just like his passion, was infecting her. The longer she stayed Beneath, the more sensitive she became to the energy flying around her. She hit him with the side of her fist, following through so hard that her whole body twisted . . . and so did his. He spun around hard and hit the wall beside him, reaching out to catch himself against it.

Asia stood there breathing angrily, both fists up in front of herself defensively, her breath huffing and her face flushed with rage. Julian was just standing there running his tongue over his teeth to make certain they were all there, then he wiped at his bloody mouth and touched fingers to the hinge of his jaw.

Okay, rule number one, don't piss off the bounty hunter, he thought wryly. To be fair, he hadn't been expecting her to hit him, and by the look that was crawling over her face, she hadn't been expecting it either. Aghast, Asia covered a mouth open with shock and held out a supplicating hand to him. She touched his shoulder gently.

"Oh my God! I'm so sorry! I have no idea why I just did that! I swear to you, I don't just go around hitting people out of the blue. I . . ."

"No. No that was my fault," he soothed her quickly. He turned to the hall and entered the bathroom. It looked strange and old-fashioned, with pull chains on the basin and the toilet. It was an odd rectangular shape and it was covered. The piping in the room was visible and it looked like it was all made of something like bamboo.

Julian went to the square basin and pulled one of the chains. Immediately it began to fill with clear water. He quickly washed his hands and rinsed blood out of his mouth. Then he pulled a second chain and the basin drained in a rapid little swirl. It was efficient and a minimum of waste, Asia realized. She had seen rows of bamboo outside and had thought it was part of the structure, when in fact it was probably piping designed to take away waste water.

"The rains fill the reservoirs above us. The tanks are above all the roof levels so turning on water is just a matter of gravity. That's why when we build we build downward," he informed her when he took note of her curiosity.

She shook that off, though, resting a hand on his arm. "Are you all right?"

"I am. I'll be sporting a solid bruise by tomorrow, though. I think I'll enjoy explaining it to the Ampliphi."

"Oh God . . ."

"I'm kidding," he said quickly. "Just a joke."

"Not funny," she said darkly.

"No, I don't suppose it was." He sighed. "Listen, I know you didn't mean to hit me. It's my fault. Rage is a powerful form of energy. You were standing so close to me you got swamped. It's my responsibility to control my emotions and I'm not doing a very good job of it."

"And I'm not making it easy for you to do so," she admitted, taking responsibility for her share of the problem. "Look, I am sorry that I'm not doing things the right way. I warned you over and over that I am not the person you need . . . I'm too stubborn. Too jaded. Too harsh. People have been telling me for years what a cold bitch I am and . . . I guess I always thought that was just an outer shell I was using to protect myself. I guess it turns out I'm a cold bitch straight to the core." There was no mistaking the sadness in her pretty blue eyes as she wrapped herself into a crooked sort of hug. "I'm sorry. I know your life is on the line here. You probably wouldn't even be doing this if there wasn't so much pressure. . . ."

"Hey," he stepped up to her, taking an elbow into his palm. "I made a very conscious choice, a very self-ishly motivated choice, the moment I saw you strut-ting your stuff down the sidewalk. You're right, I never asked you if you wanted this. I never gave you a fair chance. But know this. If you had refused to come here after I tried wooing you properly, I would have stayed on the Earth plane with you. You are my *kindra*. There's no changing that. I don't want to change that. I don't care if you are prickly like a . . . like a . . . ."

"Porcupine," she provided with a small smile.

"Yes. A porkpine. I have seen this creature with many quills. It has a soft underside, as do you. It just takes some time to find it."

"Hmph. Good luck with that."

"Thank you. I will need it." He grinned when she clicked her tongue at him. "We'll find the way to make you happy here. Let's just get through tomorrow morning. Okay?"

"Okay," she agreed.

"Okay, wait a minute. I thought you said to keep off the grass."

In fact, it was such a strict rule that there was only a single walkway leading from the colony to the cliff. And it was heavily guarded. Two guards stood inside a gate in the colony and four stood outside a second gate that was on the land.

She'd been reasonable when the outfit Lucien had brought her had been a little tight on top and had a little too much swirly fabric in the skirt. How a woman could move in it was beyond Asia's scope of understanding. She'd been very accommodating when Julian and Lucien warned her to stay between them at all times during their travel, even though it rankled her to be the protected female. She'd even been ecstatic when Julian had found her a solid stick made of a remarkably strong wood that was exactly the length she wanted.

But this . . . this gave her a bad case of the heebiejeebies. Bad enough her sister was traveling this way. After listening to Julian's description of the peopleeating *okriti*, she wasn't at all eager to get out onto their territory.

"I always thought safaris were the stupidest things," she grumbled as the first gate opened. They started out on the long walkway leading toward the land. Asia gripped the straps of the pack she wore on her back as she followed Julian across. "People fighting people, that's one thing. I'm not afraid of anyone. Even the biggest, baddest man in town has soft spots, you know? But lions and shit like that, they have claws and fangs and not an ounce of fat. Their entire bodies are dedicated to one thing—muscle—and that muscle only does one thing, it helps it to kill stupid people who go out in little cars on safari!" Then she realized, "Oh God, we're not even going to have a car, are we?"

"No," Julian agreed, "we aren't. But stop worrying so much. Lucien and I have done this plenty of times. We know how to avoid danger and we know how to handle the *okriti*."

"Are you coddling me? Because if you're coddling

me, it's not the *okriti* you're going to have to be worried about," she grumbled.

"He's not coddling," Lucien reassured her, coming to the rescue of his friend. "He's just stating facts. There's no denying this is a dangerous trip. But if you listen to us and we all stay sharp, it'll be over in just a few hours."

"And we need to get there before sunset," Julian reminded them.

"Right. Sunset bad. Got it." Asia exhaled hard as they came up on the second gate. The guards saw them coming and opened it for them.

"What report?" Julian asked of them shortly.

"All's well," a guard replied. "No sign yet of the south party you're expecting and I sent two scouts north ahead of you. They reported an easy path ahead and no sign of *okriti* or *tamblyn*."

"Okay, now what the fuck is *tamblyn*?" Asia demanded to know.

"Land fowl. They can't fly but they swarm their prey and take it down by sheer numbers. A flock can be deadly to a lone person . . . a large flock isn't afraid to take one of us down. But they will avoid groups of us because they learn fast that we can hurt and kill them. They're kind of tasty, too. It's one of the main foods served in the colonies. Tastes somewhat like turkey."

"Deadly land fowl. Got it."

Julian heard the tension ratcheting up in her voice. "Listen. They have long necks like those pink birds in Florida . . ."

"Flamingos."

Lucien chuckled at the word, especially when Julian tried to repeat it. "Just avoid their sharp bills and break their necks. They're dead in an instant," he informed her.

"Oh. Cool. I can do that."

"And don't step into any patches of sand," Julian warned.

"Do I want to know why?" she asked meekly.

"Just don't do it. Stay on the hard ground and the grass."

He wasn't going to get any argument from her. Julian was actually a little fascinated by this side of her. She was a tough girl who could handle herself; why was she suddenly so afraid?

"Because I'm a city girl," she snapped irritably. "Muggers and crackheads I can deal with. This nature shit is not my scene."

"Just stick close to us and you'll be fine," Lucien advised with obvious amusement lacing his voice. "Tell me," he said conversationally, "what exactly is a crackhead? It sounds painful."

"Oh, um . . ." She laughed a little, finding it weird to talk about the dregs of her own society when she'd been so self-righteous about the way they handled theirs. "It's someone who is addicted to crack. Crack is a drug. It's very habit forming and once you start . . ."

"You become a crackhead," Lucien supplied. "I see. Julian has told me about the recreational drugs in your society. We have something like that, but only the nightfly use it. It helps their time to pass, I suppose."

The remark sobered the group as they each recalled exactly where they were headed and why.

"So what is this place like that we're going to? What can I expect?"

"It's not easy to explain the ways of the nightfly. It is something you need to see and experience for yourself to understand. It is a culture unto itself," Julian said. "But you won't need to worry about that. You won't be put in with the main population, just the holding area."

His jaw was set so hard that she could see it even

from her position behind him. He really wasn't happy about her spending even one night at the holding colony. She wondered if there were any men in the holding colony and voiced the question aloud.

"Guards, of course, are men," Julian informed her. "There is a separate holding colony for men who commit lesser crimes. Capital crimes, as you know, are a sentence of death."

"And . . . what is the punishment meted out for the men who are guilty of lesser crimes? The women are forced to sell themselves, what are the men forced to do?"

"Hunt," they answered in unison.

They didn't need to say anything more. Hunting for game in these wilds that they were clearly so frightened of was a terrible sentence indeed. Deadly and dangerous.

They moved in silence for quite some time after that. For the most part the wilderness was really just grasslands that seemed to stretch on for miles, with only the occasional copse of trees to break the monotony. It was easy to tell, now that she was really moving, just how high up they were. The air was significantly thinner than she was used to. Also, it was decidedly warmer. It had the feeling of being closer to the sun. She wondered if they had seasons, or if it was always this warm. She could see clouds above them now as well as what she had seen below, but there weren't nearly as many. It was very curious.

She caught her first sight of the *okriti* about a third of the way through the trip. Julian stopped her and pointed out the distant herd. It was hard to make them out, but they moved like gorillas, their long arms dragging through the grasses. Julian and Lucien didn't let them sit around staring at them, and she didn't blame them in the least.

They passed two other colonies over the next hours, one much smaller than Julian's, the other astoundingly larger. Asia risked going very close to the cliff's edge so she could look at how far down the levels of the colony truly went. There were many reservoir tanks both over the entire colony and down along the sides. She couldn't help but be amazed at the architecture of so many walkways and bridges and conical houses.

They went at a fairly easy and steady pace, and when they came up on a third colony she was surprised when Lucien said, "There it is."

It looked just like the other colonies, only quite a bit smaller overall. But of course it would be. There weren't many women to begin with. The percentage that was criminal must make for very small numbers.

Asia began to get a little nervous. She wasn't stupid, after all. She was going into an unknown situation that Julian deemed dangerous. He didn't seem the type to overreact, and as long as she was a fish out of water it made her especially susceptible to the dangers around her.

They approached the unassuming little colony, and immediately she could tell there was a difference. Instead of a variety of conical houses, there was one large main building and a ring of smaller houses. The gates leading from the land to the colony were set in tremendous walls that ran the length of the colony on either side, enough to cover every mooring and every contact point between the buildings and the ground. It was clear that no one wanted any of these women escaping via the rigging that kept the colony afloat.

There were also more guards at the gates. They were all armed with a variety of strange-looking weapons just like Lucien's. Julian had armed himself for the trip as well, but the long daggers crisscrossed over his back and under his pack were more familiar to her than any of the others she saw.

The guards seemed to recognize Julian on sight, and they had no trouble gaining entrance to the first gate. However, once they had crossed the walkway, it was a different story.

"Ho, Gatherer. You can come no farther. Leave the female with us and be on your way," a guard warned him off. "Ampliphi Kloe has told us to expect her."

"She's to go into holding for tonight," Julian made certain to stress. "Not the general population."

"We are well aware of what is expected," the guard said, his half-cocked smile giving Asia an instant case of the creeps. Julian, however, didn't seem to pick up on it. He was too busy turning her to face him, gathering her face between his hands and kissing the breath out of her right where she stood on that narrow walkway.

"Be careful," he whispered against her lips. "I want you back in one piece."

For the first time, Asia began to feel fear about being left behind. All of this time she'd had Julian to guard and protect her, to help guide her every step of the way in this strange, new land. Now she would be on her own for the night, barely knowing what she was getting herself into. With her heart racing, she reached to grasp his wrists. She didn't say anything, but he could see what she was feeling very clearly in her eyes. He gently ran both hands back over her hair, engulfing her head in his large palms, his thumbs stroking against her cheekbones.

"I'll be back as soon as the Ampliphi release you. You'll be in holding for tonight, which at most will hold one or two others. It is more likely, though, that you will be alone. It's only one night. We will see to it that it is only one night."

"Julian, we have to go. We won't make it back before dark as it is."

"You'll be out there in the dark?" Asia asked, breathlessly afraid for his safety. How surreal, a part of her mused, that she had come from hating a man to hating the idea of something happening to him all in the span of a day.

"Not for long. Less than an hour." Julian hugged her close long enough to shoot a dirty look at his friend over her head. "Don't worry about me. I have Lucien. You just have Asia."

"Well, I have the better part of the deal," she joked, making Lucien chuckle.

"Hey, she'll be fine," he reassured Julian. "Try not to worry so much."

"Yeah, I'll be fine," she repeated, suddenly feeling it was the truth. She might be a fish out of water, but she was more than capable of protecting herself if needed.

"Okay." Julian reached to disarm her of her stick, sliding it into the harness that held his daggers. "Give me your pack, too. You won't need it. They'll give you everything you need."

After a few more moments of fussing, Julian finally let her go, letting her walk toward the gate without him. There was a heavy clanging of steel as bolts were thrown free, and just like that, she was through and they were closing Julian off from her.

Chapter 12

Asia had no idea when she'd begun to turn to Julian, begun to actually depend on him as a resource of support, but it had to have been the fastest turnaround in all the history of man. She'd barely been Beneath with him for a day and already her enemy had become her ally. But she was nothing if not a survivor, and that meant doing whatever it took in any given moment. Right now, it meant surviving the night in what amounted to a women's prison. But if things went as planned, she would spend the night in holding, kept away from the general population. Then tomorrow Julian would go before the Ampliphi and present them with the evidence. By tomorrow evening it would be the duplicitous Ariel waiting in a holding cell and wishing Julian were still within reach.

But, of course, things did not go as smoothly as she had hoped they would.

At first all went according to plan. The guard took her for a long walk around the upper wall and she found herself looking down on a village much like the one she had come from—with two differences. One was the insurmountable wooden wall that completely circled the buildings within. She imagined that from the inside, it would feel something like being inside a huge wooden barrel or vat. The walls were perfectly smooth without any way of climbing them.

The second difference—no nets. Even from her great height she could tell there was nothing beneath the village to catch anyone who made the slightest misstep. Just realizing that made her heart pound as she walked carefully behind the guard. She realized then that it was probably because there were no children and it made it more difficult for the inmates to attempt escape.

The guard was armed, a weapon similar to the one that Lucien had worn. He also did not speak to her in any fashion. She got the idea very quickly that it was against the rules for them to speak to the female prisoners. No speak, and most certainly no touch. It must take quite a screening process to find men trustworthy enough to be in charge of the highest concentration of women in their entire society. But she came from a world where . . . where there was a will, there was a way. Women who were guarded by men would always be at risk of everything from the consensual to rape. She instantly told herself not to trust a single one of them as far as she could throw them.

Rightfully so. The guard led her to the holding room, stood aside, and unlocked the steel door for her. She hesitated on the threshold when she saw two men awaiting her in the darkened room.

"Wait a minute . . ."

"Step into the room," one of them commanded her. So much for no speak.

"Like hell I will," she said, noticing each man held a club in his hands.

"We're not going to hurt you as long as you behave yourself," one of them said almost gently. "You will come inside, we're going to search you, then we'll leave you be for the night."

The guard at the door then withdrew a small stick from his pocket and with the flick of a wrist telescoped it into a club just like theirs. He moved to stand behind her, his silence unnerving as he braced his feet hard apart on the walkway. She looked down her right side where the railless walkway fell off into the netless village. Considering how much real estate was beneath her, she wouldn't have to worry about the endless sky beneath. She'd be killed just bouncing off the roofs and walkways on her way down.

Not seeing how she had much of a choice and preferring to have her feet on the solid flooring of the holding chamber, she stepped inside as ordered.

The door shut behind her with an ominous clang, the wheel turning like the lock in a vault. Once the glare of the sun was cut off, she could see the room was just as diffusely lit as every other room she had been in to date. The room was circular, just like all the others, and the only furnishing was a single bench that wrapped around the entire wall, save for where the door was.

Bracing her feet apart, she sized up the men before her. She could see why they had been chosen for this job. They were both powerful-looking men who seemed comfortable with the flight of their own bodies. There were no ham-handed, overweight, or awkward men here. These guys knew how to move and she could read it simply in the way they stood. Then again, what did she expect in a population that trusted their balance in every step they took?

"Let's make this easy," the same guard said, his thick accent making her realize he'd probably been chosen for his ability to speak to her. It was rather thoughtful of them, really, she thought. She was starting to catch inklings of the silent conversations going on all around her, but she was far from fully understanding any of it. Okay, so maybe it wasn't no speak . . . not any more than usual, anyway. It was just that she still wasn't used to so much silence from others.

"I'm all for easy," she replied carefully, eyeing the taller and more silent of the pair.

"Strip out of your clothes and toss them over here. We'll search them and give them back."

Asia took a deep breath, fighting the urge she had to tell them in no unfuckingcertain terms exactly where they could go and that she was not going to get naked while locked in a room with two men. But considering there weren't likely to be any female guards in this society, and she had a fair idea that she could take them if it came down to it, she decided it was best if she complied. Refusing to hesitate, Asia grabbed her top and tossed it across the room. As fortune had it, she had nothing but her borrowed clothing and a very skimpy thong. She dropped her skirt and sent it over as well, then held out her arms and did a slow turn.

"Good enough?" she asked.

They seemed to eye her critically for a moment and she got the impression they were considering a body cavity search. She didn't know how much of that was real and how much was her suspicious nature, but she was on her guard as they picked up her clothing and inspected it thoroughly. She did notice their attention wasn't always one hundred percent on their task. Their gazes drifted up again and again, until she began to wonder if they were dragging this whole thing out just so they could keep ogling her. She set her hands on her hips, refusing to cover up in any way and letting them look their fill. Eyes were just fine. It was when things crossed the line to physical contact that they were going to have problems.

Apparently they read that off her loud and clear. They finished searching her clothes and tossed them back to her. She dressed herself, constantly keeping one eye on the pair of them.

"You will remain here tonight. You will be given water and a meal. If you need to relieve yourself, you need only bang on the door and the guard will take you. However, do not abuse the privilege. We can just as easily see to it you have a bucket to use. Do you understand?"

"Yes."

"If you have any trouble from any guard in the facility, you need only press this button." He pointed his club to a large button rigged into the wall. "Again, do not abuse the privilege. There are holding cells without this precaution and you can just as easily be taken to one of them. This button is for your protection. You understand?"

"Yeah. I get it. It keeps everybody honest . . . as long as a girl is strong enough to get to it."

"You are strong enough," he observed.

"True that."

"My name is Raze. You may ask for me if you need to communicate . . . but we understand you very clearly. Again—"

"Don't abuse the privilege," she interjected for him.

"My shift ends after the sleeping hour, but I don't expect you'll have need of me after that anyway. Now be seated and become familiar with your own thoughts. Tomorrow we will know what is to become of you."

"Tomorrow I am out of here," she insisted.

"We'll see," he said cautiously. He pointed again to a seat against the far wall and she went to take it, understanding that they wanted a good deal of distance from her as they left the room. She watched as Raze used his club to rap three times sharply on the door. The door opened and both men exited.

Sure enough, the only thing she was left with was her own thoughts.

"Damn," she sighed wearily to herself.

It had been a long and arduous day. And despite all the proof they had gathered, she was still nervous about the stubborn Ampliphi. Her fate, it seemed, rested in Julian's hands. He was her only ally. It helped a little, she supposed, that he had ulterior motives for getting her out of there the next day. In fact, his life hung in the balance. And when she did get out tomorrow, he had very clear expectations and uses for her.

Asia didn't want to think about that at the moment. One hurdle at a time. For the time being, she was going to try to catch a nap.

And as she quickly got bored, it didn't take much time at all for her to do so.

Asia awoke to the loud clang of the lock turning in the door. Disoriented and not knowing how long she'd been asleep, she sat up and awaited what she suspected was her evening meal.

But the man who entered the holding cell was empty-handed and she immediately recognized something in the intent of his smile that turned her stomach over.

"Come with me," he said to her, beckoning her with a short flip of his stubby fingers. He was older than most of the men she had seen, a little heavier on his feet from what she could see, but still vital enough to be a threat.

"What for?" she demanded.

"You're being moved, human."

Oh, the way he said "human" did not bode well at

all. That was an emanation she got loud and clear. In all of this time, with all of Julian's talk about the survival of his race, it had never occurred to her that there might be members of this society who did not approve of the alien women they were forced to take in, in order to propagate. It was the first time she felt someone other than Kloe look at her with nothing but disdain in their heart.

"I'm not supposed to be moved," she argued, sliding her butt along the bench another foot until she was directly under the button that had been pointed out to her. She made it very clear to him that she wasn't stupid and she wasn't afraid to use the fail-safe.

"Plans have changed," he said thickly. "A violent offender will be coming into the holding cell and you must be removed for your safety."

"I thought there were other cells," she rejoined.

"Not tonight." He stepped closer to her, a flick of his wrist extending the same club they all seemed to carry. Except she could tell by the way he handled his that it was a much-beloved weapon. He was all too familiar with its weight and balance and he was, no doubt, very quick to use the thing. Being a sensei, Asia also knew there were lots of ways to hit a person without leaving so much as a single bruise. She knew immediately that this man was familiar with every one of those ways.

On the one hand, she didn't trust this guy for a second; on the other, she didn't have much of a choice. All of her rights had been taken away from her the minute she had walked through the front gate. Until tomorrow morning she was a prisoner just like all the rest. No one was going to care what happened to her until Julian came looking for her in the morning. All she had to do was survive until then.

Getting to her feet, Asia squared off with the man in her cell.

"I'm really good with faces," she warned him, "and I'm not going to let you hurt me without a fight. Are we clear on that?"

"Very," he said, tapping his club on the floor twice in rapid succession. On cue, two other guards entered the room. "Chaperones," he offered, his smile so full of contempt she could practically taste it.

Not seeing much in the way of alternatives, Asia walked forward. She stepped out onto the walkway with one guard in front of her and two at her back. Immediately she could see the landscape had changed. For one, it was full night. The walkways glowed in the same ambient way as everything else did. In fact, the entire village was aglow. The only exception was the sheer wooden wall that surrounded them. Apparently the material that everything was made of had some kind of fluorescent properties to it that kept everything lit all of the time. If only they had something like this stuff on Earth. The money they could save in electric bills would be extraordinary.

But back in the world of Beneath, she was being walked along at a nerve-wracking clip. It got worse when they left the stability of the high wall and crossed freely into the main village. They passed through two locked doors and just when she stepped through a third, entering the large central building, the guard suddenly reversed his path and stepped outside of the door.

"Enjoy your stay," he said to her, his grin positively evil as he shut the door and locked her in.

Oh crap, she thought as she slowly turned to look into the room around her. So much for not being in general population, she thought as she met one pair of curious eyes after another. Women all around her were sitting up or standing up with attentiveness, and she was the central focus of all that attention. The huge room seemed to go on forever, chaises and chairs and plants seemingly everywhere. It was actually the most prettily decorated prison she'd ever seen. Rich fabrics abounded. Beautiful flowering plants demarcated one cozy conversation area after another. The women themselves were all dressed in a similar fashion. Light, delicate fabrics, some of which looked incredibly expensive by the weight of the gold or silver shot through or the jewels adorning them. She could smell something like perfume on the air; the cool night breeze drifted freely in and out of the building through mesh windows made of the same lightly woven material as everything else was.

The women were all well groomed and made up, almost like they were dressed for date night. In fact, if she didn't know any better, she'd think she had just walked into a sultan's harem. And like a harem, it was almost immediately clear there was a pecking order. No one moved to come up to her, but it was clear they were curious. However, attention began to distinctly waver from her to a woman down at the other end of the building who was slowly getting to her feet.

She was dressed in deep violet, a soft silken skirt with silver filigree lining its hem and little sparkling gems of a lavender color dangling from the loops of silver. She wore a bolero-styled shirt, her long, lean midriff shown off to perfection, including the large amethyst-type gem that dangled from a piercing in her navel. She was pretty busty, so the top she wore looked like it was working very hard to keep itself together at its seams. She was a cool blonde, her long hair hanging loose down her back to well beyond her backside. The soft lavender of her eyes became evident the closer she got to Asia. It was clear that she had chosen what she was wearing expressly for the purpose of flattering her natural coloring. She was groomed to perfection, everything from the chainmail cap made of silver that adorned the top of her head to the henna-style tattooing around her startling eyes that swirled and stroked and acted like an accentuating mask. She even had two tiny purple gems somehow glued to the tips of her lashes.

She was, by far, one of the most beautiful women Asia had ever seen. When she thought of the amount of time it must have taken for her to look that way, it truly baffled Asia. Then again, if they were in prison all day long, what else was there for them to do?

In fact, Asia was getting the feeling that this was exactly what they were expected to do. It stood to reason, then, that the most beautiful women snared the best of the bachelors that came calling. That meant they probably earned the most power amongst the population as a result. But then again, beauty had nothing to do with fertility. In the end, wouldn't it be the proven breeders who would earn the most attention?

And if you had both abilities . . .

But Asia would be damned if she saw so much as a stretch mark on the woman that was approaching her. Could she really have that perfect a figure if she'd ever given birth?

The blonde came up very close to her and Asia held her breath, waiting to see which way this fiasco was going to go next.

"So. You're human."

And so was she, Asia realized with sudden surprise. The delicately rounded lobes of her ears should have been the giveaway, but in the end it was her English and a very dynamic Southern accent that clinched the identification for Asia.

"So are you," Asia returned.

"Rare," she acknowledged with a sniff. "Most human women choose purge over prison."

"Purge?"

The blonde laughed through her nose in a short burst.

"The only way you can return to Earth. Didn't they tell you? You can choose to go through a purge. They basically bake your brain. Wipe it of every memory you've ever had in your life. Everything. You don't even know how to pick up a fork. When you get back to Earth you are basically like a newborn baby and have to learn everything all over again. Even the simplest things, like walking. If you're human you should have been given a choice, purge or prison."

"I-I'm not supposed to be in here," Asia said, knowing it was a mistake the minute the words left her mouth. The entire room erupted into twitters of laughter.

"Sure, honey. You're innocent. Just like the rest of us, right, girls?" she asked over her shoulder. The entire room came back affirmative. "Except for me. I did what they accused me of."

Asia wasn't about to ask. She'd already stepped in enough shit for one conversation.

"Anyway, you're pretty enough. Leggy," the blonde observed. "In good shape. You'll fetch some fair attention if you clean yourself up a bit."

"I'm not looking for attention," Asia snapped.

The blonde rolled her eyes. "Oh, do keep from being trite, honey," she begged, exaggerating a yawn behind her hand. "You can go on about being stubborn and how you're not going to whore yourself out to the highest bidder like all the newbies do, or you can face facts. We're outnumbered two hundred to one. Men from every colony along the crevasse come here for the chance to screw us. If you want the most comfortable living you'll wise up and vie for it. Otherwise you get stuck with the duds and drips. Tonight the men come to have their pick of us. There's no avoiding what happens next, so you better wise up and pretty up so you can pick the one you want."

Tonight. Oh God. She'd been tossed into the general population on the night of some sick kind of flesh bazaar! How the hell had this happened? Julian had promised her she'd stay in holding. Considering what was at stake for him, she didn't think he'd lie to her. That meant that someone else was behind this fiasco. But who? Who would have the power and the connections to do this to her, and why would they want to? She hadn't been Beneath long enough to make so many enemies, but it seemed like she kept doing so no matter what she did.

"My God," the blonde said with surprise. "You really aren't supposed to be here, are you?" She reached out and closed a warm hand around Asia's upper arm. "I can feel it radiating off you like a sun. Lord, girl, I don't know who you pissed off, but you're in deep trouble here."

She pulled Asia aside, waving off the curious whispering women at her back. She found an unoccupied corner of the room and sat Asia down.

"Listen, once a month men come to buy women for five years' time. Everyone in this room is fair game and there's no such thing as saying no. Call it rape, forced seduction, whatever you think it is, it's going to happen for every girl in here tonight and that includes you. And unless you can vamp it up until dawn when they are forced to leave, you've got a world of trouble coming your way."

"Who are you?" Asia demanded, wanting to know

why this woman gave a damn about what happened to her. Was it because she was human, too?

"Just call me Jewel. That's what I go by around here."

"Jewel, how long have you been here?"

"Lordy, girl, what are you worrying about me for? Jewel's an old hat at this particular cotillion, honey, I guarantee you that. Seven years ago I made the choice to come here. One year in, a snake tried to take what Jewel wasn't in the mood to give and he nearly killed me for it. Unfortunately, I killed him. Murder is truly frowned on 'round here."

"I know. It didn't matter to them that you were just defending yourself?" Asia wanted to know.

"It might have, I suppose, but the scum in question was a Gatherer. One of the Ampliphi's pets, you see. And you don't have much believability when up against credentials like that. So now . . ." She raised her hands to indicate the room around them. "The ultimate irony. Now I have to take what I get handed, like it or not. I'd've been better off letting the bastard rape me."

"My God," Asia said. "This is ridiculous!"

"Indeed. But it's neither here nor there, honey. Right now we have to figure out how to get you through the night."

"Don't worry about me," Asia said softly, "I can handle myself."

"Careful, cherie. Violence has a bad price to pay. If you hurt one of the paying customers, there will be a world of trouble."

"It's Asia. And I am open to suggestions, Jewel."

"Well, as I see it you have two choices. You either pretty yourself up and go for someone you can tolerate for a single night, or pretty yourself up and go for someone you can manipulate for the night. Most of the men 'round here are the strong and studly type, as no doubt you've noticed, but every crowd has the wallflower in it. The shy one. You know, the type where you wink at them the right way and they come in their pants?"

"I know the type," Asia said with a chuckle. "All I need to do is get through the night. In the morning I'll be sprung and this will be a distant nightmare."

"Then it sounds to me like you're heading for a wallflower. If you want first pick of him, you're going to have to sex it up a little bit, honey. The shy ones are real popular 'round here. They're real malleable and easy to swallow, if you get my drift."

"Yeah, I think I get it."

"Good. We don't have much time. I think we're the same size. Mmm, honey, you need some face time with a mirror."

"No doubt."

How in hell had she gotten into this mess? Asia wondered about forty minutes later. She'd shed her simple outfit for something long and slinky, her dark hair swept up tight in a braided topknot and a frightening amount of eyeliner around her eyes. Jewel had picked a gown for her in a color three shades darker than her eyes, the result making their color seem quite stunning.

Asia watched the women around her as they all did some final primping and preening before the prospective men were let into the central building. While Asia waited, she tried to reason out who could have ordered her put into the main population. Who even knew she was there?

Kloe.

Oh, that bitch, Asia thought with venom. Ampliphi Kloe had expressly ordered her to holding. Ordered her away from her precious Julian. The minute she had her here and openly unprotected, Asia would bet her ass Kloe had ordered her put into the main population.

To what end, though? Besides humiliating her? Perhaps she was trying to make her tainted goods so Julian wouldn't want to touch her once she was freed tomorrow. Julian seemed very fixated on keeping Asia all to himself. It was very important to him that no one else even think of her in an inappropriate manner. This kind of thing could very well drive him over the edge with jealousy. It could make him act very rashly. Was Kloe trying to destroy Julian? Trying to make him pay for leaving her?

Asia refused to see that happen. No fucking way. That uppity, conniving bitch was not going to win this one. Asia was going to turn on every last ounce of charm she had and then she was going to scare the crap out of some poor guy so he'd be too afraid to touch her. One night. She just needed to make it through this one night.

Suddenly she heard the sound of a huge bell ringing. Like a church bell, it clapped out long, resounding peals. Then, before the last one had faded away, the huge double doors on the east side of the main building began to open. All of the women immediately roused to attention, sitting up and posing as prettily as they could. Asia would never have thought they would have faced this forced servitude with so much eager aplomb, yet there they were, all ready to start vying for the best man in the bunch that came across the walkway and into the main pavilion.

The crowd of men quickly became intimidating and overwhelming. It seemed there were more men being let in than there were available women. Apparently it wouldn't be just the women who were forced to vie for the best place.

Nervously, Asia stood up and shifted in the silky gown that clung so eagerly to all her curves. Now the only trick was how to determine who was the shyest man in the bunch.

But she'd barely begun looking when, all of a sudden, she found herself staring into furious pine green eyes.

Chapter 13

Julian had known.

He couldn't explain the instinct that had suddenly struck him halfway through his journey home, but he'd suddenly known Asia was going to be in trouble in the prison. It might have had something to do with Lucien constantly muttering how he didn't like it. Didn't like the idea of leaving her overnight. Didn't trust Kloe not to fuck with her.

He was only saying aloud what Julian had already been thinking.

So Julian had turned around and made his way back to the prison. Knowing they wouldn't let him in to see her, he'd quickly realized there was only one way he could make certain she was safely ensconced in holding where she should be, and that was by checking the general population to make sure she wasn't there. And the only way he was going to be able to do that was if he pretended to be a paying customer.

And yet, the minute he saw those familiar eyes across the room, he still couldn't believe what he was seeing. He couldn't believe Kloe would go to such low, underhanded lengths just to make him pay for finding his *kindra*. Why she should be so jealous was completely beyond him. That she would act so damn irrationally, so beyond what she should be doing in her role as an Ampliphi, made him sick to his stomach. That she would so abuse her power just to punish an innocent woman whose only crime was that *he* had kidnapped her and brought her into their world!

But the proof was right before his eyes, looking so outrageously beautiful it should have been a crime. And where in all the planes had she gotten that dress? It was nearly transparent and clinging to every single curve on her body. And what the hell did she think she was doing anyway? Getting dressed up so sexily and working a room full of men? Just what was she after? *Who* was she after?

Julian was so instantly blind with jealousy that he didn't even notice the way her whole face lit up with relief when she saw him. She immediately picked up her skirts and rushed across the room for him, every step she took shimmering through the dress she wore until he could feel every man in a radius staring at her and watching her approach in appreciation.

But she ignored all of them and beelined for Julian. There was a minuscule measure of comfort in that for him. The major comfort came a moment later when she threw herself into his arms and wrapped her arms around his neck. He heard her release a sound that, on anyone else, might have been mistaken for a sob. Asia was tougher than that, though.

Wasn't she?

"Julian! Thank God. Oh, thank God you came back!" She was nearly throttling him, but Julian didn't really care. All he cared about was that he had her safe in his arms and none of the other bastards around him were going to get anywhere near close enough to touch her.

"I had this terrible feeling that you were somehow going to get yourself into trouble again," he said hotly against her ear. "Just . . . something about the way our luck has been turning since all of this started."

"Julian, did you ever think that it isn't luck? Someone is doing this to us, Julian, and I'll bet top dollar that it is that bitch Kloe behind this!"

"Shh. Easy," he soothed her, his hand gliding down her supple back as the slippery material of her dress removed any kind of friction from the equation. "Careful what you say. The Ampliphi are far more powerful than you know. There are few secrets from them in this world."

"Then does that mean the other Ampliphi are going to know what that bitch has done to me?" Asia demanded. "God, Julian, can't you see? Can't you see what almost happened here tonight?"

"I know. I know," he assured her. Julian couldn't help clutching her tighter when he thought about it. He reached for her mouth on instinct, crushing her beneath his suddenly frantic kiss. His lips were numb when he started the thing, his fear still too fresh in his mind and his senses still numbed by the shock of seeing her there. Yet it took only a moment for his mouth to awaken to the recognition of her, to remember who she was to him and the undeniable link they would have now and forever. She might not have felt it, but he sure as hell did.

In fact, the entire room felt it. The minute he was locked into the kiss, his tongue seeking for hers, the synergy of the kiss took over and exploded out into the room around them, even as it resonated deeply between them. People all around them gasped or grunted, feeling on a visceral level the energy the couple gave off. Asia's heart began to race as her entire body flushed with a ridiculously eager response. She knew the desperate nature of his kiss was because of how close a call they'd just had, but knowing didn't change how it felt. He was eating at her mouth as if he was starved for her, and she supposed on a literal level he truly was. But knowing and logical thinking weren't going to help her. All she could do, all that was required, was to stand there and accept the brutal power of Julian's passion. When, Asia wondered, had she become so used to needing the way he kissed her? When had his embrace turned into an anchor?

Probably around the same time her entire world had turned into a savage and unpredictable storm. But now the storm was clutched within her own embrace and she was being swept away by it. She opened wider to the incredible masculine taste of him, her tongue seeking it with nothing short of desperation and more need than she would ever have thought herself capable of. She knew, logically, that had she been in her own world with familiar feet under her, this probably wouldn't be happening, but it didn't change the need one whit.

Asia was mistaken. What she thought was a matter of circumstance, Julian knew to be a matter of destiny. They were meant to be together. They were *kind,* and that was a connection like no other. It didn't help at all that she was so beautiful and felt like pure moving sin between his tightly grasping hands. Her body was so warm and alive, safe in his arms yet a working danger to his sanity. He had to remember where they were and the danger that existed all around them, but he couldn't seem to make himself draw away from the precious delight that was her mouth.

Julian indulged for just a moment or two more, taking the sweet taste of her willing kisses onto his tongue for a long, hot exchange of need, making sure she felt and understood the nature of the man she held between her hands and wrapped up inside her arms. Then, very reluctantly, Julian drew away from her mouth. He was breathing hard, barely an inch away from the temptation of her mouth, reveling in the rose red flush of abuse his kisses had left behind on her lips. She was panting softly, her warm breath hitting his face in rapid little puffs. Her normally cool-colored eyes were now electric blue and hot with her lightly roused desires.

"Julian," she whispered on the barest of breaths. "I want to open my mind to this, to your world and the need of your people, but it's really hard for me to do when I keep being forced to fight the dangers in your world instead. I thought your world, your colony, desperately needed me!"

"They do," he said. "You saw it for yourself, Asia. They're starving more and more, day after day."

"Then why are these women in your world so against me? Why are they so bent on destroying me? Julian, there are literally hundreds of men to fulfill their needs. Why are they doing this?"

"I wish I could tell you," he said honestly. "I don't understand it any more than you do. Especially as pertains to Kloe. I am ashamed of her. I am shamed that your experience in this new world has so been tainted by them. They think that destroying you will make me better available to them? Well, they are wrong. You are *kindra, zini*. There are no other women after you. If they take you from me tomorrow, they may as well be free to take my life. I can no longer live without you."

His words made Asia's heart clutch fearfully in her chest. It was too much. Too much responsibility, too much unlike her, too dependent . . . just too much.

"I can't Julian, I'm not cut out to be anyone's *kindra*. I've never been the type. I doubt I ever will be. I wish . . . I wish I could be otherwise. I wish I was the type of woman who could believe in happily-ever-afters, but I'm not. I don't need fairy-tale endings and true love and all of that. I need stability and the ground under my own two feet. I need to kick ass and take names. I can't just sit pretty like a queen and make babies!"

At that, Julian had to chuckle. "Sit pretty like a queen? *Zini*, what about this world have you seen that makes you think a queen would have the luxury of merely sitting pretty and making babies? The only creatures in this world who live a true life of luxury and leisure are the creatures that now surround you. But that's only because they only have one purpose in their lives. They lost their rights to all other purpose. As my queen you will be responsible for the lives and well-being of an entire colony. Every child, every woman, and every man. Every man, Asia. You cannot begin to imagine the strain living a life without women puts on our men. It sets them on edge in a way I can hardly describe. Think of the women as well. Only *kindra* are allowed to form exclusive relationships for the whole of their lives. Every other woman must leave herself open to choosing multiple partners in order to create as wide and varied a genetic pool as possible. Imagine being a woman who has fallen in love with a man, but because they are not *kind* they cannot remain exclusively together. I know. You think this is cruel, but you simply cannot appreciate the fact that this world you see all around you is dying. Every day it dies quicker and quicker. We don't want these rules, but we have no choice."

Julian lifted his gaze from hers, casting his eyes around the room and feeling the attention that had become focused on them. None of these men or women were starving, but neither were they flush and fat with energy. Just the kiss he had shared with Asia had alerted them to there being something crucial and special among them. Unfortunately, being among women known for committing capital crimes, usually pertaining to violence, could easily have them looking on Asia as a threat.

Very carefully, Julian took her under his arm and tucked her in close to his body. He kept cautious eyes on the crowd the entire time, seeing everyone there as a potential threat as he took Asia up to an exit at the far eastern end of the pavilion. There, several guards were standing about and watching the events taking place in the room.

Julian was so heavily on alert that he instantly was aware of the tension that shot through Asia as they approached the guards. Suspicion growled through Julian and he wondered if she had been misused by one of the men before him. The idea raced hot and red behind his eyes, the resulting menace so powerful that all of the guards began to grip their clubs nervously and they edged and stepped aside to give him a wide berth. Eventually there was only one left for him to broach.

"We need a room. The finest here," Julian demanded.

"Not him." Asia all but growled out the warning and Julian's tension ratcheted up until his whole body vibrated like an overtaut bowstring. "He's the one who pushed me into the general population to begin with. I don't trust him."

The guard seemed to quail a little under her accusation, especially with Julian looming angrily beside her.

"I . . . was just following my orders, Gatherer," he

stammered uneasily, his grip on his baton going white-knuckled. "I didn't hurt her. I didn't even touch her!"

"Oh, but you would have by proxy. You would have stood here and watched her be forced to trade her body for a night of survival," Julian ground out between tightly clenched teeth.

"I-I didn't—"

"Don't you dare say you didn't know," Asia hissed at him. "You knew. You reveled in the knowing of it."

"I had no choice," the guard spluttered. "The Ampliphi ordered you moved into the general population. I cannot countermand an Ampliphi! No one can!"

"True," Julian said. "But you didn't have to enjoy it so much. Take care, man," he warned darkly. "You'll find yourself answering to your choices." Then he turned to a second guard. "Find us a room so we may have some privacy for the night. And if you value your position, you will not share the location and you will not disturb us until dawn."

"Y-yes, Gatherer," the new guard said, hurrying to unlock the door.

"A room?" Asia finally thought to ask.

"Did you think these couples simply fall down into an orgy?" he asked with a small touch of amusement as they followed the guard onto the walkways. Julian still held her tight to his side, as if he couldn't be convinced to put so much as an inch of distance between them. Given how nervous she was to not have nets at the bottom of the penal colony, she gladly depended on his strength and unerring balance. "Outside of the pavilion there are many different rooms in many of the other buildings. Part of the fee we pay is for the privacy of these rooms, as well as the right to feather the nest as we will. Each woman here has rooms as luxurious as her lover can afford. If you were truly staying here, I would be responsible for finding you the best accommodations I could manage, and I will do no different tonight. I won't leave you alone and at the whim of what the Ampliphi might have planned for you."

"I see you've been disarmed. So you don't kill me?"

Julian had to chuckle at that. "I'm sure they had something different in mind, because they couldn't possibly have known of the level of frustration you bring me to."

"Ha. Ha," she said dryly. "I only meant to say whatever safety we go to in this place is only relative to just how far Kloe wants to go to see me put down. When that guard reports back to her, and he will, she is going to be furious to know her plan has failed."

"Come morning it won't matter. And there are other recourses still available to us. You must trust me to protect you. I won't let anything happen to you. Have I failed you to date?"

"You mean besides bringing me here in the first place, I take it."

"Yeah, besides that."

"No. Honestly, you haven't. If anything, I'm the one constantly failing you. You expect me to be this miracle, and I am well aware as far as miracles go, I'm nothing but a huge pain in the ass."

"As far as miracles go, I couldn't have asked for better," he retorted.

"And just how do you figure that?" she wanted to know.

"Asia, you're a strong, determined woman who'll fight to do what's right and kick ass to stay alive at all costs. This is a world that needs survivors. I don't want something delicate and precious, I want a fighter. A battler. You think your fight aggravates me when, in truth, I relish it."

"Here is one of the best rooms we have, Gatherer," the guard said suddenly, reaching to spin the door handle and opening it for them.

Asia stepped in first and then waited with a tapping foot for Julian to seal the door shut behind them. The room was actually a suite, she noted. The space she was standing in was a living room of sorts, or a parlor with comfortable furniture in rich velveteen grays. There were two other doorways, but each was hung with a sparkling curtain of beads or stones, blocking her view of their interiors.

"Now what? I have to spend the entire night wondering what the Ampliphi have in store for me come the morning?" she muttered aloud as she turned back toward Julian.

Julian had a silent but powerful reply. He closed the distance between them in a single, commanding stride, his hands reaching out to her neck, his thumbs stroking along her jaw until her head tilted back. Then his mouth was on hers, burning like a sweet acid as the rest of his body crowded up against her. This time, there was something truly desperate in his kisses, something she didn't have a prayer of calming or counteracting. Her hands came up to circle his wrists, but she didn't attempt to free herself from his grasp or his kiss. Frankly, she was so happy he was there, the new familiarity of his kisses was like a powerful balm. It soothed her frayed nerves like nothing else possibly could.

Asia almost laughed at the thought. How could a force as vital and disturbing as Julian's kiss possibly have a soothing effect on her? On the one hand it did, calming her mind away from thoughts of her narrow escape just now from tasting the fate of a nightfly; on the other hand, Julian was a force to be reckoned with, pure heat and dynamic sensuality packed like a powder keg. All it would take was the slightest flame and everything would simply explode.

"Julian," she gasped the moment she could seize the opportunity. "I can't think!"

"I don't want you to think. Not now. Not any more today. We, both of us, need to stop thinking and, for a change, just feel. Are you willing to do that, *zini*? Are you willing to feel with me?"

To punctuate his invitation, Julian drifted seeking fingertips down the front of her throat and breastbone. His hands brushed between her breasts without stopping, his caress continuing on until it was coasting over her stomach, making her tense in anticipation of where he was going to end up next. She thought for a moment that she should really stop him. She should step away and take charge of herself. There was danger and uncertainty all around them and they didn't have the luxury of losing themselves in the powerful passion that seemed to burn so easily between them. Any minute the next turn or twist could come to tear them apart.

And perhaps that was what made her suddenly wrap her arms tightly around his neck and pull her body closer to his. In a world gone mad, Julian was her only true stability. He was the one constant. The only constant. She was lost and he was true north.

Asia opened her mouth under his, using the flick of her tongue to invite him to do the same. He didn't even hesitate. The very next instant he was plunging into her mouth and devouring her as deeply as he could. With a throaty moan, Asia accepted him. Her fingers plunged into the crisp ends of his hair, then immediately curled to get a good grip of it. Fingers fisted, she used his hair like reins, turning his head to suit so she could work his mouth with the sudden and savage appetite he inspired. His light touches disappeared, replaced abruptly by the powerful clamp of his hands around her lean waist. She felt his strength wrapping around her like a too-tight belt, making her breath gasp out of her in a cross between pressure and pleasure.

Feeling her react to the command of his hold, Julian quickly adapted, jerking her nearly clean off her feet and into his body. She wasn't delicate in anything she did, and that included the way she made love. Oh, that didn't mean she didn't have or appreciate finesse, it just meant she knew what she liked and knew how to get it. Once she made up her mind to take him on, she did it with everything she had, every weapon in her arsenal. That included the curved fingers dragging down his back, her nails raking through the fabric of his shirt. If Julian wasn't hard before that, he most certainly was by the time she reached his waist. And he would be damned if she didn't know it. The little brat had the gall to laugh at him for it, her tongue lashing out impudently to lick the tip of his nose.

"Oh really?" he demanded to know. "Now, all of a sudden, you're going to be a tease?"

"I've always been a tease," she pointed out, reminding him that she'd been tormenting his senses in one way or another right from the beginning.

"Then I feel I should warn you," he said on a hot, growling breath, "that this dynamic will work both ways."

With that, Julian planted his hands on her hips and sent her spinning around in his hold, forcing her into an about-face. She barely had time to catch her balance before he was gathering up the skirt of her gown in large grabs of his fingers, baring her legs all the way up to her backside. Then his hands dove under the remaining fabric to wrap around her hips and feel the bare skin there. His mouth burrowed beneath her hair, finding the back of her neck, even as his fingers stroked forward down along the V of her pelvis.

"Hmm," he observed, "no panties. One might consider you were thinking of giving yourself to a man tonight." The accusation was clear, just as it was clear from the sudden power of his grip that his temper was roused at the very idea.

"I'm not in the habit of wearing underwear," she countered, turning her head so she could whisper the information into his ear. "Unless my skirt is so short I have no choice. So you can relax, Julian, and remember you don't know me yet nearly as well as you wish you did."

"This is true," he said darkly. "But I'm about to learn a great deal more." He punctuated the remark with the forward press of his hips against the swell of her bottom, making sure she felt him rubbing hotly into her. Asia went suddenly breathless at the aggressive feel of him, her heart racing to keep up with all the feedback she was feeling.

Julian had seen dozens of women in a state of arousal, had seen them writhe in the ultimate state of pleasure, but none of it could compare to the way Asia looked just then. Her body was an incredible work of art, but flushed with need, and braced with her aggressive style of lovemaking, it was an extraordinary sight to behold. Then she reached down to grasp hold of the gathered hem of her dress and whipped it off over her head. Suddenly Julian found himself holding on to a fully naked woman who had filled his every waking thought since the moment he'd first set eyes on her. He looked at her over her shoulder, taking in everything from perfect teardrop breasts tipped with pretty pale nipples to those damn long legs of hers. The idea of having those legs wrapped around him was too much to bear.

Asia felt him spin her back around, her hair flying and a laugh bursting out of her when she could feel the brutish desperation in the grip of his hands. If Julian was a slickly skilled lover, he wasn't showing any sign of his finesse. Why that thrilled her so much she wasn't about to fathom. He turned her in a hard swing until she hit her back against a wall, then he moved in tight to pin her up into it. His hands covered both of her breasts, their heat burning her just as much as the abrupt fierceness of his kiss did.

"You can't know," he rumbled against her mouth, his teeth flashing out to catch her bottom lip, pulling slowly on it until he let her go. "I know you don't know what this feels like for me. You aren't there yet. But you will be. I swear you will be."

She wasn't quite certain if she wasn't already there. The way he was acting, the way he moved and touched her, she felt so incredibly restless, so overpowered with craving for him. Was this what it meant to be *kind*? Was it always going to be this uncontrollable? This overwhelming? The idea injected a healthy dose of fear into the mix of emotions and adrenaline she was bathing in, but it wasn't enough to make her call a stop. She suddenly felt as though she'd been craving this man for weeks. She knew he wanted something from her, something special she wasn't sure she could give, but this she could give all too easily.

"Yes. Touch me," she commanded him, grabbing hold of one of his hands and rubbing it down the full length of her bare body.

He withdrew his hand, reaching to catch her chin in his hand and pulling back to meet her hot eyes. "I'm perfectly capable of touching you." He paused to kiss her until she was certain her toes were curling. "Must everything be a battle of wills and the power of a moment for you? Can't you simply let me make love to you?"

"No. I can't. This is who and what I am. You'll make love *with* me or not at all."

Julian understood the distinction and yet another piece of the puzzle that was Asia fell into place. He had thought she simply didn't know how to allow herself to relax, but he'd been wrong. It wasn't that she was afraid to give herself to the moment, it was simply that she was always going to take control of her life and refused to leave it up to someone else. And she was right. If he was going to have her, he had to accept that.

No problem. He'd made worse trade-offs, and this hardly compared.

"Very well," he said, reaching to yank his shirt free of his jeans. "I accept."

"Good," she breathed, helping him drag the thing off. She was eager, knowing what his clothing hid. Now that she was no longer put off by the idea that he was a serial killer, she allowed herself to hunger for the spectacular body he had. He was more than just a pretty boy, she had learned. He was a man who had been birthed from the harsh conditions of this dangerous world. And there was something undeniably sexy about that. It didn't surprise her to feel how hot his flesh was under the touch of her hands. She knew it was only a fraction of a reflection of what he was feeling. The savage speed of his hands over her skin told her as much. "Yes," she hissed as she writhed between him and the woven wall.

Julian reached for his belt, unable to bear being clothed while she moved like a sensual python against him. Like those deadly serpents, she was taking his breath away. When he thought of having her wrapped around him, contracting and constricting him, it

blinded his mind to everything else. He didn't even
realize that the passion they were sharing was sending
heavy waves of fervent energy out into the holding
colony all around them. He should have remembered
that, he should have controlled it . . . but he couldn't.
His mindheart was completely overrun with other information and an entirely different focus. Unzipping
his jeans, Julian kicked off his shoes. But if he thought
she was going to give him time to strip, he was in for
a huge surprise. She grabbed hold of his shoulders
and raised a thigh to his hip. Before he knew it, she
had wrapped both of her legs around his waist and
was reaching down the front of his pants to fish for a
handhold around the thick erection she'd inspired.

Julian groaned as she wrapped her palm around him,
the sensitive nerves of his cock screaming to life as she
stroked him. Even as she did so she closed the vise of
her legs until he was pulled up tight and snug against
her. In the next instant she was holding him against her,
bathing the entire length of him in her wet pussy as she
squirmed to bring him to the brink of her waiting body.

He wasn't used to so much aggression from a woman.
He could barely keep an anchor on the world around
him, barely keep his knees locked to hold both of their
weight up against the wall. She was like a wildfire rav-
aging him, licking and eating him up as if he were raw
fuel. And Julian didn't fight a single second of it. He'd
taken so much from her, it was high time she took from
him. And he could think of no better way.

She brought him up tight against her, toying with him
now by rubbing the sensitive head of his cock around
the rim of her entrance. He toyed right back, leaving
her bruised mouth to find one of her pointed nipples
with his teeth. He sucked hard at her, the action nearly
savage, but clearly what she liked as a fresh wash

of liquid fire bathed his waiting cock. And while she continued to torment him, he decided to do likewise by thrusting a hand between their bodies. She was denuded of all her hair, leaving him with nothing but smooth wet skin to lead him to the clit hiding between folds of slick flesh. As soon as he found it, he began to toy with her exactly as she was toying with him.

Asia's entire mind seemed to go suddenly slack as his thick and insistent fingers played against her. She moaned, trying to hold on to what she was doing, what she had wanted to do to torment him the way he'd spent the day tormenting her in one fashion or another. But it all abandoned her. Now she wanted one thing and one thing only: To have him inside her. To have him fucking her until she couldn't see or think straight.

"Julian," she panted, clearly begging him for just that as she began to manipulate him into her body.

Begging wasn't necessary. He reached to pull her hand out from between their bodies and then hooked an arm under one of her knees, hauling her up into a perfect position for his first and best thrust. He almost made it all the way inside her with just that single movement, but as wet as she was and as open and eager as she was being, he was still too big for such ambition. But it was enough to get a real satisfying gasp out of her.

"Oh God! Yes!" she cried, using the undulation of her body to force him even deeper inside her. Her shoulders against the wall were excellent leverage and she curved into his hands and against him with an arching of her back. Julian grasped her so tightly he knew she was going to be bruised for it. His chest ached with the way it felt to have her sliding down around him with raw perfection. And no sooner was he inside her than he had to leave her. But only to return again. Not that he would have much of a choice. The clench of her legs demanded he come into her again and then again. He was lost from the start of it all, completely overwhelmed by knowing he was finally inside his *kindra,* the incredible and precious thing he'd been given that no other would ever know. It was all he could do to keep from falling instantly into orgasm, so devastated with pleasure and emotion was he. The only thing that tainted the far edges of it all was the knowledge that she saw this only as the physical connection of the moment.

But he would prove to her that it was otherwise. He would force her to feel it if it was the very last thing he ever did. To that end he reached to clasp her head between both of his hands, forcing those glacial blue eyes to stare straight into his, forcing her to see the depths of his need for her even as he sought the depths of her body. He emanated his thoughts and emotions into her, flooding her with the desperate need he had of her.

"You feel me," he demanded of her through the tight clench of his teeth. "Feel me."

Asia couldn't help but feel him, but she knew by looking into the depths of his gaze that he wasn't demanding the physical from her. He was already getting that. What he wanted went much, much deeper than the hard thrusts of his hips could reach. Now, for the first time since this had started, Asia felt the first frisson of trepidation. She reached to grab for his wrists, trying to pull his hands away, trying to free her head so she could look away from him. He wanted too much. Wasn't it enough that he was inside her, turning her inside out with heat and need? Why did he have to ruin it by pushing her for more than she was capable of?

"You lie to yourself if you really believe that," he whispered to her. But then he released her and swooped in for a kiss. He knew she wanted to hide, and for now he would let her. He would make himself be content with what he had. So he took hold of her hips and used the grip to add to the counterforce of having her against the wall. He began to take her hard and wildly, driving into her again and again until she was crying out with irrepressible pleasure. Then he opened his mindheart to her and swept her mind into the equation as well. He was careful, though, not to push her too hard because he didn't want her to accidentally call the Gate to them. But just the same, she exploded into a violent orgasm, her entire body bowing with the rocketing pleasure. Julian gasped as she clutched around him tight enough to strangle him. His forehead fell against the wall behind her and he gritted his teeth and rode out the buck and beauty of her release. It brought tears to his eyes as he fought the desire to simply lose himself in the moment. But he couldn't afford to let this end so quickly. So he waited for her to fall from her crest, waited until she was gasping for breath against his ear. Then he hauled her up tighter against the wall, set his feet, and began to drill himself into the heaven of her body all over again.

Julian was relentless, his psyche devouring every cry that escaped her lips, every single time her body locked up like a high-tech vault, every wave of ultimate pleasure she succumbed to. He ignored the frantic digging of her nails into his back and shoulders, the bite of her teeth into the side of his neck, the crest of his shoulder, and even his lower lip. It was all a matter of what was closest to her at the time.

"Stop! No!" she burst out blindly, not even realizing she was trying to pull him into her even as she said it. In the end it was the clawing of her nails up over his buttocks that finally made him lose all control.

The next instant they both exploded into wild orgasmic bliss, their cries mingling together even as the wetness of their bodies did. Julian felt the release all the way to the soles of his feet, all around his heart and beyond the place in his soul that knew she was forever his.

Chapter 14

The Ampliphi lived in Justice Hall, each in their own quarters. Connected to those quarters was a second suite of rooms meant for the Ampliphi's Gatherer to stay in when they were not doing their duties on the Earth plane. Julian had always been the exception to this because he was also the ruler of his colony. In the past, Kloe had understood the reasons why he had preferred to bed down in his colony home.

But tonight both Kine and Shade were missing from their quarters as well. While this wasn't against any rules, their Ampliphi frowned on not being asked permission to have leave of them. But neither Shade nor Kine wanted to be put in a position where they would have to explain the reasons for their absences, so they figured in this case that it would be better to apologize in the aftermath.

As a result, Sydelle, Kloe, and Giselle had no better company than one another that night. Kloe was in too good a mood to be rattling around her suite on her own and she was feeling very tolerant of her contemporaries' presence.

So it came to pass that they were all together when

the raw power of the most dynamic energy they'd felt in years belted through them. Each woman gasped, Sydelle even falling out of her chair and onto her knees, one hand clutching in a fist against her chest, as they absorbed the rogue wave as best they could. It tore through every last one of them and overfilled their capabilities. Within a minute every last one of them turned fully to flesh, a state none of them had seen for decades. Giselle looked at her companions in shock as she was able to touch her own hair for the first time in ages. Her skin glowed and turned flush with the power of it, making her laugh out loud.

But Kloe wasn't laughing. The moment she became true flesh, even feeling the soft hairs on her arms under her stunned touch, she knew what had happened. Her hands curled into fists and she threw back her head and screamed out in fury. Her rage was impossible to absorb since the Ampliphi were already glutted with the positive passion of *kind* coming together.

"How dare they disobey me!" she raged, fighting to keep her fury as the swamping heat of passion overwhelmed them all. "She was supposed to be at the holding colony! She cannot be there if they are together!"

Giselle slowly gained her feet, still too amazed by her transformation to resist fondling the silken feel of her gown between her fingers. It was Sydelle who was the first to turn on her peer.

"You selfish bitch," she rasped out in a hoarse emanation. "They've created an explosion of energy so magnificent it has fed us to overflowing, and all you can do is scream about it? Have you any idea what must be happening in our colonies right now? Can you not feel that? Every one of the Ampliphi is overfull, and that means pure energy is being fed straight to the colonies now for the first time in untold ages!

No filtering, no doling it out, no piecemeal portioning or rationing based on class or importance! Praise be to all. Starving children are knowing the pleasure of a pure feed for what may be the first time in their lives, and all you can think of is your wounded arrogance? Bitter, *bitter* creature! You shame us all!"

"But I—"

"Quiet, Kloe." The command came from Christophe, who now stood in the doorway of the room. Sydelle laughed, seeing him in flesh tickling her for unknown reasons. She moved over to him and touched her hands to his fine form, feeling the strength within it and the glut of energy on him that made his eyes a vibrant scarlet color. She had forgotten how handsome the Ampliphi was. The faded energy they existed as was a means of conservation, a way of bringing their energy consumption down to the barest minimum. It had been so long. . . .

"Christophe," she emanated with great awe, "I had forgotten what a beautiful man you are."

This won her something even rarer than solidity— a smile from the leader of the Ampliphi. He reached out to her, brushing a fond thumb over the warm blush on her cheek. "And you as well," he said to her, admiring the brilliant vermilion color of her eyes and the silky mocha brown of her hair. She'd had no cause to cut or grow it, all normal bodily functions merely a waste of energy to them, but it was the same long and lush length it had been before she had become Ampliphi.

And then the moment was gone, Christophe turning his full attention to Kloe, who sat seething, turning pure, clean energy into something vicious and twisted.

"You will control yourself and stop this temper tantrum immediately," Christophe warned in a powerful emanation that made it suddenly difficult to draw breath in the room. "If the human woman has committed a capital crime as she is being accused of, she will be in the penal colony soon enough. Then this, all of this," he indicated their solid state, "will be gone forever. We will fade back to what we were, scavengers feeding weakly off others who have more than we do. Will that make you happy then, Ampliphi Kloe?"

Breathing heavily but called into check by the one being who could potentially destroy her, Kloe managed to shake her head. "I only meant that if one of us is disrespected, then all of us are. To let it pass, even because they are *kind*, is to invite all manner of insubordination! What good would any of this be if our world descends into the violent chaos you well know humans carry with them?"

"It is true that humans are a risk. But they are a calculated and necessary risk, Kloe. We cannot survive without them. What will it matter, all of this, if we are dead and dust because of starvation or because we cannot birth new generations? And these humans you so despise, they are not so different from us, Ampliphi Kloe." Christophe turned to include all the Ampliphi who had arrived into his remarks. "We get no rest tonight. Instead, we must see to it that all the colonies have benefitted from this unexpected surplus. No one will be left out. By morning we shall see everyone from all colonies just as renewed as we now are."

The group nodded as one, and each quickly disappeared to see to the needs of their respective colonies.

The bells for predawn exit rang harshly throughout the holding colony. It woke Julian and he felt instant anxiety clutching at his chest. He was lying on one of the parlor couches, Asia sprawled out naked over him like a decadent blanket. He recalled stumbling over to it the night before, utter exhaustion keeping him from going any deeper into the suite with her. They'd both slept the entire night on the narrow piece of furniture. He wasn't surprised. They'd had a hell of a day between them, not to mention not having slept for the better part of two days. It also didn't surprise him that the exit alarm didn't make Asia stir so much as an inch. She just lay there breathing deeply, her ebony hair spread all around her head and her mouth softly open against his collarbone.

Gently he took her shoulders in his hands, turning with her until she dropped onto the cushions and he could gain his feet. His movement did what the shrill alarms had not. She complained about it in a numb sort of mumble, her sleep so heavy she didn't understand what was happening around her. But he knew he couldn't leave her without saying good-bye and he couldn't stay without getting in trouble. If he didn't leave the colony before the alarms stopped ringing, he would be forcibly removed. That meant he only had minutes to get dressed and say his farewells. But if all went well with the Ampliphi this morning, then he would be seeing her again shortly.

"Asia," he called to her, giving her shoulder a shake even as he looked around for his clothes. They were scattered hastily to and fro.

"Fuck off," she mumbled, the words barely coherent. It made him smile, and that was when he realized he was getting into very deep trouble with her. Nothing she did vexed him any longer. He was beginning to trust her. What was more, he was beginning to feel very deeply for her. The trouble was, he knew very well that she did not return his fondness. Not that he blamed her. He'd done some pretty terrible things to her in the name of saving his people. But he had no regrets. Perhaps he would have wished things to have gone more smoothly, but he would not regret bringing her there. And neither would his people.

"Asia," he tried again, "I have to go."

That woke her instantly, and she raised up so fast that she cracked her head into his.

"Ow!"

"Shit!" Julian swore as he jerked back from her, his hand going to the nose she'd just smacked with her skull. His fingers came away bright pink and he cursed again.

"Man, those English swear words must have been the first thing you guys learned," Asia remarked as she rubbed the back of her head, "because you sure do have a handle on them."

"Isn't that what you call a pot calling a kettle black?" he challenged her.

"Mmm. Perhaps." But the response was more than a little distracted as she sat there staring at him, seeing him fully naked for really the first time. "Holy shit! You're . . . different!" It was the nicest word she could come up with on short notice.

What he was, was entirely free of body hair, and his legs were starkly tattooed in rings of black runic symbols, all the way from his hips to his toes. The symbology was even tattooed in a V along the inside of his pelvis, accentuating the line that ran from his navel to his cock. To be honest, she was surprised *that* wasn't tattooed as well!

Julian followed her gaze to his own body and shrugged.

"They are the markings of my Advocacy. Every Ampliphi puts their own special stamp on their Gatherer. This is Kloe's."

That made Asia frown. "Does it come off? I'm not sure I like the idea of that bitch having her mark all over you."

Julian supposed he ought to have taken the time to correct her for the way she constantly disparaged Kloe, but he was too busy being delighted by the rather possessive nature of her remarks.

"Can we talk about this later?" he said evasively, reaching to pull on his pants. "I'm about to get forcibly kicked out of your bed if I don't present myself at the gate before the bell stops."

"We never made it to my bed," she noted with a saucy little grin. It made him laugh.

"You know what I mean. Besides, I have an appointment to keep, remember?"

"Yeah, I remember." Asia frowned, her fingers plucking irritably at the couch fabric for a moment. "You know, Ariel is not a criminal. She's sick in the head, and the only person she hurt was herself."

"She's trying to hurt you," he reminded her.

"I know that. But look at what she risked. She almost killed herself to try to keep you to herself, Julian. That's the act of a sick mind. And they want to make her nightfly? That'll push her into a psychotic break! There has to be another way!"

"Not in this world," he said softly as he shrugged into his shirt. "Asia, I don't have time to talk to you about this now. I have to go."

"Then go. I'll take a shower or something and sit here waiting while you and the high-and-mighty Ampliphi decide my fate."

Her sarcasm was clear even to a man who rarely used it for himself.

"You need to stop being so disrespectful," he warned her with a frown. "I understand how you feel, but the

Ampliphi are everything to my people. They are the first and the last authority. If they hear you acting so disrespectful, you will offend people. I don't think that's how you want to start out your life here Beneath."

Suddenly the bells outside silenced.

"What does that mean?" she asked suspiciously.

"It means I'm going to get my ass kicked if I don't get to the gate." He stepped over to her and bent quickly to give her a kiss, then hurried to turn the wheel to the door. He gave her one last look before stepping out, trying to capture the picture of her lying there naked in his mind. "I'll be back for you in a few hours. Just . . . try not to get killed. Stay in your rooms. Clear?"

"Clear," she acknowledged, giving him a salute.

And just like that, he was gone.

Julian was not expecting what he found when he entered Justice Hall.

To see the Ampliphi made flesh astounded him. To see them smiling and energetic with happiness all but took his breath away. He walked into the center of the chamber, faced the row of Ampliphi, and respectfully took a knee before them.

"Gatherer," Christophe greeted him, brilliant scarlet pupils shining down on him. "How do you fare this happy morning?"

"I . . . I fare well," he responded cautiously, trying to figure out what was going on. The Ampliphi maintained an energy state for a very good reason. Why would they suddenly change that? And Christophe bordering on joviality? It was all just too strange. What next? Would Rennin give up the art of criticism?

"We are very glad to hear that," Sydelle said, practically winking at him. Wait a minute, she did wink at him.

What the hell?

"Gatherer, we don't understand your confusion," Christophe said after a moment of studying his puzzled face. "Was this not your design? You wished to make it known in no uncertain terms that the human woman was indeed your *kindra,* and I must say you have succeeded stunningly."

"My design?" Julian's mind raced as he rose to his feet and tried to search his memory of the night before. What had he done? Or rather, what had he failed to do to protect their privacy? Was all of this because of his time with Asia last night? Had the joining really been this powerful? He had expected perhaps the holding colony might feel the effects of *kind,* but had it really travelled so far and so fiercely? "Please excuse my confusion, Ampliphi, but there was no design to this. This was not at all my intention. In fact, I had no idea this was possible."

"To be candid, neither did we," Christophe admitted. "Every one of the seven colonies, as well as the holding colony, is flush to overflowing thanks to you and your *kindra.*"

"*Every* colony?" Julian could not help his shock.

"Every colony, Julian. We never knew the coming together of *kind* could be so dynamic. You have proven your claim and then some. Now all that remains is for you to prove your *kindra*'s innocence in this accusation. She claims she laid no hand on your Companion. You have proof of this?"

"I do," he said grimly. "The evidence I have will show you that Ariel's wounds were self-inflicted."

"She was stabbed in the back," Kloe emanated with

hostile fury. "You expect us to simply take her word that Ariel is somehow jointed in the way to accomplish that?"

"I expect you to see the evidence that says she propped the knife between two shelves and threw herself back onto it for the express purpose of causing this reaction," Julian said with his own hostility. "Her intention was to make my *kindra* nightfly, thereby clearing the way for her to remain my Companion."

"You mean to make us believe she nearly threw her life away for the sake of vengeance? Preposterous," Rennin said. "Ariel knows there are hundreds of men among us who are ready to worship her every step and breath. The loss of one man is easily replaced by another."

"Gatherer Julian warned us the girl was unstable before this even happened," Sydelle argued on his behalf. "And he has never been known to be dishonest with us."

"And yet he has spent years among the humans and has picked up other habits of theirs," Kloe said.

"My honesty does not have to come into the matter," Julian said darkly. "The evidence will prove what you will not believe." He turned to narrow furious eyes on Kloe. "And then perhaps after that we can ask you, Ampliphi, if you know why Asia was put into general population last evening. An evening when selection was to take place. The guard says it was by order of an Ampliphi."

"General population!" Christophe turned to Kloe. "Is this true? Were you responsible for this?"

"No!" Kloe insisted. "I believe her to be guilty. All it would take was a matter of hours to prove her so! Why would I be in a rush to make nightfly out of her? It was going to happen soon enough!"

"Not soon enough," Sydelle took note, "to avoid Julian proving his claim of *kind* and thus removing himself from your service permanently. The only way you could keep him would be if she was made night-fly and his claim of *kind* was nullified . . . but it had to be done before they could be mated. Is that why you were in such a fury last night? You realized they had established proof of *kind* and there was nothing you could do about it?"

"I was angry because I thought my orders were disobeyed! I didn't even think she was in the holding colony!"

"Well, she was, as ordered. If I had not gone back to the colony and paid the price for nightfly just to make certain she wasn't among them, she might have been sold to the first man to make claim on her. She could have been raped and impregnated. Perhaps you thought this would be added insurance . . . to try and soil her for me with another man's child?"

"Julian!" Kloe surged to her feet, outrage edging every line of her body. "I will not tolerate these disrespectful accusations! You think too much of yourself if you think I cannot train another to take your place!"

Kloe waved her hand at him and Julian suddenly felt fire racing over his skin, every inch of it, from the waist down. It was a pain he had felt only once before in his life, and like that time it brought him straight to his knees. He knew that beneath his clothes and all across his legs the runes that had been burned into his skin were now being burned away. Kloe was removing her mark on him.

It proved nothing to him except how vindictive she could be. She had no choice now but to accept that he must leave her. That was the law the Ampliphi themselves had put into place. No one who was *kind* could be Gatherer. They were more valuable to the colonies if they stayed at home and took care of their partner.

"Kloe!" Christophe warned her when Julian shouted out in pain from the demarking. "You could have warned him and seen him anesthetized! This is blatant cruelty!"

Kloe shrugged and resumed her seat with all regality. "Perhaps next time he should think before throwing accusations around without proof."

"I have proof. The guard at the prison," Julian reminded her through the clench of his body and the ferocity of his pain.

"Bring him forth, then, and have him accuse me himself. Christophe, I will not stand for this! I am not the one on trial here!"

"Not as yet," Christophe relented. "Come, Julian, you will show us your evidence."

"B-before I do . . ." Julian took a breath, forcing down his pain and getting to his feet once more, "I want to discuss what will happen to Ariel."

"One stage of this process at a time, Julian. We will see to her punishment if what you say has happened is true," Rennin said.

"This is what I must know. Ariel is unbalanced. Clearly so. To make her nightfly will push her over the edge. There has to be a better way."

"There is no better way. This is our way," Rennin said. "Unlike humans, we don't do things in half measures and allow the guilty to go free unpunished. She will be nightfly and learn to live as such."

"But she has already tried to hurt herself once—"

"All the more reason she needs to be in a controlled environment. I think you should worry less about your former Companion and focus more on getting your *kindra* out of the colony. You are wasting our time and hers with this."

Rennin was right. Every minute Julian spent arguing for Ariel was a minute longer that Asia was trapped in the dangerous nightfly colony. He wanted her out and he wanted her out now.

"Please, Ampliphi. Come to my home," he invited them softly.

Chapter 15

There was a soft rapping on the other side of the steel door. Since Asia was going a little stir-crazy just pacing back and forth alone in her rooms, she figured she'd do just about anything to spice it up. Even entertain opening the door. She'd ignored the first two times someone had come knocking on her door, but now it had to be coming around to about noon and she'd had just about enough of playing wait-and-see. Julian should have been back by then. And if this wasn't him, she was going to start ripping her own hair out. She couldn't stand the idea that her entire future was resting in someone else's hands, even if it was Julian's.

Asia swept her wet braid back behind her shoulders, one downside of Beneath being there was no apparent need for blow-dryers. She supposed she ought to just be grateful there had been a shower.

Asia went across to the door, opening it carefully. To her surprise it was Jewel standing there waiting on her. But Asia almost didn't recognize her. Gone was all the makeup and adornments. Her face was scrubbed clean, except for the faintest traces of the tattooing that had been on her face last night. Her blond hair had been swept up into a simple tail. She wore what Asia assumed was the Beneath equivalent of sweats and a tee. Only they were wide-legged pants made of a near-transparent material and tied to her body with a scarf for a belt, and the simple boxy shirt was made of the same fine material that seemed to cling to human skin like static. The color was an almost unattractive mauve, but Jewel was far too beautiful to look ugly even in the worst clothing.

"Hi, there," Asia greeted her. "How goes it?"

"Not too bad." She chuckled. "Wow, I miss that. Speech," she clarified. "Idioms. People I can talk to who will actually understand me." Jewel stepped over the door saddle when Asia stood back to silently invite her in.

"I don't know. A lot of people here seem to speak English." Asia shrugged.

"You're spoiled, then. Emanation is the most common language here. It's kind of like body language, only a little . . . harder. You get used to it pretty quickly, though. When I first got here I was afraid it was going to take brain surgery in order for me to talk to the natives. But it came. Eventually."

"Just like everything, I suppose." Asia folded her arms over her breasts and eyed the other woman. "How'd you make out last night?"

"Not as good as you did, from what I've been hearing. You've found your *kindri*. The whole colony is talking about it. Last night was . . . wow. Like, a crazy aphrodisiac! I've never seen the main pavilion clear out so fast in all the years I've been here."

"All right. Is that a good thing?" Asia frowned. "I don't see how any of this can be a good thing. You've been turned into a . . . a . . ."

"Nightfly," Jewel supplied, smiling a bit wryly. "Sounds a bit nicer than whore or prostitute, huh?"

"Not if it means the same thing," Asia said.

"It's not really. More like a mistress. But I suppose that's all semantics. The fact is, it's not so bad as far as a way to live. I think the hard part will come when I have to give birth and then give the baby away. I kind of lucked out so far. My first five-year contract was kind of a dud, not for lack of trying. He blamed me, of course."

"Of course."

"Truth is, a lot of these men were made infertile from the same disease that killed off all their women. That's a little bit of information they don't readily share with us humans. But what do you expect from a society that's predominantly male?"

"Damn. It's like there's something out to get these people," Asia observed. "It's a wonder they have any fight left in them."

"You gotta give them credit for being a tenacious bunch, cherie, that's for certain."

"Actually, I feel kind of sorry for them."

"True that. One man from one plane stepping where he didn't belong and like that"—she snapped her fingers—"an entire civilization was all but destroyed."

"It kind of reminds me of white explorers bringing white diseases to the jungle tribes of the Amazon. It's so stupid and unnecessary . . . and for what? To satisfy a curiosity? Have you seen their children? Their elderly? They can barely move."

"Not today. Today they are dancing in the streets. That's because of you, cherie."

"Maybe that's true of the people in this colony, but—"

"All colonies, cherie. Word gets around fast about these sorts of things," she explained at Asia's doubtful look, "and we don't have much to do around this

place other than primp and gossip. Seems you've
made a very powerful connection."

"Does your rumor mill have anything to say about
when the hell I'm going to get out of here?"

"No. But there's a pool. High odds say you stay
here. There's odds against you making it to the end
of the week alive."

"Yeah? Well, don't take that bet," Asia warned her.
"You'll lose your shirt."

"I rather figured that out for myself, cherie. Who do
you think is running the bet?" She smiled wolfishly.
"Which brings me to why I'm here."

"I was wondering if this was just a social call."

"Oh, it is, cherie, it is!" Jewel moved a little farther
into the suite, reaching a finger out to check the dust
level on a nearby shelf. "We're just two gals sittin'
around and having a chat." She reached out to touch
the material on one of the couches, pushing at it for
a moment before turning and sitting on it, testing it
out for comfort and seemingly finding it passable.
"Now, correct me if I'm wrong, but your man is a
Gatherer, isn't he?"

"Yes, he is. How did you—?"

Jewel waved her off, clearly feeling that was a self-
answering query at that point. "The thing about Gatherers is they are quite the precious commodity. Did
you know that each colony has only one Ampliphi and
one Gatherer?" She lifted a brow when Asia nodded.
"Here's how it works. The Gatherer goes to the Earth
plane and, using a variety of unique talents, farms
energy from human resources. Now, there's all kinds
of Gatherers and they take in all kinds of energy. They
feed that energy to the Ampliphi . . . and at this point
I am talking plural. All of the Ampliphi. Then each
Ampliphi feeds their colony. Then, whatever is left

over gets tossed to the penal colony, rather like tossing scraps to the dogs."

"I see," Asia said with a dark frown.

"Well, we have other ways of obtaining energy. Don't you worry about us," Jewel assured her. "But the real fascinating part about this is the variety of specialties the Gatherers bring. For instance, your Julian. His speciality was passion. He farmed energy by manipulating the passions of the human women he found. Occasionally, he found a woman worthy of bringing here to this little slice of heaven that he felt could hack it. He's the only one allowed to do that, by the way. The rest are strictly into bartering energy. Now Shade . . . Shade's a precognitive when he's on Earth. He has the power to see into the future. He uses that to find and manipulate the kinds of energy he wants. They say he likes to pose as a fortune teller and tells people just enough to stir up a mess of trouble. Then he harvests the fallout and sends it here."

"But I thought negative emotion was not good for these people."

"Hey, when you're starving you take what you can get. Besides, the Ampliphi can filter a lot of it. They have to. Some of it . . . Some of it's pure terror. That's Adrian or Daedalus, usually. Daedalus harvests from disaster areas. All that death and destruction, all the grief that comes with it. And Adrian." Here she shivered and it was clear it wasn't for dramatic effect. "He can walk in dreams and uses his power to create the *couche mal.* Bad dreams, cherie. He can make the vilest and most frightening nightmares possible in the human mind. The way he makes them scream. . . . They say it takes everything the Ampliphi have to filter it, just to make it palatable. Even so, they can't feed that to just anyone. They say Adrian's a beast. As twisted as the nightmares he harvests from. He's Ampliphi Rennin's Gatherer. I suppose I'd be a little twisted if I was Rennin's Gatherer."

Jewel seemed to realize she'd taken a tangent and shrugged off everything she'd just said. "I do have a point here," she assured Asia. "I mean to say, you coming here has disturbed a very delicate process. But I suppose that doesn't matter much when you and Julian can put out the kind of power you do. Though I dare say you can't let it all go all of the time like you did last night. You'll burn yourselves out. Julian should have had more care. You may have fed the world, but being Beneath takes it out of you as it is. Keep throwing away your energy like that and you'll be dog tired and sick before you know it."

"Wait, are you saying that humans can get sick like they do for lack of energy?"

"Sure. The longer you stay here, the more susceptible you become. Never on the scale they do, but it'll run you down right quick."

"Julian didn't tell me that," Asia said with a frown.

"Oh, cherie, don't be hard on him. Seems to me he's got his hands full running a colony and dealing with Kloe besides. Now he has you to manage as well. Plus he and Kloe are going to have to hunt the colony for a new Gatherer. Well, Kloe will anyway, but since Julian knows his men better than anyone, he will be her best guide."

"And this is what you wanted to tell me? To be careful with my energy?"

"That and to give you some insight into how things work around these parts. Now if I thought you'd be staying here, my advice to you would be very different. But I can tell you'll be gone soon. They aren't going to want to lock up *kindra*. They need you too much. If there's even the slightest reason to get you off, you'll get off. And count yourself lucky. The law here is a harsh mistress. You can take that from me."

"Oh, I believe you. I've already learned that the hard way." Asia paused for a moment, considering her next question. "Jewel, are you here for the rest of your life?"

"No, cherie. They figure since my murder was self-defense, I only have to stay here ten years . . . or rather two contracts. That leaves me with five years to go. And I found me a nice pliable gentleman last night. Rich as Midas, too. I'll be real comfortable these next few years."

"My God, Jewel. It seems so harsh! How can you just take it like this?"

"Well, one, because I don't have a choice, cherie. And two . . . well, it suits me. I like being kept in comfort, spending the day relaxing and prettying myself up for my man in the evening. And I like sex. You pick them right, get one that won't smack you around, maybe one that knows what he's doing in the boudoir . . . and I stay safe, clean, warm, well fed, and basically content. You can bet that wouldn't be the way of it in a women's prison on Earth."

"But, Jewel, there's danger here, too," Asia said. "Maybe from the guards, certainly from the other women. Most of them are violent offenders, aren't they?"

"And that's where having the most power comes in handy. I know this place like the back of my hand, know how to get what I want when I want it, and that's valuable to even the meanest bitches here. I'm not saying there aren't those who'd like to knock me down from my spot as head bitch in charge, but I can take care of myself."

"Jewel, just what exactly did you used to do when you were on Earth?"

Jewel smiled mischievously and rocked her shoulders back and forth flirtatiously, but she didn't answer. Instead she got to her feet and walked toward the door. "Do me a favor, cherie?"

Asia laughed. "What can I possibly do for you?" she wanted to know.

"Stay alive through to next week. I have a lot of money riding on you."

With that, Jewel gave Asia a friendly wave, walked out of the door, and shut it behind her with a resonating clang.

When Julian came for her within an hour after that, he found her much subdued.

"Are you all right?" he asked her. "Did something happen?"

"Not really," she somewhat assured him. "I've just got a lot to think about. A lot has happened to me in the past two days."

"I know. And I'm sorry about that," he said quietly.

"I know you are. And . . . I'm starting to understand why you feel you have to do the things you do. I still think some of it is wrong, but I do understand."

"Asia, I can't explain to you how precious you are. And not just to me."

"I know. I'm going to be an excellent source of energy," she reiterated.

"No," he said sharply, reaching to take her chin in his hand and making her look into his eyes. "Asia, you're a phenomenal source of energy. What you did last night . . . How can I possibly explain how shocking and fantastic that was for everyone in this world? You should have seen the Ampliphi, Asia. They looked just like you and me for the first time in decades. They were made flesh and flush, as real to touch as you or I. I've never seen anything like it. There's been *kindra* and *kindri* before . . . but never between a human and one of us. You've proven that we're on the right track trying to find ways to seed our world by using humans. No one can refute the evidence before them. Not after last night."

"Julian, I want to ask you something and I want an honest answer."

"Of course. I have never lied to you, Asia. And I never will."

"I'm glad to hear that." Asia carefully stepped onto the walkway outside her room, her heart flitting inside her chest as, for a moment, she looked down on the clouds. "Remember how you told me you spend days introducing women to the idea of what your world is like?"

"Yes."

"Do you tell them everything, Julian?" She turned to search his gaze. "I mean everything. About how the need for energy in this place will even drain them eventually? About the law and what will happen to them if they break it? About the *okriti*?"

"Don't you think," he said, "it would be very wrong of me to invite a woman to come live in this place without telling her all of those things?"

"I think it would be very wrong of you. So, is that a yes? Do you tell them everything?"

"Everything, Asia. And if you need a witness to that fact, you will soon have one. Your sister is at the colony and she waits for you even now. You can ask her what I did and did not tell her when I invited her to this world."

"I think I will do that." She began to walk ahead of him. "But not because I think you are lying to me. More because . . . I can't understand it. I can't understand how my sister could willingly walk into all of this."

"Nor can you understand why she would walk away from you," Julian added a little too knowingly. "You want to know why she left you."

"I admit that I do," Asia said softly. "I see all the risk and the danger here and . . . I see the need. It's the need that attracted her, I know that much. She would have taken one look at those starving people in your clinic and that would have convinced her to chuck everything and go."

"But still . . ."

"Yes. But still." Why had her sister turned her back on her forever without so much as a good-bye? Well, maybe she didn't have the opportunity, but didn't it ever occur to Kenya that Asia might suffer from her sudden disappearance? Didn't she care about how much that had hurt her? And the way it had happened, the way it had made her believe she'd been brutally victimized. Kenya had to know Asia would think the worst when she simply ceased to exist. Didn't she care how that made Asia feel? And did it make Asia incredibly selfish to be thinking that way when she could now see the scope of the reasoning for her sacrifice? Was she being petty?

"You're being a big sister," Julian soothed her suddenly, his hand anchoring at the bend in her waist. "You're entitled to feel hurt and abandoned. But I want you to know . . . she almost told me no, Asia. She said her big sister would never stop searching for her and she couldn't do that to you."

"But something changed her mind?" She stopped to look into his gentle green eyes. "You changed her mind."

"Yes. I helped change her mind. She didn't have the heart to leave us starving and in need. Your sister has a generous soul."

"Tell me. What would have happened to her if she had said no? She would have known all about your world. . . ."

"She would have awoken as if from a dream, and it all would have faded from her like a dream. The way I do this is almost ethereal. Nothing is real, nothing feels real, unless she's there in the dream. She says yes or no while in the dream, all the while thinking it's as real as you and I speaking here now. But if she says no, it's half gone by the time she opens her eyes. The human mind in its dream state is a fascinating thing, and for us a very useful one. What we cannot change, however, is waking memories. At least, not without doing severe damage to the mind that houses the memories. It's why we don't like being forced to send someone back to the Earth plane. The memory wipe is very severe. You lose everything. Anything. Even who you are. I sometimes think that is a thousand times crueler than trying to keep you here."

"But it is a choice. A terrible choice, but a choice just the same."

"Don't even speak of it as a choice," he said with sudden harshness. "You talk about our crime and punishment here as though it were the most distasteful thing you had ever heard of, but it would be criminal for someone to eradicate Asia from this plane and all others, erasing her until she was nothing but a blank body. Your black belt, your business, your life would mean nothing to you. At least here you have purpose and direction."

"I had purpose and direction where I was," she said, but for the first time her speech was absent of malice.

"I know. But that's gone now. One way or another, Asia, it's gone forever and you have to accept that. I pray you do and that you never even consider making so rash a choice as that."

She didn't have anything to say to that. Asia turned away from him and continued along the walkway. Her mind was weighing heavily with thoughts and she almost ran into someone. Luckily they had sharp reflexes and proved able to balance them both quickly. She realized her victim was Lucien, and she smiled at him.

"Lucien! How are you?"

"I'm wonderful today, thank you for asking. But you are largely responsible for that."

Asia had to fight off a sudden blush. Did this mean everyone knew she had slept with Julian?

Again, what a petty thought, she realized. What did it matter? Everyone was flushed and happy with satisfied appetites. Today, no one was starving. Wasn't that all that mattered?

She realized it was. It really was. And it made her feel pretty damn good, too.

"So, you're a free woman. How does it feel?"

"It's a relief," she said as he turned to lead her through the guard gate. "I know I'm innocent, but for a while there I wasn't certain the Ampliphi would care about little details like that."

"They are not wholly unfair, Asia," Lucien said in a gentle scold. "They are just . . . You have to realize that we don't have the luxury of exploring gray areas here. The Ampliphi are very black-and-white creatures. Something is either black or it is white to them. With a civilization on the brink of extinction, it is how we have been forced to become. To you it seems harsh, but we live in a very harsh world here Beneath, Asia."

"It is harsh, but at the same time I understand why you feel these are your only choices. Sometimes I wish Earth functioned more in areas of black and white and spent less time wading around in the muck of the forever gray. There are many injustices in my world because of that."

"And I am certain there are some here as well. No society can claim perfection. But perhaps you can become one of our critics, Asia, and keep us on our toes. One strong voice among us can see powerful changes made."

Julian spoke up from behind her. "And one strong voice can find purpose in a new world." She had just stepped on the solid ground outside the prison gates, and the sense of freedom that washed over her compelled her to turn to him and nod.

"Perhaps it can," she allowed. The strong surprise that flashed in his expression was quickly chased by pleasure. She gave him a little smile, feeling really happy because she was free and she was on her way to see her sister at last. Kenya was the only one she had, the only one she'd ever had. Though she was the older one, Asia had been lost without her role as Kenya's guardian and caretaker. Granted, her sister was an independent-minded woman with a strong personality, but in the end it had always fallen on Asia to watch over her and keep her safe. It had truly devastated her to think she had failed so miserably in that role.

Asia walked between the two men as they made the trek back to Julian's colony. She was still wearing the gown that Jewel had lent her, her hair slowly drying in its tight, upswept braid. The day was warm and the path a little dusty, so she picked up her long skirt in one hand.

"Julian, were you able to discuss Ariel with the Ampliphi? Did they listen to you at all?"

Julian shook his head. "I tried, Asia. I promise I did. But they said she must be punished for trying to put an innocent woman through the fate of a nightfly. It's an unconscionable act. And I have to admit, I agree with them, *zini*. I came too close to losing you . . . and my people came too close to losing the treasure that you will become to them. As soon as she is well, she will go to the nightfly colony, where perhaps she can be a useful and productive member of our society again." Julian took hold of her free hand, lacing his fingers tightly with hers. "I'm sorry. I know you do not agree with this."

"No, but I do understand. I see things today that I didn't see yesterday. And perhaps . . . perhaps I can help Ariel. I made a friend in the nightfly colony. I could ask her to look out for Ariel. Perhaps protect her from the harder parts of adjustment. It won't free her, but it can help."

Julian gave her hand a squeeze and she was aware of his grim smile. He appreciated what she was trying to do. She felt the emanation almost as if he had spoken to her. Asia was startled to realize that this was the way Julian's people spoke to one another. Perhaps it was clearer to them, but given time she would be able to understand much better.

Given time.

Asia realized then that she had all the time in the world to learn. Julian had made his point to her. There was no turning back. Everything behind her was basically destroyed forever. She could imagine her life going up in a mushroom cloud, nothing left of it but herself and her memories of what had been. And the only way they would let her go back to Earth would be to destroy that last little bit. And she wouldn't do that. She was a powerful and skilled woman. She had crucial abilities that she could offer to this troubled world. And not just the ephemeral energy they so craved, either. That was an accidental ability, an incidental skill. There were other things she could do here.

After all, any world with criminals could use a bounty hunter. Or perhaps some kind of guard or protection force. There had to be a way to be useful besides sitting around like a protected little princess. Because that much she knew she could not accept.

"I do not envy you, my friend," Lucien said to Julian with a deep chuckle. "She will not be easy to protect."

Julian frowned darkly in reply. "She is very stubborn."

"She is standing right between you," she said tartly. "Don't stand there talking over my head. My God, you people are so—"

She was cut off by a wicked-sounding snarl that seemed way too close for comfort. And sure enough, in the next instant an enormous creature came hurtling up over the side of the cliff and barreled into the trio. Julian tried to keep hold of Asia, but the beast, partly scaled and partly furred, ripped them apart even as it raked savage claws down Julian's arm, cutting deep, bright pink furrows into his flesh.

Lucien and Asia rolled with the momentum as they were pushed aside, both coming up onto their feet as two other creatures followed the first into the fray.

"*Abraxi!*" Lucien emanated to her as he grabbed for the crescent around his waist. Stepping away from Asia so he had room, he swung the gleaming silver wire around over his head and then sent the balled end of it flying toward the beast that was shoving Julian down into the dirt, preparing to maul him. The ball and wire wrapped around a raised arm until the ball caught the wire again on the opposite side of the thing's huge biceps. Then Lucien threw all of his body power into yanking the thing hard toward him.

The wire went straight through the creature's arm, cleanly dismembering it and dropping the limb to the ground. The bloody and now free wire came whipping back and Asia had sense enough to duck out of the way. Meanwhile, she had been sizing up one of the other creatures scrabbling toward them. It was smaller and lighter than the other two and she was willing to bet it was the female of the group. She hated that she didn't know a damn thing about what was attacking them, but she also knew she couldn't just stand by and let them gang up on Julian. She dug her feet in and ran at the *abraxi* with all the power she could muster in a short tackling run. She aimed for the knees, hitting it below its center of balance, plowing it off its feet and sending it tumbling over her back.

Julian now had the chance to recover, rushing to his feet and pulling a wickedly curved blade from a sheath strapped to the lower lumbar region of his back. The rune-carved blade was silver and black, for all of a second. Then it was dark pink with blood after he decapitated the injured beast, dropping it straight to the ground and opening himself up to the second male.

Asia focused on her own battle, likening it to wrestling with a lion. A black belt or two didn't make a damn bit of difference when it came to confronting a wild creature, but she was going to give it her best shot. It took her only a minute to register what she supposed were the animal's vulnerable points. The one constant in all species: the eyes. Making her fingers rigid on her striking hand, she punched down deep into the thing's eyeball socket, feeling the vitre-

ous fluid explode from the rending pressure of her
vicious strike. Then she slammed all of her weight
down on a single knee, aiming for the creature's
throat, because if you can't see and you can't breathe,
you can't fight.

Not well, anyway.

But the thing about a wounded beast was that they
invariably went berserk, lashing out on instinct. Asia
didn't move out of reach fast enough to avoid the
swipe of the thing's enormous paw. Claws sank deep
into her flank, and once the creature had hold of her,
it threw her back as far as it could. Burning pain
lanced through her entire body as she rolled with the
strike the best she could.

And rolled herself right over the edge of the cliff.

"Asia!"

Lucien only had one choice and one instant to react.
He flung out his weapon, aiming for whatever part of
her body he could see as she disappeared over the
edge. The killer razorwire spiraled around her leg,
snagging her hard. Lucien ran forward to lessen the
impact, fearing he would cut her straight to the bone,
and he was barely able to keep from plummeting over
the side himself. Luckily, Julian had already dispatched
the second male and was able to grab Lucien by the
back of his leather vest.

"Don't lose her!" he cried out to his friend, who was
down on his backside and sliding in the soft soil
against the brace of his feet as he gripped the crescent
end of his weapon with all of his strength.

"God, she's heavy!" Lucien grunted. "The wire is
going to slice right through her! You have to grab her!"

Julian let go of Lucien, trusting him to hold on while
he dove for the cliff's edge. Dropping his blade to the
ground to free his hands, he leaned out into the open

air to find Asia. She was there, barely—a good two fee
down the side of the cliff, her leg extended up toward
him, her foot just out of reach. The wire spiraled from
her thigh all the way down and around to her calf, and
everywhere it dug in was brilliant with scarlet red blood

And right below her was the narrow ledge the
abraxi had congregated on before they'd heard then
coming along and decided to attack.

"Julian!" Lucien warned, his braced feet sliding
even farther, sending rivers of soft sand down onto
Asia's dangling body.

"Let her go! Asia, you have to get that ledge! Asia!

"I hear you!"

"Lucien . . . as easy as you can," Julian begged him

Lucien nodded, sweat breaking out on his forehead
as he let himself slide as far as he dared, then dropped
forward and let go at the very last instant. Even so, he
overshot the cliff and would have fallen over if Julian
hadn't snagged him at the last minute. It had taken a
lot for Julian to take his eyes off Asia, but he couldn'
let Lucien sacrifice himself. Both men fell back onto
the dirt, dragging hard for breath. Then, after look
ing at one another, they both scrambled for the cliff
side. Looking over the edge, they both exhaled in
violent relief to see Asia lying flat-faced on the scrawny
little ledge. But if it was strong enough to hold three
abraxi, it was strong enough to hold one woman.

The trouble was neither of them could tell if she
was moving . . . or even breathing.

Lucien tried to reassure him. "I bet she's passed ou
from the pain. The wire must have cut her deep."

"Asia wouldn't pass out from pain," Julian argued
pushing back away from the cliff. "You keep an eye on
her, you hear me? I have to find something to act as a
rope."

"You could go back to the colony . . ."

"And leave her down there all that time? Bleeding and God knows what else?"

"I'll watch her," Lucien agreed.

Julian left his friend to keep watch and ran away from the trail and into the tree line. The trees grew thick ivy vines as fat around as his wrist and notorious for being incredibly strong. In fact, it was a species similar to the one that they used to make all of their homes and walkways. The only difference was, the kind they used had natural fluorescent properties that provided for ambient lighting.

Julian was searching for a suitable vine, scrambling up into the trees to reach one that was long enough. They had to do this quickly. The longer they stayed in one spot, the more dangerous it became. There could be *okriti* in the area, or other *abraxi*.

Julian used his blade to saw through the thick vine and then hurried out of the tree to gather it up in great heavy loops. He was out of breath and drenched in sweat from fear and exertion by the time he made it back to the edge of the cliff.

"Did you see her move?" he demanded.

"Not yet."

"Stand back away from the edge and loop this around your back and make sure you anchor your feet well."

"Julian, you can't go and get her. I can't hold both of you."

"Well then, what the hell do you think I should do, Lucien, because she clearly can't get up here on her own, and the longer we leave her down there, the more blood she's going to lose! And it's not as if we have a huge supply of human blood around to replace it!"

"Just . . . just give her a minute! Just a minute,

Julian. Call down to her and see if you can get her to wake up. If not, then I'll be your anchor and you can go get her. I'll find a way to do it."

Julian nodded and crawled back up to the edge of the drop-off to look down on Asia. She hadn't moved so much as an inch.

"Asia! Asia, wake up! Come on!" He continued to shout down to her while Lucien watched his back for wildlife and other dangers. "Asia! Damn it, Asia, you wake up!" he yelled in frustration.

It did the trick. He saw her twitch and then suddenly she bolted into consciousness, sending his heart into his throat when she nearly sent herself over the end of the shelf in the process. But she caught herself and threw her back up against the solid side of the cliff.

"My God!" he heard her cry out at the close call. Then she seemed to realize he was above her and she turned eyes of blue fire up to him. "These cliffs are a deathtrap, and you people are fucking insane for living this way!"

"Yeah, because the land is so much safer," he returned to her, so damned relieved to hear her voice he was on the verge of laughing at her.

"Okay . . . You kind of have a point there," she gasped as she leaned over to inspect the damage to her leg. She was convinced she was going to find herself cut straight to the bone, but to her relief the diffused spiral and Lucien's quick thinking had spared her from losing a leg. Now she was left with the quandary of whether it was a better idea to take the razor wire out of her leg or leave it be for the time being.

"I could sure use a rope or something," she remarked, temporarily opting to leave the wire alone until its owner could tell her the wisest way to remove it.

"Do you think you can climb?" Lucien asked from

over Julian's shoulder. "The vine we have is too thick
to tie off around you with any decency."

"Great. A vine," she muttered loudly. "I'm on freakin' *Gilligan's Island.*" She carefully got to her feet, grit-
ting her teeth against the pain in her leg. "Maybe we
can make me a bra out of coconuts next."

Julian exchanged a puzzled look with Lucien. Lucien
shrugged. If anyone would know what she was talking
about, it would be Julian. Since he was clearly clueless,
they had no choice but to take her literally.

"We don't have coconuts Beneath," he informed her
gravely. "And I'm sorry, but our women don't wear
bras." But neither did she, as far as he knew. He wondered why she suddenly wanted one.

"Never mind!" she shouted up at him, clearly sounding angry. Well, he could hardly blame her. She'd yet
again fallen into danger from his world. And it was his
fault. He should have been paying better attention. "I
can climb up some, but you guys gotta pull me up real
fast, too. I'm getting a little dizzy down here." Whether
it was from blood loss or vertigo, she couldn't say. She
wouldn't know until she reached the top of the cliff.

Julian hurried to drop the vine down to her, watching its progress toward her. She inspected it for
strength once she had a hold of it, but he worried she
wouldn't be strong enough to hold on, so the minute
she climbed on and shouted "Ready!" he and Lucien
hauled her up with all the speed they could muster.
When she finally popped up over the side of the cliff,
he rushed to grab her, dragging her onto the stable
and relatively safe ground.

"Thank God," he breathed roughly into her hair as
he hugged her tightly to him while still on his knees.
"I thought I'd lost you," he said, kissing her lips with
fervent fear still on his tongue.

"I'm not out of the woods yet," she remarked as gently as she could. She pushed away from him to show him her torn and bloody leg. "You couldn't think of anything else?" she asked Lucien with a small laugh.

"Sorry, it was the only thing I had." Lucien knelt down beside her leg and inspected the wire. "You may want to wait until we get to the colony. They have something to numb the pain there."

"It would be faster to go back to the holding colony," Julian pointed out.

"I'd rather wrap wire around my other leg," she said dryly.

"Here . . . I can remove the axe head and the ball so the weight doesn't pull on you. Then Julian and I can support your weight between us." He reached to do exactly that.

"I can carry her," Julian insisted gruffly.

"Not with that arm you can't," she argued, pointing out the gaping injury that had been all but forgotten. "Besides, I can walk." She stood up to prove it, but ended up mostly hopping on one leg when the wire tightened under the flex of her foot and the shift of her weight. The men quickly hooked her between themselves, Julian moving so she wasn't resting on his shredded arm.

That was the way they walked for hours, like a wicked three-legged race, moving as fast as they dared while keeping an eye out for more danger.

Asia never thought she'd be so happy to see Julian's colony. They took her through the gate and had to relinquish Lucien's help because the walkways weren't wide enough for three to walk side by side. So Lucien followed as Julian took her into the clinic.

The empty clinic.

Nothing impacted her about the events of the previous night like walking into a clinic full of empty beds. All the children, all the elderly patients—every last one of them had been sent home.

Save one.

Ariel.

The Companion was asleep when they first came in, and because the place was empty, they had the whole staff of clinicians all to themselves. They lifted Asia up onto the surgery table.

"Come, Gatherer," one of the medics said, "let me tend that arm."

"I am no longer a Gatherer," he said sternly. "I am only Magistrate. And the arm will wait. I will see Asia tended to first."

"Magistrate, it's already been several hours. I need to disinfect and stitch the wound or you will draw illness and sepsis."

"I said it will wait!" he barked at the hapless medic.

"Julian, please. I'm fine. They'll treat me just fine," Asia assured him, reaching out to touch a warm hand to his wrist. She gave him a squeeze, with just the message in her eyes insisting he listen to her. "You can sit right beside me and let them fix your arm and be able to see me the entire time."

Taking her cue, the medic pulled up a chair for him. Reluctantly, Julian took a seat and held his arm out for care. Then he affixed all of his attention on the doctors who were tending to her leg.

Chapter 16

Asia felt someone rubbing her cheek in gentle strokes and she slowly stirred herself awake, forcing her eyes open a tiny sliver so she could see Julian. After all, he was the only one who touched her in that soft, almost reverent manner.

It took her a moment longer to finally pry her eyes open.

"Hey, stranger."

"Kenya!"

Asia was wide awake in an instant, sitting up to grab her sister and hug her tight. The moment she felt Kenya's arms wrap tightly around her, the impetus of the last few months rushed up on her. She felt her throat close up as she felt her sister's warmth bleeding into her, smelled the wonderfully familiar nutmeg fragrance her hair always seemed to have. Kenya was strong, for all she was a petite thing, and she all but squeezed the breath out of Asia. She always hugged as tight as she could. She'd always been the most enthusiastically affectionate person Asia had ever come across, and this time it brought tears to her eyes.

She had believed Julian all of this time that she was

alive and well, but it hadn't been truly real for her until this very instant. Before she could get control of herself, tears of pure relief chased each other down her cheeks.

"Oh my God," she said hoarsely, hugging Kenya with brutal power. "How could you do this to me?" She wanted to know. "Didn't you know I'd be out of my mind? I'm so mad at you!" And yet she clutched her like a drowning woman would cling to driftwood.

"I know," Kenya whispered, her soft South African accent so wonderfully familiar. Their mother had been something of a free spirit, traveling the globe where the will and the wind took her. A matter-of-fact kind of woman, she'd named her children for the country or continent they'd been conceived in. After Kenya was born, their little family had lived in South Africa for five years, and Kenya had never shaken the accent from her speech. "I'm so sorry, darling," Kenya soothed her sister, running her long fingers warmly over her head and hair again and again in order to comfort her.

When Asia could bear to do so, she let up on her sister, allowing her to sit back so she could inspect her for hardship or damage. There had been so much danger since she'd arrived Beneath that she couldn't believe Kenya had survived here unscathed.

But in truth, Kenya had never looked so beautiful and healthy. She was wearing a very elegant, delicately embroidered shawl draped gently over her head and hair, the deep maroon color of it positively breathtaking against the smooth mocha warmth of her mulatto coloring. Her eyes were lined with what looked like liquid gold, her lashes touched at the tips with it as well, making her beautiful russet eyes stand out in stunning relief. Her black hair was braided with handpainted beads of maroon and gold. In the lee of her throat was an exotic hennalike tattoo with sweeps and curlicues and a finishing point that led provocatively down her breastbone and tickled the top of her cleavage.

The way she was put together reminded Asia of the haremlike feel of Jewel and the women of the holding colony. The only difference was that she could see and feel the power of Kenya's happiness.

"Can you forgive me?" she asked, touching Asia's face gently. "I never wanted to hurt you. But I hope that now you have been here a while you can understand why I couldn't turn my back on them. It's such a simple thing, a thing that I can create so easily and have in such surplus. For once I could make a difference. A child that would die would become a child that could live . . . and all because of me. People live and survive, because of me."

She spoke with such heartfelt passion, and Asia knew this was important to a soul like Kenya's. In their travels with their mother before she had died, they had seen the very worst the world had to offer. Starvation, violence, prejudice, and hatred. Death for no reason other than being born to the wrong family name. But what had jaded Asia had made Kenya determined to make a difference. Wherever there had been a need for manpower, where the efforts of volunteers meant the difference between saving homes or animals or lives, Kenya had traveled there and done her best. She'd done everything from sandbagging swelling rivers to rescuing pets evacuees had been forced to leave behind.

That was why Asia had believed Julian when he'd said she'd volunteered to come to this place. Kenya could never have the heart to say no to so much need. No matter the danger to herself. No matter the broken heart of a sister left behind. And Asia was not truly hurt by that. On some level she'd always known that Kenya's driven heart would take her away from her one day. But when Asia had thought a killer had stolen her sister from the world that needed her—that she could never have accepted. But Kenya had no idea Asia would make such an assumption. She'd never have guessed that the tenacious Asia would one day come so far to find her.

"Of course I forgive you," Asia whispered reassuringly to her, reaching to clasp her hands, unable to stop reassuring herself that she was real, vital and alive. "And I do understand. But you had me so worried. So very worried." She swallowed back more tears, the relief still toying with her emotions.

"I know, sweetie. I'm so sorry. I can't say it enough. But look at you! Here not even two days and you look like something kicked the ever-loving shit out of you!" Kenya lifted the edge of the woven blanket to peek at Asia's leg. She was bandaged from hip to ankle, the light fabric bandages stained with her blood. "For a while there they were afraid they'd need to give you a transfusion. Their medical care is competent enough, but there's not exactly state-of-the-art equipment around here. The doctor said you needed a lot of stitching. How do you feel?"

"Sore," Asia confessed. "Worn out. You picked a hell of a place to take a permanent vacation."

Kenya snickered. "It has its challenges, but I've been worse places. Your problem is you've been a metro girl for far too long. You've forgotten what it was like living in the bush."

"I remember it well enough," Asia corrected. "Enough to know I hated it."

"Spoiled."

"Me? Look at you. You look like a sultana. You're hardly roughing it!"

"True," Kenya said, smiling very slyly. "They treat women here like precious treasures. We want for nothng and, it's true, we are well and truly spoiled. On the downside, you should see how much they freak out when I insist on working in the clinic of whatever colony I am in. But I think I should be there. They can take energy from me and it heals them."

"I've been told you can burn out if you aren't careful," Asia warned.

"If you try to feed the world every night, I imagine you would," Kenya said pointedly. "But feeding little bits of happy energy to some hungry babies? I'm not worried about that."

"No, you wouldn't be." Asia sighed.

"Never mind giving me that disdainful big sister routine. You're the one who fed out so much energy you made the Ampliphi *solid*. Do you have any idea when the last time that happened was? I think it was before the last plague. That's quite a feat."

"Solid, hmm? I'd like to see that."

"I'm told it won't last. But I wouldn't be surprised if you saw one or two of them around here shortly. You've caused quite a stir in this plane, sis. Beating an attempted murder rap, mouthing off to Ampliphi, proving you're *kind*, and feeding the masses? What are you planning to do next? Single-handedly repopulate the world?"

"As if," Asia snorted. "I'm not the mothering type."

"Liar. You raised me well enough after Mom died."

"I meant giving birth and diapers and all that stuff," she grumbled.

"Well, you have time to decide about all of that. Right now you need to focus on healing. Do you need me to get you anything?"

"Do you know where—?"

Asia didn't finish. She saw a flash of movement over her sister's shoulder and reacted before she could

even think. She shoved Kenya off her bed, sending
her to the floor with a crash just as Ariel would have
struck her in the back. Instead, Asia caught Ariel's
wrist, controlling the scalpel-like instrument she held,
twisting her and forcing her down onto the bed. Still
controlling Ariel's hand and her weapon, she brought
the blade up to her throat, ready to kill the bitch once
and for all for daring to attempt to hurt her sister.

But years of restraining her own anger in all the
worst of situations served her well, and instead of
doing what she had every right to do, she disarmed
the troublesome twit and threw the blade away so
hard it thunked fast and deep into a wall.

"You know, I'm getting sick and tired of you and your
goddamn knives," she growled into the face of the
other woman. "You come near me or my sister again
and I'm going to beat the fucking Christ out of you.
You got me?"

At this point the feeble girl was crying, whimpering
in pain from the way Asia was holding her down
against her injured shoulder. She'd probably ripped
open a few of Ariel's stitches . . . she was fairly certain
she'd done so to her leg.

"Lucien, I think it's time Ariel was escorted to the
holding colony." The deep, familiar voice brought her
attention up to the open door of the clinic. "Since she
seems hearty enough to cause trouble, I think she's
well enough for the trek."

"I agree," Lucien said grimly as he moved to Asia's
bedside beside his friend. Julian was seething with re-
pressed anger as he reached for Ariel and yanked her
out from under Asia and onto her feet. The redhead
cried out in pain, curling into herself in a combination of pain and fear.

"But Julian! I'm doing this for us!" she cried. "Thing

could go back to the way they've always been! We've been perfectly happy all of this time! Then she comes and tries to kill me!"

"Enough! Everyone, including the Ampliphi, knows that you did this to yourself!" Julian gave her a shake, unable to help himself before he threw her back into her own bed. "You'll be nightfly before this day draws to a close. You're the holding colony's problem now."

"No! It's a lie! Why would you believe her over me? You don't even know her! She's a lying, violent human!"

"This violent human had me beg the Ampliphi for mercy for you." Julian rounded on her. "She owed you nothing, almost suffered the harshest fate this society has for women because of you, and yet she felt enough compassion for your sick and twisted little mind to try and help you. But I am not so compassionate. I am glad to see you go to your fate. You have painted your own picture of the future. Now you can stare at it night and day and see what you make of it. Lucien, take her away from here before I forget myself," he commanded.

"Gladly," Lucien said.

Even so, he was infinitely more careful with Ariel than Julian had been. He gathered the girl up and carried her out of the clinic; within seconds her sobs for Julian were the only thing left of her. Asia rolled onto her back with a wince, exhaling with relief that it was finally over, and watching Julian hold a hand out to her sister. He helped her back into the chair beside the bed and she rubbed her bruised bottom on one side, giving her sister a sidelong look.

"Now you know you just did that because you're mad at me," she joked.

"Hmph. I would have pushed harder had I really had time to think about it," Asia retorted.

"This from the woman who claims to love me so much."

"Hey, I followed you to another plane of existence!"

"You know, you can only take that one so far," Kenya remarked with a grin. "It's going to get old."

"Mmm. Something tells me you've been treated like a princess for way too long."

"Hey, I'm not the one who's all set up to become a queen."

The mock disconcertment suddenly became the real thing. "I'm not set up to be anybody's anything," Asia said defensively. She avoided looking at Julian, pretending to inspect her injured leg.

The fact was, her words stung him. Badly. He was trying to understand what a big adjustment this was for her and that she kept running into the darker side of his world, but he could swear she attracted trouble like a magnet and that no matter what he did, it was always going to find her. All he could do was somehow try to help her adjust, and while he was at it he had to prove to her that things Beneath weren't always about struggling to keep their heads above water.

He had thought that their coming together would make things better, that it would help her to relax and truly see the benefit she could provide to others. But he hadn't counted on just how powerful their combined energy would be, and now it was only shining sharper light on her and making her more uncomfortable. Oh, he knew she saw the plus side and that she appreciated the benefit she was to his people, but the more special she became, the more she seemed to fight it.

Kenya, on the other hand, thrived on being special. He had never seen a human being adjust as quickly and flourish so wonderfully as she had. She had even found a more valuable niche to top off the blessing she was as a source of energy. She was very useful to the colonies she visited. Not satisfied to be just a pretty face to be adored and worshipped, she lent a hand wherever she could.

Perhaps this was something her sister needed as well? The truth was, for all he felt connected to her at his soul, Julian didn't know enough about Asia to help her adjust better. Since she had gotten there, he had done little more than try to force her to accept what she could not change. Maybe, he thought, he'd been going about it all wrong. Maybe he needed to draw her sister aside and figure out the best way to help her adapt.

At the same time, Julian could feel the sudden barrier Kenya presented. Until now, Asia had only had him to depend on. He knew that was part of the reason they had become so suddenly close and in need of one another. Had there not been so much to fight against together, Asia probably would never have . . .

The thought that followed hurt even more than hearing her outright reject him. The understanding that it had only been a matter of circumstance for her really tore into him.

This didn't make any sense! Why did she not feel the same things he did? It was clear they were *kind,* but she didn't *feel* that connection. She was cold to it, as if he were nothing more than another stranger. How could she not feel it? It was a visceral sensation, one he felt all the way to his soul. So deeply, in fact, that every time she tore herself away from him, it left him raw and bleeding in places he simply could not reach. This wasn't the way it was supposed to be. *Kind* felt one another, to the point of being overwhelmed. If the Ampliphi had come simply to observe them, they would never believe they were *kind.* If not for the sating wash of energy their world was infused with, they would have called him a liar and he would have paid with his life by now.

How could he fix this? Could it be fixed? Was she simply not capable of feeling the connection of *kind?* Was it her humanity that prevented it? Or was it her human experiences that had burned the ability out of her once and for all? Was she truly so jaded that nothing could touch her anymore?

No. He refused to believe that. If that were true, then they would never have been able to produce the reaction they had . . . and she certainly wouldn't give a damn about her sister. As Julian watched them interact, it was clear to him that there was a great deal of love between them. In fact, that had been clear from the start of all of this. Asia would never have felt such a passionate hatred of him if she had not felt the deepest of love and pain for the loss of her sister. So it was clear she could feel.

The question was, how was he going to get her to feel what she was so steadfastly denying?

Yes. That must be what she was doing. It wasn't that she couldn't feel the connection of *kind,* but that she was fighting it with all of that remarkable and beautiful fury. It was more than clear how stubborn she could be. So all he had to do now was find a way around all of the walls and obstinacy. But the very idea of it was exhausting to him. If he had learned anything about Asia, it was how powerful she could be when she was fighting something.

In the end, Julian was afraid she would never need him anywhere near as much as he needed her.

It was three days before they let her out of the clinic, and by then she was going utterly stir-crazy. Worse than that, though, the glut of energy everyone had so benefited from was well and truly in fade and people were beginning to find their way back into the clinic. Like her sister, it was the children that tugged at her the most. They seemed so fragile. Little boys who should be running around and playing, getting into all manner of trouble that had nothing to do with a shortage of energy or the bogeymen that lived on the land.

When it came time for her to leave, she made the mistake of asking for her own place to live. Immediately after she did so she had this terrible feeling like she had played the part of Ariel and plunged a huge butcher knife straight down Julian's spine. She hadn't meant to hurt him or offend him. She only wanted what her sister had, a place to call her own where she could find peace and time to sort her own thoughts out. She tried not to get angry when he adamantly refused the request, angrily telling her that she would simply have to find it in herself to suffer his company.

"You cannot live on your own!" he gritted at her.

"I am perfectly capable of taking care of myself!"

"You've made that abundantly clear," he said through his teeth.

"Then I don't understand why I don't have the right to have a place of my own! My sister lives alone!"

"Your sister living on her own wouldn't shame me in front of all of my *kin!*"

Ah. Well. She hadn't thought of that. As it was, they'd had the fight in front of the entire clinic staff. Now she couldn't pretend it hadn't happened and she couldn't take it back. Again, she wondered when she'd gotten so selfish that simple things like this had stopped occurring to her. That didn't mean she wasn't right. She did deserve a place of her own. It was the least he could do considering how he had forced her into this new way of life. But he didn't see it that way. This claim he felt he had on her, that he felt gave him complete rights to her, came with cultural expectations. As it was, he had lost face with Ampliphi Kloe. She had removed her good graces and protection of the colony along with her mark on him. And the longer he took to help her find his replacement, the longer the colony would suffer for it.

For the first time Asia began to truly appreciate the amount of pressure he was under. What an undertaking it must be, to be responsible for so many, and all the while knowing nothing you did would ever be enough. No wonder he was clinging to her so hard, trying so hard to convince her she would be best off with him. On the other hand, it wasn't exactly romantic, all these ulterior motives. In fact, none of it seemed to be truly personal. She felt like a means to an end to him and nothing more than that.

Just the same, to spare him the embarrassment he spoke of, she found it in herself to share his home with him. But it was as if they were two strangers sharing space. He left her alone for the most part, not making any overtures or even so much as touching her if he could at all avoid it, and she was inclined to let it stand that way. Not that she wanted to purposely deny anyone anything, but she wasn't going to sleep with the man just because that's what everyone else wanted her to do.

The issue, unfortunately, made her sister shake her head every time they visited with one another.

"Will you please stop doing that?" Asia demanded when the sigh and clicks of the tongue became too much for her to ignore any longer. "It's bad enough everyone else stares at me like I'm the village idiot. I don't need it from my own sister."

Asia went back to chopping vegetables for the meal they were planning on sharing.

"I'm sorry. I just don't understand you," Kenya said

with a frown. "What is so wrong with him? I mean, clearly you are or were attracted to him at some point!"

"Attraction is not the issue! I'm just sick of everyone telling me what I should be doing! When have you ever known me to do what others felt they had a right to tell me to do?"

Kenya shrugged and grabbed up one of the chopped bits Asia had created, munching on it thoughtfully. "True. You've always rebelled when people told you you couldn't do something, that you weren't capable of it. But this is just the opposite. We all know you can do this already."

"Oh for . . . God! I slept with the man! So what! Does that mean I have to be stuck with him for the rest of my natural born life? I don't work that way, Kenya! I don't have relationships. When have you ever known me to have a relationship?"

"Never. But there was never so much at stake before, Asia. What has he done that's so terrible? What is it you don't like about him?"

The chopping resumed, faster and a little more recklessly. "I didn't say he did anything wrong. Or that I don't like him. He's an honorable man. He's just expecting too much out of the wrong person. And frankly, he should have thought of all of this before he forced me to come here." She glanced at Kenya. "Not that I'm not happy to see you and know what happened to you. You know that I am."

"I know. And that isn't the issue. The issue is this: Ampliphi Kloe is neglecting the colony. She is angry with Julian and she knows the best way to make Julian suffer is to make his people suffer. And yet, even though he knows they are in trouble, you have said yourself he hasn't made so much as one little pass in your direction. Do you have any idea what that must take?"

No, she didn't. And she hadn't thought about it in that way, either.

"I didn't tell him he couldn't make a pass at me," she said softly. In fact, she had to admit she'd found the whole thing damn puzzling. What had she done to put him off anyway? He'd been nothing but aggressive and overwhelming . . . and then suddenly nothing.

"I beg to differ," her sister said. "You asked for your own place, remember? You may as well have kicked him in the balls."

Asia winced. Just when the hell had her baby sister grown so damn insightful?

Probably around the same time Asia'd grown selfish and thickheaded. But she hated feeling this way! Why did she have to be the designated asshole in this situation? Didn't she deserve any independence? Any right to the way she was feeling? Any choices?

"Asia, we grew up in a half dozen different cultures. Why can't you see the cultural aspect to this? The relationship of *kind* is like . . . well, it's like happily-ever-after is on Earth. Only to a much more intense degree. It's what every person here wishes for. What they crave. And here you are with it sitting right in your lap, just waiting for you, and you keep pushing it away and want nothing to do with it. And you wonder why they look at you like the ultimate alien? And you don't attribute any emotions to the man you live with. It isn't just about embarrassment and filling a need for energy for him. It's about hurt. Rejection. It's about facing a one-way street when you've always been told to expect a two-lane highway."

"That isn't my fault," she said softly. "I didn't ask for any of this. I would never ask for something like this. I'm just not made for happily-ever-after. I never was."

"Oh? Then why did you always read me those fairy

tales when I was younger? Why would you raise me to have hope for something if you didn't believe in it?"

"I raised you to believe in Santa Claus, too," she argued. "That doesn't mean it's real or that I think it's real."

"No, but it means you believe in what it stands for. Imagination, goodwill toward men, magic in the mind of a child. Believing. You went out of your way to see that I believed in all of those things. It's what made me into the person you are so proud of."

"I am proud. Proud that you had the strength not to end up like me. Which is someone who's too jaded to believe in all of those things. I always thought that you were stronger than me in that way. Why do you think I always had to fight everything else so hard?"

"Oh, Asia," Kenya said, dodging the knife to give her a powerful hug. "I think you sell yourself short. I think all your fighting has just been your way of hanging on to what little you felt you had left. And that means it is still there. Just somewhere deep down where even you can't seem to find it anymore."

Asia dropped the knife and reached to pry her sister off her. "I can't do this. No. *I can't do this!* You're all expecting something out of me that I just can't do!"

With that Asia abandoned her sister and left her house. She couldn't stand there and go around and around in circles having the same argument. Of course her sister expected better from her than she was capable of. Her sister expected better from everyone around her! Why couldn't Kenya just accept that she wasn't that person?

Asia hurried down the walkway, the fading light around her making her aware that it was dusk and she was making a mistake by being out when the *okriti* were on the move. And no sooner did she have the thought than something huge fell from the walkway above her, hitting the path in front of her hard. She gasped, coiling to the ready, but it only took a second for her to realize who it was.

"Julian!"

"You aren't supposed to be out here now," he said with a dark frown. "You just gave half the colony a heart attack."

"I'm sorry. I was just on my way home." She tried to move around him, her arms wrapping tightly around herself. Small comfort for the way she was feeling.

"I thought you were eating with your sister."

"What, are you my keeper now, too? Am I going to have you keeping tabs on me every second for the rest of my life?"

"Probably so," he shot back. "This isn't Earth. Your independence is admirable, Asia, but here it is also a deadly thing. Are you going to use it against me that I give a damn what happens to you?"

"Of course you do," she said pushing past him. "If something happens to me, your precious village would starve to death. I get it. I understand."

"Asia!" He snagged her by an arm, turning her back around to face him. "That was not what I meant! Can't I worry about your safety without being accused of having some ulterior motive attached to it?"

"No. Everything you do has to have an ulterior motive attached to it, Julian, just by nature of who you are and your role here. Just by nature of the reasons why you brought me here in the first place. And neither one of us can do anything to change that."

"But maybe one of us can stop blaming me for that," he said sharply. "I am sorry I brought you here. I swear to you, I regret nothing more than bringing you here against your will."

And for the first time he didn't add his usual clause, "but there's nothing you can do about it."

"Thank you," she said softly, finally looking up into his eyes. She had gotten into the habit of avoiding his gaze, the emotion and depth of it so compelling she found it hard to stand her ground on any single issue. "Thank you for that. I really needed to hear you truly regret this. You've said it before, but I never believed you until now."

"Well, believe me when I say you've made me regret it these past days."

There was real pain behind those words and reflected in his eyes. It made her sister's warning about the emotions he felt ring loudly in her conscience.

"I'm sorry," she said with sincerity. "I'm not out to make you feel guilty. I just . . . I'm just not what you want me to be. I wish that weren't the case, but it is."

"And how do you know what I want you to be? Have you asked me?" He shook his head. "I don't want you to be anything other than yourself. Do you think I want a woman who is somehow different? Someone softer, maybe? Someone more delicate? I do not want that. I want you. With your incredible strength and the fortitude of several of my men, you could survive anything this world throws at you. And that, that is exactly what I want."

"You want a *kindra* to feed your people with."

"Yes. And I will not pretend otherwise. Instead, I am honest with you about it. I have been from the start."

He was right. He had never lied to her. She, on the other hand, could not say as much. In fact, it was lies and trickery that had gotten her into this mess in the first place. All of this time she had spent blaming him for her being here, but the truth of the matter was that she had gone on a pursuit of her sister and had been willing to take any road it led her down. It had led her here, and now she was trying to blame someone else for it?

"You've always been honest with me," she acknowledged. "I know that. But it's also a lot of pressure to put on a person."

"And that is why I have tried to give you your space these last days."

"But the expectation still hangs over me. Not just yours, but everyone's." She sighed. "But given their situation, I can't fault them for that." She reached out to dust away a piece of lint from his shirt, her fingers slowly smoothing over fabric and warm flesh beneath. "I suppose I should try to be just as fair to you."

"It's all right," he said softly. "I understand why you feel the way you do toward me."

"I don't hate you," she insisted, stepping closer to him so he would look into her eyes. "I don't."

Julian couldn't bear looking into her gaze another moment without touching her. Maybe she didn't realize that the whole of her palm now rested on his chest, but it was the closest thing he'd gotten to an invitation from her in days and he simply didn't have it in him to pass it by. But, very aware of the tenuousness of their honesty with one another, he was extremely cautious as he raised gentle fingertips to the crest of her cheek.

"I am guilty of many things, Asia," he confessed to her, "including forgetting to tell you how beautiful you are to me. I make the mistake of seeing how strong you are, how tough you are, and forget that even the most hardened woman needs soft words. I saw you walking up to me that first night and all the rest of the world fell away from me. It was like standing over a chasm much more dangerous than this one could ever be." He glanced down over the edge of the walkway. "I've walked a hair's breadth away from falling since the day I took my first steps in this world, but I never feared it until I thought I was falling away from you. I've been falling for days and . . . all I want is the smallest thing to catch on to. But I won't take your hand unless you want to give it freely. No matter the cost to me and mine. This means nothing to me if it means nothing to you."

Asia drew a difficult breath, her throat suddenly closing tight with unexpected emotion. It blindsided her, the way he made her feel by speaking the exact words she most needed to hear. He was willing to give her the freedom she chafed for, no matter what it might mean for the colony. No matter what it meant for his entire world.

"I feel so selfish whenever I speak to you," she said hot and fast, her breath rushing tightly with her feelings. "You give and give until your back might break from it. I swear, I think the first time you ever took anything for yourself was the day you took me . . . and even then, even then you thought of others before yourself. I don't do things like that. I never have. Everything I do or did centered around myself. My needs, my school, my money, my sister . . . my revenge. I don't know how I ever raised such a selfless girl like Kenya."

"Shh," he hushed her with the sweep of a thumb over her lips. "You are too harsh. You did what was necessary to survive. It's what you do. Don't criticize yourself for wanting to survive. You accuse my world of being a harsh environment, but I have spent years on the Earth plane. I know all too well how judgmental and coarse it can be. And I am not as selfless as you would make me out to be. For example, my desire to kiss you right now is pure self-indulgence."

Asia smiled slowly under the press of his thumb.

"You're being charming," she accused him.

"Perhaps," he said with a sly little grin, "I am being so in order to get what I want. I can be selfish in that way."

"Really?" She laughed at him, her eyes everything

disbelieving. "How terrible of you. Maybe I shouldn't indulge you."

"I wouldn't. It would send the wrong message."

"True," she agreed even as she stepped in close enough to rest her body up against his. All teasing came to a sharp halt as his eyes flickered closed in pleasure just to have her near again.

Asia reached up to cup his face in her hands and then rocked forward onto her toes so she could touch her mouth to his. She had never once fooled herself into thinking it would be a matter of a simple kiss. Their history was blatantly clear. There was never going to be anything but the rawest of heat between them. No sooner had her mouth opened against his than his fingers were diving deeply into her hair and his hands were holding her still for his total assault. His tongue swept into her mouth and brought liquid fire with it. Nerve endings she didn't even know she had flared wildly to life in her scalp, sending wicked chills chasing down the back of her neck and her spine. He took over and commanded the kiss, sweeping against her tongue in a devouring tangle of need. It was as though he couldn't help himself, almost as though he wanted to but found it a hopeless matter. And just when she needed to draw for breath, he broke away from her, stepping back and releasing her so he could turn away from her.

"Julian?" she gasped breathlessly, reaching to touch him and to steady herself in the process.

"I'm sorry," he said, reaching to wipe slightly shaking fingers across his wet mouth. "I shouldn't be like that with you. I should be patient and give you space. But . . ." He reached to grip hold of the hand she'd laid against his arm. "All you have to do is touch me and I forget. I forget everything but the way you make me burn."

She stepped closer to him once more, reaching to

run her hand up over the powerful flex of his biceps, and then she leaned in to kiss his shoulder through the ashen gray fabric of his shirt.

Julian took it for the invitation that it was. He turned back to her, circling a hand around the side of her graceful neck, pulling her up to the descent of his mouth and kissing her until he thought his entire body would melt from the fire of it. She made his very blood boil, stoking his unquenchable craving for her until he could hardly see straight, never mind keep his balance on a dangerous walkway. He broke from her mouth so they could both draw hard for breath, his gaze searching around them in a desperate sweep for somewhere close to take her.

Suddenly he reached for her, swinging her up into his arms. She wrapped surprised arms around his neck only an instant before he leapt from the walkway they were on and landed on the one directly below. They landed hard, but his powerful legs easily absorbed the impact. She was gasping for breath from a combination of fear and excitement as he turned to take her into a near building.

She didn't even question whose house he had brought her into. The moment he put her on her feet so he could shut the door, she reached to strip off the first of two shirts she was wearing. When he turned back to her she threw herself against him and seized him for a long and passionate kiss. She tangled her tongue sensuously against his until he couldn't even see straight. Dragging his fingers through her thick hair, he pulled her mouth free of his so he could turn his desperation to other places on her body. He started with her sweet-smelling neck and immediately worked his way down her breastbone. The remaining shirt she wore was no better than a tank top, only far briefer over her midriff.

Her hands were fast and hungry over the muscles of his chest and arms. She didn't stop touching him, and he didn't want her to stop. He separated from her only long enough to strip the offending material of his shirt away, it being the only thing standing in the way between her warm hands and his own bare skin. Shucking the thing off and throwing it away, he grabbed for both of her hands and returned them to their forays across his chest. She wasted no time in taking over for herself, and then moved to creep her fingers up the entire length of his back. Julian groaned softly into her mouth as he caught her up for another kiss. He wanted to do nothing more than spend hours eating his way across her mouth. Then he recalled there was plenty more he wanted to do to her.

Julian grabbed her suddenly by the backs of her thighs, close up against the cheeks of her buttocks so he could haul her up against him and wrap her long, luscious legs around him. She was very obliging as she clung tightly to him, making it easy for him to walk them through a beaded curtain and into a back bedroom. When she realized where they were, she gave him a wicked little smile.

"Just where the hell are we?" she wanted to know.

"Lucien's home. Don't worry, he won't be walking in on us or anything."

"Isn't it a little rude to be doing this without asking?" she asked even as she ran eager hands over the ridges of his belly.

"Yes. It's very rude. But Lucien will understand."

Julian then knelt on the bed and laid her back across the mattress. There was a soft creak of stressed ropes as he moved his weight over her, but it was the only protest. Not that she would have noticed. Julian had reached for the hem of her shirt and was slowly pushing it up, his mouth falling on her skin as he bared it one inch at a time.

"You always smell so good," he murmured softly against her belly. He paused just long enough to breathe her in, his eyes drifting closed in pleasure as he did so. "Especially now," he said, "when you are aroused and smelling of imminent sex."

"Hmm. Imminent sex. That sounds so dirty," she breathed, wriggling provocatively beneath him at the very thought.

"I have a great many dirty thoughts where you're concerned," he assured her.

"Oh, really? Do tell," she invited him in soft temptation.

He smiled at that, moving up to nuzzle against each of her breasts briefly before licking her flat across one of her nipples straight through the fabric of the tight little shirt.

"For instance," he said hotly just before he took a nip at the thrust-out nipple his teasing had provoked, "I can't wait to have the taste of you on my tongue. And I think you know I'm not talking about this taste." He dragged up her shirt to expose her to him, his mouth closing over her voraciously, making her cry out and arch her back.

She took several beats to catch her breath and then said, "I have no idea what you're talking about. I think you need to explain it to me much more clearly."

Now there was an idea, Julian thought as it made his entire body flash hot with arousal just to think of all the explanations he had for her. He quickly slid a hand beneath her back, lifting her up only an inch or two so he could fully strip off the annoying little shirt that was in his way. Then he reached to grab hold of her skirt around its waist and wriggled down so low on her hips that he could see the top of the soft new growth of hair that appeared without care of waxing to maintain her groomed state. He found the fuzzy black growth tantalizing in the extreme and he quickly reached to place a line of kisses down from her navel to the very edge of her waistband. He took his tongue across the new line of pubic hair, licking the taste of salt and arousal off her until she was squirming and moaning softly.

"Is this becoming any clearer?" he asked as he jerked the skirt just another inch farther down. He rubbed his chin against her through the material of her skirt, breathing deeply of the pungent musk he knew he'd caused her body to create. At this point she was breathing so hard it was all he could hear. "I want to stick my tongue deep inside you," he murmured against her skin. "I'm going to do that very, very soon, *zini*."

He earned a moan for his blatant taunting and he decided to tease her just a little longer. He reached for the hem of her skirt, sweeping it up over her legs, bringing his fingers up the insides of her thighs as he spread her knees to the outsides of his shoulders. She had long since given up wearing any underwear, figuring out that the women Beneath didn't much care for underclothing. To be honest, Julian didn't much care for them either. He liked her just the way she was, as natural as possible at any given moment.

Julian took his tongue up along the inside of her right thigh. He felt her shifting restlessly between his hands, her hips lifting as if she would chase his tongue if she could. She needn't have worried. Being this close to the sultry smell of her excitement made him forget all about teasing her and instead made him crave the taste of her. He quickly jerked her skirt down her thighs, impatiently leaving her in order to shed it and just as quickly returning to lick her right at the very cleft of her pussy. She hitched out a gasp, restless fingers suddenly finding a home in his hair, holding him where he was, as if he were going to try and escape her. In fact, there was nothing further from his mind. Her long, glorious legs wrapped around his shoulders and back and he suddenly needed to somehow be inside her. The fastest and best way he could come up with was to run a finger through her wet lips and thrust it deep into her. The act sent her hips shooting up off the bed, and his mouth was there to catch her. He devoured her flavor like a starving man, all the while feeling her body clamp down around his finger until he couldn't do anything other than take it as an invitation for another finger. He slowly worked both fingers inside her, all the while dancing his tongue across her clit.

"Oh yes," he hummed against her, making her cry out when the vibrations of it nearly sent her over the edge. "You're utterly delicious, *zini*," he told her.

And now he was wishing he had taken the time to finish undressing himself before undertaking this zealous pursuit of her taste. He was so incredibly hard it was bordering on painful, and wearing the closely confining denim from her world was driving him up the wall. Not that he was in any kind of a rush, but it was damn uncomfortable.

Julian shifted his position just enough so he could use his free hand to unbutton and unzip his fly. He hastily pushed away the material until he felt like his aching cock could breathe a little. Then he returned his focus to his woman and her vibrating body. His lips caressed her intimate folds again and again, rubbing over her until she was moaning in long chains of breath, her hands against his scalp guiding him perfectly into doing what she liked best, where she best liked it. It was so erotic, so perfect, that she exploded into a sudden orgasm against his mouth, her wild shout echoing up into the conical ceiling of the room. Julian felt her body milking his fingers in rippling waves of contractions, and suddenly it was all he could think of, feeling her wrapped around him, squeezing the very life out of him.

But Asia had other ideas. She waited until he had pulled free of her body before she rolled over underneath him, the act allowing him to move his teeth across her buttocks in slow, gnawing bites. He growled in frustration, though, when she slipped away from him, turning around so she could lean over his back and slowly kiss him down the length of his spine. Julian didn't know how much of this he could possibly take. The feeling only intensified when her wet mouth slid over the cheek of his backside, her teeth returning the naughty nips he'd stolen first from her. When she slid her hands into his pants and down his legs, he quickly accommodated her as she stripped him. He turned over as she pulled the denim free of his feet, then she set her teeth against his left shin and slowly began to nibble back up his leg. He was so hypersensitive by the time her hair fell across his erection he had to resist the compulsion to come right up off the bed. And if he thought that was unbearable, he was in for a hell of a shock when she worked her hand between his legs, her fingers molding the malleable flesh of his balls even as her hair danced tormentingly across his cock.

"Asia," he ground out. "You're driving me out of my mind."

"Mmm, what's the matter?" she teased him. "Not game for a little tit for tat?"

And as she said that she resituated herself over him so her very fine breasts came to rest on either side of his cock. The sight of her reaching for him, making sure he was set surely between her tits, was absolutely incredible. He held his breath as she worked her hand into the mix, a brief flashing lick of her tongue coating her palm with saliva as she grabbed hold of him and slowly began to stroke him through the valley of her breasts, pressing him with merciless pleasure against her breastbone as she surrounded him perfectly. Julian couldn't restrain the instinctive need to thrust against her, his groan of pleasure mutating into a fierce growl. But it was all too slow. There was no hope of any kind of satisfaction for him, and he had a sinking feeling that was exactly her plan. She had provided him with a taste of the best of decadent pleasures, yet denied him anything resembling relief. Not immediately anyway. And just when he thought he might scream from the torture, she sank down an extra few inches and caught the head of his cock in her hot, eager mouth.

"Asia!" he coughed out, his hands diving forward to grip her by her hair, his blind need to thrust seating him deeply against the back of her tongue. She twisted in his hold, sucking him in as fully as she could. Like every other thing she did, she fought for control of the situation. He was inclined to give it to her, but he just couldn't make himself relinquish the need to move. Neither could he take his eyes off the picture of his dick disappearing between her lips again and again, that irrepressible smile of power and satisfaction so damn evident in her shining eyes the entire time. He ought to have just relaxed, lay back and let her do her worst, but he couldn't find it in himself to do so. He didn't think it was possible for any sane man to keep still with such a dynamic mouth working his most intimate flesh. And he was completely neglecting to mention the work of her determined hands.

"Asia, do something!" he demanded blindly of her.

The command made her laugh against him, but she did shift into a steadier, drawing rhythm. It wasn't quite what he had meant, but it would more than do. He didn't really want her to take him all the way over the edge like this. He craved the feel of a connection between them. He wanted too badly to be inside her, making fierce love to her until neither of them could see straight. But she clearly had other plans.

Julian closed his eyes, no longer able to focus as his entire body curled in anticipation. She fondled him straight down his shaft and over his sac, working her mouth over him with deep drawing speed. Julian began to gasp hard for breath, feeling the world spin out of his control. He looked at her and thought he had never seen anything so beautiful in all of his lifetime. In the end, it was that understanding that brought him over her finely worked edge. He felt his entire body draw up tight right before he exploded in release.

He hardly expected her to continue moving her mouth over him the entire time he came, but she did exactly that, dragging him to hell and back on a train of pleasure. He shouted out her name, his hands fisting savagely in her hair as he jetted hot release into the back of her quickly working throat.

The instant he was finished he had to pull away from her. He was on a sensual overload and he simply couldn't bear to stay in her mouth a minute longer without shouting the bloody roof down around them. She didn't come easily, of course. She had to have her way in the form of an impudent lick of her tongue. Then he pulled her up the full length of his body and held her tight and close while he tried to catch his breath.

On the edges of his awareness was the ever-present buzz of the village around them. Always. So he was more than powerfully aware of the fact that a days-

long spiral of hunger and neglect had just come to a
resounding end. Kloe had not seen fit to feed her
colony even once since Julian and Asia's lovemaking
had last glutted them all. The clinic had been filling
rapidly, and tenuous holds on health had been rapidly declining. Now, once again, the powerful energy
of them coming together had restored his people to
full and satiated status. It wasn't near as far-reaching
an effect as last time, but it was enough to take care of
his people where his Ampliphi would not.

And it only took him moments to realize that Asia
was just as aware of that as he was.

"She's wrong, you know," she said with soft breathy
note.

"I know she is. But there is nothing I can do about it
except complain to the other Ampliphi—and if I do
that, it will only make relations worse between Kloe and
the colony. It's just a matter of us holding on until she
gets over her anger. The fastest way for that to happen
is a sacrificial lamb. I have to find someone I know is
going to be able to represent us well and yet have the
patience to manage Kloe's temperamental nature."

"It's not fair. One thing shouldn't have anything to
do with the other. Kloe needs to be above letting petty
emotion affect her obligation to serve this colony.
The other Ampliphi should see to it that she does.
And I don't care if she doesn't like it, you should go
to them and make them force her to behave herself."

Julian sighed. "You don't understand. The Ampliphi are an unpredictable lot. They could just as
easily side with her or opt not to do anything at all,
forcing us to resolve the issue on our own. But by then
the damage will have already been done. If I do anything further to anger Kloe, it could cost us lives."

"And meanwhile children are suffering in the clinic,"

Asia said angrily. She pushed away from him, getting up off the bed in her frustration, needing to move and settling for pacing the room. "Julian, there has to be answerability. The way it stands now, your Ampliphi are nothing more than spoiled children, a clique that sides for or against an issue based solely on whims that have nothing to do with justice! As long as they are able to rule over everyone with no system of checks or balances, your entire society is at risk and you will never recover from your plagues." She looked at him with vivid, troubled eyes. "Julian, the Ampliphi themselves are just another plague if they can get away with hurting you all like this."

He sat up in the bed, draping an arm over a raised knee. "Well, luckily for my people they have us to compensate."

She frowned at that. "They need more than that. They need to be able to depend on those responsible for taking care of them."

"I'm not saying you're wrong," Julian said, trying not to smile to see her reacting so passionately on behalf of his people. "But you see what an untenable position I am in?"

"Yes, of course I see it. And I hope you see how this is part of the overwhelming pressure I am feeling. If I don't sleep with you, people will starve? Where's the freedom of my choice in that?"

Julian felt fingers of ice crawl up his spine, his whole body going stiff.

"I would never want you to be with me out of some sense of obligation to the people around you," he said tightly. "Has that been what this was all about?"

"No, of course not," she chided him. The relief he felt to hear her say it was extraordinary.

"Good. My reasons for being here have nothing

to do with the benefit of my people. I hope you understand that."

"I'm not a child, Julian." She laughed. "I am perfectly capable of deciding for myself if I want to have a fling with someone for my own reasons. I can separate my desire for good sex from my desire to see people treated well and fairly."

She might as well have thrown a volley of knives into his heart. Feeling a bit numb with a shock he knew he shouldn't be feeling, he moved carefully to the edge of the bed.

"A fling?" he asked very carefully. "Is that all this is to you?"

She hesitated, taking note of his tension. She immediately stood still, tension lacing her entire body. He could tell the minute she felt vulnerable having the conversation in the nude because she began to cast her eyes around, looking for her clothes. She found her shirt and tugged it on.

"I didn't mean to make it sound quite that way," she said just as carefully. "Don't take anything I say too personally. I'm angry because of Kloe."

Julian took his cue from her and bent to retrieve his pants from the floor. He tugged his jeans on as his thoughts whirled around what she had said and how it was making him feel.

"Why are we here?" he wanted to know, indicating the bedroom around them. "Are you just . . . Do you just indulge in some kind of impulse of the moment when you decide to sleep with me? Is that all it is?"

She laughed at that as she found her skirt. "Don't kid yourself. You were acting on your impulses just as much as I was."

But the difference was he wasn't acting only on those impulses. For him, it meant much more than

the passing fancy of the moment to take her to his
bed. There was a lot more on the line than just the
physical for him. And once again he was being forced
to realize she didn't have that problem. She didn't
now, and possibly would never, feel these encounters
with the same depth that he did. And he was beginning to seriously doubt she was ever going to be able
to. She was too compartmentalized. Too disconnected
from her needs and her emotions. She was too different. She was alien in ways that had nothing to do with
her being human. In fact, she was so cut off from her
humanity sometimes it simply floored him.

Feeling like an idiot for thinking things had somehow changed for her, Julian got up and left the room
in search of his shirt. He needed distance, and he
needed it fast—before he let his emotions run away
with him and he ended up saying something he was
going to regret.

"Julian! Where are you going?" Asia asked, hurrying after him. "I don't want you to leave! I didn't
mean this had to end or anything!"

His only response was a short, barking laugh. He
shrugged into his shirt as he headed straight for
the door.

"Julian!" She chased him down as he hit the walkway,
reaching to grab for his arm. He turned on her with
a low, savage sound that made her come up short.
Then he pushed her hand away and started to walk
away from her.

"Julian, wait."

He shook his head and continued to walk off,
trying to put distance between them and failing miserably because she was dogging every step he took.

"Julian, are you going to make me chase you all over
the colony or are you going to stop and talk to me?" she

demanded. "Why don't you stand still for two seconds and ask me what I want instead of assuming you already know what it is!"

That had the power to stop him in his tracks. He turned to face her, surprise limning his eyes so clearly she had to bite her bottom lip to keep from laughing at him. Even so, she was afraid her amusement radiated into her eyes.

"You find this difficulty of mine amusing?" he asked severely, his outrage emanating in a sudden suffocating sweep.

"No, I find your bullheaded ideas of chivalry amusing. And while I appreciate the thought, I'm trying to tell you it's not really necessary. I'm trying to tell you to take me home so we can continue this in the privacy of our own house. I'm trying to make you understand that I want you to seduce me and that there's nothing wrong with either one of us wanting that."

Apparently, she didn't have to ask him twice. This time she had to bite back a giggle as he grabbed her hand and began to pull her along behind him. However, it took her a full minute for her to realize they weren't headed toward home. Instead, he took her to her sister's house.

"Go in to your sister. Have your scheduled meal with her. I am not going to do this game with you," he informed her bitterly.

"What game?" she wanted to know, her shock clear on her features.

"Asia, to you this is about sex and physical passions. And that's all it is. I can't play that game with you. I can't pretend to feel less than what I do just to make things more comfortable for you. Not when it comes to physical intimacy. That asks too much of me. Now go to your sister and leave me be to clear my head!"

"Stop it! Don't you dare brush me off like I'm some kind of pesky schoolgirl who doesn't know what's good for her! And don't accuse me of taking this situation lightly!"

"But you are taking it lightly." He rounded on her. "You are not willing to take it any other way, you've made that abundantly clear to me. Now you're pissed off because I won't let you play with me like a toy you can bat carelessly back and forth? You're fucking with my head, Asia! What's worse, you're fucking with my heart! And you either don't even know it or you just don't care. Either way, I'm not willing to find out what I'm going to feel like come sunrise when you decide you want nothing to do with me and mine again!"

Asia just stared at him, knowing her mouth was gaping wide open, and she couldn't even bring herself to close it.

"There you go again!" she accused him. "Making me out to be the designated asshole around here! You speak to me like I have no feelings. Stop treating me like this!"

"How else am I supposed to treat you? You keep telling me over and over again how you are not capable of the things I want from you. Now I am telling you I won't take half measures from you. You either want all I have to offer or you want nothing at all from me. You make your choice and you stick to it, damn you, because I don't know how much more of this I can tolerate! You're killing me in slow doses, can't you see that?"

She hadn't seen that. Not until he'd said as much. All of this time he had talked of her being his *kindra*, about the energy to feed his colony, about all the things she had to accept . . . what she could and could not do. But never once had he said a single thing about his heart being involved. She'd known she was hurting him, but she had thought that was through embarrassing him and wounding his ego. Until three minutes ago she hadn't heard word one about tender feelings and emotions. ·

Not that it mattered anyway, she told herself fiercely. She didn't do relationships. She wasn't capable of the emotions he was laying claim to. He was right. If he wasn't willing to do things on more shallow terms, then they shouldn't have anything to do with one another.

But then why did her chest suddenly hurt with the very idea of letting him walk away? That was easy, she told herself. He was growing on her. He was a good man, an impressive example of what real manhood should be about. Honesty, honor, responsibility, and the determination to see things were carried through to the end. He was . . .

He was going to walk away and leave her there. He was going to tear himself away from her rather than fight his way through to her. He was going to surrender the war when all the battles had yet to be fought. It didn't make sense! He'd been dogged and determined from the very beginning, yanking her through from one moment to the next fearlessly and with emphasis. Why would he give up now?

"Because I can't wrestle you for every single inch of a heart you refuse to even think about opening up to me," he said. "No one can possibly have the amount of fight you expect them to go through to prove to you they are worth your while! You have made yourself too hard, Asia! You wanted to be impenetrable and you've succeeded. Now you are surprised to see me concede?"

"I—" She didn't know what to say. Her brain was swirling with input and hard words. He was emanating such powerful anger and other painful emotions it was impossible for her to see straight.

"You win," he said softly. "Isn't that what you always want? To win? Well, you win. Once and for all. You've convinced me to walk away and give up. You want to live on your own? Fine. You can have it. You want to be with other men?" His hands clenched into fists and she could see a pulse ticking in his jaw. "Go. Take yourself to any other colony but this one and do whatever you please. I'm done. I'm done."

Julian turned his back on her and walked away.

Chapter 17

Kenya came to the door to retrieve her sister when several minutes passed without a single hint of emotion emanating from the other side. The entire colony had to have felt that horrible argument between Julian and Asia. Julian's sense of defeat and the extraordinary pain of the sacrifice he was forced to make would be felt for miles.

Kenya dragged a rather shell-shocked Asia into her living room.

"Are you okay, honey?" she asked as her sister dropped into a chair.

"I—I don't . . ." Asia shook her head. She was such a jumble of confused emotions Kenya couldn't sort them out any more than her sister could. So, instead, Kenya went to make her sister a simple cup of steeped herbs, similar to teas from home. It would have a soothing effect. Perhaps it would help.

Or perhaps not.

No sooner had Kenya handed her sister the cup than there was an awful racket against the other side of her door. Hurrying to see who was intruding on them, Asia's sister was shocked to open the steel door to the violently flickering form of Ampliphi Kloe. The Ampliphi did not wait for an invitation before she pushed past Kenya and confronted Asia with sparks of outrage jumping from her to physically touch Asia's exposed skin like static shocks.

"You ungrateful creature," Kloe shouted in Asia's face. The aggression emanating off her was overwhelming. "Have you no idea what that boy gave up for you? Have you no appreciation for the magnitude of the gift I gave you in him? Impudent girl! You would throw away the most precious thing this entire world has to offer you?"

"Hey! Back off her!" Kenya demanded of one of the creatures that had most reverently intimidated her since the day she had gotten there. But all it took was seeing her sister under attack for her to fly in the face of the Ampliphi.

"Sit and quiet yourself!"

Kenya suddenly learned why the Ampliphi were so feared. She was plucked from the air and thrown back into a chair with nothing but the power of the Ampliphi's energy.

It was the biggest mistake Kloe could have made.

No one . . . *no one* touched Asia's sister with intent to harm without answering to her.

Asia was on her feet in the very next instant, getting up into Kloe's face with the full force of all the rage and anger she'd been holding in store. A sharp electrical arc leapt from Asia to the Ampliphi, making Kloe cry out in shock and surprise.

"Don't you dare touch my sister!" Asia snarled at Kloe.

Ampliphi Kloe stood back away from the creature that had just done the impossible to her. She had used energy against her! Kloe was energy itself—how could this human beast use energy to attack her?

"You dare?" Kloe hissed in Asia's face. "You dare to attack one of the Ampliphi?"

"No! She didn't attack you!" Kenya shouted, fear lacing her entire soul.

"I'll dare that and more if you even think of touching my sister again!"

Kloe saw red. She lashed out in her rage, reaching to grab the object of the dare into her power, seizing Kenya's entire body and throwing her across the room until she hit a wall and fell into a slump on the floor. Triumphant and powerful, she turned on the human who had dared to challenge her.

Asia didn't even think in terms of solidity. She saw a threat to Kenya and she had to neutralize that threat; that was all that she saw and all that she had to consider. She grabbed for Kloe, something she didn't realize was impossible, caught hold of the Ampliphi, and threw her down to the floor with all of her power and all of her fury backing it up. She didn't realize the explosion of her own violent emotions burst out into the colony like a nuclear blast.

Kloe hit the ground so hard that she actually felt extraordinary pain. It was unthinkable. The human could not only touch her, but had taken control of her. Now she held her down to the ground with a hand around where a normal woman's throat would be.

"Ungrateful, you called me?" Asia spat into the other woman's face. "You who look down on all of these people as if they were little ants you might step on if only it strikes your fancy to do so? How dare you take one of the women these people deem precious and treat her as if she were nothing! And I am supposed to believe you've come here indignant on behalf of the man you viciously stripped from your service? I am not that stupid! This is nothing but an excuse to get up in my face! Well, you wanted a brawl, sister, and you've got one!"

Asia hauled the Ampliphi up to her feet and with an explosion of emotion sent the faded creature barreling back into the same wall she'd thrown Kenya against. By the time Kloe hit, she had become fully flush and flesh with the power of the energy Asia was sending explosively into her, so she felt the landing crack against her back, ribs, and skull.

Kloe dropped into a stunned little heap right next to the unconscious Kenya, but when she saw Asia round a chair to come after her she began to scramble back away from her in sudden and incomprehensible fear. She had woefully underestimated the human girl. She'd had no idea a human could become so powerful in their world. Where had she gotten so much energy from? How had she learned to wield it?

"On Earth, in jujitsu, it is called *ki*. The inner focus and force of personal energy," Asia answered the unspoken question. "I mastered it long ago. And maybe it's because Julian is my *kindri* or maybe it's just me, but whatever it is, it's more powerful than you are, and I am not going to let you forget it!"

Asia lunged for the other woman and Kloe was forced to defend herself. The resulting clash of energy rocked the little house like a C-4 detonation. Items in the house rattled, shattered, and fell, and the house itself shuddered on its foundations.

"I'm going to kill you," Kloe snarled. "You're a poison to this plane. You must be destroyed!"

"Yeah, good luck with that!" Asia backhanded Kloe across the face, and then focusing all of her *ki,* she hit her with a rigid palm in the dead center of her breastbone. Once, about three years ago, Asia had taken down a 350-pound man with the exact same maneuver. She figured if it worked then, it would work now.

Kloe hit the floor like a marionette, all loose limbs clattering numbly around her. The Ampliphi gasped for breath, trying to force what would not come naturally as the impact of the strike against her chest kept her from succeeding. Asia stepped over her, a looming virago ready to prove what a human being was truly capable of when pushed to her breaking point.

"So? Nothing to say? You who would rather let children starve to death than get over your petty emotions? When was the last time you fed the people of this colony? Hmm? The day Julian and I made love? You're blackmailing him, punishing him by punishing his people, and you're supposed to be *revered*? These people are supposed to respect you? More like they live under the thumb of your terrorism! You sick, psychopathic bitch! Have you nothing to say for yourself?"

"Greison," she ground out, a sudden smile of satisfaction coming over her.

Too late Asia whirled to see the second Ampliphi that had entered through the open door. Greison was on her before she could react defensively, so she tried to act offensively.

"Let's see what you'll have to say when I am through with you!" he snarled at her.

Julian felt the first blast tear through the village and knew instantly where the central point of it had been. He'd run as fast as he could, leaping dangerously from one level to the next. He burst into Kenya's house just as Greison made his threat and grabbed hold of Asia.

Julian knew the very instant he saw him what he was going to do to her.

"*No!*"

Julian was across the room and on Greison in a heartbeat. As faded as he was, Julian didn't know how he was going to have any impact, didn't know how he was going to stop him from erasing everything that Asia was. But it was pure fear and the energy of his outrage at the thought that allowed him to strike Greison. He grabbed hold of the male Ampliphi with both hands and dragged him back away from Asia. It was watching Asia drop to her knees limply, as if she'd lost all use of her backbone, that made him scream out in primal fury. And as Asia had done to Kloe, the impact of his emotional energy bludgeoned Greison until he was flush and solid. It gave Julian a target to take out his fury on, and he unleashed it with everything that was in him.

"What did you do to her?" he raged in Greison's face. "Did you take her? *Did you take her from me?*"

"You're too late," Greison emanated even as he struggled to remove Julian's hands from around his throat.

"You didn't have enough time," Julian said savagely. "You don't know her like I do! Did you even bother to find out what had happened here? Who are you to pass summary judgment on anyone? Who are any of you to treat others the way you do?"

"She had her hands on Ampliphi in violence, just as you do now! If anything deserves summary judgment, then that is it!"

"If you've hurt her, I swear to all that is precious in the land that I will kill you!"

"Face it, Magistrate. She is gone! Well and truly gone! And good riddance! We will send her back to where she came from now and let them deal with her. And this world can get back to the business of peaceful life!"

"I will never let her go!"

"You have no choice! These Ampliphi judge her to be too violent for our world. She will go back or she will be nightfly to thousands of men! You decide," Kloe said with triumph.

"There is always a choice."

The heavy, resounding statement was taken straight out of Julian's mind. Only he did not speak or emanate them. He looked up to the Ampliphi who now stood in the doorway.

Christophe. The one Ampliphi who could possibly overrule the heavy-handed sentence these two were now trying to pass down on his beloved Asia.

Or what was left of her.

"They are Ampliphi," Christophe pointed out, "but they are also answerable to a body of their peers."

Julian's eyes slid closed, unmanageable tears rolling down his cheeks. He tried to continue grasping at the beautiful rage he needed to punish Greison for what he had done, but he knew that the powerful Christophe was subverting the worst of the emotion, taking it from him and diffusing the power of it.

With a sound of disgust he released Greison and threw himself over to where Asia lay sprawled across the floor. He gathered her up tightly into his arms, clutching her to him as if somehow the power of his hold could make her memories keep root within her mind.

Greison had taken everything that she was.

All her breathtaking strength, all her powerful fighting spirit. All of her undeniable passion. Greison had taken all hope of Asia ever finding a place in her heart for Julian. And it was all his fault. He should never have given up on her. He should have been stronger. Stronger than her fear. Stronger than the things her jaded eyes had seen that had made her so damn hard in the first place. He should have trusted the bond of *kind* to come through for him in the end.

Instead, like Greison, he had thrown it all away.

"Judged by their peers?" he demanded hoarsely as he clung to the limp body of the woman he loved more than he would ever fear the Ampliphi again. "Judged from what? The only witness to what they have done here has been destroyed! They will not be made to answer for this any more than Kloe was made to answer for what happened in the prison! You mark yourselves as above and beyond judgment. There is no justice among the Ampliphi!"

"Oh, but there is," Kloe rasped. "Your *kindra* has had a taste of Ampliphi justice!"

"You will be quiet, Kloe!" Christophe bellowed. The leader of the Ampliphi looked to Julian, who seethed until he shouted up to the heavens above him, making Kloe and Greison both shudder with the impact of all of that wrath. Christophe stepped into the room and rode the powerful wave of negative emotion, the strength of it beating at him as he tried to absorb and dissipate the tempest before it shook the village from its very foundations. "Don't listen to them, Julian. Remember what you know of me and the other Ampliphi. Remember that they do not speak for us all. And if nothing else, find faith in me that I will serve you and Asia well. I won't let this pass unanswered. I swear it to you."

"Your promises mean nothing to me," Julian said hoarsely. "They mean nothing to me because they will mean nothing to Asia. He has destroyed her mind. Robbed her of everything that made her what she was." Robbed her even of the last harsh things he had said to her. Stolen away every memory of every touch they had ever shared. Gone. All of it gone.

"There is yet hope," Christophe said gently, coming to kneel across from Julian, coaxing him through the will of his mind into meeting his eyes. "You said it yourself, Julian. He didn't have enough time. He would have you think otherwise, but I can feel the doubt in his mind. Try to hold on to that small hope until she wakes. Then we will know the depth of the crime done here. Julian, take her home. Watch over her while I tend to these."

Julian didn't want to hear Christophe's words of hope. It was too painful . . . too tormenting. What if he held hope and it was all for nothing? How could Asia have ever been strong enough to fight off Greison's attack?

And then he knew the answer.

Fighting was Asia's forte.

The proper question should have been, how could Greison ever have hoped to defeat the indefatigable spirit that was Asia Callahan?

Chapter 18

Julian laid Asia out very gently in his bed, taking care to smooth her hair out from beneath her head and shoulders. He brushed a hand down her leg to straighten her skirt against her body. He had to fight back wave after wave of fear, trying to hold on to the hope that Christophe had given him, the hope that he knew Asia herself had given him just by being who she was. The same things that had once caused him never-ending frustration were now the things he prayed remained intact and able to fight for what she deserved.

She had tried to warn him again and again about the flaws in the Ampliphi, and he had lived with it for so long he had grown numb to it. Or . . . he had not lived with it enough until now. As soon as he had been of an age he had volunteered to become the liaison between his colony and the Ampliphi known as Kloe. And while all his training had shown him how temperamental she could be, he had simply accepted it as the way things were. He had seen the rest of the Ampliphi accept it and tolerate it. It was what it was.

Or so he had always thought, until he came home and found himself on the wrong end of Kloe's good graces. Then he had seen just how unfair and spoiled she could truly be. Now she had manipulated Asia into acting rashly, and Greison had been forced to come to Kloe's aid. No one laid hands on an Ampliphi in anger. No one. Not without paying a price. Asia had known that when she had gone after Kloe. But all it took was one look at Kenya's limp body and he knew exactly why she would think to take on a creature so powerful.

Asia, who had so little knowledge of how these things worked, had somehow been powerful enough to take Kloe down.

He touched her face with gentle fingertips, leaning over her to brush a kiss against her still lips.

"Please be here," he whispered over her, reaching for her hand to clutch it to his chest over his racing heart. "Please remember me. Remember you. *Be here.* I am begging you, *zini.* Nothing else is going to matter to me without you."

And if she was gone . . . if she was wiped blank and they decided to send her back for her so-called crimes, he would go with her. He would elevate Lucien to Magistrate and do what he had continually demanded of her. He would give up his world and his place within it to follow her and be the one source of support he knew she was going to need. With no parents, no sister to care for her, she would have no one to help her recover from this.

No. She would be here when she woke. She would be Asia. There to frustrate him for another day. There for him to battle so he could earn his place in her heart. No matter how much time it took, no matter how stubborn she was, he would be there to make his way through. He would teach her that she could trust him. That she could have faith in him.

That she could love him.

* * *

Asia opened her eyes, looking up at the strange round roof above her, so truly fascinating in shape and size. Then she looked at the rest of the room, finding it all so plain and empty in its way.

Then, with a surprised breath, she turned her attention in an about-face to see the man lying in bed beside her, his long boy's lashes resting heavily against his cheeks as he slept. His dark hair fell over his forehead recklessly, perfecting the image of a guileless and innocent boy. She turned to face him with all of her body, lying on her side as she watched him breathe deeply. He looked so hard asleep, as if exhaustion rode him into it instead of him having gone willingly into it.

She reached out with the softest touch she could manage, touching his whisker-roughened jaw and chin, fascinated by how several days' growth still could not detract from that boylike ingenuousness. She smiled, though, when she came to his lips, their decadent fullness far too sinful for the image of innocence to hold true.

"Julian," she whispered softly.

And like magic his eyes flew open, the confusion of sleep shed instantly as he sucked in a breath and held it for several beats. Then he was reaching to grasp her shoulder, squeezing tightly.

"What did you say?" he demanded.

"Nothing," she replied. "I just called your name."

"My name? You know my name?"

"Of course I know your name," she said, truly perplexed when he suddenly scooped her up against his powerful body and squeezed the breath out of her in a powerful hug. "Why wouldn't I know the name of the man who has plagued my every waking minute for days?" She laughed at him.

"Asia," he breathed, unrelenting as he crushed her to him. "You're here. You're all here!"

"Yes. You brought me here, remember? Where the hell else am I going to go?" Then she paused for a beat, trying to think. "How did I end up in bed with you?"

Julian pulled back a little, easing his clutch on her and trying not to feel the pang of doubt that suddenly wormed through him. "What do you remember?" he asked her. "What is the last thing you remember?"

"Um." She gave it some thought. "I remember you telling me to go take a flying fuck at a rolling doughnut."

Julian laughed. It was a sound of pure relief and she could swear those were tears in his eyes. He reached to kiss her lips tightly again and again and she could do little more than accept the strange turn in his behavior. Then, with her face held between both of his powerful hands, he looked deep into her eyes, the green of his dark with emotion.

"I love you, Asia," he said on a fast hot breath. "By saying that, I fully expect to freak you out and make you behave as friendly toward me as a hissing snake, but I have to say it. I love you. Everything about you. I love how hard and stubborn you are. I love your relentlessness and dogged determination to see justice served. You constantly think I want you to change, and maybe I have given you that impression from time to time, but I don't want you to. I don't want anything to change. All I want, all I have ever wanted, is the hope of a chance. Just a small hope of a chance that someday you will search your heart and find me in it. That is all I want. Can you give that to me? Just that small hope?"

Every emotion in the book chased through her as he made his declaration, starting with outright fear

and ending with utter bemusement. In the end, she
went with the last thing she was feeling.

"Why would you want anything to do with me?" she
asked him frankly. "All I do is vex you until you clearly
want to strangle me. What makes you think I am even
capable of the emotions you're talking about?"

"Kenya," he answered promptly. "If not for her I
might doubt you, but you love your sister even beyond
good judgment, so I know very well that you are capable. More than capable. I know that if I am ever so
lucky as to earn what I am seeking from you, you will
be just as determined to keep me and to hold me as
you have been when you have fought your way free of
me. It is a day I long for. One I am willing to wait for
and work for, whatever it takes. Perhaps if you see I am
not about to go anywhere, maybe then you will come
around and begin to trust me with your heart. The
same way you entrust it to Kenya."

Stunned, Asia stared into his darkened eyes, realizing just how determined he was. It was radiating out
of every inch of his body. But the frightening thing,
the truly scary thing, was that she considered his offer.
She knew almost everything about him, about the
parts of him that should really matter, and she asked
herself what it would take, if not him, to win over her
jaded little heart. What more could he possibly do?
What more outside of honor, loyalty, truth, and determination would do for her? What more, outside of
the overwhelming passion they shared, would anyone
be able to do to convince her to take a chance on
what she had never considered before?

"I see the fear in your eyes," he said, proving just
how well he could read her, just how well he had come
to know her. Every bitter, judgmental part of her. All

of the good and powerful she could offer and all of the stubborn and bad.

"It scares me that you know me so well," she confessed on a soft, rushing breath. "Everything about you has always scared the hell out of me. You were so much easier to cope with when I thought you were a serial killer who had taken my sister's life. I knew what to do with you then. I knew just how I was going to handle you." She paused for a breath, but she never once looked away from his frank eyes. She hoped he could see she was being just as candid. "You know," she said, "I'm never going to really need you. You understand that, right? I mean, I'm not the needy sort. I don't need rescuing and I don't need handholding or any of that weak girly crap."

"I already told you, I don't want any of the weak girly crap. I want you just as you are. All of your strength and all of your indefatigable spirit. I need you, not the other way around. And I am perfectly willing to accept that."

"You say that now," she said softly, finally breaking eye contact with him and looking down. It showed him she was afraid of much more than what she was telling him. "But maybe years down the road you won't be able to tolerate it. You were pretty pissed before, willing to just give it all up."

"I was angry and frustrated. I said things out of hurt, Asia. And I'm going to do it again. I'm going to find a lot of things frustrating about you, and I am certain the reverse will be true as well. But I'm not going to give it all up. It was bullshit. It was stupid. I almost lost you, Asia, and it nearly killed me to realize it. I'm never going to put myself in that position again."

"Lost me?" He had her full attention. "I don't understand."

"You mean you don't remember. I'll explain that to you in a minute. What I want to do right now is make sure you won't shut me out. That we have hope."

She hesitated, and he wanted to make her believe anything was possible. He wanted to prove to her she was capable of more than she gave herself credit for. She could fight for anything if she only put her mind to it. He wanted to be something she would put her mind to, fight for with all of her heart and soul. And he didn't know what else he could do to convince her to do so.

"I'm never going to be easy," she warned him.

"I know."

"I . . . I might not ever want to have children, either. Bringing babies into a dangerous world . . ."

"That will take care of itself. I am not looking for heirs, Asia. I'm only looking for you."

She nodded slowly, trying to search-her mind for more reasons why this was a bad idea, and finding she simply couldn't come up with any more. The fact was, he was the best man she had ever known. He was the one and only to ever have gotten this close to her. He was the closest thing she had ever known to being in love.

And maybe—just maybe—it was more than just being close to it. Maybe what he was looking for already existed. The very idea made her breath come quick and her heart pound. When had she come to feel so much for him? When had he managed to get under her skin so deeply? God, she would be so stupid to fall into this without caution. She had to be careful. If she wasn't careful he could . . . he could have the power . . .

. . . the power to truly hurt her. The ability to strike her underneath the protection of years of armoring.

She had tried so hard to keep him outside of it, to protect herself.

"I'm really, really scared," she confessed suddenly, the emanation of the emotions she was feeling so powerful he could taste her fear on his own tongue.

"Because?"

"Because you scare me. You tease at something I have no control over. You want me to love you and you make it so compelling. I'm afraid I'm just leaving myself open to nothing but trouble!"

Julian knew it was important to focus on what she was saying, but the wave of emotion he was feeling just then, the pure energy of it told him exactly what she wasn't able to say aloud. It floored him, made him utterly speechless.

Whether she was ready to admit it or not, the feelings were there. She felt for him more strongly than she cared to. She had already let him in, he just hadn't realized it because until that moment, she hadn't realized it.

She was in love with him. Just as much as he found her precious and was unable to relinquish her, she was unable to relinquish him. What she feared had already come to pass, and now she was afraid of the power it gave him over her.

"I'll never let you go," he promised her soft and swift, reaching to kiss her lips with a long drink of passion. "I'll never cut you loose to flounder on your own. I swear it, Asia. You'll always have me. And I'll never once take for granted the precious gift you're giving me. And I know that if I ever do, you'll take me to task for it and make me remember these promises. You'll never sit by and let me or anyone else hurt you. If you have faith in the power of yourself, then you can have faith in this. I'll fight for it, just as you'll fight for it. Together, *zini*."

She couldn't speak, emotion choking up her ability to use speech, so she could only nod for him as he came to kiss her again. For the first time they kissed with utter freedom of emotion and spirit, and they both felt the synergy of it deep down to their souls. They finally both knew what the true reciprocal influence of *kind* was meant to feel like.

There was nothing else they could do but come together. Julian kissed her so deeply and so passionately that it touched her frightened heart, strengthening it, making it beat with a rhythm that was strong and proud and much less afraid. That was when she began to see the source of strength that he would be to her. All this time she had resisted and fought, thinking this would be a weakness, but now she saw the truth. Together they would be insurmountable. Nothing could defeat Asia and Julian. Nothing had. It had tried time and again, thrown one thing after another at them, trying to tear them down and tear them apart, and time and again they had come through victorious. This thing, this feeling of love and, yes, of need, was going to be the most prevailing skill she had ever learned.

"Julian," she whispered, telling him in strong emanations of emotion what she was realizing, what she was coming to understand. It overwhelmed him, brought him low and brought him high all at the same time. It was the most glorious thing he'd ever known.

His hands were on her in the next instant, touch becoming like the taste of a starving man. He needed everything about her and he needed it now. And the minute she put fast and eager hands on him, he knew she was feeling exactly the same way. Finally. They were both feeling exactly the same way.

There was no time for finesse, and there was no need
for it; every touch was an arousal in and of itself. Every
time fingers found bare patches of skin, it was the ultimate in foreplay. Asia rolled on top of him, straddling
his hips and rising up to strip off her shirt. She reached
then to pull his shirt over his head, baring his fine chest
to the sweeping strokes of her hands. Julian drew his
hands up under her skirt, skimming over and along
her legs and straight to the heart of her. But instead of
taking her invitation as she lifted up to give access, he
reached to unfasten his pants, shove them down and
away from himself, kicking free of the denim even as he
grabbed hold of her hips and settled her down against
himself. He couldn't believe how hard she made him
so quickly, the feeling taking his breath away.

He was grateful to find that she was already coated
in a light layer of moisture, a way to alleviate the coming
friction as he dragged her up and down his hard length.
She braced her hands on his chest, her fingers curling
and her nails scraping over his flat nipples. It made him
growl soft and low in his chest, the determined look on
his face telling her he was in no mood for delays. And
since she was of a similar mind, she smiled at him in invitation. She raised up, her powerful leg muscles keeping her above him as she reached beneath herself to
take him in hand. She directed him, hovering when he
was just on the brink of entering her body under her
guidance. She hesitated only a moment, just long
enough to meet his eyes and make certain their gazes
were tightly locked as she began to lower herself onto
him. As she took him slowly into herself in several soft
undulations of her hips, he held on to her hips, the lock
of his hands all too brutal as he tried to control the lash
of heated need that was riding into him.

It was all so different. So much sharper. So much

purer than before. For the first time he felt as if they were coming together from the exact same place, and the feeling of wholeness it left behind was outstanding.

When she finally took a firm seat with him deep inside her, they both exhaled in strong, passionate gusts. Hearing one another made them laugh.

"Good to be home?" she teased him.

"Good that home is still here," he said. "I've never been so happy as I am when I am seated inside you. I never want to lose that. Just the idea of it brought me to my knees."

"You know," she said, feeling the waves of strong relief that came with the remark, "I have a feeling I'm missing something."

"Not as much as you think. And that's not here in this moment. In this moment I just want to take pleasure in you. Can I do that?"

"I don't know. Can you?" she asked impishly as she slowly rose up on her knees, letting him slide nearly free of her body before taking him back with a fast, situating movement.

"Very much so," he said nearly through his teeth as pure pleasure rippled over him. She was as tight as a fist, a true object of decadence. It felt like a guilty pleasure. Like something he should savor every single second of. And he planned to do exactly that.

Bracing his heels into the mattress, Julian pitched his pelvis forward just a little bit, changing the pressure of the seat she had on him as he helped lift her into another thrust. Her surprised gasp was heartily satisfying. Her hands lifted away from him and her palms came to rest flat and low on her belly.

"My God, that went right through me," she said as she hastened to repeat the motion. She gasped again, her head falling back, her long hair tickling over and between his thighs as she did so. Her suddenly restless hands stroked over her belly, her fingers curling with every inward stroke. As if they had the same thought, they both brought their hands up to her breasts, cupping them and shaping them together. She urged him to pull tightly at her nipples until she released a wild little groan. This time it went right through him.

Feeling her walls flex around him as she was stimulated made him more than a little light-headed. Suddenly he didn't have time for anything resembling focus. His hands went back to her hips and he watched her as they worked to ride her over him. She was so blatantly aroused, he could feel it coming off her like an exotic perfume. Everything about the way she looked, about the way she touched herself and moved over him, only served to make him harder inside her. It was at the point where it felt like a beautiful pain, the pleasure of it riding him just as gloriously as she was.

"Soon," he warned her on an out-of-control breath. "Very soon, sweetheart."

"Mmm, I can feel it," she assured him breathlessly. "It's coming off you like a breath of hot wind on a scorching day." She laughed and looked at him. "See, you've made a poet out of me," she accused.

"And a beautiful one at that. Look at you. You're a work of art. You have to hand it to the human race, you have a hell of a gene pool."

"Flatterer." She chuckled.

"Seductress," he countered. "Come. Enough. I need speed and depth."

It was all the warning he gave her before he threw her over to the side, rolling with her until he was on top of her. Now it was his knees that braced into the bedding as he gained the depth and speed he had been searching for. He hilted hard and deep time and again, hastening his pace when he knew he was running out of time. He was in no mood to come before he had seen her do so. He poured all of his focus onto her, seeking out the heart of her mind that he knew responded so very well to his.

"Oh, it's so not fair when you do that," she gasped, her legs suddenly wrapping around his waist as if she could somehow hold him to the promise he was making to her body.

"Then let me be unfair," he requested of her, reaching to take her nipple into his mouth with a brief but potent sucking. She came free with a sound of suction and it made her already singing nervous system go wild with sensation. He felt how close she was, and teasing her mind with the promise of pleasure and the devotion of love, he sent her sailing over the edge. She writhed up hard off the bed, trapping him deeply inside her body as she burst apart in a devastating orgasm.

And still it wasn't enough for him. So he gathered her back up—all the pulsing, flying pieces of her—and spun her back around onto herself.

"Julian!" she cried out, her bucking body now too much for his sanity. She was begging him to join her, and just as he put himself hard to the task of thrusting into her, she did a most miraculous thing. She traced back along the connection he was using into her mind and found his mindheart. Just the act of breaching that most private place was enough to send him off into a rushing orgasm that had no finesse, no rhythm, but all of the heart in the world.

He held himself inside her as he exploded in jetting liberation, the clawing release coming from so deep inside him that he shouted out in coarse relief. And all the while she clung to him with long, clutching legs and a body wet with passion.

Her hands were suddenly in his hair, pulling his head down to her breasts as she gasped to find her breath. He took the gesture of comfort for what it was, her need to hold him to her heart bringing sharp tears to his eyes.

"I love you," they said.

Chapter 19

Julian and Asia appeared in Justice Hall within hours. There they found the entire panel of Ampliphi sitting in state and waiting for them. Once again, every member of the panel was fully flesh and flushed with the satiation of energy. It was a damning situation for them if they were thinking of passing a hard judgment on Asia or Julian for their attacks on Kloe and Greison. They really couldn't afford to lose the power of a couple connected as *kind*. And they couldn't afford to see an injustice go unpunished. In a society as tenuously in control as theirs was, order and control were essential.

"Julian," Christophe greeted them, "I see Asia has come through unscathed."

"Not fully."

"No thanks to you all," Asia muttered.

"Asia," Julian hushed her gently. They had agreed that he would be the one to handle the Ampliphi since she had no recollection of how she had come to attack Kloe in the first place. She could not serve as witness in the matter. Although, after having to visit Kenya in the clinic, she knew she would defend her again if needed.

"Before we take this any further, I demand Kloe be held

responsible for her actions. Her vindictive nature has damaged my colony, put lives in the balance. Lives we cannot afford to spare. No life in this society can afford to be lost, and yet she toys with them like . . . like . . ."

"Like ants at a picnic," Asia supplied.

"Slander!" Kloe burst out in violent emanation, unable to sit still any longer under accusation. She even lurched to her feet out of her chair. Julian quickly sought out Shade, who was standing at Gisella's shoulder as usual. Then he glanced at Kine, who stood behind Sydelle. They had talked before coming there and it had been agreed by them all that Kloe would never be allowed to hurt Asia again. They would do whatever it took to see to that.

"I won't sit still for this," Kloe swore. "Who are they to accuse the Ampliphi?"

"He is Magistrate of the colony you are supposed to be serving, Kloe. The colony is not supposed to serve you. I think you have forgotten that," Christophe said in dark, strident tones. "I will hear you out, Magistrate," Christophe said to Julian.

"Since she stripped me of her mark, she has not fed a single soul in my colony. Children hovered on the brink of starvation because of her petty anger at me for finding my *kindra* and leaving her service. I thought that if I found another to serve her quickly enough we could appease her, but Asia made me realize that it should not be about what appeases the vanity of one woman, Ampliphi or no."

"Vanity!" Kloe shouted. "You think it is vanity that affects me when you disrespect me like this? You have no regard for the power that sits before you! You think you are above this body!"

"I think you think this body should be above criticism, and I think your behavior is deplorable! Not just you, but those who indulge you! Do I believe the Ampliphi should be the ultimate authority? Yes. But only if they do what is necessary to deserve it!" Julian turned eyes of green fire onto Christophe. "You have a duty to hold yourselves in check. If you do not see to that, then the colonies have no choice but to do it for you."

"This is . . . true," Christophe conceded, checking glances with other Ampliphi who were nodding. Rennin clearly did not agree, but he was the only dissenter besides Kloe. "So speak for your colony. Make your accusation."

"If you will indulge me, I have a witness," Julian said, holding a hand out to call forward his witness. Kenya nervously stepped into the Hall and came to stand before the Ampliphi. "Tell them what you told me."

"Ampliphi Kloe got all up in my sister's face, pushed her, and disrespected her, and then, to prove how powerful she was, she began to push me around. When she threw me so hard against a wall I blacked out, I can only imagine that my sister naturally went nuts on her obnoxious ass."

"She lies," Kloe hissed. "It was her sister's own uncontrolled rage energy that injured her sister. Let her accuse me herself if she knows otherwise."

Kloe's smug little smile told her accusers that she was well aware Asia could not remember the incident in question. How she had found out that information, Julian did not know. But he had only told Shade and Kine about it. The idea that one of his trusted friends might have betrayed him sickened him. But since he could not be certain, he turned his focus to the task at hand.

"As Ampliphi Kloe clearly already knows, Greison's assault on Asia has robbed her of all memory of the incident. It's only by the grace of God and a testament to Asia's strength that more was not lost."

"Magistrate, I beg you to understand. All I saw was your *kindra* attacking a member of this body. Kloe sent out a summons for help and I was the closest. I only did what I thought I had to do," Greison said grimly. "It is against the law to attack a member of this body. It is a capital offense. It deserved a capital punishment." He paused for a beat. "However, I did not take the time to find out what instigated the attack or who struck whom first, and that was wrong of me. I am glad you were not permanently damaged, Asia, and I ask your forgiveness for my unthinking haste."

Asia was frankly surprised to hear such a gracious concession from a member of the implacable Ampliphi. It immediately served to soften her opinion of the others. Just because there was one bad egg in the bunch didn't mean they were all bad. Greison had just proved that.

"We have a witness, albeit a biased one," Christophe observed of Kenya. "Were it not your sister's life on the line, I would take you at your word, Kenya, but you can see why I need corroborating information. As it stands now it is a matter of she said/she said."

"Does it matter? You witnessed it for yourself, Christophe. Not only did this one attack me," Kloe said pointing to Asia, "but her mate attacked Greison."

Greison sat up quickly. "Given he knew what I was about to do, I do not hold blame against Julian. I have no desire to see him punished for trying to protect his mate. The issue should be solely what is to happen to Asia."

"Very well," Christophe said, turning to Asia with a frown. "As I see it, there is only one way to settle this matter."

Julian felt his heart leap into his throat. He had been counting on Christophe. He prayed the leader of the Ampliphi would not let him down.

"We need another witness, and so we shall have one," Christophe said.

That got Kloe's immediate attention. "There was no other witness. No one else was there."

Christophe looked at her, a small smile climbing over his lips. "How quickly you forget, Ampliphi Kloe," he said. Then he cleared his throat and reached to ring the bell by his hand. The very specific tone called forth a very specific being. As soon as the dark figure appeared in the hall, Julian could see Kloe going suddenly pale. A powerful sensation of fear emanated from her, the reaction all too telling.

"When your *kindra* first came and you claimed her for yourself, I confess I was uncertain. She had not come willingly and we had to clean up quite a mess behind you, Julian. I was not willing to simply let you run free and wild among us without keeping an eye on you. So I ordered Daedalus to keep close tabs on you." Christophe indicated the Gatherer who now stood before him. "As you know, Julian, Daedalus can become completely invisible. This allowed him to follow you both wherever you went. He has reported back to me on several occasions and helped me to make choices as far as you were concerned. It was how I learned that you had told the truth about the prison guard, Asia. Someone from this panel ordered you moved into the general population for the express purpose of sabotaging your safety and your relationship with Julian. There were other things as well. Unfortunately, Daedalus was following Julian at the time and did not see the altercation between Asia and Ariel. I regret that was the case. It could have saved us all a great deal of trouble.

"But that matter has been solved. The issue at hand is the incident between Kloe and Asia. Daedalus, you were there, I take it?"

"I was," the new man emanated darkly, the coarseness of his presence riding roughly over everyone there.

Asia could see simply a man, no different in height than Julian, though a bit darker in eyes and hair and badly scarred along one side of his face, as if he had been on the losing end of a bad knife fight. He wore nothing but black shirt, pants, and cloak, the latter pulled forward in an attempt, it seemed, to minimize the exposure of that terrible scar. But his dark appearance was nothing to the deep perception of him. There was something about him that rang like guilt and accusation, though for the life of her she could not figure out what it was.

Still, that couldn't be her worry of the moment. Right now she was curious to see what he would say. He was a Gatherer. One of the Ampliphi's pets. Would he sit in support of his masters, or would he corroborate what Kenya said, what Asia believed to be the truth because it rang true and she knew her sister did not tell lies?

"Tell us what you witnessed, Daedalus. And remember you are bound by your oath as a Gatherer to tell the truth," Christophe said. "What is more, your debt to this society compels you to do what is best for it."

Daedalus nodded, the weight of the statement clearly heavy on him. Asia looked at Julian with curiosity, but Julian shook it off. Not now, the gesture said to her. But he would tell her later.

"This is what I witnessed," Daedalus said in rough English. "Julian's *kindra* was in private with her sister when Kloe came in upon her with rage and accusation. Then Ampliphi Kloe used her power to abuse the *kindra*'s defenseless sister. She threw her so violently into the wall I thought sure her neck would break. In defense of her helpless sister, the *kindra* did attack Kloe. As I saw it, it was the only way she could get the Ampliphi's attention off her sister. She was protecting her. It was the Ampliphi who was in the wrong."

Asia leaned toward Julian with a small smile. "That's gotta hurt," she said with smug satisfaction.

"Indeed it does." Christophe spoke up, turning a cold eye onto Kloe. "So now we have the truth of it. Kloe, you have done nothing but persecute this woman since she arrived, forcing her to defend herself at every turn. And then you are surprised when she turns on you in order to protect her sister? Your crimes listed here are many and varied. I see no choice left to us but to punish one of our own."

"Punish?" Kloe laughed incredulously. "You cannot punish me! I am as powerful as any of you!"

"Power can be taken away. Energy can be leeched away. The body will do to you what you have done to others. We will see you so starved of energy that there is nothing left of you but a faded shell. You will never know power again, since you cannot seem to wield it properly. You will be taken to a holding cell where you will live out the remainder of your years in isolation."

"You cannot do that!" Kloe cried. "You need six Ampliphi! Without me there will be no one to feed his rotten little colony! The lot of them will starve to death!"

"I think Julian and Asia have proven that they can keep their people fed far more easily without you than with you. And there will be six Ampliphi," Gisella said. "Isn't that right, Ampliphi Julian?"

Asia gasped and she felt Julian go tense beside her. He was holding her hand, so when he squeezed it in his shock it was a wonder he didn't crack a bone.

"I warned you," Christophe said. "I said one day he

would be the most powerful among us. That day came sooner than expected and yet right in time. Julian, we hope you will accept and join us. Shade, Daedalus, and Kine, please escort Kloe to her rooms and keep an eye on her until we can contact the holding colony and see that arrangements are made for her imminent stay."

"With pleasure," Shade said as he stepped out to confront the defrocked Ampliphi.

"Christophe, please," Kloe begged suddenly. "You can't do this! Think of the example you are setting! People will believe they can tear down the Ampliphi with mere accusations—"

"I *am* thinking of the example it sets," Christophe countered. "It tells our people that no one is above the law. Not even the Ampliphi. Everyone will do well to remember that. Especially you. Gentlemen, remove her. She fouls this fine chamber."

And they did exactly that.

Epilogue

"So does this mean you're going to walk around look-ing like a ghost?" Asia teased him for the hundredth time about his new elevated position in his society.

"No. Clearly I have an excellent source of energy always on tap," he said, reaching to smack her on her bottom. She gasped in outrage, then laughed as she tried to smack him back. He dodged her, snaring her for a kiss as a way to distract her from her purpose.

"Can you tell me something?" she asked after a long minute of enjoying his mouth.

"I will try. Always."

She smiled. "Can you tell me about Daedalus? He seemed so . . . dark. And Christophe said something about him owing a debt. Is he a prisoner of some kind?"

"After a fashion," Julian said grimly. "Daedalus is a tortured man. He holds a very heavy weight on his con-science."

"What happened? What did he do?"

"Do you remember the story I told you? The one about the girl who came here by accident and then brought back a scientist?"

"Patient zero of your plague. Yes, I remember."

"Daedalus was that scientist."

Asia gasped. "Oh my God! But that would make him generations old! How can he be that old and look so young?"

"You forget, he is not from our planes. In his world people remain younger for much longer. Knowing what he had done, Daed wanted to make amends in whatever way he could. He chose to become a Gatherer. He's Greison's Gatherer, actually. And where I was assigned to bring back the energy of passion to this world, Daed is assigned to something much more painful. His is the power to create disasters. Then, he uses his invisibility to walk disaster areas and harvest the energy of grief, pain, and devastation. It is not the most coveted form of energy, but it is better than nothing at all and it is among the most powerful."

"Oh, how awful! He creates disasters? You mean like hurricanes and tornadoes and stuff? All those people? All that death and destruction?"

"It's no different than what your own world creates for itself," Julian reminded her. "There is a great lot of things this society does that we are not proud of, but it keeps our heads above water. Perhaps, one day, if we are very lucky, every colony will be blessed with a pair of *kind* as powerful as you and I. Until that day, this is the way things will be. *Zini,* you cannot change all of this world in an instant. Take your victory over Kloe. It is an enormous step toward righting the wrongs you see around you here. Love me. Keep our colony flush with life and positive energy, and there will be less demand for the type of work Gatherers like Daedalus and Adrian do."

"I hope you're right," she said with a frown. "But I'm not going to stop questioning and trying to fix things I see wrong here. You know that, right?"

"*Zini,* I am practically counting on it."

Did you miss Jacquelyn's
SHADOWDWELLERS series?
Go back and pick up these titles today!

ECSTASY

At one with the darkness, the mysterious Shadowdwellers must live as far from light-loving humans as possible in order to survive. Yet one damaged human woman will tempt the man behind the Shadowdweller throne into a dangerous desire. . . .

Worlds Couldn't Keep Them Apart

Among the Shadowdwellers, Trace holds power that some are willing to kill for. Without a stranger's aid, one rival would surely have succeeded, but Trace's brush with death is less surprising to him than his reaction to the beautiful, fragile human who heals him. By rights, Trace should hardly even register Ashla's existence within the realm of Shadowscape, but instead he is drawn to everything about her—her innocence, her courage, and her lush, sensual heat. . . .

After a terrifying car crash, Ashla Townsend wakes up to find that the bustling New York she knew is now eerie and desolate. Just when she's convinced she's alone, Ashla is confronted by a dark warrior who draws her deeper into a world she never knew existed. The bond between Ashla and Trace is a mystery to both, but searching for answers will mean confronting long-hidden secrets, and uncovering a threat that could destroy everything Trace holds precious. . . .

RAPTURE

*The Shadowdwellers live in a realm of darkness
and sensuality, where order is prized and sin must
be punished. Yet for Magnus, the head priest of Sanctuary,
salvation rests with the one woman who can entice
him to break every rule. . . .*

She Was the Ultimate Temptation

Magnus is a man of contradictions—a spiritual leader
in a warrior's body. To him, laws are for enforcing
and visions must be followed—even if that means
freeing a beautiful slave and making her his reluctant
handmaiden. Betrayed once before, Magnus can
barely bring himself to trust another woman. Yet
Daenaira's fiery innocence is drawing them both
into a reckless inferno of desire. . . .

Daenaira grew up hearing tales of a fearsome
priest who seemed more myth than reality. But
Magnus is very real—every inch of him—and so
is the treachery surrounding them. Beneath
Sanctuary's calm surface, an enemy is scheming
to unleash havoc on the Shadowdwellers, unless
Magnus trusts in a union ordained by fate, and
sealed by unending bliss. . . .

PLEASURE

*Beyond our world lies a land where darkness reigns—
the land of the virile, sensual Shadowdwellers. Yet their
mysterious abilities are no match for the power of desire. . . .*

Double Your Pleasure

Discipline. Penance. Order. A Sanctuary priest's
life revolves around such things. But when Sagan
is taken captive and thrust into the Alaskan
wilderness, he encounters a woman who challenges
his faith and his self-control. Valera is a natural
born witch who almost lost herself to the lure of
dark magic. By rights, Sagan should shun her,
but convention will count for nothing in the face
of a passion that could change the world of
the Shadowdwellers forever. . . .

As Chancellor of the Shadowdwellers, Malaya's first
duty is to her people. Her bodyguard, Guin, knows
this only too well. For tradition's sake, Malaya must
marry, and the thought of this lush, vibrant woman in
a loveless union is impossible for him to bear. Guin
loves Malaya—not as a subject loves his queen but as
a man craves a woman. And even if he cannot keep
her, he'll show her everything she stands to lose. . . .

And here's a peek at her upcoming book
in THE GATHERERS series!

New York Times *bestselling author Jacquelyn Frank*
invites you to explore a strange and sensuous world of
darkest desire ruled by an extraordinary being who is
about to meet his earthly match. . . .

Sandman. Angus. Morpheus. He is known by many
names, except his true one, Adrian. When he departs
his world, it is to enter the sacred space of sleep, and
he is not there to sow sweet dreams. Adrian's mission
is to reap the dark energy of nightmares, work that
has twisted his soul as well as his once-handsome
face. Now, he lives only to await the day darkness
finally overcomes him . . . and to collect exquisite
reminders of what he's lost. . . .

But there is one treasure that stands apart. Having
risked everything to obtain her, Adrian soon realizes
his mistake. For Kathryn has a wholly unexpected
power over him, not only for what she represents, but
for what for she *is*: a soul with desires as strong as his
own, tempered by compassion that could save Adrian
from his self-made hell—or condemn them both. . . .

Something was pulling Kathryn, drawing her.

She had been floating in a benign gray void of nothingness. Somehow she knew that she had been there for quite some time.

But something was now beckoning her away from it.

Slowly, with a soft sigh, she came around. She opened her eyes with a hesitant flutter of her lashes.

Then she heard again what it had been that had called her back to consciousness.

A moan.

It was a low, tortured sound. The sound of someone in unbearable pain.

And whoever that someone was, he was very close by.

She sat up slowly, blinking once. She was aware of feeling stronger. Of feeling more well-rested than she had been in a very long time. She did not even feel afraid this time as she quickly looked around the strange room she was in. Of course, she wasn't quite brave enough to look at any one thing for any length of time, either.

Then the moan came again, drawing her full attention quickly to the floor beside herself.

She gasped softly.

Whoever he was, he had to be the most massive man she had ever laid eyes on. Well, maybe with the exception of the color plates of giants in her childhood fairy-tale books. Still, the difference between seeing a drawing of a mythical giant and finding yourself sitting and staring at a real one, was quite vast. Why, the width of his shoulders might be nearly twice the length of one of her arms from fingertips to shoulder! Of course, she was a little small according to some people.

She bit her lip and leaned closer with irresistible curiosity so she could get a better look at him.

He was on his forearms and knees, his face burrowed into his hands. He was dressed entirely in black. The clothing, what she could see of it, was alien to her in its fashion. Even the fabrics looked strangely coarse. It was nothing she had ever worked her needle through, and she prided herself on being a remarkably fair seamstress.

She could see the back of his large head. His features were further hidden by an outrageously thick and long tumble of silken black hair that sprouted from his scalp, tumbling forward over his neck and face. She followed the line of that neck, picking out the distinction of his bold spine through his shirt fabric and the spreading of the back of an immense ribcage. In relativity, his waist was narrower, though probably still as wide as her thigh from hip to knee. His hips were less so wide, but also in a similar fashion to the rest of his physique. The legs, tucked in a rather fetal manner beneath himself, were the size of good-sized and very sturdy tree trunks.

Sweet Father, he was twice the size of any man

anywhere! She suspected he would dwarf her own husky father!

Another tormented groan rose from the object of her fascination, snapping Kathryn's attention back to the huge man's obvious distress, as well as her present situation. She warned herself to exercise caution. She might be a scrapper, but there was nothing she could expect to do against someone so much bigger than she was. It was likely, she told herself, that this was the person who had all the answers to what was going on.

Well that meant she needed him to talk. And he wasn't likely to do much of that if he was hurting. And besides, he sounded almost sad as he made those painful little sounds.

She scuttled off the bed, approaching him slowly and carefully lowering herself to her knees beside him, she leaned over him and laid her hands on his shoulders as comfortingly as she could.

"Can I help you?" When she received no immediate response, she moved forward a little further and sought to gain his attention by placing her hand in his hair at the back of his head. "Here now, let me help you. Please."

Kathryn gave a yelp of shocked surprise when he suddenly lurched away from her touch, stumbling and crashing heavily to the floor again, trying to crawl away from her. He barely progressed another foot away before collapsing face first into the carpeting. He whined piercingly, like an animal in raw, anguished agony, making the hair on the back of her neck raise up as if someone had just trod across her grave.

Kathryn's heart stuttered and her eyes widened. She had never heard such a horribly inhuman sound before. It was terrifying. But as he whimpered softly again, she knew it was the most pitiful thing she'd ever heard and there was no way she could even pretend to ignore him. Bolstering her courage, hesitating with each movement, she slid herself cautiously back to his side.

"Please," she begged softly, "let me help you."

She touched him again and he reacted as if she had burned him. He recoiled, an agonized roar splitting her ears as it tore from the huddled black mass before her.

"Leave me alone!"

She fell back away from the booming power of his voice rattling the treasures around them in their casings. It must be the acoustics and the vastness of the room that made it amplify in such an ominous way!

She felt icy cold fingers of dread stroking at her throat.

There's something familiar about that voice.

Her nightmare! He was the one who had been in her . . .

But no! Then that would mean it . . . all of this . . . either all of this was still the same dream or—

Or it was all real? If so, then he was the one who had touched her time and again in unwelcome ways. It didn't seem possible, by why else would she know his voice if it hadn't somehow been real? And it was this monstrous man who had somehow spirited her away from her home and had subjected her to all this awful terror and fear! Trapped her there like one of these shiny baubles to be gaped at and toyed with.

Bastard! she thought with unaccustomed vileness. *Soulless bastard!* Her family had been dying and he had violated them and her by stealing her away! Kidnapping her!

"Bastard!" she screeched, the thought of her

abandoned and helpless family riling her up like a madwoman. "You bloody bastard of hell!"

She was no longer sympathetic to his pain as she flew into him, pummeling him with her relatively small fists. Somewhere in her enraged mind, a quiet voice told her she was probably doing him little or no harm. He was so much bigger than she and Kathryn could now feel the thick masses of muscles beneath her battering hands. But regardless of that, it made her feel better to fight back. Then she, who had never wished harm on the slightest of creatures, felt joy that he was in pain. Utter, mind-numbing joy.

She was completely unaware of the ripple of re-newed strength that was shuddering through her victim. She was oblivious to the fact that his agonized moans were replaced with a soft sigh of something slightly but distantly akin to pleasure.

The next thing she was aware of was a bone-chilling, wickedly rolling laugh. Then he was surging up before her like a monolith of black rage.

She froze, her entire body locking. No breath. No blink. Not a glimmer of movement as her shocked eyes tried to absorb the impact of the face looming above hers.

He was hideous!

She had never seen such a grotesque compilation of features and was paralyzed with panic that she was seeing it now. The entire face was bloated over warped, distended bones. His forehead and jaw jutted out in a way that would give his profile a crescent-like shape. Cheekbones, fat with flesh, protruded starkly before falling into the contrasting concave cheeks themselves. His eyes were enormous, though sunken, the lids above and under colored in brown shadow in severe contrast to the pristine white of the rest of his complexion. The eyes themselves she had seen before. They were such a brackish, swamp-like black and green. The blackness in them twisted into horrifying shapes and mysteries her mind could not bear.

But the worst of it. The utmost horror of him was his mouth. The upper lip was abnormally larger than the lower one. And as he released a malevolent laugh, she saw the wicked gleam of two fangs.

Vicious, monstrous fangs.

10/10- 6